THE WOLF

Leo Carew is a Cambridge graduate of Biological Anthropology, currently studying medicine at Barts and the London Medical School. Apart from writing, his real passion is exploration, which led him to spend a year living in a tent in the High Arctic, where he trained and worked as an Arctic guide.

Praise for Leo Carew and his work:

'The next George RR Martin – *Mail on Sunday*

'Imagine *Game of Thrones* rewritten by John le Carré . . . A marvellously accomplished debut' – *Guardian*

'*The Wolf* is a work of extraordinary imagination and perhaps the most captivating first novel I've ever read' – Michael Dobbs, author of *House of Cards*

'Full of dark conspiracies, larger-than-life characters, and tense battles, Leo Carew has created a rousing cross between *The Magnificent Seven* and *Game of Thrones*' – Paul Hoffman, author of *The Left Hand of God*

'As bleak and brutal as the northern snows, a new voice in epic fantasy' – Gareth L. Powell, BSFA Award winner

'A confident first novel . . . It's a cliché to compare up-and-coming authors with David Gemmell or George RR Martin. So instead let's imagine this shouldering in between James Abbott's *The Never King* and Joe Abercrombie's *Half a King* series' – Dave Bradley, *SFX*

'The characters are memorable and entertaining . . . and this is a striking debut' – *SciFiNow*

'Gripping and ambitious . . . twisty in its political maneuverings, gritty in its battle descriptions, and rich with a sense of heroism and glory' – *Publishers Weekly*

'An action-packed and blood-splattered tour de force . . . Carew is the real deal-an exciting new voice in fantasy' – *Kirkus Reviews*

THE WOLF

LEO CAREW

First published in 2018 by
WILDFIRE
An imprint of HEADLINE PUBLISHING GROUP

First published in paperback in 2018 by
WILDFIRE
An imprint of HEADLINE PUBLISHING GROUP

16

Cataloguing in Publication Data is available from the British Library

ISBN 978 1 4722 4702 5

Map illustration © Morag Hood

Typeset in 10.5/13 pt Zapf Elliptical 711 BT by Jouve (UK), Milton Keynes

Printed and bound in Great Britain by Clays Ltd, Elcograf S.p.A.

Headline's policy is to use papers that are natural, renewable and
recyclable products and made from wood grown in sustainable forests.
The logging and manufacturing processes are expected to conform to the
environmental regulations of the country of origin.

HEADLINE PUBLISHING GROUP
An Hachette UK Company
Carmelite House
50 Victoria Embankment
London EC4Y 0DZ

www.headline.co.uk
www.hachette.co.uk

For Mum, with love

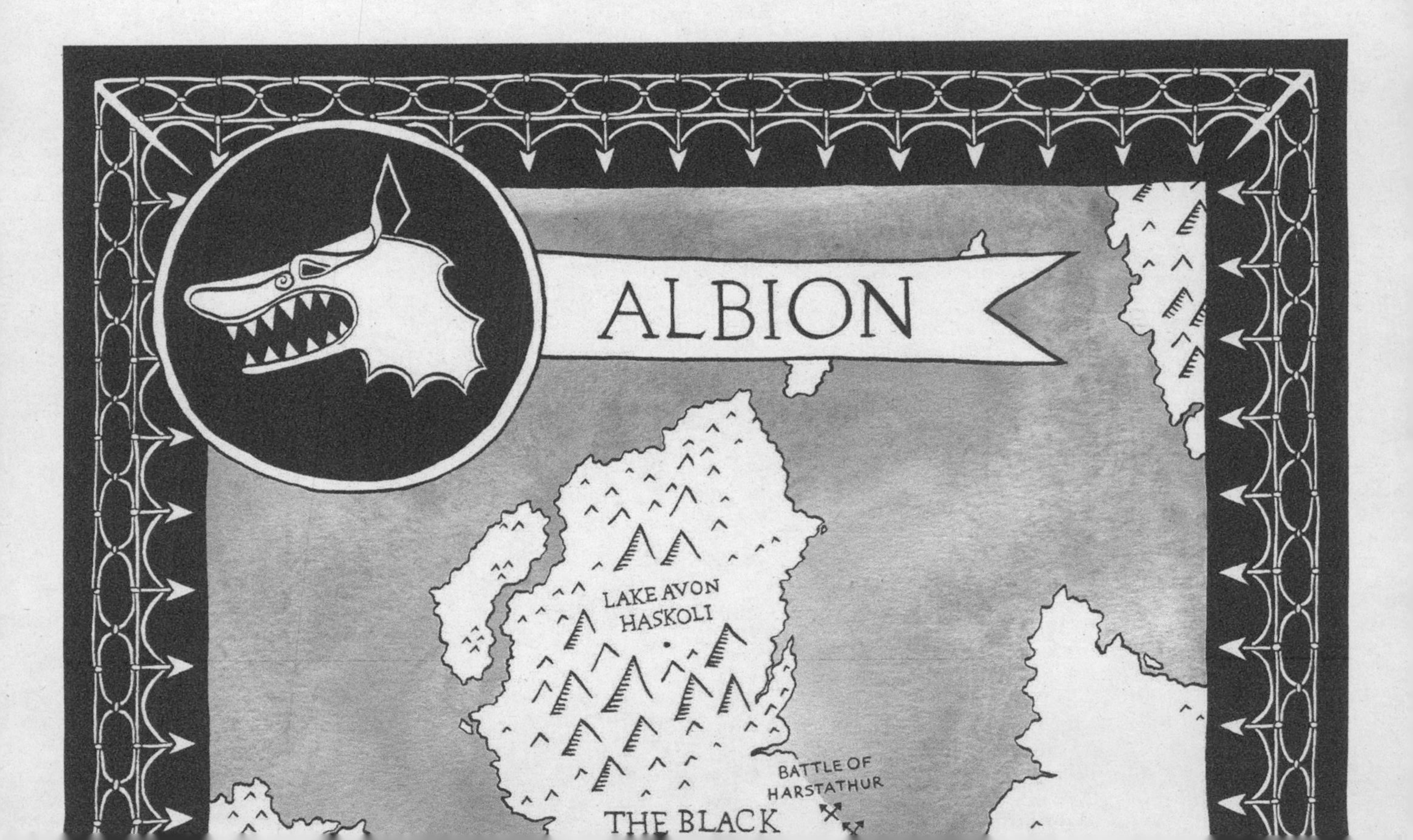
ALBION
LAKE AVON
HASKOLI
BATTLE OF
HARSTATHUR
THE BLACK

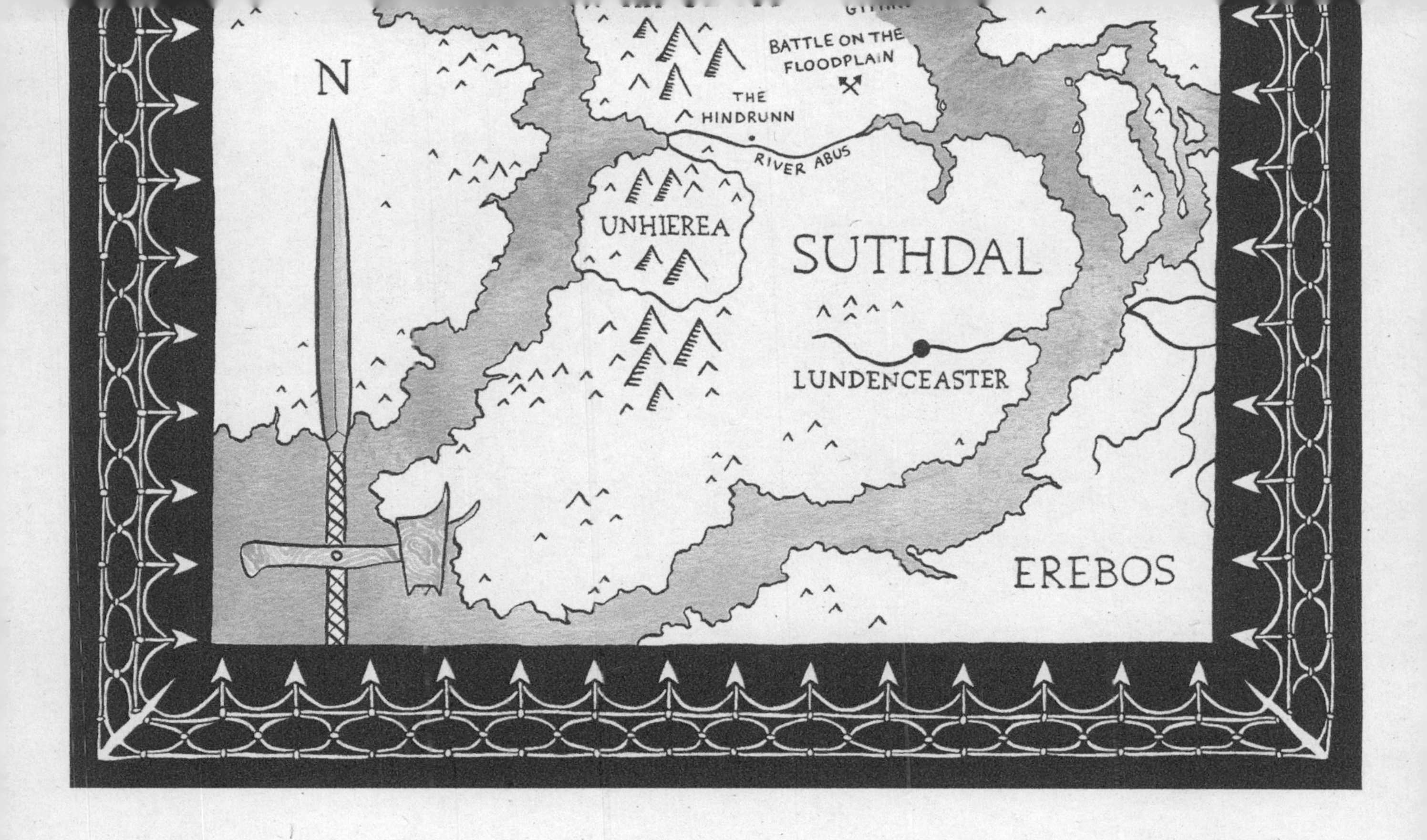
N
BATTLE ON THE FLOODPLAIN
THE HINDRUNN
RIVER ABUS
UNHIEREA
SUTHDAL
LUNDENCEASTER
EREBOS

Contents

Part III – Spring

Prologue

It rained as though the world was ending. In a cobbled street made dark by the clouds that covered moon and stars, a hooded figure struggled towards the door of a stone house, dragged back by a bitter wind. The figure leaned forward against the rushing dark, one hand grasping the top of its hood as the wind threatened to unmask it. The roof of the house ahead was unravelling and the air was thick with swirling reed. So great was the pressure the wind exerted on the dwelling that, when the figure reached it and lifted the latch, the door swept inwards and rattled off the stone behind. Within, the darkness was complete. No candles burned, no lamps were lit and there was no natural light on this wild night. Water was pouring somewhere in the dark.

The figure hesitated on the threshold for a moment, casting around. Then it groped inside, forcing the door shut behind. The wind stopped roaring and began to moan instead as it was banished from the room. In the pitch-darkness, the figure lowered its hood.

Footsteps were ringing through the dark.

The figure stood still as light began to erode a corner of the blackness. Into this growing pool of light strode a tall, dark-haired man; his fine features illuminated by a candle which he clutched in a pewter holder. There was a touch of grey at his temples and his eyes were narrowed. He stopped dead at the sight of the figure by the door and dropped his hand to a long dagger at his belt. 'Who's that?'

The figure stepped forward into the glow of the candle and resolved itself into the form of a golden-haired woman, hair tied back and gleaming with rain. She smiled and the man's mouth fell open. He stared at her for a moment. 'You've been wandering the streets alone?'

'Nobody's out in this,' replied the woman. The man took a couple of steps towards her so that the candlelight was able to bring her face into greater resolution. Her clothes were dark with rain, but so fine they obviously belonged to a woman of the highest birth. But here her resemblance to the other noblewomen of the land ended. She was not like them: paled, painted, adorned, frail and delicate. Her beauty was harsher; in the bones of her face, the lines around her eyes and the ease of her stance. She wore no gold or silver and her skin was not chalk-white but browned and lined by the sun.

'Where is His Majesty?' asked the man.

'Sleeping. His physician has administered one of his brews: he won't wake up. He fears the lightning.' The golden-haired woman rolled her eyes.

He observed her for a moment. The wind whispered through the cracks in the door, making the candle flicker. 'You're mad.'

She smiled and raised her eyebrows a little, her eyes slightly narrowed. 'That's what the court says about you. "Be careful of Bellamus of Safinim, Your Majesty. The upstart is not right."'

Bellamus of Safinim held out an arm and she crossed to him, placing one of her own about his waist and supporting his upon her shoulder. Bellamus looked down at her upturned face, her eyes still narrowed, still smiling, and he kissed her. He raised his hand from her shoulder and inspected a finger and thumb, shining with moisture from her clothes. 'You are in need of a fire.'

They turned away and into the dark. The candle fought silently with the void, briefly revealing the pool in the centre of the hall into which water fell in sheets from an aperture in the centre of the roof, and then, as they moved on down a corridor, illuminating faded frescoes on the plastered walls. The queen turned her head as they passed to follow one of a boar being skewered by a spear; then another of a bull-necked man in profile, surrounded by leaves and dancing figures. The plaster on which it had been painted had shrunk and cracked and the queen could smell the dust it gave off as it silently disassembled.

At the end of this corridor was a more consistent glow and the two figures emerged into another stone room. This one had a hearth crudely chiselled into a wall, with one wooden chair by the fire that burned within, and another drawn up to a glassless window on the other side of the room.

'You were awake?' asked the queen, glancing at the fire.

'Watching the lightning.' Bellamus steered her into the seat by the fire and snuffed out the candle between finger and thumb. He crossed the room to fetch the chair by the window and a blanket that lay next to it, bringing both back to the woman. He gave her the blanket and drew up the chair beside her. 'So what did the king say?' he asked.

'He said you're going to war.'

Bellamus let out a slow breath. 'We're invading?'

She raised her eyebrows a little in response, staring into the hearth.

Bellamus laughed; at first a gentle chuckle, until he lost control of it and it became a full-throated roar of triumph. It carried him onto his feet, and he turned towards the queen to perform a little bow. 'Well done, Your Majesty,' he said, and he leaned forward to kiss her again, his fingers digging into her shoulders. He broke away but did not resume his seat. 'How did you manage that?'

The praise ran off her. 'We both managed it. You scared him wicked, the fiery snakes and the flooding put the fear of God into him, and I directed both those fears.'

The fiery snakes. The night before, a cool evening with a clear sky, the sound of wails and screams had drawn Queen Aramilla to her window. Looking out, she saw a sky stained unearthly green. As though a veil had descended from the stars, swaying and billowing in a breeze that stirred this apparition alone. It intensified, resembling a giant pot of emerald ink that had been spilled among the stars, flowing in rivers from one horizon to another. Aramilla had watched, entranced and awed, as the city beneath her began to cry. The streets emptied, some people fleeing for their houses; others to the church to pray for deliverance from whatever this omen signified. It had gone on through the night until the clouds preceding the storm rolled in, obscuring the sight.

'They were beautiful,' said Bellamus. He sank into his seat again. 'They did not look like an ill omen to me, but I'm glad if the king saw things differently.'

'Well, they were not an ill omen for you,' replied the queen. 'They may yet be an ill omen for the king. I made sure he saw it that way, anyway. The flooding, the plague and now the snakes in the sky. He thinks God is furious.'

'I am impressed. Was he not worried by launching a campaign so late in the season?'

'He was more worried at the thought of enduring a winter with God's anger unchecked.' She placed a hand on his cheek. 'But I've sent you to war, my soldier. Don't make me regret it.' She sounded a little amused, but he grasped her hand anyway.

'You won't,' he said. 'I always come back.'

'Bring me something back from beyond the Abus?' Her pupils were wide, drinking in the sight of him.

He glanced at her. 'What should you like? The Anakim have no treasures. They don't value anything that can't be put to use.'

'What do they have?'

'Weapons,' said Bellamus. 'Bigger and better than anything in the south. I could bring you a splendid axe?'

'Keep thinking,' she said, amused. There came a pause. 'I'd settle for the antlers of a giant elk.'

'A trifle,' said Bellamus. 'But I intend to present something special to the king. You will not be happy unless you have something equally magnificent.'

'What will you give him?'

Bellamus nodded slightly to himself. 'The skull of the Black Lord.' He still spoke mildly.

She looked at him out of the corner of her eye and then leaned into his chest. 'My upstart. I don't envy the Anakim having you as an enemy.'

Silence fell for a time. A flash of white light allowed the queen to see this room as it might appear in daylight for the merest instant. Then the darkness swallowed it once more. The queen counted ten heartbeats before a roll of thunder rumbled by and she shivered comfortably. 'I wish I could come north. I want to see the Anakim before you wipe them out.'

Bellamus had lapsed into thoughtful silence. He stared into the flames, playing vacantly with her hair.

'Have you ever killed one of them?' she asked. 'An Anakim?'

'Once or twice,' he said. 'Never a fully armed and armoured warrior though. I leave those to greater heroes than I. But like all of us, they are considerably less formidable when caught by surprise.'

'Is it true about their bone-plates? Or was that just another way to frighten the king?'

Bellamus grinned. 'If we are to survive this game, we must stick to lies that won't be uncovered. That one is true. From groin to neck, they are exceedingly difficult to pierce.'

'My father scoffed at that. He said it was a rumour of war.'

'Earl Seaton is fortunate enough never to have met an Anakim in the flesh. Our borders have been so safe for so long that people have forgotten how severe that threat really is. It is no rumour, my queen.'

She squirmed slightly in his arms. 'So why disturb them, then?' she pressed him. 'I thought they fascinated you. And however uneasy, the peace has held for years. Why risk it all to silence them?'

Bellamus was quiet for a moment and she knew he was wondering how much to reveal. Eventually, he said, 'You must pick a side, and then advance it with all your might – must you not? The other side will assuredly do the same. Only by doing it harder will your side triumph.'

She thought about that. 'I have a side.'

'I know who you fight for,' he said pointedly.

'The same person you fight for.' She smiled up at him. 'Me.'

Part I
AUTUMN

1

Broken Clockwork

The rain had not stopped for days. The road was under six inches of brown water. Everything was underwater. Roper's horse stumbled and collapsed onto its knees; it was all he could do to stay in the saddle.

'Up,' said Kynortas. 'You must be twice the man you expect your legionaries to be.'

Roper dismounted to allow his horse to rise before swinging himself back into his saddle. The legionaries behind had not noticed; they marched on, heads dipped against the rain.

'What effect will the rain have?' asked Kynortas.

'It will shorten the battle,' Roper hazarded. 'Formations are easily broken and men die faster when their footing is unsure.'

'A fair assessment,' Kynortas judged. 'Men also fight less fiercely in the rain. It will favour the Sutherners; the legions are more skilled and will struggle to assert their dominance in rain.'

Roper drank the words in. 'How does that change our battle plan, lord?'

'We have no battle plan,' said Kynortas. 'We do not know what we will face. The scouts report that the Sutherners have found a strong position to defend, so we know we must attack; that is all. But,' he went on, 'we must be careful with the legions. They take hundreds of years to develop and because they will not run, they can be destroyed in a single battle. Remember this above all: the legions are irreplaceable. Preserve the legions, Roper.'

Marching at Kynortas's back were close to ninety thousand soldiers: the full strength of the Black Kingdom. The column, lined with countless banners that hung sodden and limp, stretched miles back down the road and far out of sight. Even now they marched in step, causing waves to pulse through the flood water. There had never been a call-up so vast in Roper's nineteen years. No man liked summoning all the legions beneath a single banner; the propensity for catastrophe was too great. As Kynortas had said, the legions were irreplaceable. Losing them was the collective fear of every echelon of their nation.

On this occasion, there had been no choice. Their enemies had gathered an enormous army that threatened to capsize the balance of power in Albion. The force, a composite of Saxon and Frankish soldiers, with mercenaries from Samnia and Iberia, was so big that nobody knew how many men their enemies commanded. But it numbered many more than the legionaries under Kynortas.

'Why do we not do as the Sutherners do, lord?' asked Roper. 'Unify all our peoples under a single banner?'

Kynortas did not countenance the idea. 'Can you imagine any king surrendering control of his forces to another? Can you imagine a dozen kings all agreeing to back the same man?' He shook his head dismissively. 'Perhaps one man in a million could unify the Anakim. Perhaps. But I am not the man to do it, and neither will I surrender the legions to any foreign sovereignty.'

Roper could not imagine a lord greater than Kynortas. As strong in face and limb as were his faith and convictions. Straight-backed and stern, with a thunderous brow and a face as yet unscarred by conflict. His men regarded him; his enemies despised and respected him in equal measure. He knew how to court an ally, cow an enemy and read a battlefield like a poem. He was a tall man, though Roper almost equalled him in that regard already. Theirs was reckoned a strong house, with Roper a promising prospect as Kynortas's heir, his two younger brothers indemnifying the lineage.

At the head of the mighty column, the Black Lord and his young heir crested a hill to reveal a great flood plain. Across almost a mile of wind-rippled water lay a ridge of extraordinary length. Whether a natural formation or some ancient battle-works thrown up in this scarred land was not clear, but it stretched almost from horizon to horizon. Its northern flank was guarded by a great forest and on it was arrayed the Suthern horde. Thousands lined the ridge. Tens of thousands; protected by the mangled and rain-slicked slope. Their banners were as wilted as those of the legions but Roper could make out halberdiers, longbowmen, swordsmen and some who shone greyly on the wet day and must surely be men-at-arms. At the southern edge of the ridge, a vast mass of cavalry sat malevolently.

It was to be Roper's first battle. He had never seen one before. He had heard them, rumbling and crashing from afar like a heaving ocean beating against an iron-bound coast. He had seen the warriors return, most weary and bereft, a special few energised and inspired; all filthy and battered. He had seen the wounded treated; watched as surgeons trepanned the skulls of unconscious men or extracted slivers of steel from their forearms, thrown off by the clash of blades. His father had discussed it often, indeed talked of little else to his heir. Roper had studied it; had trained for it from the age of six. His life had so far revolved around this sacred clash and yet he felt utterly unprepared for what he saw before him.

Laying eyes on the enemy, the Black Lord and his son spurred out of the column's path. Kynortas snapped his fingers and an aide trotted to his side. 'Deploy our army in battle formation, as close as possible to where the flooding begins.'

Kynortas rattled off a list of where each legion should be placed in the line, concluding with the observation that all their cavalry would be on the right, 'save for those from Houses Oris and Alba, who take the left'.

'That's a lot of orders, lord,' said the aide.

'Delegate.' The aide complied. 'Uvoren!'

A mounted officer detached himself from the column and rode to join Kynortas. 'My lord?' His high ponytail, threaded through a hole in the back of his helmet, identified him as a Sacred Guardsman. A silver eye was inlaid into his right shoulder-plate, his helmet covered his eyes and he grinned roguishly at his master.

'You know Uvoren, Roper,' Kynortas introduced them. Roper had heard of Uvoren; there was no boy in the Black Kingdom who had not. The Captain of the Sacred Guard: a role every aspiring warrior dreamed of playing. There could be no higher endorsement of your martial capability than appointment to such an office. Over his back was slung his famous war hammer: Marrow-Hunter. It was said that Uvoren had had Marrow-Hunter's gorgeous rippled-steel head forged from the combined swords of four Suthern earls, each put down by the captain himself. When hope had seemed a distant memory at the Siege of Lundenceaster – the greatest of Albion's settlements, far to the south – it had been Marrow-Hunter which had at last cleared a foothold on the wall. At the Battle of Eoferwic, its great blunt head had broken the back of King Offa's horse and then smashed the downed king's head like a rotten egg, crumpling his gilt helmet.

Yes, Roper had heard of Uvoren. Playing in the academy far in the north, Roper had always pretended to be Uvoren the Mighty. The little stick he wielded had not been a sword but a war hammer.

Now, he nodded silently at the captain, who beamed back at him. 'Of course he does.'

'Captain of the Sacred Guard and model of humility,' said Kynortas acidly. 'Uvoren: parley. Roper will accompany us.'

'You'll enjoy this, young lord,' said Uvoren, curbing his horse next to Roper and gripping his shoulder. Roper did not respond beyond staring wide-eyed at the guardsman. 'Your father's good fun when treating with the enemy.'

The three of them rode together down onto the flood plain, accompanied by another Sacred Guardsman bearing a white flag. 'Carrying a white flag comes naturally to you, Gray,' Uvoren called to the guardsman. Gray's reaction was merely to stare unsmiling at his captain. Uvoren laughed. 'Stay calm, Gray. And learn to laugh.' Roper looked to Kynortas to see what to make of this, but the Black Lord had ignored the exchange.

They splashed into the flood waters which proved to be no more than a foot deep. Beyond the water, atop the ridge, a group of horsemen detached themselves from the Suthern army and rode out to them. To Roper, there seemed a significant disparity in power between the two groups. He, his father, Uvoren and 'Gray' numbered four; riding against them were close to thirty. Three unhelmeted lords led the party, accompanied by two dozen knights in gleaming plate armour, visors down and horses billowing in embroidered caparisons.

'Will this be your first battle, little lord?' Uvoren asked of Roper.

'The first one,' confirmed Roper. Being taller than most already, he was hardly little but the term did not feel strange from a man as elevated as Uvoren.

'There is nothing like it. Here is where you will discover what you were born for.'

'You loved your first one?' asked Roper. He was not accustomed to struggling with words, but stuttered slightly when addressing Uvoren.

'Oh yes,' responded the captain, beaming again. 'That was before I was even a legionary and I bagged my first earl! Fighting these Sutherners is not hard; look here.' They were drawing close to the group of horsemen.

Roper had never beheld a Sutherner before and their

appearance shocked him. They looked like him, just smaller. Though all were tall among Anakim, not one of Roper, Gray, Uvoren or Kynortas stood below seven feet in height; even on horseback they towered above their enemies, who were on an altogether smaller scale. The disparity in power vanished.

Now Roper came to inspect them more closely, there was something different about the faces of these Sutherners as well. They were somehow child-like. Their eyes were expressive and their emotions and characters stood out on their faces with a clarity that made them almost endearing. Their features were softer and less robust. By comparison, Kynortas's countenance might have been carved from oak. These Suthern faces put Roper in mind of something domesticated, like a dog. Something far from the wild.

Kynortas raised a hand in greeting. 'Who commands here?' Though he spoke good Saxon, he delivered these words in the Anakim tongue. The knights shivered slightly as the speech of the Black Kingdom washed over them.

'I command here,' said a man in the centre of the group in a halting, accented version of the same language. He rode towards Kynortas, seemingly indifferent to his size. 'You must be the Black Lord.' He sat straight in his saddle, wearing a suit of plate armour so bright that Roper could make out his own reflection in the breastplate. He had a dark beard and a mane of curly hair. His face, what could be seen of it, was reddened by drink. 'I am Earl William of Lundenceaster. I lead this army.' He gestured to his left. 'This is the Lord Cedric of Northwic and this,' he gestured to his right, 'is Bellamus.'

'You have a title, Bellamus?' demanded Kynortas.

William of Lundenceaster answered for him. 'Bellamus is an upstart without any sort of rank to his name. Nevertheless, he commands our Right.' Earl William regularly substituted Anakim words that he did not know with the Saxon equivalent, knowing that Kynortas understood anyway.

Kynortas looked intrigued at the earl's words and Bellamus raised a hand in acknowledgement. He was good-looking, this upstart, with a touch of grey at the temples of his dark, wavy hair and he appeared prosperous. He alone of the Sutherners present was not dressed in plate armour but instead wore a thick jerkin of quilted leather, with gold hung at his neck and wrists. His high boots were of the finest quality, so new that they looked as if they might rub. He wore a rich red-dyed tunic beneath the jerkin and sat on a bearskin draped over his horse. He also had the two outermost fingers missing from his left hand. Next to the austere, armour-plated lords, it was the upstart who stood out.

The Black Lord looked back at Earl William.

'You have invaded our lands,' said Kynortas, his voice harsh. 'You crossed the Abus which has been a peaceful border for years. You have burned, you have plundered and you have raped.' Kynortas advanced his horse, bearing down on Earl William. His huge physical presence was more than matched by his implacable bearing. 'Leave now, un-harried, or I will unleash the Black Legions. If I am forced to use my soldiers, there will be no mercy for any of you.' He cast an eye over the ridge behind the Suthern generals. 'In addition, I doubt you can bring an army like this here and have left anything to defend your homelands. You have violated our peace and once I have decimated your army here, I will advance to Lundenceaster and strip it to the bone by way of reparations. The violence,' he leaned forward, 'will be extreme.'

Uvoren laughed loudly.

'We could withdraw,' suggested Earl William, who had not flinched as Kynortas advanced. 'But we're very comfortable here. We are well supplied; we have a strong position. And the reason you even offer us the chance of withdrawal is that you do not want to lose soldiers. You value them too highly and they are too dearly replaced. You do not want to attack us.' Earl William had a slight squint. He gazed frankly at

Kynortas, who waited for the offer that was about to be broached. 'Gold,' said the earl softly. 'For the lives of your legionaries. Thirty chests would make our time worthwhile. That and the meagre plunder we have already taken from your eastern lands.'

Kynortas did not respond. He just stared at Earl William and allowed the silence to stretch.

Roper watched. Thirty chests was an absurd figure to propose. The Black Kingdom's wealth was not based on gold; it was based on harder metals, beyond the manipulation of the Sutherners. They could not provide thirty chests of gold, as Earl William would surely have known; not if they scoured the country from meanest hovel to most magnificent castle. The earl had also been provocative in his demand of the tribute, though not obviously so. All of which led Roper to one conclusion; he did not want his offer to be accepted, but was trying to pretend that he did. The Sutherners had some kind of plan and had already decided how they wanted these negotiations to play out. Roper suspected Earl William was trying to goad Kynortas into a rash attack, where the legionaries could be killed trying to scale the mud-slicked ridge.

Kynortas himself – wiser, battle-hardened and more experienced – had no such suspicions. Foolish, ignorant Sutherners. 'We have no value for metal of such limited use,' said Kynortas at last. 'We do not have thirty chests to satisfy your greed for things that are soft and impotent; nor would we supply you with them if we did.'

Kynortas suddenly jerked forward, leaning out of his saddle in a great creaking of leather harnesses, and seized the top of Earl William's breastplate. Earl William's face reddened still further and he leaned backwards desperately, trying to pull his horse out of Kynortas's reach, but the Black Lord had him fast. The Sutherner was panicking, terror transparent on his face as Kynortas's alien hand touched his flesh. With a mighty wrench and a screech of yielding metal, Kynortas tore the shining breastplate clean off, causing Earl

William to spring back like a willow-board. Beneath his armour was revealed leather padding, soaked in sweat, and Kynortas snorted as he flung the breastplate aside. It had all happened so fast, Earl William's knightly bodyguard had had no time to do anything more than look shocked. Earl William himself quivered, thunderstruck.

'Worthless,' said Kynortas, sitting back in his saddle. 'And beneath, a feeble sack of bones. You cannot fight my legions. They will cut through your plate like carving a ham.' He smiled bleakly at Earl William, who had drawn his right arm across his vulnerable chest as though violated. The upstart Bellamus was looking across at his general with eyes crinkled in amusement. The two were evidently not friends. 'Your last chance, Earl William. Withdraw, or I will release the legions.'

'You use your precious bloody soldiers, then,' boomed Earl William, his voice quivering with rage. 'Watch them flounder and die in the filth!' He dragged his horse away from the encounter as though he could not bear to be in Kynortas's presence a moment longer. The Black Lord stood his ground and watched the retinue file away until it was just Bellamus staring back at him. The smaller man broke the silence first.

'Being blessed with bone-armour, I cannot imagine you know how it felt for Earl William to have his defences taken so contemptuously from him. Before this battle is over, I will show you how that feels.' His Anakim was flawless; he might have passed for a subject of the Hindrunn had his stature been less mean. He had spoken mildly and nodded at the four Anakim before clicking his tongue to coax his horse away and back up to the ridge. He rode slowly, raising an arm in retrospective salute.

'Do negotiations always end like that?' asked Roper as the four of them turned back to their own forces, still assembling on the plain.

'Always,' said Kynortas. 'Nobody negotiates in negotiations. It's an exercise in intimidation.'

Uvoren snorted. 'Your father treats negotiations as an exercise in intimidation, Roper,' he corrected. 'Everyone else goes into it genuinely hoping to avoid battle.' Uvoren and Gray laughed.

'They didn't want to negotiate anyway,' said Roper.

Kynortas cast a glance in his direction. 'What makes you say so?'

'The way he phrased the offer; the fact that he'd have known it was beyond our means anyway. He was goading us into attack.'

Kynortas brooded on this. 'Perhaps. So they're over-confident.'

Roper stayed silent. Who could be over-confident going into battle against the Black Legions? There must be a reason for their belief. They must have a plan. But Roper did not know the way of these Sutherners. Perhaps their numbers gave them confidence. Perhaps they were just a confident race. Roper did not know and so stayed quiet.

'Stay with me,' Kynortas said to Roper. 'Watch as I do. One day, you will be responsible for the legions.' The Black Legions were advancing into the flood waters. Holding the right wing, with the vast majority of the cavalry, was Ramnea's Own Legion; the elite soldiers of the Black Kingdom, second only in martial repute and prestige to the Sacred Guard. On the left was the Blackstone Legion; veteran, battle-hardened and with a reputation for savagery. Some men said the Blackstones were even more efficient than Ramnea's Own as line-breakers. Most of those men were Blackstones themselves.

The legates – the legion commanders – had each ridden out in front of their legion. On horseback they presented themselves to their warriors and held their arms high to the air as a pair of legionaries rode up behind them and invested each with a vast rippling cloak of liquid-brown eagle feathers. These were fastened over the shoulders, draping much of the horse as well, and flashed and glimmered as the legate dropped his arms. Clad in this holy raiment, they rode along the front of their advancing legions, holding out before them a branch of holly, an eye woven from the pointed leaves at the top of the branch. The eye looked over the ranks, inspecting their courage for the combat to come and blessing those who were worthy.

Roper and Kynortas trotted behind the battle line, a clutch of aides following in their wake. Kynortas sent them streaming out in all directions with instructions to hold fast, keep the line together, discharging regards and advice to the legates. He was so calm, the Black Lord. So still. His confidence, his faith in the legions, radiated around him like the ripples his horse made in the flood waters. Roper watched his father, hoping to absorb his presence and character by looking. Even when they had advanced into the shadow of the ridge, when longbow arrows began to spit into the waters around them, bouncing off the armour of two of the aides, the Black Lord appeared unfazed.

The Sutherners on the ridge above were chanting. Swords thumped on shields, polearms rattled together and the men screamed and jeered. Devils, the Anakim were. Demons. Freaks, monsters, destroyers. They worked themselves into a frenzy of drumming and screaming to drown the awful, gut-wrenching fear they had of the giants they opposed. 'Kill!' screamed a lord.

'Kill, kill, kill!' roared his men.

'Kill!' the lord insisted.

'Kill, kill, kill!' bayed his men.

'Scream at them!' bellowed the lord. 'They're the murderers of the Black Kingdom! Scream at them!' His men screamed. 'These are fallen angels, cast down from Heaven! God wants these demons banished from our lands! Do your duty this day by God!' The shields and pikes began to thump in time and the Sutherners stamped their feet. The sound, like a mighty drum being pounded, was enough to create ripples in the flood waters through which the Anakim marched.

The Anakim had their own drums, but they were not like their enemy's. Each legion beat its own tattoo on the advance, the drummers standing in the rear ranks and driving their warriors forward. The noise was not feral and savage like the Sutherners'. It was mechanical and crisp; a regular wave of sound.

Thousands of banners rose forest-like above the Anakim ranks. They had the great squares of embroidered linen that the Sutherners flew, but also long tapestries of woven silk, held aloft by up to six standard-bearers and depicting ancient battles in stark Anakim colours. Next to these stood giant eyes, woven from leafy withies of holly, willow and ash, or perhaps a great stretched bearskin, or a pole suspended with half a dozen tattered wolf pelts that swirled raggedly in the breeze. Where the legates rode, enormous bolts of linen impregnated with eagle feathers were held aloft, rippling and flashing in the wind. All of these banners but the last would be dropped when their bearers joined combat.

The legionaries themselves did not scream or shout on the advance. They did not clash their weapons, as the Sutherners were doing. They sang. Low, eerie battle hymns spread across the line, clashing and swelling; growing in volume and emotion until the Sutherners were sick with the unfamiliarity of it all. The music reflected the tangled wilderness which surrounded them; the grey agitation of the sky above and forests that rustled and shifted on their flanks. The breeze was intensifying, as though the Sutherners were surrounded by Anakim allies who answered the call of that unearthly singing. This was Anakim land. The Black Kingdom: every inch as barren and unholy as the Sutherners had feared.

On the Suthern Right, Kynortas could make out the upstart Bellamus riding along the front of the line, roaring at his men. In his wake, men stood straighter and hefted their weapons. Kynortas took note: *One day*, he thought, *I will have to face an army commanded by that man alone.*

No sooner had this occurred to him, than the Suthern Right broke. Perhaps Bellamus had over-excited them to the extent that their officers had lost control. Perhaps, after all, he knew no more about war than his lowly station suggested and he was foolhardy in the face of his steady enemy. Whatever the cause, Sutherners had begun to flood down the ridge, slipping and sliding through the mud in a mad charge against the Blackstone Legion. They broke formation and so lost the only advantage they had held: the ridge. Thousands surged forward, screaming for Anakim blood.

Kynortas had not expected such an easy opening. Disordered and chaotic, the Sutherners would be shredded in open combat. 'Release the Blackstones!' From a trumpet behind him soared three glorious notes, commanding the Blackstones, who needed no second invitation, to attack.

Once, perhaps a decade ago now, Kynortas had seen a mechanical clock. Envoys from Anakim-held lands to the south had sought an audience, proposing an alliance in which they were to act as anvil to the Black Kingdom hammer. To be wrought: the Sutherners' central Ereboan territories. Into this alliance they had quietly rooted a trade agreement – favourable, they had said, for both parties. They had presented samples of the goods that the Black Kingdom could expect to flood their markets. A hull load of beautiful, dark timber said to be the best in the Known World for ship craft. Weightless sacks of eider down. Wine-red crystals that are precious to the Black Kingdom for the potent metal that can be extracted from them. And a mechanical clock; the first Kynortas had seen. In the Black Kingdom the length of an hour differed with each day of the year and was judged from the passing of sun and moon. If they needed to measure short periods of time, they would use a water-clock. They had no need of a mechanical timekeeping device and yet Kynortas had been entranced by the inscrutable object.

It was held together by an exoskeleton that laid bare its inner workings. It was half machine, half organism. Its heart was a little spring; perfectly weighted and animating the busy cogs with which it was enmeshed. There was no flaw in any one of its workings. It ticked and clicked with quiet order and, twelve times a day, a bell would chime out the hour. It was unnecessary, of course. A frivolous waste of good steel, but Kynortas was convinced that he had seen the future. One day, such craftsmanship could build a boat that would man itself, or a harvesting machine that could cut down an entire field if it were just set moving.

Now, he thought of his legions as clockwork. The epitome of flawless, synchronised cooperation. The Blackstone Legion armed itself as five thousand blades were swept clear of their scabbards. It surged forward in ten waves, five hundred abreast. Kynortas was extending his influence through the flood waters; they were his harvesting machine and he had set them moving. Two lines, one calm and ordered; one frenzied and chaotic, splashed through the flood waters to meet each other. It would be a slaughter.

The clockwork failed.

The Blackstones began to stumble and fall into the waters. Legionaries started to drop by the handful, with more and more falling until the front rank in its entirety had dropped below the surface, no longer howling but crying in pain. Those who followed met the same fate, staggering and plunging into the flood waters. Kynortas spurred towards his Left, straining his eyes at the scene. Why were his soldiers falling? Was the footing treacherous? But this was Suthern trickery; the water around the Blackstones was turning red with blood. Beneath the flood waters, a trap had been laid.

The Blackstone Legion had stopped dead in their tracks. Every man that attempted to advance stumbled and fell. The Sutherners on the ridge jeered and hooted and their charging warriors, who had seemed to be in chaos, stopped seventy yards short of the stricken Blackstones. They were longbowmen; so lightly armed and armoured that they would never have stood a chance against legionaries in open combat.

They had charged to bait the Blackstones and now revealed their true strength: their great curved yew bows. These were unslung, arrows nocked to strings and deadly shafts poured into the legionaries. Their fletching whistled as they hurtled forward; a noise like a sky-full of whirring starlings. At this close range, some of the steel-tipped arrows were able to penetrate tough Anakim plate armour. The legionaries, unable to move in either direction, dropped into the flooding to try and limit the damage of this swarm of arrows. They cowered in the waters, seemingly completely mired. Kynortas was witnessing the near perfect destruction of one of his legions at the hands of the Suthern upstart, Bellamus. The Anakim Left was ruined and they had yet to kill a single Sutherner.

'Roper, with me!' bellowed the Black Lord. He spurred towards the Raptors, shouting that the trumpeter should signal the halt. The Anakim line juddered to a standstill, so that they could not outstrip the mired legion and leave their flank exposed. But this left them vulnerable to the longbow shafts that rained down upon the line from the ridge. These arrows were more distant and so had less force, but they still withered the Anakim ranks.

Roper and Kynortas sped towards the Blackstones, Kynortas looking first for the problem, and then for a solution – any solution. But the Black Lord, so calm, so confident, had strayed. He feared for his legion and could not understand how the battle had escalated beyond his control so quickly. So he rode towards the problem, seeking a solution.

And a gust of arrows took him and Roper.

They struck plate armour with a clang like the splitting of a bell, the force enough to knock the Black Lord from his saddle and stagger his heir. Kynortas's boot became entangled in the stirrup and he was dragged through the water by his bolting stallion, straight towards the Suthern line. His body left a trail of blood through the flood waters.

Roper, staggering and with an arrow protruding from beneath his collarbone, spurred his horse after his father.

Kynortas was not resisting, lying limp as he was pulled through the waters towards his enemies and Roper spurred hard enough that the horse's blood and his own mingled and dripped from his stirrups. Arrows spat into the waters around him and more clanged off his armour as his father was dragged further and further from his reach.

Blood-crazed Sutherners were swarming towards him. Roper drew his sword in anger for the very first time and hacked down. There was a ring of metal on metal and a juddering shockwave ran up Roper's arm. He struck wildly once, twice, three times; his eyes always on the body of his father which had now been dragged into the heart of the Suthern mass. Men drew wicked knives and converged on the body to claim the rich prize: a fallen king. The Black Lord was dead and his son was dying.

Roper was spraying vile curses at the men between him and his father, trying to drive his horse onwards. A hand seized his boot and dragged him from the saddle. He crashed into the flood waters and for a moment could neither see nor hear as he was engulfed. There was an awful, puncturing sensation in his thigh and he knew he had been stabbed. Panic lent him strength and he thrashed to the surface, finding his sword still in his hand and sweeping it from the water. He was pinned to the ground by a spear thrust into his leg but he could still swing his sword and aimed it wildly at the Sutherners who surrounded him, blocking attacks as best he could. One lunge made it through and smashed into his head, where it opened a gash to the bone but went no further. Whilst Roper's head was ringing, his vision a clouded white, another thrust hit his chest, puncturing his plate and through to his bone-armour where, again, it was stopped.

Roper had no idea of it but he was screaming; a vile shriek of distress and ferocity as his sword flailed through the air, seeking to strike back at someone. He was alone in these waters, which were steadily turning pink with his own blood. He could barely see the sky, the view blocked by lunging Suthern bodies. There was no noise at all; he was enslaved by the overwhelming instinct to keep himself alive for a few seconds more.

An improbable freedom had descended upon him. His self-doubt was gone, his mind wiped clean for one great, dynamic effort. His vision, which no longer felt like vision in the ordinary sense, had become tunnel-like and responded to motion alone. He could not think, he had no control; Roper was stripped to his core. He was a cornered wildcat. There was nothing in him beyond his hauling lungs and swinging blade. Dark shapes were pressing in on his prone form.

And then there was a break in the wall of flesh which surrounded him. The light of the grey skies poured down on Roper.

A dead Sutherner had crashed into the waters at his feet in a spray of blood and there was a shout of alarm. A flash of light carved through another two Sutherners who were hurled backwards and an enormous shadow stepped into the gap they had left. The figure raised its great light blade again and sparks sprang away from it as it swept along a Suthern weapon, taking the top of a man's skull off as if it were an apple. Like rows of wheat, the Sutherners were falling before this harvester until Roper's final two attackers fled, splashing away through the waters.

A hand seized Roper's collar and dragged him up and out. Roper screamed again as the spear was ripped from his flesh but his rescuer took no notice, hauling him from the scene. The shock almost made Roper drop his sword, but his groping fingers managed to just clutch the pommel as he was hauled away. 'My lord father!' he roared as he was dragged back. 'The Black Lord! He's there! Get him!'

More hands seized Roper and Anakim swarmed around him, flooding between him and the Suthern ranks. 'Release me!' he shouted. It was the Sacred Guard. The finest fighting unit in the world had arrived, honour-bound to preserve the blood that surged through Roper.

Roper received as little mercy from their treatment as had the Sutherners. His protestations were ignored as he was dragged from the front line and violence erupted all about him. He was allowed to collapse at last, dazed and bleeding, into the waters forty yards from the melee. His eyes focused on the man who had held his collar and who had surely rescued him from death. It was a Blackstone, though Roper did not know his name. He demanded it of the man.

'Helmec, my lord.'

The words 'my lord' jarred with Roper, though he could not have said why. 'I'll make a guardsman of you, Helmec.'

Helmec stared. Enough sense was returning to Roper for him to be able to take in some of the man's face. He must have been young, but it was difficult to tell beneath a mask of scars. One of his cheeks was so shredded that the interior of his mouth was visible through the old wounds. He held himself with the demeanour of a veteran: weary and assured, though there had been no weariness in his defence of Roper. 'My lord . . .'

There it was again. Lord.

Men were gathering around Roper like lost sheep, though seemingly not daring to ask anything of him. A vague sense of responsibility began to press against him.

'A horse,' murmured Roper. Perhaps things would be clearer on horseback. One was brought to him and when he could not mount on his savaged leg, Helmec was there again to help him into the saddle. 'Obliged,' he muttered, turning the horse towards where the Sacred Guard had turned the flood waters a boiling red.

Uvoren was in the thick of the fighting, Marrow-Hunter in hand. Roper watched him take a great overhead swing at a Sutherner, dismissing the feeble block raised against him and flattening his opponent. The rest of the Sacred Guard were shredding the lightly armoured longbowmen they faced, but outside this martial mismatch the Anakim were in dire trouble. The Blackstone Legion appeared to have dissolved into the flooding as arrows continued to rain down on them, and the rest of the army was scarcely in a better position. Still stationary, they endured the sting of arrows from the ridge without shields to hide behind. Bone- and steel-armour were limiting the damage but the effect on morale was worse. The Sutherners had not advanced, content to let their arrows work for them.

'Lord?' said a voice behind Roper. He turned to see half a dozen mounted aides staring at him. Roper nodded at them and turned back to the battle. *Almighty god, what now?* It did not feel as though there was any way back from here. His Left could not advance; something beneath the water was preventing it. If the rest of the army moved forward, Roper was not even sure that they would be able to climb the slick ridge. They would take many casualties; that much was certain and their Left would be exposed to flanking attacks. *But what is the alternative? What if we retreat?* He could hardly breathe. Or maybe it was just that his breathing had ceased to be effective.

'Lord?' Again, more persistent. Roper was trembling now. His mouth formed several words but none of them made it past his lips.

What now? Almighty, help me! What now?

'My lord!'

Preserve the legions, Roper.

'We retreat,' said Roper, inflecting the order as though it were a question. 'Retreat,' he said again, agitated. 'The cavalry are to cover us.' He almost added: *I think.*

The aides stared at him. 'Lord?' said one, confused. 'That isn't . . .'

'Retreat!' insisted Roper. 'Retreat!' A thought struck him. 'Keep the cavalry clear of the waters around the Blackstones.' One of the aides nodded and pulled his horse away, signalling to a trumpeter. The others followed suit and the trumpet sounded. The legions juddered into life again. *Discipline will save us*, thought Roper as the legions about-turned and began to march away, arrows still spitting into the water around them. As the Sutherners saw the forces of the Black Kingdom begin to turn away, there came a great cheer and howl of derision from the ridge. A rumbling began, so deep that at first Roper thought it was distant thunder. Then he realised that the Suthern cavalry had begun to surge after the legions.

Then Uvoren was by Roper's side. He was on horseback and began snarling orders, sending aides scurrying across the battlefield and a string of trumpet notes blasting out. The cavalry was called into action and rode forward to cover the legions' retreat. Uvoren glanced at Roper. 'You have an arrow in your shoulder, Roper.' Almighty god. Roper swayed in his saddle. Uvoren stared for a moment, seeming fascinated.

Across the waters, behind the Blackstone Legion that was staggering away from the battle leaving behind as many as were able to retreat, Roper saw a familiar flash of steel. Earl William was there on horseback, surrounded by his knightly bodyguard, and he had found a new breastplate, quite as magnificent as the one Kynortas had torn from his chest. His horse stood among the longbowmen who still peppered the retreating Blackstones and he was gesticulating at a trumpeter, who appeared to be pulling the strings of the Suthern cavalry. Bellamus was nowhere to be seen; it seemed Earl William had assumed command of this corner of the battlefield.

Suddenly, there was screaming from Roper's right. He turned just in time to see a figure bolting through the flooding; a dark blur of striking rapidity. Alone, this warrior was charging for the Suthern ranks, changing direction violently and somehow sprinting right through the first line of soldiers. Sutherners were pushing towards him, trying to stop him but always left swinging at thin air as the figure seared through their loose ranks. Roper's mouth fell open; the warrior was heading for Earl William. It was a Sacred Guardsman, his ponytail exceptionally long, single-handedly charging the Suthern leader. In his wake he left a trail of spray and bamboozled Suthern warriors and he hurtled right through the enemy ranks and into the clear waters behind.

Uvoren had seen him too. 'Make room for your lictor!' The Sacred Guard obeyed, surging forward once more and driving a wedge into the Suthern line. They were evidently seeking to open a return path for the nameless warrior who was now nearing Earl William.

Earl William's bodyguards had spotted the radical. Half a dozen armoured knights, lances lowered, charged. The guardsman changed tack, heading for the outside of the formation and drawing his sword. It was the work of an instant and a whirl of metal: the figure, dwarfing the riders he faced, had beaten aside two lances and slipped between the knights. He was through, with nothing standing between him and Earl William. The latter had realised the danger he faced and desperately pulled his horse away, attempting to spur for safety.

He had left it too late. The guardsman was upon him before his horse had taken more than a few strides and he had seized Earl William's boot, dragging him from the saddle to crash into the water. The blade rose high and then plunged into the obscured form in the water; twice. The guardsman straightened up and held up something soaking, turning around to show it to both Suthern and Anakim army.

Earl William's head.

His long curls were held in the guardsman's enormous hand and water and blood trickled from beard and neck. The guardsman cast it aside contemptuously and turned back to the knights, who had now turned and converged on him. He disappeared from Roper's view, hidden behind thrusting horses.

Somebody smacked Roper in the back of the head. He turned and Uvoren rode past him. 'Move,' he called over his shoulder. 'Pryce has given us some time. We're leaving.' Pryce? Roper looked back to the guardsman who had slain Earl William and could scarcely credit his eyes when he saw that he had re-emerged. Two horses lay in the water, screaming in pain. Another one had no rider and the remaining knights were not pressing their attack, wary of the guardsman who had begun to run again. The Sacred Guard had opened a corridor for him in the Suthern ranks and held it as the lone hero returned.

So this is war.

The Black Legions were in headlong retreat. They were marshalled into columns by their officers, who threw confused looks at where the Almighty Eye of the Sacred Guard flew and where they knew somebody must be in command. Thousands of Anakim bodies lay in the flooding, arrows protruding from their flesh and bodies weighted down by armour. Only the Sacred Guard had shed Suthern blood and that because they had been forced to in defence of Roper. Trumpets were pealing out across the battlefield as the Anakim army condensed and the Suthern cavalry tore after them, searching for an opening. They were being held back by the Anakim cavalry, which was charging and re-charging, using their discipline to extricate the legions.

Pandemonium. Hundreds of Blackstones were half crawling, half swimming after the retreating soldiers. The other warriors, no longer in neat ranks but wading as quickly as they could through the flooding, were streaming away from the ridge where the Suthern infantry had begun to advance.

The Sutherners were after them.

2

The Hindrunn

There was always one oasis of calm in the Black Kingdom. Regardless of what war ravaged the rest of it, the great fastness at the border, the Hindrunn, would be safe. Built over centuries by one of Roper's ancestors, it was a thirteen-hundred-year-old honeycomb of black granite, lead and flint. Its presence, so dark and malevolent when observed from Suthdal – the land below the River Abus, occupied by the Sutherners – was the reason the border had barely changed over centuries. Within its tangle of broad, cobbled streets dwelt the legions.

When these returned, tradition dictated that they should be greeted by the women and children of the fortress. Crowds would line the streets, armed with little bunches of herbs to be thrown into the path of the legions. The bitter smell of rosemary, lemon balm and comfrey, crushed underfoot, was an evocation of celebration and relief. The warriors had returned home and once again they had been successful. Word would already have reached the Hindrunn of who had fought with particular bravery or skill and their names would be called out by the throng. The young boys would watch their warriors, imagining the day when the armour of the Black Kingdom would fit them and when it would be their turn to march through these streets.

The Sacred Guard would be first to enter the Great Gate. They would march in step, always in step, up the cobbled street; the crowds on each side ever-optimistic about the gap through which their legionaries could squeeze. People would lean from the upper windows of the houses to throw their herbs and the warriors, stern and proud, would try not to grin. Roper had been there once; part of the crowds that welcomed back the legions. He had not imagined taking his father's place, resplendent on a white horse at the front of the column, but a little further back, wearing the armour of a guardsman. Black Lords might be rare, but they were born. A Sacred Guardsman was self-forged; made through his own merits. There could be no more splendid thing and it had been decades since the Black Legions had failed on the battlefield.

The crowds were not accustomed to defeat.

So it was that when news reached the fastness that the legions had been whipped, that they were marching home with their tails between their legs and that the great Kynortas, Black Lord of forty years' dedicated service, had fallen on the battlefield, the reaction was first one of incredulity. It was simply unthinkable that the legions could have failed so badly and the report of tens of thousands of Sutherners swarming across the Black Kingdom must be exaggerated. Then the stream of refugees began to arrive, confirming that at their back was a marauding enemy force, and the incredulity turned to anger. Some were claiming that the army had not even fought the Sutherners. They had just turned and run in the face of a strong defensive position and a swarm of angry arrows. This was not just a defeat: it was humiliation. What seemed even clearer was that Roper had wilted in the crucible, as so many are wont to do, and having inherited command, had panicked and insisted on retreat. He had not even stayed long enough to retrieve his father's body; it had been left to be stripped and degraded by the Sutherners.

Roper was not sure who had commanded the army on the bleak march back to the Hindrunn. It did not seem to have been him. Nobody came to ask him for orders and Roper did not know to whom he should volunteer them or what form they should take. Indeed, he had been ignored by all but two people on the march. The first was a surgeon, who had silently extracted the arrow from his shoulder and staunched his wounds. Roper had gritted his teeth as the head was dragged from his flesh and had no more than a couple of deep breaths to sustain him before a glowing brand was pressed into the wound. He made no sound, but the hiss and smell like cooked meat had been too much. His vision faded into white and he swayed where he sat. When it was over, he was unsure whether he had stayed conscious or not.

It was at the same time that Roper's second visitor approached: Uvoren. He stood quietly and watched Roper setting his jaw, again apparently fascinated by the wounds, though he must have seen many. He smiled roguishly at Roper. 'A troublemaker, eh, lord?' Lord. 'Never seen our army's leader ride alone into a press of the enemy before.'

Roper looked up at Uvoren, teeth gritted. 'Not fast enough.'

Uvoren shrugged. 'You couldn't have saved him, lord. He was dead already. It was bold to try, but not clever. But having retreated . . . well, you'll need to be careful from now on. The Hindrunn won't take kindly to it. As we enter the fortress tomorrow you must ride at the head of the column.'

'I must?'

'I would advise so. Your subjects must know that you unquestionably command this army.'

Roper nodded. 'I understand.'

Uvoren glanced down at Roper's battered plate armour that lay resting against the surgeon's supplies. The chestplate had been punctured by a thrust of considerable power; damage sustained during Roper's struggle for survival in the flood waters. 'You must find some new armour as well. The

Black Lord should appear invincible. You don't want people to know you've been brawling like a gutter-rat.'

Roper nodded again. Uvoren stared at him a little longer before turning away, a strange smile on his lips. Roper did as he was told, donning fresh armour and taking the lead of the column as the shadow of the fortress fell over the horizon. The legionaries looked up at him with accusatory eyes as he rode past, though they said nothing. Roper hunched into the unfamiliar horse that he had had pressed upon him on the battlefield, looking away from his soldiers.

There was no shout of welcome as the Great Gate opened; just the clunk of the locking bars being withdrawn. It was a sapphire dusk; nearly nightfall. The first stars had begun to glow overhead. The rain had stopped but moisture clung to the air, creating a chill. Roper led the first ranks through the gate and saw that the streets beyond, as ever, were thronged with women and children. But they bore no herbs.

Roper straightened his back and stared ahead. *Steady, now.* His home had never felt so unfamiliar. Where usually they would have been cheering and calling out, the crowd was breathtakingly silent. The only movement as Roper rode past was of eyes: hundreds of eyes following him. His horse's hooves sounded indecently loud on the cobbles and suddenly, in his shiny new armour, Roper felt abashed. The silence stretched.

And held.

He could hear the guardsmen trying to soften the pounding of their boots behind him; those heroic men attempting to withdraw inside their armour altogether. A low hiss escaped one of the spectators and was taken up by others around. It crossed the deserted road and rose like a waterfall on both sides. Roper's lungs seemed to fill impossibly as the hiss grew and grew, as though it were Catastrophe herself, the great chain-mailed serpent that would overturn the world, rising from the earth. The hiss burst, and suddenly the crowd was in open disdain, hooting and whistling as the burning-faced legionaries entered the Hindrunn. A girl called that the legionaries should leave their weapons with the women; they would acquit themselves more honourably than their men had. The crowd laughed and jeered.

Roper rode alone at the front, burned by the contempt radiating from either side and the hatred at his back. He would be blamed for all of this. It might be the worst humiliation the legions had ever suffered and it was all his.

But this was not the worst realisation that was breaking over him. Another far worse, far more significant thought had invaded his mind. Accidentally, with no will or intent, Roper had made a terrible enemy.

Roper sat alone at the end of the great table that occupied the Chamber of State. The table was made of vast lengths of oak, so enormous that they could not have come from any living tree. Kynortas had explained to Roper that the wood had been extracted from a simmering bog to the south which preserved the ancient line of trees that had once dominated Albion. Now, the table dominated a large granite chamber, whose floor was covered by bearskins and which was well illuminated, even at this hour, by two-score oil lamps. Flames stirred in a brutally heavy stone fireplace that had been chiselled into one of the walls.

He had been here many times before at Kynortas's side, brought to witness negotiations, campaign plans and even disciplinary hearings. He was not sure why he was here now.

An aide, one of the young warriors seeking a role in high command some day, had arrived at Roper's quarters to tell him that he and Uvoren were to meet here as soon as Roper was able. Roper had hobbled down to the room as fast as he could on his damaged leg, expecting to arrive late to a full war council where the legates debated how to stem the tide of Suthern soldiers now sweeping across the Black Kingdom, aides galloping through the corridors outside to prepare their warlike nation's revenge.

Instead, the room had been deserted.

Roper had sat down at first in his usual seat, to the right of the seat his father occupied – the Stone Throne. Soon afterwards, he had shifted to his left; he should occupy his father's place. He had now been seated there for an hour. Only one person had come; an irritable legionary who trimmed and charged the oil lamps. He did not acknowledge Roper and Roper did not know what to say to him. He felt foolish sitting silently on the Stone Throne, and even more foolish after the legionary departed and he was left alone in the chamber.

Roper was tormented by the realisation that had come to him as he had entered the gate and left him more and more desperate as he sat alone in this room, waiting for Uvoren.

The Captain of the Guard arrived after an hour and a half. He threw open the door and marched for a seat at Roper's end of the table, followed by ten companions. From the crests that they bore, Roper counted four Sacred Guardsmen, two Ramnea's Own legionaries and two legates. With them were a pair dressed in embroidered robes: a Councillor and a Tribune. The final Sacred Guardsman, who drew his own chair as though he scarce had time for sitting, was in possession of an exceptionally long black ponytail that reached down to his waist. Where the others all looked strained, this man appeared merely impatient.

Uvoren did not introduce Roper. Indeed, he did not acknowledge him. 'We have plans to make,' he said shortly.

'Make them quickly,' said the man with the long ponytail. 'Jokul has summoned me for two hours at my earliest convenience. I don't want to spend this entire night in council.'

Uvoren smiled at the man. 'Two hours with Jokul? Just one might kill you.'

The ponytailed man nodded. 'I'm worried it might not.'

There was a slight pause and then the table rippled with laughter.

'That man gets thinner every time I see him,' said one of the Sacred Guardsmen.

'I've seen buzzards follow him around when he goes outside,' said Uvoren. They all laughed again. Roper joined in, but stopped when Uvoren stared at him, that smile on his lips again. 'You shouldn't laugh at Jokul, Roper.' Roper. 'He is a public servant of many years. Nor should you be sitting in the Stone Throne. It remains unoccupied for three days after the death of the Black Lord as a mark of respect.' He gestured to one of the places further down the table.

Roper did not move for a moment. He did not believe Uvoren and stared at him stubbornly. He felt the combined gaze of the table focus on him and realised this was a contest of will he could not win. Retreat, again. He stood and moved further down the table. The ponytailed man watched him dead-eyed as he sat down. 'What is your name, Guardsman?' Roper asked, looking for some initiative.

'Lictor,' responded the man.

'That is a title,' said Roper.

'Yes. It is my title.'

And my title is Lord, thought Roper, though he said no more. He knew this man by reputation, if not to look at. A lictor was the disciplinarian of a fighting unit, charged with ensuring that the soldiers do as they are told. He had the remit to beat his fellow soldiers to death if he wished, though they could not lay a hand on him. It was an influential position, traditionally given to a man of surpassing self-confidence and bravery. Evidently the role fitted the ponytailed man like a glove: it was he who had killed Earl William.

Roper knew his name and his reputation well: this was the sprinter Pryce Rubenson, twice honoured with a Prize of Valour. He was almost as famous as Uvoren himself; known throughout the Black Kingdom as one of the finest athletes it had ever produced and as much a hero to the young women of the land as to its warriors.

Roper learned much over the next hours.

The legate of the Blackstones told what had been happening beneath the flood waters. 'Clever bastards. Caltrops. I've seen them before in Samnia: jagged iron spikes which always face upwards, sprinkled in front of my legionaries, thick as grass. They baited us with a false charge to make sure we were running when we hit the trap.' The legate had shaken his head. 'Now that was clever. And the nerve, to get the timing just right. I'm rather sorry you killed Earl William, Pryce. It can only hasten the rise of Bellamus. In him, we have a worthy enemy.'

'I'm not sorry,' said Uvoren. 'The bickering between Bellamus and Lord Northwic was all that stopped our retreat turning into a full-blown disaster.' He had turned to look sourly at Roper.

'I ordered the cavalry to keep clear of the Blackstones,' Roper blurted. This elicited a stony silence from the other men at the table.

'Be silent, Roper,' said Uvoren finally. 'You have no idea what you're talking about. Your father was just passable as a leader; limited, but passable. You have absolutely nothing going for you.' Everyone at the table besides Pryce laughed. Uvoren grinned. 'What are you doing here?'

'You told me to come,' said Roper. He wanted to say more, but knew Uvoren would undermine him, whatever his words.

'He told you to come?' put in another guardsman with a sweaty face. 'If you can do exactly as you're told, you might rule after all, Roper.' The table laughed again.

Roper kept quiet. He knew his first taste of command could scarcely have been worse, but he had not expected it to be met by this naked aggression. Uvoren, who had seemed so charming and friendly under Kynortas's gaze, had turned on Roper. This was his enemy: Uvoren the Mighty. The most esteemed man in the country and its most glorified warrior. They had started playing a game and Roper had not even known. That was why he had told Roper to change his armour: so that it would look as though he had commanded and panicked from afar, and not been involved in the fighting.

That was why he had asked Roper to ride at the head of the column: so that the blame was placed squarely on his shoulders.

The laws of succession were clear; Roper must rule. But Uvoren, one of the most influential and respected warriors of the age, at the head of the Lothbroks, one of its greatest houses, was trying to make Roper's position so untenable that an exception would be made. Uvoren had seemed to support the retreat but it was Roper who had taken the blame for it. After that, and with such an obvious and capable rival to his succession, who would support Roper? What chance did a nineteen-year-old with no experience and no name other than that bequeathed to him by his father stand against the greatest warrior alive?

He had no idea where to begin; no idea where he would find the allies to support his claim. But he knew where to find his enemies.

They were right here; at this table. Uvoren's war council.

Roper memorised them all. He remembered their names, their stations, their countenances. He observed who was personally close to Uvoren, who merely a crony. He watched the way they sat, deduced their characters and weaknesses. Was there resentment in the eyes of Uvoren's sons, Unndor and Urthr? Was Asger, the sweaty-faced second-in-command of the Sacred Guard, rather unintelligent? He found himself particularly transfixed by the Sacred Guardsman next to him: Gosta. He said very little during the council and was rarely asked for his opinion. Sometimes he was given an order which he accepted with a mute nod. Roper knew nothing of him, but Uvoren treated him as though he were a faithful hound. The other officers appeared wary of Gosta. Even Pryce was leaning away from him in some distaste.

Before Roper was arrayed an influential power block: men of wealth and prestige who would support Uvoren's claim to the Stone Throne. If Roper wanted to rule, he would have to break them all; one by one.

And, of course, there was Uvoren himself, who now spoke. 'Forget Boy-Roper, he isn't relevant. Our position is dire. The Blackstones are at half-strength, morale has plummeted and we did not anticipate returning the legions to the Hindrunn. We need more food. The Skiritai have suggested that the Sutherners do not intend to besiege us; they'd rather harry our eastern lands. We must put a stop to that. That is tomorrow's task. Until then, I'm going to bed.' Uvoren stood and so did the rest of the council. The long-ponytailed Pryce did not wait to be dismissed, stalking past Roper and out of the Chamber of State. Roper remained in his seat. Uvoren stared at him, eyes narrowed. Roper returned his gaze stubbornly. 'A Blackstone reported to me today, Roper, informing me you had made him a Sacred Guardsman. Don't ever try and put your own men in my unit again.'

'That is my right, Uvoren,' said Roper, flushing.

'You think so?' Uvoren sounded incredulous. Then he laughed at Roper's furious expression and leaned over to pat him on the cheek. 'Calm yourself, Roper.' He chuckled, now pinching Roper's cheek. 'You take life so seriously. You're not upset about your father, are you?' Roper said nothing. Uvoren laughed again. 'It was a good death,' he said, carelessly. 'Peers, tomorrow. Goodnight.'

They filed out of the chamber, leaving Roper alone again. He stood and moved back to the Stone Throne, obstinately sitting back down. He rubbed his fingers over the smooth arm rests; polished by the grip of a dozen Black Lords and, most recently, his father. The Black Lord does not cry. So Roper howled instead.

3
The Inferno

'It was a good move, Bellamus,' said Lord Northwic carelessly. The lord had once been a shining young warrior and, though he was now an old man, his experience made him an invaluable leader. He might have been in his late sixties but was still fit and mobile. A beard the colour of faded copper extended right up to his cheekbones, above which a pair of rheumy eyes, draped in deep folds of skin, probed the landscape. He looked tough, which he was, and harsh, which he was not. 'You have seen the spikes used in battle before?'

'The caltrops? Yes; in Safinim. My father was a pikeman.'

'A pikeman?' said Lord Northwic with a snort. 'Good God. You really do come from nothing, don't you?' Bellamus supposed that Lord Northwic had meant this as a compliment of sorts. 'A shame about Earl William,' continued Northwic.

'Do you really think so?' asked Bellamus, eyes crinkling in amusement. Seeing Lord Northwic's shock, he tried to mollify his tone. 'It was quite a spectacular death,' he said, remembering the great figure who had come storming through the flood waters. Half a dozen of Suthdal's noblest knights had been made to look inadequate by that single, immense warrior.

'No denying that,' allowed Northwic.

The two generals sat on horseback atop the ridge from which Roper's forces had retreated. The rain continued to thunder down but they were kept dry by a canopy, borne by four aides who waited patiently at each corner, water dripping down their faces. Most of the Suthern army was elsewhere, committing the Black Kingdom to the torch and the sword, but below them several thousand soldiers worked in the flood waters.

The pale, rain-bloated Anakim corpses were being stripped and searched for anything valuable. Their prized arms and armour, of which the legionaries had been so proud and which they had treated so lovingly in life, were piled haphazardly to be melted down and re-forged to a more useful size. The rough woollen clothing, though utilitarian, was robust enough to be put to further use. But the most valuable plunder was within the corpses themselves.

Bone-armour.

The Sutherners sliced through the rain-softened skin to expose the overlapping bone-plates beneath. They sawed and wrenched at the ligaments that held them in place, hauling out the flint-hard plates and piling them up. These were not the stark-white or light-cream of other bones; they had a reddish, rust-coloured hue to them. They were lighter and harder than any steel developed by the Sutherners, and Bellamus had very particular ideas about how he would use such a material.

After the battle, an enormous corpse had been dragged up the ridge for his inspection. It was different from the others. Bigger; more magnificently equipped. Those who had seen the individual felled by an arrow to the throat reported that he had been an officer of some kind, mounted on horseback. Bellamus recognised the face. 'So we got you,' he had said sadly to Kynortas's body. 'And if you're dead, that means your lad now rules.'

Bellamus frowned down at the body. 'Fetch me his helmet.'

The master of the horse which had dragged the corpse unbuckled the great war-helm from Kynortas's head and passed it up to Bellamus. He ran his fingers over it, turning it over in his hands. As he had thought, it was not steel. It was some kind of alloy, duller than steel but also more beautiful. It was almost marbled, with shades of cloud, gloom, iron and moonlight merging and overlapping. 'The famous Unthank-silver. Never before have I seen it used for anything other than a sword.' It felt too light for the brutality of combat, though Bellamus knew the Anakim did not suffer equipment that was just for show. War was their business and if this battle helm felt light in his hands, that was no more than a demonstration of how little he knew. He tried it on: much too large for his head.

'Unthank-silver, lord?'

'I'm not a lord,' said Bellamus to the horse-master. 'Just a commoner, like you. It's the alloy that Anakim make their swords from. Can't say I know how it's made but I hear that when two Unthank-weapons meet in combat, they shed white sparks like a blacksmith's anvil. Maybe there's a clue in that.'

If there was, it mystified the horse-master.

Bellamus took the helmet off and examined it once again. 'Magnificent.' A metal crest ran from the front to the back of the crown, with a perilously sharp blade, shaped like the edge of an axe, on the front of the crest. Overlapping plates which would provide flexible protection for the owner's neck ran down the back and an alloy visor and cheek-plates concluded the comprehensive defence. 'A shame for the Jormunrekur to lose it; I'm not sure they could afford its replacement nowadays. We shall send it back to them.' He tossed it back to the horse-master and bade him reattach it to the corpse. He had intended to send the king Kynortas's skull. But the king could have another present. He had a different use for this one.

Bellamus discovered a mighty sword still in Kynortas's scabbard. It appeared to be made of the same metal as the helmet and so was light and strong, but it also glittered strangely in the grey light of the day. The edge was shining somehow. It was too long to be practical and he could barely close his hand around the grip, which was built for a hand on an altogether different scale. Even so, Bellamus strapped it on. There was more than one way to use a weapon like this.

Bellamus had told Lord Northwic that Kynortas was dead, though he had neglected to mention that his body had been recovered. Now he and the lord rode along the crest of the ridge together, moving slowly enough for the canopy to keep up with them. Thunder was beginning to rumble in the mountains to the north and a bolt of pale lightning splashed shadows across the battlefield. It made the flood waters boil where it struck them. 'This is a bleak country,' said Lord Northwic, staring down at the labourers who toiled over the Anakim dead. 'We must rid ourselves of the Anakim, but beyond that . . . it isn't worth the taking.'

'They have been beset by unusual quantities of rain just as surely as we have,' said Bellamus mildly. 'I can imagine this looking quite beautiful in the sun, in a rugged sort of way.'

'Wilderness,' replied Lord Northwic dismissively. 'These mountains are the cankers on the face of the earth. Below the Abus, good ripe soil; tilled, farmed and ordered. It is a little closer to paradise. This . . .' he flicked a clawed hand at the forest that occupied one end of the ridge, tree tops shifting in the wind. 'This is the country of the wolf and the bear and the wildcat. Their villages are isolated by the distance and the wild. They share their land with the barbarous and the chaotic. No wonder they are so wild themselves.

'I wonder, can it even be pacified? When we have defeated the Anakim, can this land be tilled, or is the earth too shallow and too filled with rocks? Will the site of the forests support pasture land for cows and sheep, or is the earth too sour?'

'We shall have to keep the Trawden forests standing,' said Bellamus. 'By all accounts a legendary hunting ground.'

Lord Northwic grunted. 'So this is your plan. Take the north and you shall be its master.'

Bellamus smiled briefly. 'Nobody else seems to want it. His Majesty even speaks of building a great wall and forgetting that half of this island lies to the north. Give the north to me; I'll pacify it.'

'Is it just the north you want, Bellamus?' Lord Northwic was looking sidelong at him and Bellamus knew at once what he was referring to. 'I was as young as you once. Even younger. I can see how you act around Queen Aramilla. She is the only one of us you keep your distance from.'

'Better not to play with fire,' said Bellamus, not returning Lord Northwic's gaze.

'Yes, it is,' said Lord Northwic forcefully. 'In the eyes of both God and man. Be careful with her.'

'I barely know her,' said Bellamus.

'I know you both,' said Lord Northwic. 'She is inscrutable. But you are hiding something.' Lord Northwic spoke harshly but Bellamus knew that, whatever his words, the old man rather liked him. In any case, he was in no danger. The man who suggested to the king that his wife was having an affair was at greater risk than either of the accused. The two men rode in silence for a time. 'Perhaps we should move to take the Hindrunn,' suggested Lord Northwic.

'Bad idea, Ced,' responded Bellamus. Lord Northwic was relaxed in his leadership and did not object to the informality. 'With the legions still inside, that nut is un-crackable. They would like nothing more than for us to attempt a siege.'

'More plundering, then,' said the lord, unenthusiastic.

'More plundering,' agreed Bellamus. 'The more loot that floods the south, the more warriors will come to our cause. It is also our best hope of bleeding the Black Legions from the Hindrunn before we have to attack it.'

'And what do you know of their new leader, the lad Roper?' asked Northwic.

Bellamus had risen to prominence as the Anakim-specialist

of Erebos – the continent to which Albion was tethered. Nobody navigated the shadows quite like the upstart and nobody had the same ability to speak to Anakim on their level. He understood them: their motivations, their customs, their concerns. He had spent time with them in the Alps, in Iberia and now Albion. They had become his trade. Most observed the hopeless shortcomings of the Anakim tongue, their crude silhouetted art, their baffling, nonsensical maps, their lack of writing and their barbarous ways, and gave up trying to treat with them. Not Bellamus. His fellow Sutherners intrigued him. The Anakim fascinated him.

Bellamus had charmed and bullied and bribed to achieve what the nobles of Suthdal had considered impossible: a network of reliable Anakim spies within the Black Kingdom itself. In previous invasions of the north, their knowledge of the enemy they faced and their tactics had been woefully inadequate. Bellamus had made himself indispensable through knowing more than anyone else; and had shown a scarcely credible flair for command to boot.

'He was always said to be promising,' he answered Lord Northwic. 'But whether he actually commands is in doubt. I am told that a senior officer in the country, a warrior named Uvoren, has been making arrangements to take command should Kynortas die in battle. We met him, incidentally,' he added, glancing at Lord Northwic. 'He was the one with the war hammer, on Kynortas's left side. And the wildcat engraved on his chestplate.'

'Kynortas in the middle, who embarrassed poor Earl William,' said Lord Northwic, screwing up his face so that his eyes disappeared from view completely in his effort to remember. 'Uv . . . Uvora?'

'Uvoren,' corrected Bellamus.

'Uvoren on the left with the war hammer. Roper was the big lad on the right. What about the other one?'

'I don't know,' admitted Bellamus. 'A Sacred Guardsman, from his armour.' The two rode in silence for a while longer,

Bellamus content to stay quiet; absorbing the saturated landscape and delighting in the smell of the rain.

'I'm not sure this is a campaign we'll get to finish,' said Lord Northwic, at last.

Bellamus looked shocked. 'My lord?'

'For goodness' sake, Bellamus,' Northwic snapped. 'If I ever actually told you anything you didn't know already, I'd feel disappointed.'

Bellamus laughed.

The news from the south was that King Osbert, who truly feared the Anakim, was minded to withdraw the army now that Earl William had been killed. Letters had streamed north, illustrating a king who thought he had done enough to placate God's anger, and who thought, too, that they should take all they had gained and retreat. Northwic, though a powerful lord, was not considered to possess quite the level of vaunted nobility required to lead an army north of the Abus. Winter was fast approaching, and the first battle had gone better than anyone had dared hope. The rumours said King Osbert was considering leaving the campaign at that and calling it a success. It could only get worse from here.

If true, it would spell disaster for Bellamus's ambitions. He had invested every favour, every piece of influence and wealth he had in this push north. To have it ended so soon, or else to have to deal with another earl sent north by the king to replace Earl William, could ruin everything. But he had few worries. At the first letter, he had sent a reply south with a swift rider, asking Queen Aramilla to intervene on his behalf. She had not failed him yet.

'I'm sure His Majesty will see sense,' Bellamus said after a time. 'It would be madness to leave the campaign here. We have an opportunity that is unlikely to present itself again.'

Northwic nodded. 'So who killed Earl William?' he growled.

'I can only guess at that, but one man does fit the description,' ventured Bellamus. 'Another Sacred Guardsman of considerable renown called Pryce Rubenson. He's a famous sprinter. They say he's faster on foot than a horse with a rider over any distance and any terrain. And perhaps the most courageous warrior in the north.'

'See if you can confirm that,' said Northwic. 'And make him pay.'

'As you wish,' said Bellamus.

'You're a valuable man, Bellamus.'

'You know how to use me, lord.'

Lord Northwic snorted. 'Yes, I do. Let you do exactly what you want.'

The Black Kingdom was being overrun. The defeat on the flood plain, which had been so humiliating that nobody had wanted to name the battle, had left the Sutherners free to rampage north of the Abus for the first time in centuries. It was as though each soldier had endured that wait personally, such was their appetite to loot and burn.

Especially to burn.

It was common enough, when at war, to set villages and granaries ablaze as you passed through them. It weakened the enemy's morale, hampered their ability to resist and signified the helplessness of the occupied territory.

Even this, however, did not explain what was happening to the east of the Hindrunn. From atop any one of the great granite walls, or the towers that surrounded the Central Keep, an immense cloud cast the east into shadow. It smothered the light from the sky and stained every sun- and moon-rise a bruised red. Every soldier in the Hindrunn had seen it: the very sky swamped by the atomised infrastructure of their country. Scouts were flooding in, reporting a conflagration so dense that they could not pass through; a wall of flame that swept clear the lands at the back of the Suthern army.

The news grew worse.

The Anakim had always been outnumbered by the Sutherners, but their warlike society and forbidding reputation had made most think twice before attempting an invasion. Now, with the news that they had won a great victory, Suthern reinforcements were streaming north, swelling the ranks of the army that was now commanded by Lord Northwic. He was commanding well, this lord, and seemed content to keep clear of the Hindrunn, seeking instead to vaporise the land around it and so draw the legions swarming angrily from their nest.

Uvoren would have none of this. He met every day in the Chamber of State with a full council of war, the immense oak table crammed with all fourteen legates; representatives from the great houses of the realm; the heads of the offices of state; the Chief Historian and her deputy; and the leaders of various towns who had sought refuge in the Hindrunn from the Suthern horde. Roper was there too, listening as the same voices clamoured again and again for an audience. They would stand and repeat their perspective, either to a rumble of agreement or baying dissent. It seemed that most of those around the table who spoke shared Uvoren's thoughts on the matter.

The legions should be kept in the fortress. It was regrettable that the surrounding lands were being put to the torch but they had to look to the long term. Within the Hindrunn, they would outlast any attack. As long as the real wealth of the Black Kingdom – the legions – was kept safe, then they could retake all they had lost.

The Chief Historian was one of the few prepared to speak out against this course of action. A woman of steel-grey hair, angular features and unswerving rectitude, her role was to provide perspective on the situation, drawing the council's attention towards historical precedents. 'You should all realise that this may be the first time the Hindrunn has been used so defensively. Its construction was justified as a wasps' nest, not a strong-box. In all previous invasions, the councillors have concluded that we cannot survive without supplies provided by the kingdom, and we have met our enemies in the field. Outside the walls of this chamber, the Black Kingdom is in flames.'

'We are the Black Kingdom,' growled Uvoren. There were not many prepared to speak out against him; it was obvious which way the wind was blowing.

So the legions sat inside the Hindrunn. And waited.

At his first full war council, Roper, trying to limp as little as possible on his damaged thigh, strode straight-backed to the Stone Throne and sat down in it, coldly meeting the gaze of anyone who looked at him. That had raised eyebrows, but Uvoren had not dared repeat his lie about three days of mourning in front of so many. Beyond that, Roper had no idea how to progress. He had tried to speak in the councils but Uvoren had snarled at him to be silent, followed by the rumble of agreement. That was becoming Roper's default position. Silence.

Five full days after the legions' return to the Hindrunn, they were still there. Another council had ended with the decision to weather the storm behind granite. It had further been decided that the gates were to be shut to the swarm of refugees arriving at the Hindrunn. Uvoren said they were to stay outside the walls, citing concerns over hygiene. As the numbers of refugees grew yet greater and became a restless mob at the fortress gates, Roper suspected the decision would be attributed to him.

Roper stood from the Stone Throne as the council filed from the room. He watched as the Chief Historian arrested one of the other councillors, placing a hand on the man's shoulder and whispering in his ear. The man, who, Roper had learned, was called Jokul, stood motionless and listened, still facing the door. The other councillors, thwarted and frustrated, had eyes only for the exit. They split around the pair, before finally Jokul turned and looked directly at Roper, locking eyes with him. The Chief Historian was still murmuring in his ear as Roper and Jokul shared a long appraisal. Finally, Jokul nodded. He had not said a word. The chamber drained until it was just the three of them, Jokul and the Chief Historian both examining Roper. Uvoren was last out of the door and looked back at them. He snorted, calling something to the sweaty-faced Guardsman Asger, who laughed uproariously and tried to steal a glance at 'Boy-Roper' before Uvoren shut the door.

Roper knew about the Chief Historian, and had been watching Jokul over the last few days. He was one of the few who had stood against the idea of sheltering in the Hindrunn. Even more unusually, when he spoke, his words were not treated with scorn by Uvoren and his baying supporters, but warily considered. He was treated delicately, like one of those toxic-mouthed snakes that sometimes arrive on trade ships from distant lands, which even Uvoren dared not enrage. There was no obvious reason why. He had no reputation in battle, he was not backed by any great house that Roper knew of, and he was certainly no orator. Indeed, when he spoke, it seemed to suck the energy from the room.

'May we speak, lord?' the historian asked.

'Of course,' said Roper, resuming his seat heavily. He still felt a penetrating ache whenever he employed leg or shoulder. The Chief Historian strode nearer and Jokul drifted in her wake, both taking seats on Roper's left.

'Do you know who we are, lord?' the historian asked, her voice steady.

'You are the Chief Historian,' Roper said. 'Frathi Akisdottir. And I know your name,' said Roper, turning to Jokul. 'But not your station.'

'No,' said Jokul, his voice small and crisp. 'My title is Master of the Kryptea.'

And suddenly this figure made sense.

Roper stared at him for a moment, his mind swirling. He glanced at the old historian, who looked back unshakeably, tapping a finger on the table as though trying to raise the tempo of this meeting. Roper turned back to Jokul and, in the end, managed a slightly aggressive: 'Well?'

'You know of the Kryptea, but our function is purposefully obscure. I would not kill the Black Lord in front of the most reliable witness in the kingdom.' Jokul gestured at the Chief Historian.

Roper licked his lips. 'Then why are you here?'

Jokul sat back in one of the yew chairs that lined the table, legs folded over one another. He was excessively thin. Had a tangle of veins not wound around his forearms, he might have looked like a corpse. Roper remembered Uvoren's words about him a few days before: *I've seen buzzards follow him around when he goes outside.* Jokul was playing with a silver coin of some sort, twirling it between thumb and forefinger. 'We preserve the stability of the Black Kingdom,' replied Jokul. 'It is true that in the past this has sometimes manifested itself in assassinating members of your family who enjoyed their power excessively. But you have no power at the moment. Do you?'

'None,' admitted Roper. 'None.'

'Well, then, you are hardly a threat to the country.'

'You're interested in stability,' blurted Roper. 'It would make everyone's lives easier if I wasn't here and Uvoren commanded.'

'That is not our opinion,' said the Chief Historian. Jokul, still playing with the coin, shifted to a new position in his chair that made it look as though he was trying to see how little of it he could take up with his narrow shoulders. Roper's gaze switched to the woman, but found her no easier a resting place. She was more rigid, resembling a scaffold of oak in comparison to Jokul's mess of coppiced willow. And to look at her, Roper had to meet those unshakeable, white-blue eyes. 'We've both kept eyes on you as you grew up,' she went on, her voice softer than her glare. 'We were hopeful that you might become a leader some day. Not a ruler. A leader. Somebody who might command the love of the legions, as proficiently as your father had their respect. Unfortunately, your father died before you were prepared to take command.

Doubtless, Kynortas thought he had more time, but time is short for us all.

'What do you know of the Sutherners?' she demanded unexpectedly, leaning forward to hear his answer.

'They're small,' offered Roper, shrugging.

'Eh? Small?' She sat back again and pretended Roper had not spoken. 'The most important thing you must know about them is that they do not live longer than a century. That is why they are such a voracious race. They have no time, and so they must consume. They each want to see change in their own lifetime. We know that we just have to wait and change will come.'

'I don't know anything about them,' said Roper.

'Nobody seems to. The Academy,' she said, referring to the sisterhood which she led, 'and the Kryptea,' she gestured at Jokul, who sat scrunched into his chair, 'have a similar complaint. We have fought against the Sutherners for thousands of years and nobody has bothered to interpret them.'

Roper had little interest in the Sutherners at that moment. He glanced at Jokul. 'So you will just sit by in the contest between me and Uvoren and do nothing?'

'It is very rarely that the Kryptea is required to act,' replied the pale man. 'Most of my task is to gather information, and of late the Sutherners have presented a much more real threat to the stability of our lands than your family has. Between the Wolf and the Wildcat . . .' Jokul named Roper's and Uvoren's house banners, his eyes narrowed. 'There is no need to intervene just yet.'

'So can't you make us march on the Sutherners?' demanded Roper.

'That would be an abuse of my position,' replied Jokul. 'The Kryptea is not here to rule; but we make certain that the right person does.'

'I am the right person—'

'Are you?' Jokul cut Roper short, pale eyebrows flying upwards. 'Certainly not in the opinion of the Black Kingdom, which mostly regards you as a coward.'

'I did the right thing,' said Roper quietly. He had no idea if that was true.

'I wasn't there,' said Jokul, managing to imply that he still knew more about what had happened than Roper did.

Of course you weren't, thought Roper. He had never seen anyone so un-warrior-like.

'Neither of us was,' cut in the historian. 'Where we agree is that we don't much want Uvoren to succeed your father. He has his talents. He knows the business of war, he is well supported and he brings the welcome backing of the Lothbroks.' Uvoren's house. 'But his temperament is a problem. He acts in his own interest and he is not wise. I do not want him ruling the Black Kingdom. Do you understand why he delays?'

'Self-interest,' said Roper bitterly. 'He won't risk anything for others.'

Jokul gave a little tut. 'Do not despise Uvoren,' he said. 'Hatred is not a man's emotion.'

'Don't patronise me,' snapped Roper. It did not surprise him that Jokul did not believe in excessive emotion.

The historian waved a hand at Jokul, dismissing his intervention. 'Do not react,' she said, still unfazed. 'Just think. Uvoren does not leave this fortress because he knows that it is you who takes the blame while the Black Kingdom burns. You are nominally in command and he is waiting until frustration against you reaches boiling point. He is waiting, Lord Roper, for the point when he can usurp you and know that the reaction will be one of relief. Time is against you, so you must act fast.'

'If a single man would support me,' said Roper, 'I'd happily lead the army to attack.'

The historian raised an eyebrow. 'What do you need?' she asked, watching the effect of her words closely. It was an obvious test and Roper, cornered by the pair of them, did not respond to it. 'We're not going to secure the Stone Throne for you,' continued the historian, manoeuvring round his resistance. 'I don't have that power. But I'd like to see if you can do it for yourself. Uvoren has influence, wealth, reputation and allies. You'll need all of those, if you are to take him on.'

'I need allies first,' said Roper, 'and my house does not have the power to challenge the Lothbroks.'

'Your father was a strong ruler,' said the historian. 'Strong rulers have no need to elevate their family any more than another, but it has left your throne precarious. Even those in House Jormunrekur who do still enjoy positions of status will be reluctant to support you; they must join other powerful factions or find themselves smothered. But Uvoren has many enemies. They are quiet now, fearing a rise in his power. You must wake them up and bring them into the open.'

'So who are these enemies?'

The historian gave a little shrug before answering. 'Finding out is your task. This is your test. It looked as though the throne was to be yours by birthright but you're going to have to earn it. Let us see if there's enough talent in you to topple Uvoren.' Her tone was soothing, but her gaze unsettled Roper. 'If there is, you will be the most deserving Black Lord for centuries, because you'll need everything you've got. This will take all you can muster, and I doubt even that will be enough. All your charm, all your strategy, all your luck. He is a mighty warrior and the greatest warriors can fight in any theatre.' By her side, Jokul had finally stopped twirling the coin and slapped it flat upon the ancient oak table.

So let us begin, thought Roper. 'He is a mighty warrior and one with many times my experience, who knows infinitely more than I about this "theatre". This is not an even contest, but I will make it one. Where do I start?'

Jokul, seemingly more reluctant to offer help, stayed silent. Again, it was the historian who answered Roper. 'With a guardsman named Gray Konrathson,' she said. 'He was Uvoren's greatest competition for Captain of the Guard and, had sense prevailed, he would have won the contest. He has no great house, it is true, and holds little formal power. But he is Uvoren's most vocal opponent and is highly respected. Win Gray and you will have secured two valuable allies.'

'Two?'

'Gray's protégé: the lictor named Pryce Rubenson.'

'Pryce?' said Roper blankly. He had committed the name and the face to memory in this very room. 'He's a member of Uvoren's war council. And he doesn't seem interested in helping me.'

'I doubt he is,' agreed the historian, with a heave of her brow. 'But he sits on Uvoren's war council because he is the most admired man in the Black Kingdom, so Uvoren wants him on his side. People fawn for that man's approval in numbers that Uvoren can only dream of. And Pryce listens to just one man. So win Gray. That is where you start.'

Roper ran his fingers over the stone arm rests. 'There can be only one conclusion to this,' he said.

'Civil war,' finished the historian.

'At a time when we face invasion. My father declared it the greatest evil a nation can succumb to. And it has happened on my watch . . .' Roper turned his head to stare bleakly into the fire.

'This is your father's fault,' said the woman. Her unfaltering presence reminded Roper of Kynortas. 'You have been left in a poor position. That is why we are helping. Uvoren has made it clear that he would allow this country to burn to the ground in order to occupy that seat beneath you.' She indicated the Stone Throne. 'So you need allies. Public allies especially.'

'Marriage?' asked Roper.

'Marriage,' she said, nodding slightly. 'Work out with whom.' She stood and Roper was astonished to discover that Jokul was already on his feet behind her. The pale man's presence was so faint that Roper had not noticed him rise. Roper struggled up to join them and it was Jokul who spoke next.

'Your most immediate concern is a man whom you can trust to defend you. Uvoren has seen us meet; you are in more danger now than ever before. Do you know a warrior who may help?'

Roper thought hard. 'Perhaps.'

Jokul nodded. 'Make him your man. Uvoren has informants everywhere.' He folded a fraction at the waist and turned for the door, leaving the historian still standing by Roper.

'Do not disappoint me, lord,' she said. 'I suspect we will need you.' She turned to follow Jokul, who was holding the door for her. As she passed through it, Jokul turned back towards Roper, one hand resting on the handle.

'You were, of course, correct, lord. Stability would indeed be improved by your death. And one way or another we will need firm leadership in the times to come. Do what you must, my lord. Or the Kryptea will do what they must.'

4

The Severed Head

Queen Aramilla processed down an aisle of trees, a gaggle of courtiers trotting behind her and the king in front, restraining a pair of hounds. Copper leaves strewed the filthy path, which bisected a royal forest. Aramilla did not care for the hunting for which this forest had been preserved. Her sport this day would be with her retinue. The elaborately frocked and painted women who followed her were engaged in a constant struggle to adapt to her wildly varying fashion. On the last occasion they had walked here, the weather dry and mild, Aramilla had appeared in the most outlandishly extravagant piece she had been able to lay her hands on; bristling with so many pearls that she resembled a hail-cloud and fairly rattled as she walked. She had declared to her pragmatically dressed ladies-in-waiting that wherever they were, their standards must never drop. Now, to her great satisfaction, all had attended this muddy march absurdly overdressed, flinching away like sheep from the mud that speckled their costly skirts. Aramilla had reverted to darker and more practical garb, and threw amused glances over her shoulder at those who trotted unhappily in her wake. By her side was the only other woman in on the joke: a dark-haired favourite of hers enfolded in a dusky cloak much more appropriate to the day.

'Some fun, Maria?'

'Of course, Majesty,' said the dark-haired woman.

Aramilla reached out and grasped a low branch that overhung the path, dragging it with her for a moment before releasing it, allowing it to jerk back into position. The leaves shivered and displaced the droplets they carried over the two women who followed behind, dousing them in a freezing shower.

There was a silence.

Aramilla looked back to see both women with their shoulders hunched by their ears, faces twisted with shock. The queen smiled and there was a smattering of nervous laughter, most of it relief from those who had not been singled out for the jest. One of the women who had been doused smiled quickly in response to Aramilla. The other simply met her eyes, face in open horror and disdain. Aramilla stopped walking, fixing the horrified woman with an expression that fairly dripped with sympathy. 'Oh my dear, Lady Sofia; I didn't mean to shock you so.' She advanced to Lady Sofia and captured her arm, dragging her back into motion. Lady Sofia's countenance was determined, furious calm as the queen squeezed her elbow and fell into step beside her. 'There, it isn't so bad,' she said, sweetness giving way to impatience before the sentence was over. 'The walk will warm you again. Are you enjoying the country air?'

'I'd be enjoying it more without your claws in my arm, Majesty,' said Lady Sofia, staring straight ahead.

Aramilla only smiled in response. 'You'll calm down soon and feel silly that you reacted so to a few drops.'

Lady Sofia tried to drag her arm away but Aramilla's fingers tightened on her elbow, hard enough to make her gasp. Lady Sofia struggled for a moment more, but the queen was relentless and she sagged, allowing herself to be drawn along in the royal wake. There was silence for a time and when Aramilla examined Lady Sofia's face from the corner of her eye, she saw unhappiness but no longer rage. On reflex, she shifted her approach. 'I very much like your dress, my dear,' she said, admiring the other woman. 'Where was it made?'

'It's Frankish,' said Lady Sofia dully. 'A tailor in Massalia.'

'You must give me his details. Such silk: it appears he can train spiders into willing employment.' That drew an unwilling smile from Lady Sofia, who was capitulating. Aramilla left it there, squeezing her elbow once more. 'I think I shall go and speak to my husband.'

The queen broke into a trot, leaving her ladies behind to join the plump King Osbert ahead. He was as preposterously dressed as most of Aramilla's retinue, wearing a helmet circled by a gilt rim and a vast shaggy bear fur about his shoulders. Each hand gripped the leash of a straining hound and the king was fussing over the hurt they might be causing themselves.

'May I have your arm, my love?' asked Aramilla, drawing level.

The king bowed elaborately. 'My queen.' His mighty voice made the air around Aramilla quiver. The dogs were passed to a nearby steward and the queen threaded her arm through her husband's proffered elbow. She could feel the damp heat as he sweated beneath the fur.

'How wonderful to be away from Lundenceaster,' she said with a sigh, leaning into him as they navigated a tawny puddle.

'Quite so,' said King Osbert, approvingly. 'I have rarely felt so light.'

'The city is restless,' Aramilla agreed sympathetically, giving his arm a squeeze. 'There are fewer worries here without the courtiers and priests constantly demanding your attention.'

The king flapped a gold-weighted hand. 'The Anakim, the Anakim. That's all I ever hear from them.'

'Maybe the day is approaching when you will not hear those words again. The tidings sound well, from the north.'

King Osbert raised a finger and waggled it before him, twisting his head to give her an indulgent smile. 'Not so, my dear lady. I fret about my men north of that dark river, now that they are no longer steered by the experienced hand of dear Earl William. A fine man: may God take him. I am minded to recall them all. The campaigning season is over already. We bloodied their noses and we can retreat with the loot we have claimed and the wrath of God placated. And without wise Earl William there to guide them . . . I fear for those soldiers.' His melodious voice sounded close to breaking under the pity that loaded it.

'Quite so, Your Majesty,' said Aramilla, nodding. 'A seasoned warrior. Which campaigns did he lead? I recall him being at Eoferwic. And in Iberia, of course.'

The king shook his head a little. 'Indeed, indeed, but neither was his finest hour.'

'No,' said Aramilla sadly. 'I fear both are remembered fondly by the Anakim. At least more so than the campaign currently under way.'

'Well, quite,' said the king. 'Look what he achieved in the first battle. But when one leads from the front, one takes great risk upon oneself.'

'So what did he achieve? What did the dispatch from Lord Northwic say?' probed Aramilla.

'Oh, it paid tribute to his bravery. It was most warm on that subject.'

'How did he defeat them?'

The king's head wobbled from side to side on its neck. 'Well, Northwic claimed that Bellamus of Safinim was instrumental in that, and that his plan crippled the Anakim and forced them to retreat. I can scarcely believe that of a commoner, though there is little doubt that he is a capable man.'

Aramilla snorted. 'I am thankful Northwic leads our men

in the north. Bellamus? A mercenary upstart able to defeat the Anakim? There is little he is good for. He has no business anywhere near a battlefield.'

'Now, now, my queen,' rebuked King Osbert. 'Let us not be unkind. I often believe he is cleverer than others recognise.'

Aramilla was quiet for a moment. When she spoke, her voice was warm. 'You have been truly generous in your support of him,' she said, leaning into her husband again. 'I have always admired your ability to see beyond his origins.'

'We must be generous in all things if we are to rule effectively,' said King Osbert sagely.

'And you are generous too, not to recall them. If Bellamus was truly responsible for that first victory, then you could leave him and Northwic in charge,' she said. 'Northwic is noble enough to command the army's loyalty and Bellamus can compensate for his lack of experience against the Anakim.'

'Perhaps, perhaps,' said the king, distractedly. 'But I would like a noble of higher standing in the north with them. Perhaps I shall send your father to join them. He is a man of true cunning and would be a fine representative.'

Aramilla stopped walking abruptly, though she retained her grip on the king's arm, dragging him to a halt too. She looked at him, her eyes wide. 'Please don't send my father north to fight the Anakim, my love.'

King Osbert blinked. 'No. Of course.' He planted a kiss on her forehead. 'How thoughtless of me, sweet woman. He shall stay safe in the south with us. Yes. Yes, we shall leave it to Northwic and Bellamus.'

Helmec knocked at the door to Roper's quarters. It was an honour, being summoned to the Black Lord's private quarters. Or it had been under Kynortas. Roper was simply relieved the guardsman had turned up, and he called him in at once. Helmec entered, his house crest emblazoned on the right side of his tunic: an upright spear capped with a split battle helm. House Baltasar.

Roper, sitting behind another table of rich bog-oak, stood to meet him, trying out the charm that Kynortas had been able to unleash. 'Helmec,' he said with a smile, leaning forward and offering the guardsman his hand. Helmec took Roper's hand in a huge scarred paw and bowed, an evidently irrepressible grin spreading across his ruined face.

'My lord,' he said. Lord. Indoors, away from the horrors of battle where he had seemed somehow more appropriate, Helmec was a hideous spectacle. His mangled cheek, through which a constantly working jaw complete with yellowed molars could be seen, was more withered space than flesh. He was missing an eyebrow and whatever had taken it had almost split his left eyelid. The very light grey eyes beneath looked almost ghoulish and his body was a compact box of muscle rather than the broad shoulders and triangular torso so stylised in Anakim carvings.

Roper invited the guardsman to a chair on the other side of the table and the two sat opposite one another. 'Helmec, I wanted to thank you again for the services you rendered me in battle, which amounted to no less than saving my life.'

'My honour, lord,' said Helmec loyally. 'I did what any man there would have done.'

'Were you scared?'

'Scared for you, lord,' said Helmec, the smile reappearing on his face. 'I thought you'd be dead before I could get there. But you've got some speed with that sword of yours.'

Roper nodded, so intent on winning over Helmec that the compliment did not register. 'We need more of your sort, Helmec; even in the Guard.' *Too much,* he thought to himself. *More subtle.* 'I trust you have been welcomed into your new unit?'

'Of course, lord.' Roper did a double-take at the guardsman, as though Helmec had just let something slip that he had not meant to. Helmec's answer had been convincing, but Roper could guess how Uvoren had treated a man appointed to the Guard by Roper.

'Uvoren has been good to you?'

'Yes, lord,' said Helmec, a touch more feeble this time.

'Go on.' Roper leaned forward in concern, as though Helmec had begun to condemn Uvoren but restrained himself.

'He has been good to me,' said Helmec stubbornly.

Roper sighed and looked down at the ancient oak. 'Uvoren is a great servant to the country and one of our mightiest warriors. But he guards his unit jealously. He will often exclude those who have more right than most to be in the Guard.' Helmec hesitated. 'I am firmly against the practice. To be the unit they can be, the Sacred Guard must fight as one, undivided by petty rivalries. He tried to turn the rest of the unit against you?' A wild guess.

Helmec looked a little dismayed. 'Yes, lord,' he said, at last.

'I'll do what I can to help you. You have earned that much. Rest assured, Uvoren will not know that you confided in me.' Helmec nodded curtly, already looking ashamed of his admission. Roper kept his face detached, but he was pleased. His man, indeed. 'Now, Helmec. I have some special duties I would like from you.'

'Certainly, my lord.'

'I want you with me for the next few days. You will be assisting me as we attempt to drive the Suthern horde from our lands.'

'That would be my honour, lord,' said Helmec dutifully. He could hardly refuse; not now he had confided his discontent with Uvoren's leadership.

'Very good,' said Roper. 'Then I will settle it with Uvoren.

To your station, Helmec.' Helmec, looking bemused, stepped outside Roper's quarters and stood guard over the door.

And Roper had his first ally.

Beyond the Hindrunn's southernmost extremity, from outside the Great Gate, Uvoren dispatched a messenger. A handful of subterranean tunnels aside, the gate was the only way in or out. It pierced the Outer Wall; a one-hundred-and-fifty-foot-high wave of dark granite that marked the edge of the fortress. Studded with bronze cannons and crowned with all manner of siege-breaking equipment, it was reckoned near-enough impenetrable. But that was no concern of the messenger, for the gates, forty feet of iron-sheathed oak, were opening before him. Behind: a deep stone well that tunnelled through the Outer Wall, ending in a far window of light. As the messenger continued and the passage was sealed behind him, the darkness pressed against his eyes. Just discernible above as deeper pools in the blackness were the charred 'murder-holes', through which sticky-fire would pour onto any soldier who made it through the Great Gate.

But the messenger had passed this way many times before, and the defences were not his concern. His journey to the Central Keep would take him through many structures as intimidating as this. At the end of the tunnel, he emerged into the residential area of the Hindrunn. Beyond him stretched a road of dense cobbles, brushed clean by unwilling legionaries. The roads fed a tight neighbourhood of sturdy stone dwellings, all remarkably alike; built from granite, roofed in slate and guttered with lead. A newcomer would notice that, although this was a cold land, well to the north of Albion, the glassless windows were frequent and large. A newcomer too might wrinkle their nose in preparation for the smell of raw sewage that would greet them in their home town or any of the great fortresses that they had visited before. But it would not come. The air smelt of baking rye bread, charcoal smoke, freshly dyed-cloth, hay, horse dung and of growing things. These last emanated from the small corridors of wilderness that bordered each of the dwellings. Hawthorn bushes laden with maroon haws climbed up the side of the buildings; crab-apple trees and raspberry canes swayed gently in the breeze and lingon bushes bearing pea-sized rubies packed any remaining space. As the messenger passed by, geese marched angrily towards the edge of their gardens and hissed at him.

He moved onwards, automatically bounding over the small clear streams set in stone beds that sometimes cut across the cobbles. Familiarity made him blind to the many intricacies that might strike a newcomer, particularly if that newcomer were a Sutherner. The carved outlines of hands, impressed into the walls of some of the houses, or of bare feet, ground into some of the larger cobbles. Wings of eagles, falcons and hawks hanging from the doorways or beneath the gutters. Twin stone pillars that stood close together and seemingly at random on top of some of the roofs. The occasional black cobble, strewn amongst the grey. Semi-circular instruments on some of the walls that a Sutherner might think were sundials, but had only four markings. There was a din coming from somewhere to the messenger's right and some of the residents were making their way towards the noise, laden with sacks of woven cloth or driving a little flock of geese.

The messenger moved on and presently came to a second wall; another mighty ripple of dark grey granite. Through another gate: another district, this one more pungent. He passed ripe pigsties and sheep-pens; flint and slate but better insulated than the dwellings occupied by their Anakim masters. These gave way to more intense drystone enclosures in which geese and ducks swirled as though draining into the watering hole in the centre. And so far, the fortress had exhibited barely a single piece of wood, with everything worked in unyielding stone.

Next, the weaving-houses received sacks stuffed with

wool, loaded onto pallets and craned high into upper windows. Then the tanneries: deer-, ox- and boar-hides piled outside, the air bitter with the smell of tannins and saturated with the taste of brine. After this, were buildings that received cartloads of barrels, but did not smell like breweries. Instead, the sour aroma of curdling cheese wafted from the windows, and the tight-laced barrels were filled with milk. At the end of this district, surrounding the third wall of this enormous hive, were the barracks. Weapons and helmets were supported on racks outside (carved exquisitely from rugged stone, with wood disdained even for this meagre duty) and ale and warm food wafted from the frenetic kitchens situated at the end.

Through another gate in another wall, the messenger crossed another river running through the fortress, this one powering a constantly-chewing water-mill, fed endlessly by wagon after wagon of grain. Then another row of buildings, instantly recognisable for the smell of yeast, wood-fired ovens and baking bread that suffused the air. He went past the brew-houses, the mouth-watering smoke-houses receiving wagons of carcasses into a collective maw and spewing wagons of skins back out to the tanners. All the while, the noise and smell were growing ominously. The air had begun to clang and hiss and ring, and the smell of hot metal and charcoal was all around before the messenger had arrived at the smithies. Swords, spearheads, arrowheads, helmets, armour, horseshoes, axeheads, buckles and more, much more, were pumped out by this rough community. Sparks drifted across the street, and here the messenger was briefly reminded of a story he had once heard, that the Sutherners thought the Anakim were fallen angels. In this ringing place of metal and smoke, it was difficult not to be reminded of hell. To a Sutherner, that might seem to be where this road leads: a pit, or a staircase that leads down, down, down.

Rearing above all this, behind one last curtain wall, were two structures. One was the messenger's destination: the

Central Keep. The other, nearby, was the summit of a vast stepped pyramid, capped by a shining silver eye. It had been visible for some minutes now, watching sleepless over the inhabitants of the fortress.

The messenger passed through that last wall, which was not a single wall but a system of them. Each gate led to a courtyard surrounded by potent weapons of slaughter, though for now they were filled with horses, munching contentedly on a nose-bag apiece. Through all this – defences and resources almost without limit – the messenger came at last to the Central Keep and, hidden until now by the defences, the Holy Temple. The Temple was an upturned cauldron of stone, caulked in acres of lead, and ghoulishly observed day and night by the desiccated corpses of ancient warriors. Sheltered in stone alcoves, the bodies of these old heroes were held erect by armour; one withered hand resting upon the hilt of a sheathed sword; teeth bared by retreating lips. One foot of each corpse was set slightly further forward than the other, as though the cadaver had been caught in the act of advance.

Beside the Temple, the Keep was three hundred vertical feet of tightly laid stone, braced by a dozen external towers and wearing a barbaric crown of crenellations.

Somehow, though it was all built with slaughter in mind, the fortress felt a good place. Throughout, fresh water flowed along custom-made paths, willing in its assistance of Anakim business. It was open and light, with no construction more than two-storeys high save the towers, Central Keep and the eye-capped pyramid. It was fresh and clean; un-soured by waste, sewage and plague. And everywhere were those little gardens of fruit-bearing trees and bushes, adding life to this stone colony. Something about it spoke of clarity of thought and purpose. There was no confusion here; no compromise. Only will, and wild.

The messenger's journey was not yet done. He climbed a broad flight of steps that led to the main doorway of the

Central Keep. Through this door was a vaulted stone hall, unadorned other than brackets for oil lamps set every few feet into the wall. A dozen doors branched off the hall and the messenger took the nearest on the right, coming to a narrow spiral staircase. He rose up the outside of the keep, the stairs dimly lit by arrow-slits that flashed past every dozen steps, until he came to another door some four storeys up. On the other side was a corridor, and at the end of the corridor was Helmec. The messenger tried to stride past him, but was halted by a firm hand on his chest. He spoke with the guardsman for some time; the messenger shrugging at last and turning away. Helmec watched him go, and then turned to knock on the door behind him.

'My lord?' Helmec peered around the door. 'A message from Uvoren. He says there is something outside the Great Gate that he needs your authority to deal with.'

Roper was tending to his equipment in his quarters. His cuirass gleamed from the table, and the room smelt of oil and beeswax. He looked up at Helmec, dropping the oil-soaked rag he held and on his guard at once. 'He's going to try and embarrass me.'

'I don't know, lord.'

'Ask him to provide more information.'

'The messenger was quite insistent, lord,' said Helmec, apologetically. 'Said it must be as soon as possible.'

Roper wondered whether he could refuse. It could be the wise course, but he still hoped that there might be a genuine need for his presence. He had few enough opportunities to lead without turning them down when they presented themselves. He bade Helmec accompany him and together they took a pair of horses from the stables below the Central Keep. They clattered out onto the cobbles, riding for the Great Gate. Helmec, prodded by a question from Roper, began chattering about where his two daughters were. 'They're both working in the freyi, lord, teaching medicine to the young girls there. I had word from one of them yesterday. She said the usual plants they use at this time of year are nowhere to be found: everything has been covered by the flood waters.'

Roper was not really listening. As they reached the gatehouse, he spotted Uvoren atop it. He was leaning against the battlements and laughing raucously with Asger, the Lieutenant of the Guard. Uvoren saw Roper and waved at him before pointing at something that Roper could not see behind the gate. 'Have a look!' he shouted, before gesticulating to a guard that the gate should be opened. The locking bars grated backwards and the counter-weight was released so that the gates ticked open.

Roper, still mounted, could not immediately see anything through the gateway. The great grass plain before the fortress appeared to be deserted, which was in itself strange. For weeks now it had been home to the thousands of refugees who fled the Suthern invasion, but now only their meagre possessions were in evidence. Their owners seemed to have scattered. Roper rode forward, straining his eyes and casting around. He half expected the joke to be that the gates would shut behind him, so he left Helmec behind to guard against any inclination that Uvoren might have to lock him out. Then he spotted it: an upright stake of some kind, planted in the earth fifty yards away. There was a dark mass on top of it.

Roper had realised what it was long before he reached it. The stake was a spear, butt-spike planted in the ground and there was a helmeted head impaled on top of it. Roper's face was drained of colour by the time he reached it, moving more and more slowly the closer he got. He stopped at last, a few yards short of the head. It was suspended at his eye-level. He stared at it for a long while and his father stared back.

So this was what Uvoren had wanted him to see. He turned to look back at the gate and saw that Uvoren and Asger were still watching him, though he could not make out their expressions. He turned back to the head. 'Hello, my lord,' he said, softly. A single tear welled over his eyelid and splattered onto his armour. An expulsion escaped his lips; the plosive sound of the letter 'p'. He took a sharp breath and straightened his back. 'I'm glad you're here.' His father just stared, eyes half-open, as if in a drunken stupor. Roper leaned forward and tried to pull the head from the spear, but the vomit rose in his throat and his hands felt so weak that he could not do it. He tried until he retched. He pulled back, trembling and panting. The head reeked.

'So what do I do now?' he asked the head, voice quivering a little. 'Almighty god, what do I do now?' The head looked at him blankly. 'I have an enemy, my lord,' Roper continued. He spoke haltingly, as though he were talking to the living Kynortas. He would have had little patience for these emotions. 'It is Uvoren and I think he is going to kill me. I want to die on the battlefield. Please, let me die on the battlefield. He could do it now and I don't think anyone would stop him. But he'll play with me more.' Roper took a deep breath again and blinked. For the first time, the thing before him appeared dead. 'And I'm going to kill him first. Do you hear me, Father? I'm going to kill Uvoren. I'm going to win the loyalty of this army. I'm going to break his traitorous council into a thousand bloody pieces. And then I'm going to *kill* that exalted bastard.'

Roper stopped abruptly and took a deep, steadying breath. He could hear a pair of crows calling to one another behind him. *Enough words. Actions now.* He seized the shaft of the spear, hauling it from the ground. Holding it up high, he turned back to the fortress and cantered back through the gates. On the other side, Uvoren and Asger had descended from atop the gatehouse and were waiting for him. They both grinned and Uvoren leaned to Asger and muttered something that Roper could hear plainly. 'I told you he'd weep.'

Roper stopped in front of them. 'Thank you for summoning me, Captain,' he said as calmly as he could. 'I hope you feel you can ask for me whenever you need help.' Uvoren was straight-faced, a touch of humour in his eyes. He had heard Roper, but his words were barely worth considering. A nineteen-year-old was no more than a wasp to the Captain of the Guard. He was the most esteemed warrior in Albion. The lad was weak. Roper did not have his skill, his strength, his experience or his resolve.

'He'll summon you whenever he pleases, Roper,' said Asger, glancing knowingly at Uvoren, who had eyes only for Roper.

Roper snorted at Asger's words. He had developed a deep disdain for the Lieutenant of the Guard, whose face was glistening even on this cool morning. He was Uvoren's lapdog; a yapping irritation who possessed no great talent at anything and yet had somehow managed to make it to his elevated position on Uvoren's coat-tails. If Uvoren made a joke, he was the first to start laughing and the last to stop. If Uvoren made a comment, Asger would agree with it fervently until Uvoren decided that perhaps he had not been right after all, at which point Asger would say how wise that was. He would talk happily with anyone, until Uvoren came into a room. Then he would look superior and aloof, regularly looking over at Uvoren and rolling his eyes as if to say that this company was not worth his time.

'You'll refer to me as "lord", Asger,' said Roper. He paused. 'You're always sweating. It must be warm, spending so much time with your head up Uvoren's arse.'

Even Uvoren laughed at that. Asger bristled but Roper just nodded to them and spurred his horse forward, Helmec falling in behind him. He felt a not inconsiderable glee at enraging Asger.

Roper took the head to the physician in the Central Keep and requested that the flesh be stripped from it and the skull returned afterwards. The wire-haired man he left it with seemed surprised but pleased to help. Roper would bury the skull somewhere in the wilds, where Anakim bones belonged.

He then returned to his quarters to drop off Kynortas's valuable battle helm, which, in truth, he was glad to have recovered.

There was work to do.

His quarters were on the highest floor of the keep, in one of the many towers that braced its exterior. The spiral staircase outside took him down to the foundations. Here, in a cave-like chamber twenty feet high and capped with vaulted stone, Ramnea's Own Legion, the Black Kingdom's finest, had their training hall. Thick stone walls and dozens of shafts, lined with polished copper alloy which directed cold air and golden light into the chamber, kept it cool and light all year round.

Following Roper was a fully armed and armoured Helmec. Roper himself wore his plate armour (patched and sealed by the Hindrunn armourers) and carried one of the great swords of his own house, Jormunrekur. It was called Cold-Edge and had been bequeathed by his father four years before when Roper had reached the age of fifteen. It was one of the most distinctive weapons in Albion: a straight-bladed cleaver of the very finest temper and alloy. The Jormunrekur had all the best swords. His father's war-blade had, perhaps, been even finer. Bright-Shock, it was called. Its blade glittered with diamond-dust, embedded in it during its forging. Even against other Unthank-weapons, it had been known to break them apart before the fight was over. An uneasy legend had also grown up around the sword. People said that Bright-Shock thirsted for blood like no other blade and that, if its thirst was not satisfied during battle, it would drive its bearer to commit murder. That weapon had been lost: it had been in Kynortas's scabbard when he was dragged into the Suthern ranks.

Roper was glad of Cold-Edge and the memory of its receipt when he saw the legionaries' faces. Those who were running around the great track that encircled the hall stared at him with hostility as they passed. A squad of legionaries at sword-play beyond the track fell still and gazed at him with aggressive curiosity, their lictor joining them in conspicuous inactivity.

'Wait here for me, Helmec,' said Roper. Helmec had bristled at the lictor but did as he was told, standing by the door as Roper crossed the track and stalked towards the legionaries. The lictor said nothing as Roper approached. Nor did he bow, though it would have been the expected level of deference.

'What are you staring at, Lictor?' asked Roper, coming to a halt before the officer. Roper was taller than he and stared down at the smaller man, standing as his father had taught him. Back straight, shoulders back, hands joined behind his back.

'Nothing,' responded the officer, returning Roper's gaze.

'For your sake, I shall assume that your shocking lack of respect is because you do not know who I am,' said Roper, taking a step closer to the man and raising his voice. 'I am, after all, new to my role. My name is Roper Kynortasson, of the House Jormunrekur. I am the Black Lord; your master. You refer to me as "my lord".'

'I know,' said the lictor.

'I know, what?' repeated Roper, leaning very close now.

'I know, lord,' said the lictor sourly.

Roper straightened up. 'Your men should still be training, Lictor. The Second Trumpet has yet to sound.'

The lictor blinked and stared at Roper for a moment before turning back to his soldiers. 'Did I say you could rest?' At once the legionaries began sparring again. Roper regarded the lictor coldly.

'Where does the Guard train?'

'Why, lord?'

'I don't answer to impertinent lictors. Answer me, man. Where does the Guard train?'

The lictor gestured to the centre of the hall, where Roper could now make out the banner of the Sacred Guard: a silver eye on a black, starred background, hanging from one of the pillars.

'What is your name?' Roper asked the lictor, still staring at the banner.

'Ingolfur, lord.'

'I shall remember you,' said Roper, looking the legionary up and down. 'Carry on, Ingolfur.'

The lictor, still refusing to bow, turned back to his soldiers while Roper marched towards the silver eye. This he had learned already; men in a group might condemn and scorn him, but they grew much less brave if singled out.

While others stopped to stare as Roper passed, the Sacred Guard, when he finally reached them, did not even acknowledge him. They were also sparring, using the heavier, blunted steel blades that were employed during training. When in battle they used the lighter, Unthank-silver that all the best Anakim blades were made of; it was almost miraculously easy to wield. The echoing clang of the blades made the training hall sound like a foundry.

The guardsman closest to Roper was another face he had memorised: Gosta, one of Uvoren's war council. Most of the rest of the Guard fought with tight, economical movements; disciplined and fit. Gosta was more like a rabid dog, slashing harvestman-style at his evidently intimidated opponent and spitting vile curses as he forced the man back. Suddenly, Gosta lunged and beat aside his opponent's blade; his own sword ricocheted back towards his opponent's head and delivered a mighty, edge-on stroke to the man's unhelmeted head. The crack of that blow cut through the training hall, making even hardened guardsmen stop to look up. A couple of pairs even stared open-mouthed as Gosta's opponent crashed to the ground. Gosta turned away and moved to take a sip from a water-skin behind him.

'Almighty god, what was that?' muttered Roper, watching Gosta's victim lie unconscious on the floor, hair shining darkly with blood. Roper looked up and met another pair of eyes he recognised: lightning blue, framed by a face of surpassing handsomeness. Pryce; whom Roper remembered as the protégé of the man he sought named Gray.

'You're on half-rations for the rest of the week, Gosta,' said Pryce, turning back to his sparring partner. 'You play too rough.'

Gosta said nothing, staring expressionless at Pryce as he took another sip of water. Roper stepped forward now, over the prone guardsman, and hailed Pryce, who did not acknowledge Roper and would have begun sparring again had not his partner held up a hand and motioned in Roper's direction. Pryce turned back to Roper.

'I need a service of you, Lictor,' said Roper. 'I wish to know where the guardsman named Gray is.'

Pryce gave a snort and sheathed his sword, turning away from Roper and towards his own water-skin. Roper looked from the departing guardsman to the partner he had left behind, who also sheathed his sword and offered Roper a bow.

'You are Gray?' asked Roper, inspecting the guardsman. He wore a black tunic with the Almighty Eye over his heart. On the right side of the tunic was the crest of House Alba: a rampant unicorn.

'Yes, my lord. Gray Konrathson.' The guardsman straightened up. He was tall, this guardsman. Tall, broad and straight-backed. His face was plain but for a pair of engaging, dark-brown eyes that peered from it. And Roper realised he had met this man before. This had been the guardsman carrying the white flag when they parleyed with Earl William before battle.

'Gray,' said Roper, 'we've met before, you and I.'

'We have, lord. On a day that I would rather forget, excepting our encounter.' Gray had an air about him; relaxed, unhurried. But his words made Roper suspicious. After weeks of enemies, kind words were hard to believe.

'Walk with me, Gray. I require your service.'

'Of course, lord.' They skirted around the training guardsmen and headed for the outer circuit, Gray casting an eye over Roper's sword. 'Cold-Edge,' he said, with a nod. 'One of the great blades of the land. I always preferred it to your father's weapon, lord.' He meant the lost sword Bright-Shock.

'Why so?' asked Roper. He wanted to know what sort of man Gray was.

'The balance,' said Gray. 'A devastating cutting weapon but equally good as a thruster. And for the serious fights, you need to use the point.' Gray looked as though he had seen his fair share of serious fights. He would have been one of the older members of the Sacred Guard, with perhaps a hundred seasons behind him and many scars to show for it. The high ponytail he wore revealed he was missing an ear and Roper also noted a little finger gone from Gray's right hand. 'You know what the handle is, my lord?' asked Gray.

'Tell me.'

'Mammoth ivory. The tusks of a great beast, long since gone from this world. But they roamed this land in their thousands when our ancestors first arrived.' Roper looked down at the cream and black marbled handle of Cold-Edge, wondering if that could be true. 'They arrived to find a frozen land. The landscape sliced apart by rivers of ice and earth so cold that trees could not grow, if the Academy is to be believed. Our ancestors, the first Anakim, carved out a home in the ice. They made fire from animal bones and shale and turf dug from the ground when they had no wood. They built their houses from ice or bone and shared this land with animals that today we would think of as monsters. Can you imagine such an existence? Were they driven to it by conflicts in the south? Or did they choose that life?'

'Do you admire them?' asked Roper.

'I do, lord. Either they did not know what they would find when they advanced north, or they knew it was a frozen wasteland and came anyway. They made our home and now, we cannot even retain it. The Black Kingdom burns and the Sutherners are rampant.'

'Perhaps you can help me with that,' said Roper, as the two began walking around the track. 'I would like nothing more than to unleash the legions and gain revenge on the Sutherners.'

'Forget revenge, lord,' said Gray firmly. 'But I can certainly help you regain this country.'

'I wonder if you'd say that if you knew what it will take.'

Gray looked shrewdly at Roper. 'It will take one of two things, lord. The easier option by far is for you to flee the Black Kingdom. Perhaps defect to Suthdal? Head for King Osbert's court. I hear he is obsessed by Anakim and would surely welcome you as an advisor, no doubt shower you with land and titles as well. Wherever you go, it would leave Uvoren unchallenged as commander of the legions. Then he could not afford to delay, as the considerable heat currently being directed at you would turn to him.'

Roper did not speak, knowing that Gray had more to say.

'That might well save this country. As your father will no doubt have taught you, the Black Lord is the ultimate servant of the realm. Regardless of the personal disgrace; regardless of your thwarted ambitions, that is the honourable course if you believe it to be in service of this burning nation.'

'Do not presume to tell me my duty,' Roper managed.

'The option evidently does not appeal,' observed Gray. 'Understandably, lord. Which brings us to your other choice: you stay; you acquire allies and you break Uvoren. And then, perhaps you can see to the task at hand and reclaim our eastern territories. But to justify such a course, you must truly believe that you are a markedly better leader than Uvoren. Otherwise, it is far easier to give him command.'

'Uvoren is a self-serving snake,' hissed Roper. 'He would be a disastrous leader.'

'Do not hate him, lord,' said Gray, echoing Jokul's advice.

'He has many qualities. But he will ignore yours; do not return the favour.'

'He wants to kill me. He has extracted every possible advantage that he could from the death of my father. He keeps the legions in the Hindrunn and allows our country to burn because he knows I will take the blame. If he does not deserve my hatred, nobody does.'

Gray looked disappointed by Roper's vehemence. 'As it happens, I want what you want.' A pack of legionaries ran past them on the track but Gray did not bother to lower his voice. 'Your house is not spent yet and I will die before letting Uvoren sit on the Stone Throne. He and I are not friends, but I do not hate him. Soldiers master their emotions. Hatred would only cloud my ability to fight.'

'Uvoren is a cancer of this country,' said Roper firmly. 'And together, you and I shall cut him out.'

'Yes, lord,' said Gray, and there was suddenly a touch of darkness in his voice. 'Well, for that, you have me at your back. Pryce too.'

'It doesn't seem as though Pryce will follow me,' said Roper dryly.

'Pryce will follow me, though,' said Gray. 'He is my brother.' He meant brothers in the way that men who fight together in the battle line are brothers. Who have seen each other at their most terrified and their most exhausted under the great pressure of the fray. Who, having seen each other stripped to the very core, know every wrinkle of each other's character; have relied on one another utterly, placed their lives in the other man's hands and found their comrade up to the challenge. Brothers by choice.

Roper had two blood brothers of his own: twins, the effort of whose delivery had killed their mother. They were further north, in one of the haskoli: academies set amongst the mountains to train the young warriors of the country. Prospective heirs to the Stone Throne were no exception: at the age of six they were taken from their mothers and transferred to the haskoli, deliberately constructed in areas as cold and steep as possible. The boys would learn to use the sword and spear, but, most of all, the haskoli taught grit. The strength to take punishment again and again without complaint. The fortitude to face overwhelming force and not indulge in the luxury of panic. To bear the burdens and expectations of being part of the finest army in the Known World. In short, to create the kind of character whom you could call brother.

Roper had not thought of his brothers for weeks. No doubt they would have heard the news of Kynortas's death by now, but they were probably in considerably less danger than he. There would be no sense murdering the second and third in line to the Stone Throne while its primary still lived.

'So I can rely on your support when I speak in Uvoren's war council, Gray?' asked Roper.

'Certainly, lord,' said Gray. 'But I would suggest that you shouldn't play your hand too soon. Currently, Uvoren does not believe you can seriously challenge his leadership. Make sure that the first he knows of your gaining influence is when you have enough power to force his hand. You need to marry and gain the backing of another of the great houses. Even then, this is a near impossible task. The influence you have at the moment may persuade some to back you, but to take on Uvoren directly, you will need to prove yourself as a leader. And it is difficult to see Uvoren allowing you an opportunity to do that.' Gray lapsed into silence.

'Let me worry about that,' said Roper. 'I have a plan.'

'I hope it's a good one, lord,' said Gray as they reached the archway by which Helmec waited. 'I said I'd die to keep Uvoren off the throne, but I'd really rather I didn't have to.' He offered Roper his disarming smile. 'Have you given thought to who you might marry, lord?'

'Many thoughts, few conclusions,' said Roper grimly. The thought disturbed him quite as much as taking on Uvoren.

'Pryce has a cousin; Keturah Tekoasdottir, who would be

about your age. It is time she was wed, and that would be a worthy alliance.'

'Tekoasdottir?' said Roper, nervously. Pryce's uncle, Tekoa, was the infamous head of House Vidarr. Roper had never seen him at the war council but had noted that a seat was always kept empty for him, even when the great table was crowded, lest he should decide to attend.

Gray suddenly relaxed his face into a look of childlike terror, causing an unexpected peal of laughter to escape Roper. 'Don't worry, lord,' he said. 'His bark is worse than his bite. But all the same, winning him round will be a challenge.'

'Thank you, Gray Konrathson,' said Roper holding out a hand, which Gray took with a bow. 'Perhaps Pryce could speak to his uncle on my behalf and soothe the beast before I come face to face with it.'

'Lord, safe to say that nothing enrages the beast more than talking to Pryce.'

Roper smiled and departed, leaving Gray to walk back to the centre of the hall where the Guard still trained. Pryce was sparring with another guardsman so Gray took a skin of water and sat and watched his young protégé. He was not very refined. Many of the Guard could do extraordinary things with a blade, bewildering opponents and onlookers in ways which Gray knew he could not achieve with a lifetime of training, but Pryce was not one of those. His movements were often wild and savage. Those who could defeat him easily in training were the technically advanced swordsmen, who could spot and exploit an exposed wrist or throat. The likes of Vigtyr the Quick or Leon Kaldison should be able to cut him down with relative ease.

Even so, there was a saying among the legions: 'Never fight Pryce.' His movements might be wild, but they were an order of magnitude faster than any man Gray had met. He was also well-balanced, with exceptional footwork and any who had seen him fight in combat understood the saying all too well. *Never fight Pryce.* His brutality and energy overwhelmed most of his opponents, and he appeared invulnerable to pain. The theory was that even if you could deliver a lethal blow to Pryce, he would still have the time and inclination to savage you with his own sword or, if you had somehow disarmed him, simply tear into you with his teeth and fingernails.

The Second Trumpet blasted across the hall, indicating that the legionaries should cease training to eat. Gray waited as Pryce clapped his opponent on the shoulder and laughed with him, gesticulating rapidly in an impression of one of their bouts. The guardsman looked absurdly pleased that he was laughing with Pryce; everyone was pleased when Pryce showed an interest in them. Gray had his own measure of respect, but knew that people did not fawn for his approval like they did for Pryce's. The young sprinter was a force of nature.

Pryce clasped his opponent's hand, bade him farewell and re-joined Gray. 'So how was your conversation with Boy-Roper?'

'Satisfactory,' said Gray as they began to walk together to the mess hall. 'He knows what he has to do.'

Pryce frowned. 'So you're going to back him? That child who inflicted the ignominy of a first ever retreat on a full call-up?'

'That was the correct decision,' said Gray without hesitation. 'We might still have won the battle if he'd advanced, but at a terrible price. Honour is everything, but I refuse to accept a definition of honour that places higher regard on tactical suicide than it does on the security of future generations.'

'You may be right,' deferred Pryce. 'But still: a boy, on the Stone Throne?'

'He has shown much promise, growing up. And the alternative is a bleak one. Your uncle won't rule; it's too much like hard work for him. So that leaves us with either Roper or Uvoren. I know which one I'd choose. With the right support, he may even be exceptional.'

'How can you tell?'

Gray smiled into the distance. 'I don't know. Once you've had as many peers standing next to you in the battle line as I have, you learn to tell very quickly who you can trust with your life. There's something about Roper. He's clever, he understands leadership and, most importantly, he's calm. His emotions are differently calibrated from most here.' Gray waved an arm at the chattering legionaries, all moving for the mess hall. 'He masters himself, and those can be the best leaders of all.' Gray smiled again, tapping Pryce in the small of the back. 'You are with me?'

'You know I am.'

The Black Lord would usually have had a pair of guardsmen standing watch over his quarters, day and night. However, as far as Roper knew, there were only two, perhaps three guardsmen he could trust not to turn on him if Uvoren gave the word. Since he could not have Gray and Helmec guarding him at all times, Roper had dismissed any sentries. He would sleep unguarded and simply trust that Uvoren was not as underhanded as Roper believed he was. He was trying desperately not to hate the captain, but simply saying to himself over and over again: 'There's no need to hate him; just defeat him' was having no effect. He despised Uvoren.

It was late. The moon was high; the sun long since submerged beneath the horizon. The Central Keep was indented with small alcoves, purpose-built to provide shelter for a population of owls, whose tenants now called glumly to one another. As committed as any servants of the Black Kingdom, the owls fought the only army to have ever successfully occupied the Hindrunn: its rats. Besides this, the fortress was quiet. The legions and their families had retired, too accustomed to the sickly orange glow on the eastern horizon for it to trouble their sleep.

Roper sat at a table that faced a leaded window. He had done his best to banish the dark from this little corner of his quarters and the collective effort of three oil lamps was providing him with light by which to plan a speech. Anakim had no writing, but when memorising long verses they used small, crude pictograms in linear fashion to be broadly representative of a theme and to ignite the memory. Roper scratched out a chain, the ink black as the night. It smelt faintly of soot, making Roper pause, standing the quill in the ink pot and staring through the rippled glass. A feathered, moonlit knife cut the dark as an owl slid past the window.

This would be his first speech. He had no idea whether he would get a chance to deliver it, but he must be ready to take the opportunity when the time came. Roper could not afford to leave to chance anything that was within his control. He took up the quill once more and carved another symbol onto the page: a warrior, this time. It sounded odd. He looked at the tip of the quill, frowning.

And heard the noise again.

It was a creak. The slight strain of thick leather as it is stretched; insignificant as a cat's footfall. But Roper heard it. *And I wouldn't have done if I was asleep.*

As quietly as he could, he extinguished the lamps by retracting the wicks and slid his legs to the side of his chair so he could stand without the need to move it. Three quick, silent strides in the dark and he had reached his weapon chest; iron-bound oak behind the door, on top of which lay Cold-Edge, its handle rich with wax from his ministrations.

The noise came again from outside the door: a boot contracting slowly as its owner brought their weight down upon it. Roper eased Cold-Edge from its scabbard, eyes wide as he tried to adapt to the gloom. The window glowed with just enough moonlight for Roper to be able to see the latch on the door lift (for he could not hear it). It swung open by ten inches: enough for a dark-clothed figure to slide through and re-latch the door. Whoever it was had not seen Roper; their attention was focused on Roper's bed and the un-made woollen blankets, piled enough to give a passable impression of a figure sleeping within.

Roper was certain that the assassin must hear his heartbeat. He could hear almost nothing else as the blood roared through his ears and his hands jumped in time with the savage thump. The figure was masked. He must act. He must kill the man, who would realise at any moment that Roper's bed was empty.

Roper stepped forward. Fear slowed his movements as though his blood had turned to tar. The assassin had heard him at last, was turning, drawing a short sword with a black blade and Roper screamed, swinging Cold-Edge with all his might at the man's neck.

Roper did not see where the sword struck but he felt the impact. It was less the jolt of blade clashing on blade, more firm resistance. The assassin was knocked flat; poleaxed by the blow. Roper's darting eyes saw the black sword drop oddly noiselessly onto a deerskin on the floor. He roared again, raising Cold-Edge, wanting to keep his advantage; waiting for the next attack. It did not come.

The man lay prone, flooding Roper's floor with thick, dark blood. His head, still masked, was tipped right backwards, like a flower that has had its stem broken. Roper had half-decapitated him.

It was over. He was dead.

Roper shook, hauling in deep breaths. Cold-Edge's tip dropped slowly until Roper released the handle and it fell to the floor. He dropped onto his knees and each heartbeat was so wild that it felt like a hiccough. 'Shit,' he said. 'Shit.'

He had killed a man. He had caught him unawares and struck before he had time to defend himself with the black short sword that now lay next to Cold-Edge. *Almighty god.*

Roper leaned forward and pulled off the mask with shaking hands. He did not recognise the slack face beneath; did not want to look at the inanimate features that so resembled the decapitated head of his father. He examined the mask instead. It was dark-brown leather, supple and soft. There were only two holes: one for each eye. Not for the mouth or the nose. Instead of a face, the wearer of this mask would bear the stamp imprinted on the dark leather: a spread-winged cuckoo, head turned to one side.

The mask of the Kryptea. Roper recognised the black-bladed short sword as well. Easier to use at close quarters and alloyed matt-black to make it near invisible in the dark. Kryptea.

Jokul, for all his words, wanted to kill him. The Kryptea could not be stopped.

5
House Vidarr

Roper spent the remainder of the night positioned behind his door, Cold-Edge propped in the corner next to him. After much searching for a better location, he had placed the Kryptean agent's body in his own bed; replacing the mask and covering him in rough woollen blankets. If there was another attacker, perhaps they would believe it was Roper.

Dawn filled the room with painful reluctance. The walls of Roper's quarters were bronzed by the early light, illuminating the pool of congealed blood on the floor and the wool-covered corpse in his bed. Being able to see the remnants of last night's panicked slaughter scarcely improved matters, but furnished an exhausted Roper with sufficient courage to strap on his armour and sit upon the chair at his desk. He tried to distract himself by seeing how much of last night's speech he could remember.

It was in this position that Helmec discovered Roper. Finding his knocks ignored, Helmec entered hesitantly and first spied the cracked puddle of blood on the floor before travelling up to see Roper, searching the young lord for any sign of a wound. 'What happened, lord?'

Roper could not bring himself to admit last night's scene.

Who would support a man being targeted by the Kryptea? Instead, he nodded curtly at the bed. Helmec crossed to it and drew back the blankets, staring at the masked face beneath. He glanced at Roper, noting Cold-Edge's blood-stained blade, and removed the mask.

'I know this man,' said Helmec, quietly. 'You have killed one of Ramnea's Own, my lord. Aslakur Bjargarson; House Algauti.' Roper had not digested Helmec's words. Helmec was looking at him, and then crossed the floor to place a hand on Roper's shoulder. 'It's over, lord. You killed him.'

Roper's eyes were glazed for a moment and then flickered into life, glancing up at the guardsman. 'House Algauti?' he said, finally seeming to register what Helmec had said. A possibility was stirring in his mind. 'Helmec, fetch the guardsman Gray Konrathson for me at once.'

'Lord.' Helmec bowed and departed, returning before long with Gray. Aides from Roper's own house, Jormunrekur, were summoned to clear away the body, watched closely by Gray and Helmec, both resting their hands on their sword-hilts. 'Strip it,' commanded Roper. 'Find a pike, plant it in the ground and impale the body.' Gray looked at Roper quizzically but did not question him in front of others. 'And summon Jokul,' said Roper, grimly.

He could not hide the fact that he had been attacked, so he would use it as best he could. Impaling a Black legionary might make him hated, but it also gave him an edge; the beginnings of something approaching respect. He had killed one of Ramnea's Own in single combat. At that moment, Roper preferred hatred to contempt. Perhaps he would no longer be thought of as a boy.

Jokul arrived without delay. His pale eyes took in the blood on the floor before staring at Roper, flanked by Helmec and Gray. 'Are you going to execute me, lord?' he asked in his dry, quiet voice.

'So you admit that in spite of your words, you have tried to have me killed,' said Roper vengefully.

'I admit nothing,' said Jokul. He knelt before Roper, who kept the surprise from his face. 'On my honour,' said Jokul, holding forward supplicatory hands that Roper took. 'On my station; on my life. That assassin was no Kryptean.'

'He wore the mask,' said Roper sternly. 'He carried the sword!'

'Stolen,' said Jokul. 'I do not want you dead. I do not want Uvoren.'

'Rise, then,' said Roper and Jokul stood, becoming hardly more physically imposing than he had been on his knees. 'The man was Aslakur Bjargarson of House Algauti.' It was almost a question. If anyone could confirm Roper's suspicions, it was the Master of the Kryptea.

'That tells you all you need to know, my lord,' said Jokul simply. House Algauti were vassals of House Lothbrok, Uvoren's family. They were a minor servile house, rewarded by the Lothbroks for their loyal support with wealth, status and protection. This assassin, if Roper believed Jokul, would have been sent by Uvoren and tricked out as a Kryptean. If the assassination were successful, it would be the Kryptea who bore any heat for the murder and Uvoren would be best placed to occupy the Stone Throne. If it were unsuccessful, then it could not be traced to Uvoren and might have the added benefit of driving a wedge between Roper and Jokul, whom Uvoren had seen parley.

It was brutal and clever. It had Uvoren written all over it and Roper was reminded forcibly of the Chief Historian's words when they had met in the Chamber of State: *The greatest warriors can fight in any theatre.* Roper needed a response. He needed to become someone who could not be killed without uproar ensuing, making Uvoren think twice before attempting such a tactic again.

'I am by your side from now on, my lord,' said Gray. 'Send for Pryce as well. You need him.'

'Do not dismiss me again, lord,' echoed Helmec. 'We'll keep you alive until you can take Uvoren.'

Roper looked at the pair of them, quite moved. He had few reasons to trust anyone at the moment, but he trusted these two. 'What have I done to deserve the service of two such fine warriors?' he asked. 'Thank you.' He turned to Jokul. 'Uvoren has abused the reputation of the Kryptea for his own ends. What are you going to do about it?'

Jokul gazed at Roper for a moment. 'We preserve the stability of this country. It is certainly not in our interest to kill him. But this will not stand. We will find out who took the mask and blade and they will die. We will warn Uvoren. And . . .' he examined Roper a moment longer – 'you have a reprieve, for the moment, Lord Roper. I will give you a month to gather your strength and then we shall reassess.'

'It's all I need,' said Roper.

Bellamus sat within a pavilion, his desk adrift in an inky sea on the little island of light cast by two oil lamps. The rain thrashed onto the canvas walls, beading them with cold glass droplets that slipped from the roof and down the sides to pool at the edges. There were no windows, the opening was sutured tight, and within, little daylight was admitted. The only connection with the twisted acres that stretched beyond the walls was the drum of the rain, rolling through the darkness.

This was where he met with his spies, where he interrogated his enemies, where he disciplined his soldiers and where he interviewed captured Anakim. The character of each conversation was much the same, and the pavilion was all part of that, designed in every detail to place his informants at ease. Bellamus had learned long ago that the right environment was often all that it took to dismantle someone's defences. The soft glow emitted as oil became air lent the space a conspiratorial atmosphere, eliminating distractions and focusing the mind on the conversation. The light was reminiscent of the hearths by which humans of all kinds had sat since their earliest years to spill secrets to those close to them.

For the Anakim informants, Bellamus had ordered a chair constructed to suit their larger proportions, and one for himself as well, so that the two of them could sit on the same level. Every word of his introduction, every gesture, he had trialled before. It all depended on that, he had discovered. If the right tone was not set at the beginning, there was no hope for the interview. Any hint of antagonism, and Bellamus would find himself frozen out. They were stubborn folk, these Anakim, perhaps unsurprisingly when there was an army camped on their land.

Bellamus had spoken to one of them that morning: a woman named Adras. It had been just the two of them in this space, along with a jug of wine which Bellamus had unstoppered, decanting generous measures into two goblets. The potent smell of fermentation made the Anakim woman wrinkle her nose as he pushed one of the cups towards her.

She stared at it, then back up at Bellamus, saying nothing. She was almost entirely rigid, each muscle braced against its antagonist. Bellamus did not appear to notice, taking up his goblet and leaning back in his chair to take a sip. He glanced over the rim at the woman and, when he removed the cup, his face was sympathetic. 'That cup is yours.' He spoke in Anakim. 'Whenever you want it.'

The woman made no move for it beyond a glance.

'This must be your home, that we are camped in now,' Bellamus continued. 'My very great apologies for that. We'll be moving along soon and, by that time, we'll have had a good conversation and you'll be free to stay here.'

'What are we going to talk about?' asked the woman.

'You,' said Bellamus, smiling gently. 'You must forgive me for being so personal. My trade back home, in the south, is my knowledge of your people. And I wouldn't be of much use if I didn't keep that knowledge sharp. I won't remain unique in my skills for long. Others will see the value in them and try to catch up: I must always remain a master of my subject. At least, relatively speaking. So if you'll be very kind, perhaps you could help me with these words.' Bellamus took the top parchment off the table with his free hand and cast an eye over it. '*Kip-sun-ga*? Am I saying that right?' He leaned closer to the woman. '*Kipsunga*?'

'*Kipsanga*,' corrected Adras.

'*Kipsanga*. What does it mean?'

Adras paused, staring at him for a time. 'It is the best kind of friend.'

'Explain for me,' said Bellamus, taking another sip of wine.

The Anakim stayed silent, and then took up her own cup. She sniffed it for a moment, glanced at Bellamus (who appeared to be consulting his list of words once again) and took a sip. 'A *kipsanga* is a friend whom you both respect as a person, and get on with particularly well.' She stopped there but, confronted with Bellamus's hopeful expression, gave a small smile and continued. 'Maybe you share a very similar sense of humour, or have an especially good time with them. But you also respect their character.'

'And are there other kinds of friends, beyond *kipsanga*?' pressed Bellamus. 'Its opposite, perhaps?'

'We talk about three kinds of friends,' said Adras. 'A *kipsanga* combines the two most important elements of friendship. An *unga* has only one of them: it is someone you get on with very well, but do not admire as a person.'

'Could you give me an example?'

Adras shrugged. 'Perhaps they are kind to you but unkind to others. Or maybe they are good company but sometimes try to manipulate you. Or . . .' She thought carefully. 'Maybe they are lazy and fearful, and unwilling to confront their own shortcomings.'

Bellamus was scribbling furiously. He saw Adras looking curiously at his paper and held it up to show her. 'Writing,' he said. 'We use it to store words. I suspect we Sutherners have less good memories than your kind, but it is helpful to be able to remember things exactly. Memory can twist what has happened. Please, go on.'

'The third kind is the opposite of an *unga*. A *badarra*: a person for whom you feel great respect, or distant affection, but with whom you don't get on particularly well. They might be a serious person, but one who is especially kind and generous. Or one from whom you have very different opinions, but you appreciate how well reasoned theirs are, and that they think them for the right reasons. Or maybe just someone you don't have much to say to, but you still greatly respect.'

'Fascinating, fascinating,' said Bellamus, absorbed in his parchment. 'Your people have a very objective view on those they are close to.'

Adras shrugged. 'Of course.'

Bellamus liked to start with the easy questions: the words. He had known what *kipsanga* meant. He had mispronounced it deliberately, to bleed the first little piece of information from Adras. He had known about *unga* and *badarra* too. It was how he opened his informant, and how he gauged how willing they were. It was just hard enough an explanation to require some effort, but not a difficult concept. By broaching the topic of friendship, Bellamus also hoped to positively dispose Adras towards this conversation. Then he could progress to the harder questions.

What was the significance of wilderness?

How was the Anakim manifestation of memory different from his own?

Why did the Anakim not run in the face of his advancing army?

Why was it, that in spite of their harsh and unyielding way of life, they never rebelled?

How was such tight control maintained in a land which had no writing?

Such questions were not easily answered and required

an informant of unusual thought, willingness and eloquence. Bellamus had to use every advantage at his disposal so that, when one as promising as Adras came along, he was prepared.

He was learning more simply by being north of the Abus, in this place which had seemed so nightmarish from the other side of that dark stretch of water. The southern bank was tilled and manipulated: neat furrows creating levels on which crops could be raised and some measure of order imposed. Here, in the Black Kingdom, the land was so twisted by the roots of giant trees that there could be no hope of tilling it, or perched so steep on the sides of mountains that it was a wonder that earth clung there at all. And yet the Anakim clearly had no difficulty existing here. The forests the Sutherners torched were suffused with ghostly ruins – the stone skeletons of great towns and temples that had sheltered the ancient creatures who lived in these lands. Now the gaping houses were dens for the enormous, short-muzzled bears that terrorised his foraging parties, and the villages had been taken in by the trees, as though in solidarity. They grew around and atop one another, just as the Anakim roads grew around the landscape. They were seldom visible before one had stumbled upon them, and they seemed to go to painstaking lengths to accommodate the hills and trees, not cutting a clean line through the obstacles like many in the south, but twisting around them.

It was a land of unusual intensity, grown from earth so rich that it rotted when overturned. The birds that flew overhead called like phantoms. The cries of the animals that echoed between the trees were so strange that Bellamus was struggling to imagine what sort of beast they might belong to. His sleep, usually so deep and untroubled, was disturbed by exquisite dreams. At night, towering shadows, extraordinary creatures and smells filled his mind. Fear too, was present in his dreams to an extent and clarity that was utterly unknown to him. He would often think he had awoken with a start, only to hear strange, unearthly music beyond the walls of his tent. Three times now, in the dead of night, Bellamus had stumbled through the fluttering tent flap and into the land of silver shadow beyond, seeking the source of that distant music. But every time it had faded slowly, leaving him standing still in a silent and moonlit forest, wondering if the music had just been the afterglow of his bright dreams. It must have been, for each note had been heart-cramping, and Bellamus could remember none of the melody. He was left only with the memory of how it had made him feel.

History was altogether less distant here. In the south, the land was turned over and recycled so quickly, and the dwellings made of materials so readily consumed by earth and fire, that little survived more than a few generations. Bellamus was forced to breathe the Black Kingdom in with every mile he travelled. No matter how much he tried to brand his presence into the north, there was always more forest. Attacking the Black Kingdom was like venting rage on a mountain. It looked on at his efforts, indifferent to them. And look on it did. In some way, this land was powerfully reminiscent of a single organism; one of incalculable age and significance.

Bellamus shook his head, dismissing the encounter with Adras that morning and the alien world outside, and looking back towards his papers. The words written thereon were incomprehensible. Senseless chains of letters, randomly divided into unpronounceable words. Bellamus set down his cup and ran a finger along the top paper, staring up at his own furrowed brow. 'Ah!' He glanced around the desk and, from beneath one of the papers, extracted a cracked rectangle of wood, scarcely thicker than the paper before him and with several dozen little windows cut into it. Bellamus laid the wood carefully over the parchment, each of the tiny windows perfectly framing one letter beneath. These letters, read in sequence and with some guesswork as to where the spaces and grammar were supposed to sit, were rendered thus:

My upstart – as requested I have twisted the Royal Arm very hard and you shall not be recalled, nor burdened with another earl. I –

Bellamus flipped the piece of wood over, being careful to hinge it about its lower edge, revealing the lines of text concealed further down the page:

. . . also seeded the idea of you as Master of the North in the Royal Ear. We will see how it grows. Don't forget my present. A

Bellamus had many informants, and used many cyphers. This one was reserved exclusively for his correspondence with Aramilla. There were two copies of the piece of wood that Bellamus had used to decode it, and the other was with the queen.

Bellamus did not trust many people. He did not really trust Aramilla either. He knew she felt affection for him (based, he thought, on an interested regard), but he did not believe he was of particular importance to her. She would try to help him because she enjoyed this game and the risk that came with it, and she enjoyed him too. He entertained her, but if he were to task her with anything that might mean sacrificing something she valued, he knew he would face her cold amusement. He could not trust her, but he trusted her subtlety. He had never seen her pour words like wine into the king's ear, but he had often relied on her efficacy. Once or twice, he had felt the force of those words and had noticed how she steered the conversation in such a way that the thoughts she wanted to plant were never out of place. If it did not go in the direction she wished, Aramilla would say nothing, preferring silence to discovery.

The entire court was in her thrall. The weapons she used shifted imperceptibly, so that as soon as you felt you were beginning to resist her, you would realise you were capitulating in some other way. If you were a man, she would start with a look of undecided interest, as though you were somebody different, but she was not sure what to make of you. *Impress me.* When, inevitably, you made a clumsy joke, she would meet it with a laugh; a noise Bellamus thought he had only heard her make in earnest a few times. It sounded like a magpie, or the rattle of dice in a wooden cup. Her attention was entirely yours. Where she proceeded from there depended on how self-assured you seemed. For the confident: more encouragement, more laughter; then perhaps a prickly comment. *You're not there yet. Keep trying.* For the fragile: they were hers already. Gentle teasing, stretching their relationship until, ultimately, they thought little of her requests.

If you were a woman, her methods were more relentless. She would shift between charm, humour and callous mistreatment, until you were persuaded of the futility of resistance. To argue against her was as exhausting as it was fruitless, and, if you did not, then she was good company. Capitulate and she could be a generous mistress. Just do not forget your place.

There were a score of minor houses in the Black Kingdom and perhaps three major ones. Roper's own house, Jormunrekur, had faded in recent years despite being the lineage from which the Black Lord was drawn. The consummate leader elevates based on merit, which Kynortas had done in order not to show favouritism to his own kin. It had resulted in House Lothbrok, of which Uvoren was the foremost son, superseding the Jormunrekur in wealth and influence. Now Roper needed to break Uvoren, for which he would require support from the third major house: Vidarr.

Though it was necessary, entering into negotiations with

House Vidarr was a daunting prospect. They were led by Tekoa Urielson; Pryce's uncle and legate of the Skiritai Legion. Roper had never met him, but knew he was a man of unbending will. Roper remembered words that Kynortas had once spoken of him: 'Tekoa would be a fine servant if he didn't have such monstrous self-regard.'

When Roper had asked Pryce how he could best win over his uncle, the lictor had replied: 'Entertain him.'

These thoughts circumnavigated Roper's head as Helmec rapped on the door of Tekoa's house. Roper had tried summoning him to his own quarters in the Central Keep but his messenger had returned shaken, delivering the news that if Roper wished to see Tekoa, he would have to go and meet where Tekoa could have a comfortable chair and goblet of birch wine.

The door before them was opened by one of Tekoa's household warriors, a full legionary with the crest of House Vidarr: a monstrous serpent armoured in chain mail, destroying an even larger holly tree. 'The Black Lord, Roper Kynortasson of House Jormunrekur, has come for an audience with Tekoa Urielson,' announced Helmec. The legionary smirked and stepped aside with an air that said: *You're welcome to him.*

Roper, Helmec and Gray entered, finding themselves in a granite reception room. Chairs of split yew lined the walls and a fire stirred in a raised hearth. This house was larger than most within the walls of the Hindrunn. Tekoa was a wealthy man but a true subject of the Black Kingdom and had furnished it austerely. The walls were bare but for lamp brackets and a single silk tapestry of cream and black, showing the same tree and chain-mail snake that the legionary bore on his breast. As with all Anakim art it had no colour; only outlines. The stone floor was barely visible beneath an assortment of deerskins, though Roper could see a couple of carved footprints in the bare patches. Now he looked, Roper could see some handprints carved into the wall as well, including one very small and very low down that must have belonged to a child.

The legionary who had shown them in asked them to wait in the chamber whilst he went to fetch Tekoa. He departed through an oaken door, next to which was a low table. On this sat a spherical object supported in a wooden cradle. Roper moved towards it, reaching out a hand to examine it.

'Don't touch it!' cried a voice behind him.

Roper's hand recoiled and he snapped around. Standing behind him, evidently having emerged from one of the rooms that came off this chamber, was a woman. She was extremely tall – almost Roper's own height – and had eyes of a ghostly pale green and extremely long, gossamer-fine blonde hair. Her skin was so fair as to be almost translucent; Roper could see the veins at her temples. And she was painfully thin, her white linen shift looking as if it contributed considerably to keeping her upright.

'My lady?' said Roper, noting that her hair was tied back in the manner of a married woman with children; a full subject of the Black Kingdom. 'Why not?'

'You mustn't touch it!' she insisted. A servant girl, appearing almost ludicrously short by comparison, emerged from the room to stand next to the woman and stared at Roper accusingly, as though he had disturbed her mistress deliberately. The tall woman strode forward, stopping uncomfortably close to Roper and almost staring right through him with her ghostly eyes. 'Who are you?'

Roper took a half-step backwards before answering. 'Roper Kynortasson. I have come for an audience with Legate Tekoa.'

'You want Keturah? That's why you're here, isn't it?' demanded the woman.

'I just want to talk to the legate,' insisted Roper.

'Keturah is precious to us. You *must not* hurt her!'

'I'm not planning to hurt anyone,' said Roper. 'Please, lady, I am just here to speak to Legate Tekoa.'

All at once, the tall woman seemed to have lost interest in

him. She turned away in an arc like a ship under sail and shuffled towards the fire, holding out her hands as she approached the flames. 'You mustn't touch it,' she repeated, her voice thinner and calmer now. 'That globe is unholy . . . sickening . . .' And then, very suddenly: 'Why does he keep it?'

'What is your name, my lady?' tried Roper, speaking to the woman's back.

'I am the lady of the house,' said she. 'Skathi. Do not distress my husband, he is a good man.'

Roper was utterly nonplussed. The servant girl approached Skathi and took one of her outstretched hands, leading her in another gentle arc back towards her room. Skathi seemed quite happy to be steered in this way and did not glance at Roper on her way out.

'Let's sit by the fire in your room, my lady,' said the servant girl kindly. 'Your weaving is nearly finished.' She shot another cross-glance at Roper as she drew the door shut behind her, setting the latch into place with a click.

Roper glanced at Gray. 'Tekoa's wife,' said Gray softly. 'She's not had an easy life. Keturah is her eldest living child but she lost five sons before that; four on the battlefield, the last as an infant.'

'Ah.' Roper nodded abruptly and turned back towards the globe that sat on the table, more entranced than ever after what Skathi had said about it. He leaned close.

It took Roper some seconds to realise that this was a model of the Known World. He picked it up, turning it in his hands. Crammed into one tiny corner was an island, the outline of which he recognised from a captured Suthern map that hung in his quarters. His island. Albion. It was so small! A rock, surrounded by endless ocean. Above it was a great jagged crown of white, which at first left Roper confused. Then his memory sparked. Ice. Enough to cover the top of the world. South and east of Albion, across seas of varying width, stretched some lands he had heard of, most he had not.

Landmasses and empires that shrank his island to insignificance. And in the west? A vast sea and a shadow. A mere sketch of coastline, behind which was darkness. Unknown lands. To the extreme south, across six inches of polished wood representing unimaginable stretches of kinetic ocean, lay another cap of ice, as if the world could be either way up.

Roper felt nauseous. The sensation this object gave him was like being at the top of the keep's very tallest tower and standing leaning over the edge, one foot flirting with emptiness. The globe was swelling beneath his feet. It stretched out around him, each angle containing incalculable leagues running through lands that could not be more different from his own. That ice: there could not possibly be trees there. And there could therefore be no fire. The very ground would move beneath your feet. There would be nothing to connect you to the world in which you existed; no scents, for every smell would be frozen; no mountains or hills, no plants, no memories. Just an endless sea of white, stretching out in every direction, and perhaps a barren wind for company.

Footsteps sounded from the stairs to Roper's left and he recovered, withdrawing his imagination from the disturbing object whilst at the same time wondering who would choose to keep such an item in their home. He returned the globe to its cradle and had just managed to sit down in one of the yew chairs beside Gray and Helmec when someone who was unmistakably Tekoa Urielson entered.

It was the way he carried himself. Imperious. Energetic. He looked like an older version of Pryce; dark-haired, handsome and unscarred. He halted suddenly when he saw Roper still arranging himself on the chair and glanced down at the globe, which had been replaced lopsidedly, as though it had been as sickened as Roper by their encounter. Tekoa looked at Roper through furrowed brows and straightened the globe. 'You little bastard,' he growled. Gray and Helmec made noises of anger but Tekoa flapped at them impatiently to be silent. He seized a chair and drew it towards the fire. 'We shall talk by the fire,' he declared. Aware that he was on the back foot already, Roper stood and dragged his own chair to the fireplace. The legionary returned, furnishing Tekoa with a goblet of birch wine. 'You are old enough for wine, Roper?' demanded Tekoa.

'I am old enough for wine and senior enough to be called "my lord",' admonished Roper.

Tekoa glanced at him appraisingly. 'Well, then, why are you bothering me, my lord? To what do I owe your magpie-like presence in my house?' He raised a hand to the legionary, who supplied Roper with his own goblet.

'Because I think neither of us wants Uvoren on the Stone Throne. We came very close to that state of affairs last night.' Roper sipped the birch wine. It was delicious. Tekoa's house might be austere, but everything in it was made by the most devoted craftsmen.

Tekoa laughed. It was like the boom of a cannon. 'Ha! I hear the Kryptea are after you.'

'Jokul swears not,' said Roper. 'And I believe him. The assassin was from House Algauti.'

'Hmm,' Tekoa gazed into his cup. 'Perhaps the more convincing evidence that he was not Kryptean is that he botched the job.'

Despite himself, a little chuckle escaped Roper. Everyone else had tiptoed around the disturbing encounter, but Tekoa was not so sensitive and Roper found it a refreshing change to be able to laugh about such a thing.

'Perhaps,' he allowed. 'So Uvoren wants the throne and will do whatever he can to obtain it for the Lothbroks, including killing its current occupant. There was a time when that was called treason.' Tekoa grinned and Roper could tell that that had amused him. He went on. 'And the Vidarr . . . who knows? Perhaps you yourself intend to stake a claim and between us we can tear the Hindrunn apart while the Sutherners do the same to our country.' He took another sip of wine.

'Tempting, tempting,' murmured Tekoa. 'So the obvious alternative you propose is an alliance between the Vidarr and the Jormunrekur.' He brooded. 'Which means you want to take one of my daughters off my hands.'

Roper was taken aback. After a pause, he said reasonably, 'The natural way to seal an alliance.'

'Well, this is all terribly equitable of you, Roper,' said Tekoa sourly. 'Most equitable. You gain the Stone Throne, a powerful ally, and one of my own dear daughters. What do I inherit from this accord, besides Uvoren's displeasure?' He spoke harshly, but Roper thought Tekoa might still be enjoying himself.

'With you at my back, my throne will surely be secured beyond doubt,' said Roper. 'As my father showed, we reward those who help us.'

'Prospective gains!' Tekoa leaned back, steepling his fingers and looking at Roper. 'You can't say fairer than that. Except, of course, by offering actual gains. And naturally Uvoren has already approached me with some rather more concrete advantages than you can offer. So why choose you?'

'Because you already rejected Uvoren,' said Roper, hoping very much that this was true. The laughter exploded out of Tekoa.

'I was rather hoping you'd make me a more convincing case. Why would I reject Uvoren? He is the safer bet. A much safer bet.'

'It is a safe bet that you would get a warrior of great renown and unsurpassed self-interest,' said Roper mildly. 'Better to gamble.'

'He does show very little flair for leadership,' admitted Tekoa. 'I'm surprised you two don't get on.' Roper ignored this. 'So I've made my bed, have I? Let's allow your prospective wife to decide.' Roper looked stunned at this. The conversation was escalating more rapidly than he had imagined. When he had seen his father discuss political matters, it had always been so subtle and so steady, to the extent that

Roper had become bored. Tekoa did not seem to do subtle.

'Send me Keturah!' called Tekoa to his legionary.

'I don't know where she is, sir,' said the legionary, re-entering the room through the oak door.

Tekoa twisted in his chair and examined the legionary nastily. 'Harald, I have literally no idea why you would bother me with information like that.'

Harald frowned, a slight smile on his lips. 'You want me to find her?'

'That's very perceptive of you.' Harald bowed and left. Tekoa turned back to Roper. 'While we wait you can tell me how last night's assassin came to suffer the ignominy of dying at your hand.'

Roper explained as they waited. They had moved on to Kynortas's death by the time the legionary returned. 'I was sorry about that,' said Tekoa. 'And not merely because it has plunged us into an underhanded civil war. Kynortas and I did not see eye to eye, but he was a warrior through and through. He was good for this country.'

'Miss Keturah,' announced the legionary from the door, bowing as Tekoa's daughter entered. Roper, who had been suppressing a sense of mounting anticipation, stood to look at the woman who might be his future wife.

Keturah was tall. At barely an inch shorter than Roper himself, she was every bit as tall as her mother. She also shared Skathi's pale green eyes, though perhaps because she had inherited her father's black hair and rather less fair skin, they appeared vivid to the point of poisonous, rather than ghostly. She was appraising Roper sceptically as she approached. Her walk bore all the confidence and easy grace of her cousin, Pryce, and her father, but with more of a swagger. Tekoa and Pryce came across as aloof. Keturah was equally poised but looked as though she was more interested in other mortals.

'There you are, my sweet,' said Tekoa, not bothering to stand and waving her to bring another chair to join them. 'I have found you a victim.'

'Miss Keturah,' said Roper, taking the hand she offered him. He could feel his face warming.

'The Black Lord,' said Keturah.

Is that a hint of mockery in her voice?

'Ostensibly,' she finished.

Yes. 'Please take a seat,' said Roper, offering his chair. She took it and Roper fetched another, receiving a wink and a grin from Helmec as he faced him momentarily. Roper sat on Keturah's right, opposite Tekoa, who was looking greatly pleased.

Keturah was gazing at Roper. 'Father, you wish me to marry the man who was not able to defeat the Sutherners with a full call-up?' Roper's face burned and Tekoa blasted him with more cannon-fire. 'So what do you do?' she asked him. 'Why should my father secure your position for you? A line like yours can't have produced something completely lacking in talent.'

'No more than yours could have produced an individual with normal levels of self-esteem,' said Roper, drawing a smile from Keturah.

'You've met my cousin?'

'Pryce? I've had that pleasure.'

'It's not much of a pleasure,' said Keturah waspishly. 'I suppose he runs very quickly, but he has that in common with you.' Her eyes glittered.

'Now, now, my little spider,' intervened Tekoa with evident glee. 'The Jormunrekur are more fragile than we. The lad can't be of much use to us if you shred his self-confidence. Besides, imagine your guilt if the next assassin is more competent than the last.'

'If I marry your daughter, I may wish that were true, Tekoa,' said Roper, inadvertently speaking the truth for the first time.

Father and daughter beamed at each other. It seemed the Vidarr were as happy receiving abuse as they were distributing it.

'So where does your skill lie, my lord?' Keturah pressed Roper, mocking him again with his title.

'I am a leader,' said Roper. 'That's all. That is what this country needs. And if I am ever given the opportunity, that is what I will show.'

Keturah rearranged her hair, flicking her vivid gaze at her father before returning it to Roper. 'So why did you retreat from battle?'

'Because it was the right thing to do,' said Roper. 'The Sutherners fought cleverly. Perhaps we could have won, if I'd advanced. Maybe I should have forced the legions to endure the slaughter of climbing a slick ridge while being deluged with arrows. Only, then they'd have had to fight through men who outnumbered them by thousands with an exposed flank. Maybe I should have insisted on that course of action and saved myself the castigation I have endured since my return. But a victory where we lose half the legionaries is no victory at all,' Roper finished, his voice slightly raised. The injustice still rankled. He was hated by the very men whose lives he had saved; by the women whose husbands, brothers and fathers he had brought home safely, and by the fortress whose long-term future he had secured.

'Fear has possessed our subjects,' Roper added. 'Possessed. They have allowed themselves to become a baying mob that follows the thoughts of only the most unstable and vicious among them. It is time we restored their faith.'

Father and daughter looked at him steadily. 'You were there, Father. Do you take his assessment?' asked Keturah, eyes still on Roper.

'I command the Skiritai,' said Tekoa. 'The Rangers. I was out in front of the army, in the thickest arrow-fire and could not believe my ears when I heard the trumpet sounding the retreat. Before we had even shed Suthern blood? Full legionaries, heroes who have trained for war their entire lives, were going to turn tail and run in the face of a few arrows? I have scarcely been more furious, Roper.' Tekoa drained the last of his birch wine and set the goblet on the floor. 'You wish to know why I turned down Uvoren's offer of alliance? Why I am countenancing yours? Because retreating that day *was* the right decision. And it was the hard decision. I recognised that even in the midst of my fury. I thought I could follow a man who takes such hard decisions. And now I have met you . . .' Tekoa watched Roper intently, as though expecting him to spontaneously combust. 'You are hopelessly out of your depth,' he declared at last. 'You are a butterfly in a tempest. But still so calm. Still unbowed. Still curious enough to play with my bloody possessions. I could gamble with you. What about you, Keturah? Will you gamble with me? Is this a man you could follow?'

She, too, appraised Roper. 'I believe so, Father,' she said cautiously.

'Well, then!' roared Tekoa, snatching up his goblet again. 'Birch wine!' The legionary Harald hurried over, supplying Keturah with a goblet and refilling Roper's and Tekoa's cups. 'To the Black Lord,' said Tekoa solemnly, raising his goblet. 'And my daughter.' They drank.

This was no time for Roper and Keturah to marry. They exchanged an oath of commitment within the walls of Tekoa's household, each swearing themselves to the other. Then Roper revealed his plan to a sceptical Tekoa. 'This is insanity, Roper.'

'My title is "lord".'

'This is insanity, my lord.'

'That doesn't matter. We're going to do it anyway.'

Roper had Uvoren's measure.

So it was that, that afternoon, he forced Uvoren to call a council. Tekoa sent word to Uvoren that either he could call a full council, or Tekoa and Roper would call one that excluded Uvoren. 'After all,' his messenger had said, 'the Captain of the Guard does not customarily sit at council.'

The Chamber of State had begun to fill just hours later. Lately, the council meetings had been stale. The legates were sick of circular debates ending in inactivity. This one was lent an extra edge by the news of Roper's foiled assassination, which had by now filtered throughout the Hindrunn. The legates buzzed as they took their seats, leaving two empty: the Stone Throne and one at the far end of the table for Tekoa.

As Roper entered, hush descended. He was armed and armoured and had Gray and an irritated-looking Pryce at his back as he took the throne.

'Heavily armed, Roper,' commented Uvoren.

'Somebody seems to want to kill me, Captain,' responded Roper.

'And do you think they're going to try again in this room?' There were titters from Uvoren's supporters.

You tell me.

Roper was saved having to provide an answer by the arrival of Tekoa. The silence intensified as he entered, not deigning to look at a single one of the councillors. His presence was almost unheard of.

'Legate Tekoa,' said Uvoren dryly. 'How good of you to join us.'

'It's more than any of you deserve,' growled Tekoa, staring at the man nearest his seat until he shuffled his chair further away to give Tekoa more room. The legate sat.

Uvoren was staring from Tekoa to Roper, a sour expression infusing his face. He leaned close to Roper. 'You little shit,' he whispered, grinning at Roper. 'I still have the support of the rest of this council. I'm giving you nothing.'

Roper grinned back. 'You'll give me everything I ask, Captain,' he said happily. 'Just watch.'

'I'll do more than that,' said Uvoren, leaning away again and meeting the eyes of Tekoa, who was smiling unpleasantly at Uvoren.

A hush had descended over the table. Most were looking

from Tekoa to Uvoren and then sparing a glance for Roper. The councillors seemed almost excited at the prospect of what they were about to witness.

Roper stood and no sooner had he done so than Uvoren was on his feet, growling that he should sit down. 'Back on that chair that you so unworthily occupy.'

'Seconded,' barked the sweaty-faced Asger, from Uvoren's left. 'Roper has nothing of value to add to this council.'

'That's rich, Asger,' said Tekoa nastily. 'As you are literally the mouthpiece of Uvoren's arse.' Asger looked ruffled. He stirred, offended, but offered no response. Tekoa turned to the Captain of the Guard. 'By what right, Uvoren, do you try to forbid the Black Lord from speaking at his own council? Did you not swear yourself to his service when Kynortas was amongst us?'

'I swore my oath to Kynortas himself,' said Uvoren. 'His death releases me from obligation to his puppy! His puppy, who oversaw the first retreat of our forces in the field in two hundred years and the first ever retreat of a full call-up of legionaries. I fail to see why we should be listening to a boy of no merit, who so lightly discards the honour of the legions.' Uvoren licked his lips and added maliciously: 'In any case, I hear he is not long for this world, wanted as he is by the Kryptea.' These last words were met with a great hoot of raucous laughter from Uvoren's supporters.

'Be silent!' bellowed Tekoa. And silence there was. 'It ill-befits this noble council for half its number to bay like a pack of dogs. Possession.' Tekoa cast the word in their direction and it sobered his enemies at once. There were a number of cardinal sins to a subject of the Black Kingdom. Foremost was self-pity. Then perhaps jealousy. Second to these alone was possession: acting as part of a mob, rather than as an individual. Allowing base emotions like hatred, scorn and even adulation to cloud one's judgement and turn one into an unproductive, unthinking animal.

'Wanted by the Kryptea, is he?' continued Tekoa. 'Forgive me, my lord,' he looked at Roper, 'but perhaps before you speak we should put these claims to the Master of the Kryptea, who sits among us. What say you, Jokul? Did you send your men to take the life of the Black Lord, as is your right?'

Jokul stood before the councillors, pale eyes locking with Uvoren's. 'On my honour,' he said, 'on my office, on my life: the assassin, Aslakur Bjargarson, was no Kryptean.'

Uvoren scoffed. 'While I would never question Jokul's honour, the rest of us are bound by different laws than he. We cannot expect the Master of the Kryptea to divulge the orders he has given to his men.'

'That sounds very much as though you are indeed questioning his honour,' said Tekoa. 'Given that he swore on his honour. You must admit, Uvoren, your insistence to pin the blame on the ancient institution of the Kryptea makes this business look decidedly murky.'

'What are you suggesting?' enquired Uvoren, dangerously.

'In summary, Captain, that you have no need to be out of your seat. The Black Lord is about to speak.' Those Vidarr at the table, who were many, rapped their knuckles on the ancient oak in support of Tekoa. Roper noted the Chief Historian adding to the noise, her unshakeable gaze fastened on Uvoren.

Uvoren sank slowly back into his chair and then leaned across to Asger and began hissing in his ear.

'Thank you, Tekoa,' said Roper, inclining his head in the legate's direction. He glared around the table, steely eyed and straight-backed. 'Peers,' he employed the term of honour that subjects use between themselves, 'we find ourselves at an impasse. The Captain of the Guard, Uvoren, counsels that we should stay within these walls, conserve our strength and await our moment to strike back at the Sutherners.' Roper inclined his head to Uvoren. 'It is an honourable course, and I cannot question his motives. We have all heard and seen how many warriors Marrow-Hunter has put down. Nobody could accuse Uvoren Ymerson of cowardice.'

'Be quick about what you have to say, Roper,' snapped Uvoren. Asger rapped his knuckles on the table.

'I will say what must be said,' replied Roper. 'Uvoren's aims are honourable. Has he not proved many times how much he loves himself?' Roper stopped for a moment, then blinked, shook his head and snapped his fingers. 'Ah! I meant, loves this country. Sorry, Uvoren. I always make that mistake.' At first there was a disbelieving titter from the table. Then it opened up into a full-throated roar of hilarity. Roper even spotted Randolph, legate of the Blackstones and one of Uvoren's closest supporters, laughing. Uvoren's best course would have been to grin along with the others. But his inability to laugh at himself was one of the reasons that the joke had gone down so well. Instead, he fixed Roper with his narrowed glare, just as Roper had hoped. He sensed the sympathy of the council shift slightly in his direction. This was a game of chess and Roper had just taken a bishop.

He allowed the laughter to subside and then raised his hands, as if he might speak seriously for a moment. 'Peers, we must look to our own motives. We here, in the Hindrunn, are not the Black Kingdom. No more are the legions.' Roper stood aside so that they could see the rain-flecked window and the smoke that lingered on the horizon. 'The Black Kingdom is out there. It is the grass being flattened by a swarm of Suthern boots; the rain-sodden ash that once made our greatest towns. It is the fire that rises from this land, every flame a vaporised part of our precious forest; somebody's home, harvest or family.

'And we here have one purpose alone. We are the Black Kingdom's greatest assets. This fortress and our brave warriors are here to defend that which the Sutherners destroy so contemptuously. They rape and enslave our women. They murder our peers and children. They raze to the ground trees that have stood for thousands of years, uproot our ancient villages and carry all they can find back to their gluttonous countrymen.

'Our martial reputation lies in tatters. Nobody stands before this horde as it commits atrocities. This land used to be entirely dark to the Sutherners. For every man who set foot north of the Abus, a severed head was thrown back onto its southern bank. Invading armies were met with uncompromising steel. We torched their lands with impunity when they threatened our people. The Sutherners whispered about us. We were unconquerable: a hornets' nest that they dared not kick for the vengeful swarm that they would unleash upon themselves.

'Where is that swarm now? Those who once feared to tread upon our lands now flock across the Abus in thousands. And those figures who once haunted their nightmares now sit at this table and preach patience.' Roper let his eyes linger on Uvoren. 'Their victory is assured as long as we skulk behind high walls, facing none of the terror that those outside experience. I am ashamed! Our subjects have placed all their trust in the legions and we have shackled them. Our women sacrifice their sons, brothers and fathers to our army with a glad heart, knowing there could be no destination more valiant or force more committed to the defence of this realm. They work tirelessly to support our ability to resist. Imagine their dismay in knowing an invading army is on their doorstep and we do not even have the guts to take them on. Our lads train and compete from the age of six to wear the armour of our realm and carry the badge of their legion into battle. How can you commit so fully to a life that we strip of honour by lingering in safety while families are slaughtered and rounded up as slaves?

'Do you know what they use Anakim slaves for, in the south? We are beasts of burden. They yoke us to carts like oxen, or strap loads to our backs like mules. Our women are turned into breeding machines; their one purpose to give rise to a race of hybrid slaves that will toil on the land until they die.

'We can allow not one more son or daughter of the Black

Kingdom to undergo this fate. We cannot delay another moment under this disgrace. I shall tell you what we will do and you can see whether you find my plan or Uvoren's more in keeping with your honour. I will take a force – any force – and we will fight a battle. Any battle. The legions cannot disgrace themselves more shamefully than we have forced them to thus far. Defeat would be of little consequence. We must fight.'

As Roper finished, the Vidarr and even a good few others rapped their knuckles thunderously on the table, but Uvoren was straight on his feet. 'Roper makes an admirable appeal to sentiment,' he declared over the hubbub. 'Where was his fighting spirit when he was last on the battlefield?'

'You should have seen it, Uvoren,' said Roper coldly. 'It was much in evidence when I rode after my father's body. Or when I fought alone in the waters. Tell me, where were you then?'

This was met with silence. Several councillors shifted in their seats, eyes turning to Uvoren. The captain was gazing at Roper with flint-hard eyes. Roper stared right back.

'Roper should apologise at once,' intervened Asger. 'He has questioned Uvoren's honour and should count himself lucky if Uvoren does not make him pay for it.'

More silence. Gray clapped Pryce on the shoulder and the lictor moved to stand behind Asger, who sat very still in his seat, looking to Uvoren. His master offered no helping hand. Roper's chess pieces were intensifying their pressure on Uvoren's, seeking a victory on this small portion of the board. His pieces were in the better position: now Roper had to convert that into a victory. He did not move his eyes from Uvoren as he replied. 'Asger, if you are to speak, you will refer to me as the Black Lord. If necessary, Pryce will make that clear to you.' Asger appeared to be holding his breath. Over his shoulder, Pryce looked impassive.

Roper continued. He did not want to give Uvoren time to speak. 'Here is our course of action. I will take the Skiritai, the Pendeen, Ramnea's Own and five auxiliary legions. The Sacred Guard will also accompany me. I will take the battle to the Suthern horde, and I will secure this country. I will leave Uvoren as commander-in-chief of the Hindrunn in my absence. He will have the Blackstones, the Greyhazel and four auxiliary legions: more than enough to keep the Hindrunn secure from the greatest of armies.'

The table seemed to rustle at this proposal. Pryce and Gray looked swiftly at one another, Pryce wearing an expression of disgust. Tekoa sat back in his chair with a slight sigh. Uvoren's jaw had swung open. A slight smile began to pull the corner of his mouth as he glanced at some of his supporters. Roper took note of whom: Tore, legate of the Greyhazel; Baldwin, Legion Tribune.

'That's bold,' said Uvoren, licking his lips. 'Very bold.' He was not talking about the prospect of battling the Sutherners and everyone at the table knew it. Roper could see some of the Vidarr looking betrayed, turning hurt or angry eyes to Tekoa, who had steepled his fingers and was staring at the table before him, wearing a slight frown. 'Very well, my lord,' said Uvoren. Lord. 'I shall safeguard the Hindrunn against all invaders. I pray you triumph over the Sutherners.' He leaned forward and offered Roper his hand, beaming with his whole body. Roper, every inch as tall as Uvoren, clasped the captain's hand.

'I shall re-enter these gates victorious,' he told Uvoren, smiling gently.

Excited chatter broke out at the table on both sides. Some of the Vidarr stood, purple in the face with rage, but Tekoa smashed a fist down on the table before any of them could speak, muzzling them. Several of Uvoren's supporters were embracing with delighted laughter.

For it was a desperate gamble on Roper's part. Once he had removed his legions from the Hindrunn, there could be no way back in. He was leaving the greatest fortress in the Known World, with enough men to defend it twice over, in the hands of a ruthless enemy. He was leaving Uvoren in complete control.

If Roper wanted to re-enter the Hindrunn, it would have to be with battering rams, siege weapons and slaughter.

It was civil war.

6
Ash

Roper and Keturah married the next day. As he had no parents, the affair was witnessed simply by Roper's bodyguards (Gray, Pryce and Helmec) and Keturah's own parents, Tekoa and Skathi, as well as two Skiritai officers. Skathi – escorted by the same serving girl who had scowled at Roper when he appeared in Tekoa's house – was calmer and more distant than she had been on their first encounter. She spoke twice. The first time, she addressed Roper, sternly commanding that he put her daughter above all things on this earth.

'I will, my lady,' promised Roper.

The second time, she seized Keturah's hand and spoke at length about how she wished for her happiness. Roper expected Keturah to bat her away with one of her waspish retorts, but instead she clasped her mother's hand between her own and paid close attention throughout. Her expression was serious and when her mother was done, she beamed at her and planted a kiss on Skathi's cheek. 'Thank you, Mother,' she said softly.

One of the legates wearing the mighty eagles' wings led the prayers in the Holy Temple, a stone's throw from the Central Keep, before Roper and Keturah exchanged vows and a pair of identical silver arm-rings. Roper swore to always keep her safe; she to be a dutiful wife. They finished by both saying the words, 'You bury me' to one another, expressing the wish that they should die before being parted.

Tekoa remained unhappy that they were about to cede the fortress to Uvoren, but nonetheless presented Roper with a wedding gift of some splendour. It was a horse. A monstrous destrier, fully trained for battle. 'Zephyr is his name,' Tekoa had growled, leading the beast over to him. 'He's twenty hands. Probably the biggest ever produced in a stable of the Black Kingdom, certainly ever in a Vidarr stable. Your enemies will see you coming on this one.' He patted the beast's pale grey flank.

Roper had learned much since he last passed through the Hindrunn's Great Gate. The last time, Uvoren had humiliated him in front of his people, dressing him in untouched battle-gear and parading him at the front of a shamed army. Now, Roper kept his own counsel. He would leave as he had arrived, in resplendent plate armour at the head of the army, but the effect would be quite different.

They mustered the legions that would be under Roper's command in front of the Central Keep. Though it was scarcely more than a half-call-up, close to forty thousand men, rank on rank with armour sand-burnished and gleaming, they still made a magnificent spectacle.

And Roper led them.

Cold-Edge was sheathed at his side. He was dressed in his steel cuirass, oiled and polished, with overlapping layers of steel providing a flexible defence for his shoulders and upper arms. Inlaid into the cuirass in silver wire was a snarling wolf and a skirt of chain mail protected his thighs. High leather boots inlaid with concealed strips of metal covered his calves and a black cloak enfolded him. He wore Kynortas's battle helmet, the helmet of the Black Lord, with his hair threaded through the back in the style of a Sacred Guardsman. He looked every inch the warlord; the visor and cheek-plates of the helmet even hiding his young, unmarked features. Even Uvoren on seeing him had smiled slightly and nodded. 'You cut an impressive figure, my lord.' He and Roper had been civil as they bade each other farewell, both knowing that they now led two opposing armies.

The sun had broken through the dark blanket that had covered it for months and bathed the Hindrunn in watery gold. Roper led the army through the streets that were lined once again with women and children. Eyes penetrated Roper's armour like nothing else as he rode Zephyr towards the Great Gate. There was no ridicule this time. Perhaps it was the assassination attempt that Roper had foiled alone. Or perhaps it was the fact that he was leading the army that was finally to take on the Sutherners. Or maybe it was just that he now looked so much the part, riding his immense battle-steed. Whatever it was, he was being accorded something approaching respect.

Roper's gamble was more than simply ceding the Hindrunn and a host of armed men to Uvoren's control. He faced dreadful odds in battle against the Sutherners too. He led forty thousand men and eight thousand heavy cavalry. Nobody knew how large the Suthern force they rode against was, but their best reports indicated that it had increased by half again since the last time Roper had fought them. Some said they were moving against an army of two hundred thousand men. Roper did not believe that, but there was no point denying that they were drastically outnumbered. Plans of campaign were normally met with fevered anticipation, but when Roper had summoned the legates and bade them follow him to war against this Suthern horde, he had seen the shock on their faces. He had issued his instructions and witnessed a surreal haze descend on the room. The legates had made no reply. They staggered from the room, gaping at their own hands. The armoured men who marched behind Roper bore that same expression. The women who lined the roads read it and stood with white knuckles and slender lips. The atmosphere was one of shocked farewell. This was so sudden, and victory so implausible. How could they possibly triumph?

Roper ignored it all. His face was set, his doubts hidden behind it and able to escape only when he opened his mouth. So he said nothing. Gray, riding behind him, wore no expression at all. He stroked the neck of his horse with a gloved hand and smiled every now and then when he caught the eye of one of the onlookers. Tekoa, next to Gray, was unyielding.

The two great sheaths of iron-clad oak were hauled open before Roper and he drew his sword in preparation at passing through the Outer Wall. He raised Cold-Edge over his head in a retrospective salute to the crowds who lined the street, wondering if he would ever re-enter this fortress.

And to his very great surprise, somebody behind him cheered. The noise swelled as the crowd took it up and began to applaud. Roper had not even considered what leading the army would do for his popularity. It had been a way for him to gain enough allies and martial repute to flatten Uvoren, as well as banish the Sutherners from this land. He had forgotten that the people of the Hindrunn would love it. This was the most warlike race in the world. Their love for the legions and any who commanded them ran to the bone.

Absurdly pleased, Roper trotted Zephyr through the tunnel and onto the plains beyond, where the refugees still gathered, sheltered crudely beneath old cloaks and blankets. And even they, who had been shut out of the fortress for weeks after the destruction of their homes, got to their feet and cheered him. Roper acknowledged the applause with a raise of his sword, still beaming uncontrollably. He moved to the right to allow the column marching behind to pass him and turned back to look at the wall. Atop it stood a lone figure.

Uvoren.

Roper held Cold-Edge aloft, tip pointing at the Captain of the Guard. A salute; of sorts.

Uvoren raised a hand in acknowledgement, a wry smile discernible on his face. Let us play.

Leading an army was more complicated than Roper could ever have predicted. The legionaries were trained from the moment they entered the haskoli at the age of six to forage and procure their own food. Nevertheless, keeping the legions fully supplied was a near impossible task. Close to fifty thousand soldiers (including the troopers of the Cavalry Corps, whom Roper had discreetly removed from the fortress before Uvoren realised he was taking them), eight thousand horses and god knew how many beasts in the baggage train required vast granaries of wheat, beans, barley, oats and rye, as well as a small army of sheep for slaughter. They had taken supplies for two weeks with them, each warrior carrying much of his food on his back, but they would struggle to find more out in the field.

They were two days' march out from the Hindrunn when someone realised that while each legionary had, as always, brought his own bow, they had no arrows with them. The legates informed Roper that this was usually the duty of the Skiritai. Tekoa, who commanded them, exploded that they had been working harder than anyone had a right to expect and that it had been somebody else's responsibility to bring the bloody arrows. Men were sent back to fetch them.

Hours after the men had returned with wagons of arrows (still not enough; they would blaze through them in just a few minutes of battle), a trooper of the Cavalry Corps had reported to Roper that they were low on horseshoes. Roper had asked how that was possible just two days out of the Hindrunn and was informed that they usually had more notice if they were going on campaign. More men were sent back for horseshoes.

It was late autumn. Ordinarily, the campaigning season would be over already. The Sutherners had left them nothing; Roper's forces moved through a scorched land.

They trudged over blankets of hot, damp ash that had once been great villages. Forests had been felled and added to the conflagration. Sheep carcasses, sucked dry by the hungry Sutherners, were scattered liberally over the hills. Grain pits, granaries, storehouses: all had received special attention to ensure not so much as a bean survived obliteration.

And everywhere, there were human bones. Some black, grey and half-consumed by fire. Some white and gleaming, washed clean by the rain, resting on a bed of ash. Skulls. Vertebrae. Teeth.

At one village, they found a massacre. Anakim bones, bearing savage cut-marks that showed their owners had died by the sword, protruded from the ash. They were surrounded by axe- and spear-heads, the wooden shafts long destroyed by flame. 'Ribs. Not bone-armour,' said Gray with disgust, kicking through the ash. 'Not a single piece of it.' He looked up at Roper, eyes filled with rage and hurt. 'These are women. They were here, fighting with axes and spears while we cowered behind granite!'

Roper looked down from Zephyr's broad back. There were children's bones amongst the women's. Boys younger than six or girls below seven, who had not yet been sent away to their academies. With the legions called away in the Hindrunn, the women had mounted a last stand in defence of their village. 'You once told me,' said Roper quietly to Gray, 'to forget revenge on the Sutherners. Fight them for those that are still alive. What do you say now, my friend?'

Gray drew a deep breath. 'There is no need for revenge. But our lands are better off without creatures that would do this.' He gazed down at the bones. 'They *must* be defeated.'

Roper nodded. 'Spread word amongst the men of what is here. We will need all the motivation we can get if we are to defeat this horde.'

The legionaries had all known this land when it bloomed with health. The fire caught them. It fed the rage inside them with each ruined village; each well and river poisoned by animal carcasses; each Anakim bone that peered so starkly back at them. While some of the soldiers' families had fled into the refuge of the Hindrunn, most had stayed at their homesteads. These legionaries wandered the places where they thought their houses had once stood, seeking bones they might recognise. Some even picked up those that they found, eyes brimming, sure that they held in their hands their wife; their daughter; their son.

The rage in each man grew, smothering the fear of the enemy they hunted. Morale was low, but any thought of desertion or retreat was out of the question. A desire for vengeance flourished and Roper encouraged it, though Gray cautioned that this was not the way of the legionaries. Such all-consuming emotion was possession, pure and simple.

Finding the Sutherners would not be difficult. An army of such vast size could hardly stay hidden; all they had to do was follow the smoke that rose steadily from the horizon. Roper sent the Skiritai, the army's skirmishers, lightly armoured and chosen for speed and fitness, out in all directions. They searched for supplies, survivors and errant Sutherners.

Survivors began to appear first. They fell into the army with enough gratitude to make Roper ashamed. They wept at the sight of the legions marching to their salvation after being helpless for so long. At the van marched the Sacred Guard: men so highly esteemed that many survivors ran to embrace them or fell sobbing at their feet, assuming that their presence meant victory.

And Roper? They stared in awe at this great warlord. It had been whispered that the Jormunrekur were spent and the Lothbroks poised to succeed them. But here was a shining warrior: tall, stern and covered in steel, atop the biggest horse they had ever seen, riding at the front of a great army. They blessed him, thanked him and swore loyalty to this new lord.

The legions had less faith in him, but Roper was working on that. Each night, he insisted on pitching his own camp, setting his own fire and even did his bit to fortify the encampment with the legionaries, driving sharpened stakes into the earth around the tents. He would then move between the fires where the warriors cooked, exchanging the odd word and passing them the latest information on how far off the enemy were thought to be. 'Twenty leagues of rough country,' he told a hearth of Pendeen legionaries one evening. 'We're heading into the hills.' They chattered at that.

'There we have the advantage,' observed one.

'How are we to fight them, lord?' asked another.

'We're not short of choices on that front,' said Roper breezily. 'Guerrilla tactics are an option; make this land a frightening place for them. I favour pitched battle, though. Let's make sure they know they only got this far through luck.' There was a murmur of agreement at this and Roper bade them goodnight, moving off into the darkness. Everywhere he was followed by a combination of Gray, Pryce and Helmec. With Gray and Pryce in particular, it enhanced his esteem to be seen with such men, and it did not hurt that they had taken quickly to Helmec. The three had become something of a triumvirate and were often to be found laughing together.

Many of Uvoren's supporters were also with the army, Asger among them. As its second-in-command, he led the Guard in Uvoren's absence. Roper itched to replace him, but his influence was so insignificant that he was not worth the trouble. However, Roper was ever wary of Gosta, another of Uvoren's supporters. He was another of the Algauti, a minor vassal house of the Lothbroks. Even for an Algauti, Gosta possessed surpassing loyalty to his master. Roper thought of him more as a dog than a man. It did not matter what the situation was; Gosta could be relied upon to enact Uvoren's will to the last detail. It was not clear how Uvoren commanded his loyalty so utterly when Gosta appeared to despise all other men, but he was a powerful ally. In him, Uvoren had a fighter quite as uncompromising as Pryce, if not quite as swift.

Both Gray and Tekoa had cautioned Roper that Uvoren might well try to have Roper killed again in the hope that the legions he commanded could be brought to heel, rather than slaughtered. Roper was guarded at all times.

They marched into the wild. As the terrain grew steeper, Roper was forced to lead Zephyr on foot. The rain restarted and the steed lost its steel-grey colouring to mud. The worse the conditions, the happier the legionaries became. This was what they were born for. If not on campaign, the full legions, Ramnea's Own, the Pendeen and the Skiritai, would be engaged in exhaustive battle training inside the Hindrunn. As for the others, the five auxiliary legions: they would be working in the forges, the quarries, the forests; performing the million small tasks that kept the country functioning during peace and war. Campaign was a release for them all.

The survivors they encountered were able to point out to Roper's forces the places they had buried their food supplies, supplementing the legions' rations as they advanced. And, seven days after marching from the Hindrunn, they found their first Sutherners. Outriding Skiritai discovered a band of stragglers, slowed down by half a dozen enslaved Anakim women that they dragged with them. The Skiritai made short work of the Sutherners, releasing the women. From that point on, they encountered pockets of stragglers every few miles. Knowing this must mean they were drawing near the main Suthern horde, Roper sent the Skiritai ranging further than ever before, scouring the hills for leagues around the army.

On the eleventh day, they discovered the enemy.

A pair of mounted rangers reported to Roper. They had found soldiers by their thousand, perhaps six leagues, they said, to the north-west. 'Show me,' was all Roper said. He mounted a courser (a horse of Zephyr's size would not have the stamina for such a mission) and followed the two guides into the hills, Gray and Helmec with him.

The horses made heavy work of the mud and it was nearly four hours of picking their way between tree trunks, over beaches of ash and threading between mountains, before they arrived at the edge of a great valley. The Skiritai knew their business and had been careful to avoid detection, tethering the horses out of sight behind a ridge before approaching the rim of the valley on foot. They crawled the final few yards and peered down into the valley.

There lay the Suthern army. Or, at least, some of it. Tens of thousands filled the valley in which a semi-permanent camp had been established. Tents studded the floor with cooking fires generously interspersed among the men, most of whom were sitting and tending to equipment.

'They don't even know that we've left the Hindrunn yet,' said Roper, watching over the scene. 'Can anyone see any sentries?'

'There,' said Gray, scouring the valley with an experienced eye, and pointing at a miniscule pair of figures standing on the other side of the valley. 'And there . . . And there.' The five of them sank lower to the ground. This valley had once sheltered a forest, but the trees had been stripped, cut and piled at the sides in a firewood stack that doubled as a crude barricade. It was as though the Sutherners thought you could not camp in a forest: there was either space for soldiers or for trees, but not for both.

'They get nervous when they can't see, don't they?' said Helmec.

'They have struggled with our country, lord,' said one of the Skiritai. 'We have found Suthern skeletons everywhere we've scouted, usually killed by bears or wolves. That is why they clear the forests. Those we capture are usually grateful that we've found them. Until they're executed.' The other Skiritai laughed.

'Gestur; Margeir,' said Roper. He had discovered the names of the two Skiritai rangers from Tekoa before they had departed and they crawled a touch closer. 'I trust you have the measure of these interlopers,' said Roper, with a smile. 'I would be grateful if you could assess this army thoroughly. I need to know how many men they command and how many cavalry. Tell me how they are feeding themselves when they are clearly so ill-at-ease here. Tell me if they have split their forces. Gather as much information as you can and be back to the army before dusk tomorrow.'

The rangers obediently returned to their horses and departed.

'As for us,' continued Roper to Gray and Helmec, 'back to the army. We can do no more until we know what we are facing.'

The three mounted their steeds and retraced their tracks. They were forced to tack up some of the steeper hills, so slippery was the terrain. Back with the army, Roper established extra fortifications for the camp and asked Tekoa how the Skiritai could best keep an eye on the surrounding landscape without drawing attention to themselves. 'Figure-of-eight patrols,' Tekoa had replied. 'Parties of three on foot, orbiting the camp in overlapping figures-of-eight. The centre of the "eight" is the camp, so they can collect fresh news and orders before heading out again.'

'Very good,' said Roper, nodding. 'And I have some more specific requirements of your men.' Tekoa's eyebrow rose as Roper explained what he needed.

'It sounds like you're planning something foolish, my lord.'

'I have many plans. This one I hope not to use.'

'It is as well to be prepared,' said Tekoa dubiously.

They had a secure perimeter and well-fortified camp; now they just needed to wait. Roper walked among his men, moving from fire to fire with the news that the enemy had been found. 'Not long now, lads,' he declared. 'We're waiting on a more thorough assessment but I assure you, there are enough Sutherners to go around. You will all need to do your part.' He encouraged the legionaries to rest and eat well, as well as to make sure their weapons and armour were in peak condition.

Roper did not expect the two rangers, Gestur and Margeir, to arrive much before dusk the next day and, suspecting that inactivity would be bad for the legions, he set them to work. Some were sent out to forage for food, some to assemble pikes and some to rehearse marching on a potential battlefield that Roper had identified. None of this needed doing. Roper doubted he would use the pikes. There was no problem with more food: they were still well-supplied with rations and there would not be much to forage in these hills in any case. And the world's best-trained soldiers certainly did not need to rehearse marching. But Kynortas had been of the belief that idle men, particularly idle warriors, make trouble. And it does not do to spend too much time thinking on the eve of battle.

Roper stayed in camp and waited for the rangers to return. They arrived just as night began to drape the hills and all the legionaries were back in camp, bearing disturbing news.

'The army is vast, lord,' said Gestur, who sat at Roper's fire wolfing down hoosh that the Black Lord had prepared himself. Roper had been eating with Gray and Tekoa when the Skiritai returned and had asked that they join him.

'Be specific,' insisted Roper.

The rangers glanced at one another. 'A hundred and fifty thousand,' said Gestur, the more voluble of the two. 'It was hard to work around their sentries, lord. Even so, we are confident that it is above a hundred and thirty thousand infantry and twenty thousand mounted knights.'

'Twenty thousand knights,' said Gray mildly. 'Damn.'

'There aren't twenty thousand knights in the whole of Albion,' said Tekoa. 'Not even ten thousand. They must have support from the continent.'

'So it sounds as though we can assume we are outnumbered four to one,' Roper surmised. He took another spoonful of hoosh, frowning into his bowl. 'What else?'

'They have kept their forces together: all of them are within the valley. And they are getting their supplies from a huge wagon park in the north.'

'We thought that was so that their forces were defending it from our likely direction of approach.'

'Eh? A single wagon park in the north for the entire camp?' pressed Roper.

The two rangers nodded. 'As far as we could see.'

Roper brooded for a moment. 'Gestur, Margeir: I thank you for your services. Please take your food and excuse us; I must plan with my companions here.' The two Skiritai picked up their bowls carefully and bowed to Roper, heading for a nearby hearth at which some of their peers cackled with laughter.

'Twenty thousand knights is a daunting prospect,' said Tekoa as soon as the rangers were out of earshot. 'We will need to find a location that nullifies their cavalry.' Tekoa glanced at Roper, aware that he had already been asked to locate just such a site.

'Agreed,' said Gray. 'Somewhere we cannot be flanked, where quality counts for more than quantity.'

'Even in such a location, it is too many,' said Roper bluntly. Gray and Tekoa glanced at one another.

'My lord,' said Tekoa, sitting up straight on the log he was using as a bench. 'I admit I have been impressed with your leadership thus far. Notwithstanding that, here, you do not know what you are talking about. You have seen one battle; Gray and I have seen fifty between us. You must trust our judgement and I say that the legions are of a different quality to the Suthern soldiers. You must trust our judgement, and our legionaries.'

'I agree, my lord,' said Gray firmly. 'If we find the right

location, we can fight the Sutherners. The alternative would be to retreat again. Forget the shame, forget the dishonour: your command would not survive it twice in a row.'

'Perhaps we could win,' conceded Roper. 'Let the Sutherners wash over our line again and again until they break; hope that our cavalry can somehow contain twenty thousand knights. But we would lose thousands, perhaps tens of thousands. There is also a good chance that we would lose the battle. Do you deny it, my advisors?'

'Better than the alternative,' growled Tekoa. Gray simply stared at Roper, his brown eyes boring into Roper's green.

'What are you saying, my lord?' he asked, finally.

'I'm saying the price of victory is too dear. We must defeat this army with our own forces intact.'

'You fear you will not be able to retake the Hindrunn if we lose too many men?' Gray pressed.

'Forget the Hindrunn,' said Roper. 'That comes later.'

'It doesn't have to, lord,' Gray said. 'Do not forget why we are here. You say it is to drive the Sutherners back to their lands, not to secure your own legacy. I fear that you will not be able to do both.'

'I tell you, my mind is not on the Hindrunn,' insisted Roper. 'It is on the future. If we lose half our army here, we would win the battle but lose a war that will last for generations. We must preserve the legions in the course of victory, otherwise all we have done is pay blood for time. We cannot repel the Sutherners for ever, not unless our victory here is overwhelming.'

There was a pause as Gray continued to look shrewdly at the Black Lord. He turned his gaze to Tekoa. 'I accept that, Legate,' he said respectfully. 'Let's hear his alternative.' Tekoa's face was flushing a familiar deep red and he glowered at Roper. In the end, he nodded curtly.

'The Black Kingdom will not tolerate such a horde for long,' said Roper. 'It will shake them off, if given time. But we must help it in that regard, and I need you two to back me in front of the other legates. Everyone must agree, otherwise we will surely destroy ourselves.'

'So the Black Kingdom is to defeat the Sutherners on our behalf?' demanded Tekoa.

'It is to help us,' said Roper. 'We shall weaken the Sutherners together, and when the moment comes, when their forces are rotten with fear and pinned by the sea, we shall finish them.'

Roper built up the fire and found some more logs to provide seating around it before summoning the legates. There were nine of them, including Tekoa and the commander of the cavalry. Gray, Asger and Pryce were there also to represent the Guard, making thirteen around the fire.

The legates' mood did not match Roper's own. They arrived talkative and full of good cheer. Even with soldiers as robust as the legions, the mood on campaign was not always so positive, but Roper's understanding of small gestures and the impact they had on morale was telling. So far he had been everywhere; he had let no one see him asleep. He had kept the watchmen company on the camp perimeters; had shared his fire and his hoosh, and appeared to know the names of every soldier under his command. Any time he was questioned, he had an answer, both frankly honest and reassuring. He appeared secure, calm and serene and was beginning to exert the kind of influence that Kynortas had had early in his reign. Despite his flighty reputation, the legionaries were coming to admire this new Black Lord. He showed willingness, energy and what appeared to be competence.

Roper waited for the legates to settle and then called for silence. It was his third campaign council and silence fell more quickly than the last time, which itself had been faster than the time before that. 'Peers, perhaps you have heard by now that the Skiritai have brought worrying news. The enemy have forces in excess of one hundred and thirty thousand warriors, with twenty thousand mounted knights supporting them.' Not a councillor batted an eyelid at this. They continued to stare unmoved at Roper. 'I have considered the threat posed by such a force and concluded that it would be unwise to meet them in pitched battle straight away.' This elicited a response. There was a restless stirring among the legates and Asger tutted loudly.

'You object, Asger?' Roper called him out.

Asger was on his feet at once. 'More cowardliness from a second-rate leader, who proves himself yet again unwilling to commit to combat,' he said importantly. There was an unease around the circle that suggested he was not alone in this opinion. 'You haven't the stomach for this, Roper.'

'Regardless of your opinion, you call me "lord",' said Roper. 'Your comments have been noted, Asger.'

'You propose to retreat, lord?' said another legate impatiently. His name was Skallagrim; legate of the Gillamoor, one of the five auxiliary legions travelling with the army.

'No, I propose to use our country as best we are able to weaken them before we fight them head on.' Roper paused and then allowed himself a rueful smile. 'I think everyone here knows that we have nowhere to retreat to. The Hindrunn gates are locked to this army.'

'Nonsense,' objected Asger.

Roper let that comment receive the silence it deserved for a moment. 'You always interested me as a choice for Lieutenant of the Guard, Asger,' he said at last. 'I have never seen it first-hand, but have been informed several times that you do not really have the martial capability to be a guardsman, let alone Lieutenant of the Guard. Nor is your leadership held in high regard.' Asger's face was flooding with colour but he dared not respond. Pryce, sitting next to him, had shifted on his log so that he was directly facing the isolated lieutenant. Roper continued, slowly and deliberately enraging Asger. 'There are even those who doubt you belong in Ramnea's Own Legion, though I cannot believe every story of cowardice that comes to my ears. Despite all this, your rise to prominence has been nothing short of meteoric since your childhood friend Uvoren came to captain the Guard.' The assessment, coming from the mouth of one so young and directed at a man as proud as Asger, could blister. Several of the legates were biting back smiles as they listened. Asger, so transparent in his motives, was not popular. 'And I think, with all of this taken into account, you have spoken insolently once too often. You are relieved of the lieutenancy. Gray will take over your duties from now on.'

'Finished, Roper?' spluttered Asger, purple with rage.

'Why, yes,' said Roper, 'I believe you are.' Pryce and Tekoa snorted with laughter and several of the legates applauded gleefully. Asger stood, filled with boiling energy, glanced down at Pryce who was still staring at him steadily, and stormed from the circle.

'As I said,' Roper continued, 'we will diminish the Sutherners before fighting them.'

'How?' Skallagrim spoke again.

'An attack,' said Roper. 'But one aimed at their supplies, rather than their warriors. We launch a diversionary raid, and when they swarm to rebuff us, our cavalry rip the baggage train apart.'

'You are fighting a huge army, lord,' said Skallagrim. 'If the diversionary force is caught, it will not be in a location of our choosing. We would be surrounded and totally destroyed.'

'That is why they must not be caught. But nor shall it be. There is no way this bloated force can move through our country as fast as we can.'

There was a sceptical silence.

'I think it a rather obvious deception,' said another legate. His name was Sturla Karson and he led Ramnea's Own Legion. 'And one with an extremely high chance of disaster. Our force is already drastically outnumbered. To split it in half seems to be inviting disaster.' There was a murmur of agreement.

Roper inclined his head in the legate's direction. 'It is a valid objection, Legate. But consider the Suthern mindset. They have been raised at their mother's knee on stories of our barbarous and brutal race. They have seen our lands: mountainous, untamed and, to their eyes, ghastly. To them, we are vast unholy warriors with impenetrable armour concealed beneath our skin and terrible weapons of destruction. They are here because they have been whipped into a fervour of terror and righteousness; but with such savagery, comes recklessness. Their psyche will be their own undoing. When they see our soldiers, they will not think as hard as they usually do about why we are there. They will not approach the battle as calmly and rationally as they are able. To overcome their own fear, they will respond with utmost force to any attack of ours.

'Yes, they have won an early battle. I tell you now, they are not thinking how easy this invasion will be and how overrated our warriors were all along. A single encounter is not enough to overcome a lifetime's education. They still fear us. They will still rush to the attack like a dog whose puppies are under threat. They will be thinking about us, and not their baggage train.'

The warriors around the fire still looked sceptical, but Roper knew he was right.

'I understand these people,' he said again. 'And the worst that can happen is they do not take our bait, we outstrip them on the retreat, and we can try again. But that won't happen. Is not a surprise attack at dawn a powerful weapon in its own right? Why, when panicking that your sentries have been overwhelmed, would you do anything other than respond directly to the threat at hand?'

The silence was broken by Gray. 'It is a strong plan,' he declared generously. Tekoa grunted his agreement through gritted teeth. There was a pregnant silence. Roper could tell someone was about to try and quash the idea.

Then, much to Roper's surprise, Pryce spoke. 'I back my lord,' he said firmly. That swung it for him. Nobody would argue against the triumvirate of Pryce, Gray and Tekoa.

'So what do you command, lord?' asked a hesitant Skallagrim. Roper told them. And the next day, they marched north.

7
Out of the Mist

Bellamus struggled to rouse himself in the mornings. He liked to play a game with his manservants, challenging them to conclusively wake him by any means besides a pail of water. One, by the name of Rowan, had proved particularly adept at this game and surprised Bellamus that morning by introducing a pony from the baggage train into the sleeping chamber of his tent and sprinkling oats on his master's chest. Bellamus had awoken from one of the startling dreams that haunted his sleep in the north, to find the beast gently sucking on his woollen blankets.

'It's always a surprise with you, Rowan,' Bellamus said sternly to the straight-faced manservant on his way out of the tent. 'I preferred the bacon method; you have permission to repeat it.' The last time Rowan had woken him had been by luring him from his chamber with a plate of smoked bacon.

Bellamus ducked through the canvas flap and out into an exceptionally cold morning. The clouds had lifted during the night and any energy that had clung to the sodden earth had fled into the cosmos, leaving the mud brittle and unyielding. The waters all around had frozen over, down to an inch thick. Even the broad river threading the centre of the valley had marbled plates of ice affixed to its banks; a narrow liquid band still stirring gently between the river's cold edges. A dense mist had tumbled into the valley and Lord Northwic's pavilion, twenty yards away, was a mere sketch. Still, it promised breakfast.

Bellamus entered to discover Lord Northwic, as ever, long awake. He sat at the end of a heavy oak table dressed in split-leather leggings and a cotton shift, with a woollen blanket draped around his shoulders, nursing a mug of something steaming. As his eyes were no longer good enough to read, a servant standing in a corner was reading a classical history to him.

'Bellamus,' he growled in welcome, tapping a place at the table next to him. Bellamus took the seat and turned to wink at a servant behind him. The servant grinned and departed, returning almost at once to Bellamus's fervent thanks with a chunk of hard bread and a bowl of wine, watered pink.

Lord Northwic, who clutched a mug of pine needles steeped in hot water, eyed Bellamus's breakfast in disapproval. 'For a man whose father was a pikeman you have certainly embraced a decadent lifestyle, Bellamus,' he observed.

'It's very much about the contrast, my lord,' said Bellamus, removing the bleeding bread from the bowl and taking a bite.

'I trust you were not disappointed with your servant's efforts this morning?'

'Rowan is a good lad,' said Bellamus, his mouth full. 'You saw the pony?'

'I did,' said Northwic, snorting slightly. 'Though you are too familiar with them.'

'I see no need to be a tyrant,' said Bellamus mildly. Silence fell for a moment. 'It is cold. I think I shall never complain about a billet again.'

'We should never have launched a campaign so late in the season, but . . . His Majesty would not be dissuaded. Perhaps we should restore the roofs to the next village we come to and shelter until we are ready to leave,' said Lord Northwic, sipping his brew. 'Though the Anakim buildings are scarcely more comfortable than this tent.'

'They are a hard race,' said Bellamus. 'But when you live for two hundred years, perhaps you accept that no dwelling will last as long as you will and so resign yourself to rebuilding it many times?'

'It's just a poor land,' said Northwic dismissively.

'The Hindrunn will impress you. And there are said to be larger, more solid villages further north. Perhaps if we find one we could turn it into a permanent encampment and wait out the winter north of the Abus.'

Lord Northwic nodded. 'I don't want to cede everything we have gained to the winter. Thank God His Majesty thought better of recalling us. Perhaps we shall build a fort of our own. Still, it is a lot of men to support in a barren land and we shall struggle to persuade the fyrd to stay.' The fyrd was a militia force, roused into action by promises of wealth and fear of the Anakim. They were poorly equipped and trained, but made up for it in sheer weight of numbers.

'Sometimes . . .' said Bellamus, then paused.

Lord Northwic grunted that he should continue.

'The Anakim do not lead like we do.'

'What of it?'

Bellamus wondered how much he could say to a man as tight-laced as Lord Northwic. 'They separate their leaders and their men by distance alone. They sleep in the same way, eat the same food, carry the same burden.'

'Then the Anakim leaders will be tired when it comes to battle,' said his lordship. 'And we shall have the advantage.'

'That's possible,' conceded Bellamus. 'But I believe the Anakim are inspired by example. They will gladly follow the Black Lord, because he is the best of them. He works harder than they do and takes less rest. Under his gaze, they fight more fiercely.'

Lord Northwic's rheumy eyes glared at Bellamus, a touch suspicious at first. Then they seemed to soften. 'As you say, they are a hard race. Perhaps it is not possible to command the respect of such hard folk without leadership through deeds, as well as words.'

'Interesting,' said Bellamus, arching his eyebrows. He could do business with Lord Northwic so much more easily than with Earl William. 'I do not suggest following their example,' he explained. 'But there is so much that they do which is different; it is well to consider it.'

'I defer to you in all things Anakim,' said his lordship, taking another sip from the steaming mug.

'When we are done here, I think I shall study the Unhieru.' The Unhieru were the third race of men that dwelled in Albion. They inhabited the hills and valleys to the west of the island and were a huge people, even compared with the Anakim. They were famed for irrepressible savagery and barbarism, and said to be ruled by the almost mythical Gogmagoc, a giant-king as old as Albion itself.

'You think you would survive long enough in their company to study them?' enquired Lord Northwic.

'It is simply a case of learning to speak their language,' said Bellamus reasonably. 'But I think . . .'

What Bellamus thought never became clear, for he stopped suddenly.

A horn had sounded.

It moaned low and faint through the mist. It came once. Then twice. Then a third time.

'*Enemy Attacking*,' muttered Bellamus. Lord Northwic was on his feet at once, barking orders at his servants who now scurried out of the pavilion to fetch his armour, saddle his coursers, find out how far away and in what direction the enemy was, and half a dozen things besides.

Bellamus drained his bowl and darted out of the pavilion to discover chaos outside. Men dripping with weapons and chain mail were dissolving and reforming in the mist as they prepared themselves. Somehow a herd of goats from the baggage train was loose and was hurtling through the camp, bleating angrily. One man ran through a campfire and upset a pot in a great burst of sparks and steam.

'What's the news?' Bellamus called to no one in particular, weaving through warriors in an effort to reach his own tent.

'The Anakim, lord!' said the young lad Rowan, almost hopping with excitement. 'Their army has attacked at the mouth of the valley!' Rowan threw a finger into the air, pointing to an unearthly cloud of mist rising above them, visible over the morning fog against the faint lightening of the sky above. It was the manifest breath of thousands of warriors.

'Good lord.' Bellamus took just one moment to stare down the valley. 'My courser this instant, Rowan!' He was already wearing his war gear. He did not fight in battles. He preferred to give orders from an unobscured vantage point and so wore two thick layers of leather with chain mail in between to protect him against arrows. His horse was brought to him and he mounted, turning back to Rowan. 'Tell Lord Northwic I'm going to hold them. I'd be much obliged if he'd come and finish them before they finish me.' He raked back his heels and lunged into the mist. The faster members of his retinue were hauling themselves onto horses and joining him, so that half a dozen mailed warriors were soon with him, thundering into the white.

His tent was towards the centre of the valley and the Anakim had attacked from the south. Because of the vast size of the army, Bellamus was some miles from the front on which the Anakim descended. He might be too distant, but decisiveness was a disproportionate advantage in war. One word was ringing through his head: *attack*. The Anakim's advantage lay in facing an unprepared enemy whose resistance would be scattered and half-hearted. If Bellamus could assemble something unexpectedly stubborn, there was a chance he could hold them. If he could hold them, Lord Northwic would be able to bring reinforcements and overwhelm them. He doubted they were facing the whole Anakim army. The chances of a full call-up approaching undetected were negligible. In any case, his spies had told him of the leadership crisis unfolding in the Hindrunn. It seemed unlikely that one general had managed to gain control over the whole army. This was a splinter force: it had to be, and together he and Lord Northwic could turn this surprise attack on its head. But he had to be fast, and he had to be decisive.

Bellamus could hear none of the sounds of battle. He could see no figures through the mist. He could smell no smoke on the frozen air. But billowing above him, visible against the sky above, was that malignant cloud of mist. The horn called faintly through the mist again: *Enemy Attacking*. They were here.

There were a score of riders with him and a dozen more were unveiled by their progress, dithering about a lord with a thick black beard. 'With me!' shouted Bellamus, startling them into movement. 'With me! All of you, run or ride now to defence of your home!' From all sides, soldiers coagulated on his form. Some had ferociously gritted teeth and a naked sword, but no armour. Some hurried wide-eyed after his growing band, seizing shields at random and cramming tousled heads into helmets. Bellamus led sixty, then ninety, then one hundred and fifty: swordsmen, horsemen, spearmen, longbowmen, all keeping pace as he advanced. Their enemy could emerge from this mist at any moment, but they built a reassuring momentum that swept up the valley; a pulse of men surging in resistance.

Bellamus kept his eyes forward, sweeping the bank of white that swallowed everything except the spluttering river to his left. Were those hoof beats he could hear? They were: growing louder every moment. Huge figures consolidated in the mist before him, swarming against his patchwork band. Bellamus swore, fingernails the only weapons that occurred to him. But one of the retainers by his side held out the shaft of a spear, which Bellamus seized with a fevered nod of gratitude. 'Charge!' he shouted, as his band faltered. 'We stop them here!'

But as the figures before them solidified, they too baulked and shied away from the conflict. Bellamus allowed the charge to continue for a few heartbeats more, spear held as a lance and eyes gaping, before he realised. These were Sutherners: his own men, fleeing the Anakim at their back. 'Halt, halt! Form on us! Back now, back!' and he gestured them back the way they had come. The fleeing soldiers, most of them unarmed, milled around until swept up by Bellamus's more purposeful band. They began to move as one, more warriors still emerging from the tents to either side, bringing spare weapons to those who had none.

As they clattered up the valley, the atmosphere became more oppressive, silencing the excited jostling of his band. There was an energy developing, so potent that Bellamus half expected to see sparks jumping between the rings on his fingers, curled tight around worn leather reins. There were hundreds of men with him now. None of them spoke: they just panted and stomped in silence.

A clatter came from high up on their right and Bellamus turned towards the sound so forcefully that his horse almost turned with him. The mist was shallow, lying close to the ground, but still he could see nothing moving on the steep slopes of the valley. Then he spotted a small rock avalanche tumbling down the slope above him. 'Keep moving!' he shouted. If they were around him, there was nothing he could do about it. This Bellamus had learned first of all: whatever your plan is, execute it with utmost certainty.

Bellamus strained his ears into the fog and, for the first time, thought he could hear his enemy. Sounds carried unnaturally far in the still mist and the first noise that reached him was not the loudest, but that which travelled best on the milky air. It was a faint tinkling; though discordant, deceptively sweet, like water slipping over rock. It could have been the silver music that filled Bellamus's dreams; bells chiming to the finest touch.

More human noises began to reach their ears. A retching

shriek of pain that visibly knocked some of the advancing Sutherners. Howls of wholly unnatural savagery. Breathing so laboured that it sounded like moaning. Coughing as warriors pressed every breath from their lungs in levels of exertion ordinarily beyond them. The sounds of fighting are infinitely more terrible from the outside, before you have joined them; and they seemed so close. Bellamus was certain they would happen upon the scene with every heartbeat, but the fog was deceptive and they kept advancing into the void. On all sides, there were still upright tents and a steady stream of men retreating from the bank of noise joined with Bellamus's band, reinforcing them with numbers but bringing with them a creeping nausea. 'We're all there is!' shouted Bellamus over the heads of those around him. 'Nobody else is going to save you! Shed your fear, grit your teeth and put the horror of men from the south into the Anakim. Knock them back; do to them what they think they've done to us! Shock them! Hold them! And Northwic will be at our backs!'

Finally, they came upon the first evidence of the fighting. Bodies draped half out of the wreckage of their devastated tents and strewn across the valley floor. Light flickered from burning barricades, shaded by the mist. Most of the bodies were still alive, crawling on their hands and knees to the sides of the valley, or beneath the shelter of a wagon bed. The noises of fighting sounded as though they were fading a little and Bellamus wondered whether the Anakim had begun to retreat. 'Faster!' he roared. 'They're on the run! Faster!'

The floor of the valley was rising and they strained upwards, Bellamus unable to believe they had yet to happen upon the Anakim. But there was nothing. Just more bodies, more ghostly fire, more of this damned mist. He strained his eyes.

Nothing.

Then three dark smudges appeared in the white before him, and were gone. He quickened his horse a little, pulling out in front of the line, gazing forward and holding his breath. The outlines of three horsemen gathered themselves from the mist, so huge that they were unmistakably the enemy he sought. 'There! After them!' He charged, the spear still clutched in his hand, his retainers raking back their spurs beside him and the other riders surging out past the line. If the Anakim were retreating, he could pin them down and make them pay for this attack. They accelerated away from the foot soldiers at their back, galloping after the three shapes that had disappeared into the mist again. The three riders came back into view: Bellamus was gaining on them. Or maybe it was because they were still climbing and beginning to emerge above the haze.

Abruptly, they were out of the suffocating mist. The valley opened up around them, bathed in watery winter sunlight and smothered in fragments of bright frost.

It swarmed with Anakim. Thousands crawled over the hills, every immense warrior gleaming as though coated in dew, polished as bright as steel would allow. They were climbing the side of the valley, heading up towards a chip below the rim: a col slumped between two powerful shoulders of rock.

'Whoa, whoa, whoa!' Bellamus dragged his horse to a halt and those around him did likewise. They stared, every warrior silent and transfixed by the three figures before them. Scarcely fifty yards away, the three horsemen they had pursued were staring back. They were facing them, watching Bellamus's few hundred horsemen intently, so still that the hooves of their horses looked rooted to the ground.

The central horseman was huge. Even among fellow Anakim, he towered over his companions. Or maybe it was just that he sat atop the largest horse Bellamus had ever seen: a pale grey beast piled with muscle, hooves the circumference of a medium-sized barrel. The man astride it was black-cloaked, with shoulders of steel plate immense and brooding, and a helmet that Bellamus recognised.

The Black Lord. Their enemy stood before them: still, cold and watchful.

He wants to see how we're responding. Bellamus looked up at the col. It was perhaps two miles across, with a knotted outcrop of rock to each side rearing some two hundred feet over the col. A fearsome defensive position, with a perilously steep approach. There, the first Anakim were arraying themselves, hundreds of banners silhouetted against the sky behind. 'This stinks,' said Bellamus. 'Every bit of this. They've planned it.'

'Planned what?' asked one of his retainers.

Bellamus shook his head. 'I don't know. They've got something in mind.' He glanced at the man who had spoken and winked. 'Strip your shirt. Let's go and ask them.' Nobody else was better equipped to discern the Anakim plan, and in any case, there was nobody else on the scene. Whatever was at play, Bellamus needed to uncover it. He turned to another retainer. 'Would you head back down the valley and halt our little band? Let's not show our hand just yet.' The man departed and Bellamus affixed the filthy white shirt presented him by the first retainer onto the head of his spear. He held it up as a dismal banner and, with two companions, rode forward to meet the Black Lord.

They advanced and the three horsemen before them waited for them to close the distance, until Bellamus and his companions had drawn up before them. The central figure – the Black Lord – looked up at Bellamus's pathetic flag of truce. In Anakim he asked: 'Is that supposed to be a white flag, Bellamus?'

'You know it is, my lord. And as I have heard you are an honourable man, I know you will not violate such a gesture,' said Bellamus. He paused, trying to spot a house crest that told him whether he addressed Roper or Uvoren beneath the Black Lord's battle helm, but he could see none. 'I see you received the helmet I sent for you.'

The figure was still for a moment. His two companions

looked to him for a response and Bellamus wondered whether he had gone too far. He had no doubt who would win a contest of strength if the Anakim decided not to accept his feeble flag. 'I did,' said the warlord, at last. 'I wish you'd sent it attached to the rest of my father's body.'

Roper. 'You don't have many men, my Lord Roper,' observed Bellamus, looking up at the ridge. 'Enough for a surprise attack, not enough to repel our forces. Unless there are more that I cannot see, I think you will struggle, even with your good position.'

'We have enough,' said Roper, as though surprised Bellamus would think such a thing. 'Where is Lord Northwic?'

'Below, with the army. You wouldn't gain much by killing me here.'

The stern exterior cracked and Roper burst out laughing. He glanced at Bellamus's bodyguards, who could not understand the plosive words he and Bellamus exchanged and sat tense upon their horses. 'I'm not so sure about that. I hear Lord Northwic is capable, but you? You're something a little different, aren't you?'

'Perhaps a little, my lord,' said Bellamus modestly. Roper was smiling to himself and Bellamus found himself unexpectedly liking this lad.

'Well, Bellamus, we won't kill you. Not here. Not under a white *flag*. But I'd like to know what you did with my father's sword.'

'Bright-Shock, was it?' queried Bellamus. Roper did not object. 'It's being put to good use,' he said. He saw Roper's eyes rake his person, searching for some evidence of the blade, and Bellamus chuckled. 'Forget it, my lord. You won't get it back. I must congratulate your smiths on its quality, though.'

Roper grunted. 'It is hard to see which Sutherner would have use for an Unthank-silver blade. Well, Bellamus, did you have something you wanted to discuss? Because I must say we have conclusive ideas about what's about to happen.'

'What is about to happen?' asked Bellamus, bluntly.

The Black Lord laughed again. 'You should attack us, Bellamus,' he said. 'And you will find out.' He nodded at Bellamus and turned his monstrous horse back towards the col, followed by his two companions. Bellamus watched them go for a moment before turning back towards the mists.

'A general who rides a destrier?' said one of his bodyguards as soon as they were out of earshot. 'What is the range of that thing, four hundred yards?'

'A strange choice,' agreed Bellamus. More appropriate would have been a courser: faster, lighter and much better suited to spilling orders over a battlefield. A destrier – a full and heavily muscled battle horse – was a shocking beast to ride into combat but would tire quickly beneath a general. Still, Bellamus had been impressed by Roper, who seemed to have grown into his role in what must have been testing circumstances.

They collected the horsemen who waited below and descended back into the mist, Bellamus silent and his face crinkled. Swallowed again by the haze, it was not long before he discovered his restless infantry waiting for him. Lord Northwic was there on horseback, pushing his way up to the front of the line, followed by a great banner featuring a black bear on a white background.

'You've seen them?' he called out to Bellamus.

'I've spoken to them,' said Bellamus, pulling his horse about, next to Northwic. 'Roper is in command, riding what looks like a hippopotamus.'

'A what?'

'Forget it.'

'How many of them are there?'

'Perhaps thirty thousand,' supplied Bellamus. 'And they're defending a col further up the valley.'

Lord Northwic frowned. 'Why? They're hoping we'll attack them?'

'I doubt it,' said Bellamus. 'They're up to something. This is planned.'

The mists were dissolving in the sunlight that permeated the valley, obliterating the frost that encrusted the grass. Thousands of men were gathering around Bellamus and Northwic, and knights dressed in their full plate armour were beginning to appear on their flanks.

'Well, we know where a sizeable portion of their army is,' said Northwic. 'Let us wipe it out.'

'Yes, yes, but what are we missing?' said Bellamus, distractedly.

Northwic raised an eyebrow as if to say it hardly mattered. He turned away and began assembling the soldiers, barking the longbowmen into an advance, pulling those warriors with shields to the front of the line, pushing the knights back in reserve.

Bellamus ignored all this. He rode aside from the preparations, the frown still on his face. *What are they trying to achieve here? If this is a diversion, it's a big one.* He looked up at the col, becoming visible as the mist continued to evaporate. It was a formidable defensive position, but gave the Anakim few options for springing surprises. So if there was more to this situation, it was unlikely to be here. *What if it is a diversion? What are they distracting us from?* There was one obvious clue to that: they had attacked the southern end of the valley. If this was a diversion, it was probably calculated to tie up their forces away from the northern end. *And what is at the northern end?*

Bellamus grew still. 'Dear God.' He looked around for Lord Northwic, who was by this point a hundred yards away. Bellamus did not immediately react. For a moment, he merely stroked the mane of his horse gently. He patted its warm neck a few times. At the northern end of the valley: the wagon park. Their supplies, their equipment; their lifeline in this alien world. At that moment, the vast majority of their army was flooding towards this Anakim force. They had responded mindlessly, like a pack of dogs, to this simple threat, and had left the irreplaceable undefended. Bellamus had no proof, but it suddenly seemed glaringly obvious. 'And we'll be too bloody late,' he said bitterly. He snapped his fingers and looked up. 'Lord Northwic!' he bellowed. The old lord half turned towards him, eyebrows raised. 'Lord Northwic!'

8
Two Hanged Corpses

The fortress was always deathly still after a march-out. Even with only half the legions gone, the energy that usually animated the Hindrunn had dissipated. Those who remained were subdued, waiting for the moment their husbands, peers and brothers appeared again on the horizon. Many preferred it so quiet. The legions were absent more often than not and some of the Hindrunn's women had become accustomed to the peace, the space and the community they had grown without the warriors.

Not Keturah. She loved the throng as the legions returned. She loved the vigour of the feast that followed a successful campaign and the euphoria of the markets as legionaries who had been on marching rations for months bought everything they had desired in that time. She loved the talk of what had happened at war: the stories that circulated of campaign and the inevitable rash of betrothals that followed. She loved the return of her friends and admirers among the legionaries. But most of all, she just loved that more happened when the legions were resident. She felt part of something greater: a community of souls with a synchronised purpose. There was a sense of cooperation; that they were contributing to the symmetry of the earth.

That day, Keturah walked alone up one of the Hindrunn's cobbled roads, a leather sack over one shoulder and her face, though relaxed, stained with an expression of slight impatience. She was thinking about her father's departure. She had thought of little else for the past several days, for it had been uncharacteristic. Clad in his mighty eagle-feather cloak for the march-out, a helmet held beneath one arm, he had fussed excessively over his equipment, claiming he could not locate his task-knife.

'You have a dagger,' Keturah had said, pretending not to know that her father had no equipment problems and almost never had. He delayed because he had something to say.

'Keep your suggestions to yourself, Daughter. God knows how the estate will look after a month or so in your hands but I take it you'll do your best?' She nodded, looking at him flatly. 'Don't let anyone swindle you when you sell. And don't buy anything either . . . And we need more rams at Loratun, but just leave that. And don't talk to the estate manager at Trawden, he'll just confuse you . . . Actually, it's best if you just do nothing at all, Keturah.'

'Yes, Father.'

Tekoa looked sour. 'You acquiesce far too readily. On my return, I shall look for the column of smoke which means you've attempted something unwise. Look after your mother.' He had turned away, preparing to stride from the room. Then he faltered and turned back to her. There was a brief pause. 'Stay safe.'

Keturah was delighted. She laughed and took a few steps towards her father, placing an arm over his shoulder. 'Are you worried for me, Father?'

'Worried for whoever has to deal with you while you're unsupervised.' And then he had shocked her. He took her hand gently from his shoulder and held it in his own. 'You have declared a side now, Daughter. And most of your allies are about to leave this fortress. They may never return.'

She rolled her eyes. 'You will return.'

'Maybe. Whether or not that is true, Uvoren is the ultimate power in the Hindrunn as soon as we have left. You will have to tread carefully with him. As I said: stay safe, Daughter.' Then he had turned on his heel and was gone, his cloak lingering in the doorway for a brief moment before it too swept out of sight.

It had been sufficiently out of character to give Keturah pause for thought, but she had not taken it seriously until she had first encountered Uvoren two days later. There was more swagger in his walk. He was more insistent, more confident and had shown a great interest in Keturah. She supposed that her marriage to Roper had brought her to his attention, which was not welcome.

A right turn and the market appeared before Keturah. A rope trickled down the face of the building to either side of the path, each noosed about a corpse that hung fourteen feet from the ground. The sight had been shocking to Keturah when the bodies were fresh, their throats cut and their guts spilling out. Now the guts were gone, taken by carrion birds, and the corpses had shrunk and stiffened as the moisture left too. The mark on their forehead was still visible though: a spread-winged cuckoo.

The mark of the Kryptea.

These were the two legionaries responsible for stealing the Kryptean effects that had been used during Roper's attempted assassination. They had been hanged unseen beside the market, one of the busiest places in the fortress, as a mark of Kryptean subtlety. *They can act whenever and wherever they like,* the corpses said. *Do not steal from the Kryptea.* Since then, nobody had dared cut the bodies down, not even the poor souls whose houses they hung against. They could not be sure whether the Kryptea considered them their own property so the corpses were left, staining the stone walls behind, teeth bared by shrivelled lips.

Keturah barely noticed them now. She had passed this way often enough and they were easier to look at now that they did not so much resemble living flesh. She was heading for the market, which was more subdued than usual but scores still moved among the covered stalls and voices called out to her as she passed. 'Congratulations on your marriage, Miss Keturah!'

'Fruit leather for you and your mother today, my lady?'

'A sight for sore eyes, Miss Keturah!' She smiled at each of them, cocking her head and giving them a few words in return, though she could not linger.

'My dear!' called one woman from behind a stall laden with bolts of fabric, a softly bulging sling joining her shoulder and hip.

'Sigurasta!' Keturah stepped towards her and embraced the woman over her wares. 'Thank you for the last time,' she said, employing the fond greeting of the Black Kingdom. 'How's your beautiful girl?' With care, Keturah pulled back the edge of the sling to reveal a sleeping baby, its head turned into its mother and wearing a stubborn frown.

'Healthy, so far,' said Sigurasta. 'I hear you have a problem of your own to take care of?'

She referred to the Vidarr estate which had been left in Keturah's control. 'No problem,' said Keturah. 'Father likes to complain but it is a minor responsibility. I have some timber to sell so I must move, before Avaldr is inundated. Will you come drink wine with us tomorrow?'

Sigurasta said that she would and Keturah gave her and her baby a kiss on the cheek before they parted. As she turned away from them, her face resumed its impatient repose.

The woman was Sigurasta Sakariasdottir, wife of Vinjar Kristvinson, Councillor for Agriculture and close personal friend of Uvoren the Mighty. Roper's business was now Keturah's business, and Roper needed Uvoren's war council to be destroyed. Vinjar Kristvinson had to fall and perhaps his wife would have the key to that. Keturah thought of herself as much a warrior as any of those away on campaign.

This was her battlefield and Sigurasta, whether she knew it or not, was one of her allies.

Keturah headed for a stall around which a small crowd had already assembled and behind which was a short, stocky man, evidently enjoying the attention he received. His wandering eyes caught Keturah's and opened wide. 'Almighty preserve me!' He threw up his hands in mock dread, a look of horror crossing his face. 'No, not today, Miss Keturah. I am stretched enough as it is without one of my encounters with you.'

She laughed at this and slid through the ranks of other customers, placing a hand on his arm. 'Avaldr, I am here to do you a favour.'

'She always says that,' Avaldr declared to his other clients. 'What is it this time, Miss Keturah: a mighty bog-oak? A crystal from the Winter Road?' Avaldr always liked to share his jokes when he saw Keturah and now he had an audience. 'And what shall you have as payment? The stall itself? My shoes?'

'There's no need to be so melodramatic, Avaldr. I've some fine ash for you today but there's always Bjarkan or Parmes, if you don't want it.'

'Not while the Ulpha are away on campaign,' said Avaldr slyly, referring to the legion in which his two rivals served.

Keturah was amused. 'It's timber, Avaldr. It will keep until they're back. I've no desire to sell it to you while you think you're the only buyer in the fortress.'

He gave her a delighted smile. 'But I *am* the only buyer in the fortress!' He gestured at the customers arrayed about him.

'But Avaldr, we're such old friends.' She reached across to his cheek and gave it the lightest of caresses. 'You're still going to give me your best price.' Avaldr threw up his hands again and gestured as though to shoo her away, though he looked mightily pleased.

'It seems that I have little choice. How much have you got?'

'Three tons, twenty-foot lengths.'

'Green?'

'For now. Felled two weeks ago at Trawden.'

The two shaped an agreement, Avaldr agreeing to bring iron to Tekoa's household in payment for the timber, which was being stored outside the fortress walls. Keturah bade him farewell, extricated herself from the crowd and went on the hunt for a stall selling yarn. She found one and traded some copper for it, extracting it from the leather sack hung at her shoulder and handing it to the woman behind the stall who used a broad chisel and hammer to gouge a few chunks off the copper, handing the rest of the ingot back to Keturah. The next stall along had goose eggs and, using the rest of her copper, Keturah purchased a crate of them nestled in short straw. Looking to her right, she spotted a familiar face.

'Hafdis,' she said, placing an arm at the back of the woman next to her. Hafdis was tall (though still several inches shorter than Keturah) and attractive, with an upturned nose, blue eyes and chestnut hair that fell midway down her back. Her beauty was tempered by an almost constant expression of distaste that she wore, as though perpetually disenchanted with those around her. But her clothes were finely woven layers of overlapping wool, her boots softest leather, and she was paying for her goose eggs in a rare currency: bolts of silk. This was Hafdis Reykdalsdottir, wife to Uvoren the Mighty.

Hafdis turned to Keturah and managed a watery smile, embracing the younger woman. 'My, my, Keturah. Are you well?' Without waiting for a reply, she said, 'Isn't it dull with the legions away?'

'There's certainly less laughter in the household since my father left,' said Keturah. 'Though that was mostly him enjoying his own company. But I'm glad that the Sutherners are finally being challenged.'

'Oh, yes. I suppose you're looking after your mother,' said Hafdis carelessly. 'It's too warm today.'

Keturah was too used to Hafdis's wandering mind for it to bother her unduly, though privately she thought that of course it was warm beneath all those layers of wool. Out loud, she said sweetly: 'You're dressed for cooler weather, my dear. I hear Unndor and Urthr were married: my congratulations.'

The look of distaste on Hafdis's face magnified several times. 'I had hoped for better for both of them. A nobody from House Oris and another from House Nadoddur? My husband has a great deal to answer for.'

'Did the boys not want the marriages?'

'Neither had met their wife before the betrothal. Both girls are dull and plain: there is little desirable about the arrangement.'

'I'm so sorry,' said Keturah, shaking her head and suppressing the look of sardonic amusement with which she would usually have greeted such news. In Roper's absence, Uvoren had sought to increase his hold over the Hindrunn by marrying his two sons to prominent daughters of undeclared houses. House Oris and House Nadoddur were both minor and unable to lend much weight to Uvoren's cause, but it increased the momentum behind his claim for the throne. Roper must surely fail in the field, but Uvoren was ensuring that, even if Roper returned to the Hindrunn, popular support would overwhelmingly be his. The move was relentless. With the odds so firmly in his favour, there was scarcely a need to garner yet more support. Uvoren had his foot on Roper's throat and was only intensifying the pressure. But Unndor and Urthr were both, by all accounts, furious at the arrangement. Keturah had even heard that Unndor had spent his wedding night well apart from his new bride.

'I must get back to my mother, dear Hafdis, but will you come and share some wine with me overmorrow? It would be my great pleasure to see you.' Hafdis agreed it would be a great pleasure while Keturah privately congratulated herself on the levels of self-sacrifice she was prepared to undergo for her new husband. She chose her friends carefully and Hafdis was not the company she would usually have sought, though there could be nobody better to provide her with Uvoren's secrets than his disillusioned wife. Another ally of Keturah's: this battle was going rather well.

She was about to depart when the atmosphere around her changed abruptly. Silence rippled through the chattering stalls. Traders fell quiet and turned towards Keturah, the collective attention of that portion of the market focusing on a point above her right shoulder. Hafdis had gone very still.

Keturah turned, knowing what she would find, and came face to face with Uvoren the Mighty, standing directly behind her. He wore a great deal of steel for a man not dressed for war. His belt was studded with plates of it, his woollen shirt fastened at the front with thick clips of it. A great sheathed strip of it hung at his side: a long dagger that he never wore during battle. His cloak was fastened by it and a fine coil of it held his hair in that high ponytail, reserved for lords and members of the Sacred Guard alone. The sight caused Keturah to raise her eyebrows: Uvoren was certainly flirting with the borders of excessive personal adornment.

The silence that had spread was replaced with an excited muttering and Uvoren flashed a grin over the marketplace. 'Good morning, my friends. Please, carry on!'

The marketplace barely reacted beyond a slight flutter.

With Uvoren stood Baldwin Dufgurson, the Legion Tribune. Tall, black-haired, thin of face and narrow of limb, he surveyed Keturah imperiously, as though suspicious that Roper's wife was in such close proximity.

'What are you doing here, Tekoasdottir?' he asked coldly.

Keturah pretended to look startled and surveyed her

surroundings. 'How odd, Tribune, I thought I was in the market. Wait . . .' She cast around again. 'Yes, I am in fact in the market. So I'm trading.' She treated him to her iciest look.

Uvoren laughed, giving Baldwin an affectionate shove which the latter did not seem to appreciate. Then his eyes came to rest on his wife. He maintained his smile. 'And you? Why are you here?'

'Buying eggs,' said Hafdis, uncertainly.

'Shouldn't you be weaving?'

'I was tired of weaving.'

'Well, now you've had your break, you can return to it,' said Uvoren, still smiling. Hafdis glanced at Keturah, bade her a quiet farewell and headed for home, a basket of eggs clutched beneath one arm. Uvoren's eyes had moved onto Keturah and lingered there as his wife moved out of sight. 'What are you trading, Miss Keturah?'

She shrugged. 'Some timber arrived from Trawden, Captain, to be sold. And I needed yarn. Yarn and goose eggs.'

He smiled. It was a smile so charming, so full of warmth and confidence that she almost forgot who he was. She almost liked him. 'You intend to spend some time weaving yourself?'

'With my mother. It is hard for her, when my father is gone. She needs distraction.'

'Ah! Well, I hope she finds it.' Uvoren glanced at Baldwin, who was still wearing his supercilious expression. 'Off you go, Baldwin.' The Tribune swept past Keturah and into the marketplace. Uvoren watched his back for a moment and then drew a little closer to Keturah. She stood her ground. 'I pray your husband returns victorious.'

'Of course you do, Captain.' Keturah was very tall but, up close, Uvoren the Mighty was truly enormous. Even unarmoured and unhelmeted, his shoulders seemed to have the breadth of an eagle's wingspan and his arms were thick as the chains that raise the portcullis of the Great Gate. Even

Keturah, used to the presence of Tekoa and Pryce – men who others found quite as intimidating as Uvoren – felt daunted by this monstrous individual. When he spoke, his voice seemed to reverberate through her chest and up her throat.

'It must be hard for you, being left by both Roper and your father. Especially with your mother so unwell.' Keturah still stood her ground, even as he drew very close. 'You are always welcome in my household, if you ever feel too alone.'

She laughed at that, placing a hand on Uvoren's chest, at first lightly, as a caress, then brought the palm more firmly down and pushed him backwards. With the laugh, he was disarmed and sweetened. With the push, he was defeated. He allowed himself to be pushed backwards, infected by her laugh, smiling a little and playing the game.

'Come, come. Surely you have no loyalty towards the boy Roper yet?' he said.

'He is the Black Lord,' Keturah replied, raising her eyebrows at Uvoren and still smiling. 'I thought we were all loyal towards him.'

'Black Lord in name alone. We both know what's going to happen to him.'

'I thought you prayed for his victory?'

'I do. But victory or not, he isn't coming back through the Great Gate. You don't need to think about him.' He spoke consolingly, as though his advice was a balm to her.

Keturah tucked her hair back behind her shoulder and sighed. 'I am the paragon of a dutiful wife,' she said. 'While my husband lives, I think about him.'

'Well, we'll see what we can do about that. Perhaps—'

'Your wife seems unhappy, Captain,' interrupted Keturah, softening the change of subject with a half-step towards him.

'She always is,' he said.

'Perhaps you should see to that?' she suggested sweetly.

'Not possible.'

'Well, then, you can help me –' she looked pointedly at the box of eggs and straw – 'I have forgotten my cart.'

Uvoren grinned and gave an ironic bow. 'My lady.' He bent to pick them up and she led him back towards Tekoa's household. Under normal circumstances, Keturah would have moved from her father's house to Roper's upon marrying him. But these were not normal circumstances. Her mother needed care, her father needed the estate to be looked after while he was gone and Keturah needed some defence while her allies were out of the fortress. All were easier in Tekoa's household.

She and Uvoren walked side by side for a time, Uvoren making jests, she providing a tart audience. After a time, she interrupted him again. 'So what's going to happen to my husband when he returns?'

Uvoren looked wry. 'We both know that it depends on how he approaches the gates.'

'I'm not sure it does,' said Keturah. Both spoke as though the topic was amusing to them. To Uvoren, Keturah thought it genuinely might be. For her, it was only a lifetime of habit which kept her voice light. 'You're going to kill him whether he comes as a supplicant or a warlord.'

Uvoren just smiled, staring straight ahead, which Keturah took for confirmation.

'There are better ways to die than sticky-fire,' was all he said. She supposed that meant that if Roper came as an invader, he would be killed in a conflagration before the gates.

'Are there? I'm sure it's painful, Captain, but for all that it's quick. A few moments of pain is nothing next to the life you have lived. People get too worried about the act of dying itself: it is usually brief.'

'It's better not to know that it's coming,' said Uvoren.

Keturah tutted impatiently. 'Why? You can prepare yourself and those around you if you know it's coming. You can die as you'd planned; in the way the person you'd like to be remembered as would die.'

Uvoren raised his eyebrows. 'You've experienced a lot of death in your twenty years, Miss Keturah?'

'Not as much as you, I daresay, Captain,' said she. 'But I've seen it close and I've seen many of the faces it wears. It is better to know that it is coming.'

'If you say so.' They crossed over the running track that skirted the Hindrunn just before a pack of women ran by, wearing the black tunic of the Academy that marked them out as historians. Uvoren turned back, eyes following them. Most stared back and a few smiled, looking at the captain as they passed and sparing a glance for Keturah, wondering what they were doing together.

'Eyes front, Captain,' Keturah said. 'And what about my father?'

'I hope your father will come round to my side when Boy-Roper falls.'

'He's a stubborn man,' said Keturah. 'A change of mind is not something that comes to him readily.'

'I respect your father,' said Uvoren, with a shrug that made the box in his hands heave. 'He's just chosen the wrong side. With a man like him, I could be generous. With Boy-Roper? He is no loss to anyone really.'

They had reached Keturah's household. 'Leave the box there, Captain,' said Keturah, indicating a spot next to the door, which she opened before turning back to Uvoren. 'Thank you. Look after your wife: the poor woman just needs a little care.'

'You are ever wise, Miss Keturah,' said Uvoren. She raised an eyebrow, eyes humorous as she shut the door. Then her face dropped and she leaned against the wood.

Have I given him too much? She did not know, but she thought she knew him and that the push she gave him would barely have made an impression. He would remember the laugh and the caress that had preceded it. He would not remember the push. She had to give him a little more each time. Enough so that he would think that he might be able to win her by charm and not have to resort to force; not so much that she ran out of room before her father returned. She needed him back soon. Time was running out for her.

Keturah took a deep breath, tucked her hair behind her ears, straightened her back and walked to the hearth, by which her mother sat staring into the fire. 'Mother,' she said, giving her a kiss, 'what shall we do this afternoon?'

9
Guard Him

Bellamus and Lord Northwic had taken their horses a little way up the side of the northern end of the valley. Spread beneath them was a butcher's floor. A grisly carpet of corpses lay darkly at the valley base and the river, choked with bodies and shattered wagons, was beginning to swallow the surrounding land in glittering water. Some of their soldiers were picking over the remains, dragging survivors clear of the rising waters and furtively looting in equal measure. They did what they could for the wounded, but often what they could was as simple as a knife to the heart. The seagulls and crows had already descended and were picking out the eyes, lips and tongues from the fallen. They wheeled beneath the gathering clouds, resembling the specks of dust in a column of light.

Bellamus shivered. The wind was picking up and it felt as if more rain was on the way. He had been right, of course. Roper's attack in the south was nothing but a diversion to draw their forces swarming away from the wagon park in the north. Then the Anakim cavalry had thundered into the valley, sweeping away the feeble resistance they encountered and tipping the precious wagons of supplies into the river. Bellamus had begged Lord Northwic for a force to take north and counter the attack he saw as inevitable, a request the lord had graciously granted. On the way, Bellamus heard the horn desperately calling *Enemy Attacking* from the north, but nobody had responded, assuming it was merely a delayed echo of what was occurring in the south. He arrived to find the attack, which had clearly been wonderfully synchronised, long concluded. Bellamus left his men there to guard against the cavalry returning and hastened back to find that Lord Northwic was clutching at shadows. Roper's diversionary force had retreated soon after Bellamus had departed, and though Northwic had pursued, they had been less well prepared than the Anakim, were moving through unfamiliar land, and were evidently not as fit.

The losses sustained had barely impacted the number of men at their disposal. Even so, this was a hammer blow. It was scarcely possible to maintain a supply train through such a hostile land. The food now saturated by the river had been instrumental to their hopes, a fact obvious to all within the valley's steep walls. Bellamus had seen how the gait of his men had changed in the aftermath of this defeat. They moved in little more than a shuffle, heads so resolutely dipped that it looked as though they feared the valley would pour ferocious soldiers down on top of them, if only they were to raise their eyes to the valley rim.

'What's the tally?' asked Bellamus.

'Tally?' asked Lord Northwic with a sniff. He looked across at Bellamus with more than a little suspicion. 'Twelve thousand men are dead. More numbers for those records of yours.'

Bellamus did not much care about Northwic's tone. It could have been worse than twelve thousand.

'More,' continued Lord Northwic quietly.

'More what?'

'It's more than twelve thousand. We have twelve thousand dead, but now we've been crippled so dismissively, we'll lose twice as many again through desertion.'

Bellamus was sceptical. 'They'd be fools to leave. Sutherners alone, north of the Abus? They'll be lucky to survive a night.'

'"Sutherners"? You have spent too long among your spies.'

'You are being cold, Ced, though I have no idea why since I played more than my part today.'

Lord Northwic was silent a while. 'I know.' He continued staring down at the scene below. He shook his head bitterly. 'I know.'

'There's nothing we can do now,' said Bellamus, his voice more gentle. 'We have survived. Now we must resupply. We still far outnumber this Anakim force, we still have our knights. We will fight again another day and we will triumph.' He looked across to Lord Northwic and was surprised to see tears brimming in the old man's eyes. They built absurdly, threatening to overflow the eyelids until Lord Northwic blinked and cuffed at them. He looked pale and was hunched into his horse, eyes shadowed by a heavily laden brow and hands clutched tightly before him.

'It feels . . . it feels as though my lungs are bruised,' he said, voice growing thinner and thinner as though he scarce had the heart to finish the sentence.

Bellamus supposed this had weighed particularly heavily on Northwic, who bore ultimate responsibility for this army. It was his organisation which had been so ruthlessly exposed by this attack. Bellamus knew how that felt. He had seen defeats that left him utterly bereft; empty to the extent of feeling physically shrivelled, each breath like trying to swallow butterflies. At that moment, Bellamus himself felt more as though he had been slapped in the face. The word Northwic had used to describe this raid had lodged in him. *Dismissive.* The masters of this dreamworld had appeared at last and treated their efforts with contempt. Northwic and Bellamus had torched their way through the Black Kingdom, and the response had been silence. In retrospect, that silence seemed ominous.

There was a bitter taste in the valley. Though Bellamus would not admit it, he was beginning to feel lost in this wasteland. From afar, the Anakim had fascinated him. In context, surrounded by an order that was alien to Bellamus, they were more disturbing than fascinating. The haughty, snow-dusted peaks were the overseers of this capricious wilderness, at whose whim you operated. On their return from pursuing Roper, Northwic's forces had turned a corner on one of the tortuous Anakim roads and startled a grazing aurochs. The enraged bull had marauded through their ranks, lobbing soldiers over the heads of their fleeing compatriots and killing four of them, wounding another score before retreating back into the trees. Every day they lost a dozen foragers to packs of startlingly ferocious wolves, or rogue giant bears that did not behave like the beasts on the south side of the Abus. It was not clear to Bellamus what his men were doing wrong, or how they incurred the wrath of these predators, who seemed to tolerate the Anakim so peaceably.

What kind of people belonged to such a world? In the south, Bellamus had been determined to deconstruct them; certain he nearly understood them. Here, he felt as wide-eyed as any of his men and had felt the breath catch in his throat when the horn had called *Enemy Attacking* through the mist-smothered camp. He had been foolish. He had not thought any harder than the animal desire to defend, and that had been used to pluck something precious from them. It was a lesson for which he was not sure he could afford the exorbitant fee.

'There is not a single Anakim body down there,' said Lord Northwic. 'I was looking. Monsters.'

'So now we know that the Anakim are clever, not indestructible.'

Lord Northwic looked flatly at the younger man.

'Warfare of the mind,' elaborated Bellamus, unwillingly. 'They lost men. Of course they did. But they've removed the bodies to discourage us for the next time we fight them. They want us to believe they are invulnerable.' Both were quiet again. 'What a waste,' said Bellamus quietly. And then, to himself: 'You bloody, bloody idiot.'

Lord Northwic jerked his head as though to dispel the mood. 'We shall move the army to the coast,' he said. Food was more plentiful there than inland; they could take fish, crabs, kelp and shellfish. There was also the option of being resupplied by ships from Suthdal. 'We shall replenish our resources and send a message to the king saying we have seen off a minor raid.'

'It would appear,' replied Bellamus slowly, 'that Roper knows what he is doing. My God, we will have our revenge.'

The day was beginning to fade by the time the Anakim had come to a halt. Most of the legionaries were silent as they assembled the camp; in equal measure exhausted, elated and shocked. Physically and mentally, the effort it had taken to march through the night to come down on the Sutherners at dawn, sweep through their camp, ascend the col fast enough to avoid being caught and then retreat so swiftly as to discourage anything other than token pursuit, was at the limits of what even the legions were capable of. Roper had wrung every last drop from his soldiers and been rewarded with an overwhelming victory; though of course they had lost peers as well. Men had watched friends of a dozen campaigns fall raiding the encampment, dampening the light-headed wonder at what they had achieved that day. Crushed by his exertions, Roper was attempting to help the Sacred Guard assemble some rough fortifications, but working so slowly that Helmec took him gently by the shoulders and steered him towards the fire, pressing a bowl of hot hoosh into his hands. Roper stared blankly down at the thick stew for some time before taking up a spoon and beginning to shovel it absent-mindedly into his mouth.

The Black Lord in particular had been at the heart of that effort. He had not ridden alongside the legionaries. He had walked with them, sharing each league, blister and flooded road. He had stumbled with them in the dark of a moonless night as they approached the Suthern encampment. On the advance he had led from the front, and on the retreat from the back; at each stage more exposed to danger than any other man. He wore the risk lightly, joking with those around him and seemingly oblivious to the threat of the Suthern army. When they had at last reached the Suthern encampment and swept down upon it, the Black Lord, oblivious of what might be waiting for them in the mists, had finally mounted Zephyr and rampaged far ahead of his soldiers, Gray and Helmec tearing to keep up and preserve their lord.

If one of his men slipped, the Black Lord would not help them up, marrow-drained though they were. He stopped with them, making jokes, until the fall seemed a small thing and righting it even smaller. There had been no special arrangements for him: he did not use the great, many-chambered constructions of canvas that Lord Northwic and Bellamus brought on campaign with them. He slept beneath the charcoal clouds, wrapped in his great black cloak, a saddle for his pillow.

He did not address his soldiers by rank but by name. So many names, it was a miracle that he knew them all. His secret was that every spontaneous interaction was planned; before he joined a group of men for the march, he would consult their officers. He cooked his own meals, tended his own weapons, minded his own mood and that of every man around him.

These efforts diminished Roper. Sometimes, marching in obscurity with the legionaries, he could not be found to make decisions and the legates would have to take temporary command of the column. Placing himself at risk also placed the army at risk: if he was caught by the Sutherners, or blundered into a sentry, the army would be thrown into chaos. Sometimes Roper was so weary he could barely see, let alone lead the legions effectively. But he always kept that to himself. He had made his choice. This was how he led: by example and without compromise.

Presently, their work finished, a dozen guardsmen joined him at the fire. Pryce sat on his left and Gray on his right. Others filled in the gaps at the hearth, each bowing to Roper as they walked before him. It was a formality that should have been observed all along, but Roper was too weary to notice how his reputation was changing. Word of how he and Zephyr had marauded single-handed through the valley was spreading quickly. The guardsmen took their hoosh from a blackened communal pot hung above the fire on a tripod of greenwood and sat in companionable silence, beginning to eat.

'That was a triumph, my lord,' said Gray, breaking the silence after a few minutes. The guardsmen thumped their feet on the grass in affirmation.

Roper looked up from his bowl with a faint smile, a little hoosh dribbling down his chin. 'Wasn't it?' was all he managed.

'And how was your first victory, lord?' asked Pryce. Of every man Roper had seen, the athlete seemed the least affected by the day's exertions. His handsome face was marred by a split over his left cheekbone, surrounded by bruising and scales of dried blood, but he was ignoring it. The irrepressible guardsman did not even seem tired.

'I loved it, Pryce,' confessed Roper. 'I know there were thousands of dead; I know we have lost many brave peers and that this didn't even qualify for the full glory of the battle line . . . but I have never been so enthralled.' He shook his head, not able to articulate what he had felt.

'It is what we live for,' said Pryce, approvingly.

'You were born for this role, my lord,' said Gray. 'You cannot tell before you throw a man into battle for the first time how he will respond. I have seen martial prodigies of the haskoli and the berjasti who could not stand the slaughter. They shy away from it, despising the brutality and incapable of seeing past the death, to the wider necessity and vitality of combat. Not everyone can curb their empathy in the way that is required. True warriors discover a side to themselves they did not know existed before their first taste of combat. When a man strikes at you with a sword for the first time, you find the keys to a room which must never be opened except in battle. Some men have it, some men don't.'

'Peace is boring,' explained Pryce, more glibly. 'Nothing compares to the thrill of one-on-one combat once you have tried it. Everything afterwards seems . . .'

'Flat,' suggested another guardsman and Pryce shrugged, accepting the word.

'But there are those who will judge and despise you for loving the fight, lord,' continued Pryce, impatiently. 'They will think you a barbarian, incapable of controlling your base instincts. They do not feel what you feel and cannot appreciate that neither you, nor they, have the power to change their own nature. But they rationalise their own nature, and like to deem it superior to other men and imagine they have tamed something that you cannot.'

'Everyone tries to rationalise their own nature,' said Gray, neither in support nor disagreement of Pryce's words. 'Were you scared, my lord?' Dimly, Roper recognised that Gray was mentoring him. These were the questions that his father would have asked him, had he been alive. They would have unpacked the fight together; discovered what sort of man Roper was and what sort of warrior he would become.

'No,' said Roper, confused. 'I thought I would be but truly, no.' He had spent his whole life training against the fear he had been told would obscure his thoughts and make his limbs weak, but it had not come. There had merely been assurance, euphoria and pride. Roper wanted to say more but was not sure these men, many of whom seemed merely bereft, would understand.

'You are one of a rare breed,' said Gray. He gestured around the fire. 'Some of these men are like you. True warriors. Pryce is one. Leon is one,' he gestured at a hard-faced guardsman sitting opposite them. 'I am not.' He smiled. 'I have to control my terror before each enemy I face and even after a victory like today, all I can think of are the casualties we have taken. Do not worry that you enjoyed it.' Gray read Roper's silence exactly. 'It is as Pryce says: you cannot change your nature. It does not make you a worse man, but it might allow you to be a better leader. I find battle harder and harder to endure and one day I shall not be able to advance through my own dread.' He grinned again. 'I hope to be a bureaucrat by then.'

The guardsmen chuckled appreciatively.

'That is why this is the best man in the Black Kingdom,' said Pryce, pointing past Roper to Gray, who waved his hand dismissively. 'His courage is far superior to mine as he is always acting in spite of fear which I do not feel. It is one thing to be born for this role. It is another to make yourself fit for it through total mastery of your emotions.'

'I am far from alone in fighting through my fear,' said Gray, sternly.

'You are different, though,' said the guardsman named Leon in a bear's growl of a voice. 'Do not deny it, Konrathson. You have more awareness than any other man and yet I've never seen fear slow your hand or falter your step. Your consciousness of danger is extreme and yet you hold as many Prizes of Valour as any man alive.'

Gray gave a grunt and a little lift of his eyebrows. 'Well, then, if we're speaking on this subject, I will share with you all my dream, to which I dedicate my life. It is neither deep, nor particularly advanced. I try to be a student of fear. I want to understand it, why it is I feel it, and how it can be truly mastered. If it is possible, I want to transcend it. I want to lose all selfish desire for life and live only to be a servant to others. One day, I dream of advancing into battle with every bit of awareness of my own mortality that I possess now, knowing that I will likely die, and not caring. I wish to feel gladness alone, that I am able to lay down my life for those I love. That is my quest.'

'And does this goal grow closer, or more distant?' asked Roper. 'Is it indeed possible?'

'I believe that it is both possible, and grows a little closer,' said Gray, cautiously. 'I do not want to achieve it through weariness of life or battle, but I am inspired daily by those around me. My young protégé here,' he indicated Pryce, 'inspires me. He is heroic indeed and there is something very special about his courage, though it is not what I seek for myself. Not quite, but it is close.

'But I will tell you all a story and then I'm going to shut up. It concerns the death of Reynar the Tall, who, I believe, was closer than any man I have met to achieving the dream of which I speak.'

As one, the guardsmen looked up from their bowls, weariness and bereavement banished from their faces. Reynar the Tall was widely regarded as one of the greatest warriors of any age. He had held more Prizes of Valour than any man in history, having died in the act of achieving his fourth. Only Gray and two others had seen him die, and of those, Gray was the only witness yet alive. To the certain knowledge of all there besides Roper (for the tale was eagerly sought), Gray had never confided it to anyone besides Pryce.

'Most of you know that when I joined the Guard, I was given Reynar as my mentor. What more could I have asked for? Three times winner of the Prize of Valour, guardsman for three quarters of a century already and reckoned one of the bravest ever to have lived, even in his own time. I confess to you that it did not make me glad. I already believed myself to be hopelessly out of my depth. I had never sought the Sacred Guard; guardsmen die too readily and I was not prepared for that. I was unworthy of this band, and to be paired with Reynar . . . well, it was hardly the obscurity I was looking for. I was filling space in the Guard which should have been for another warrior and now the talents of this hero were going to be wasted on me as well. So it was in spite of my own wishes that I began training and fighting next to one of the greatest warriors who has ever lived.

'Does anyone here remember Reynar on the battlefield?' Gray looked around and chuckled. 'Of course not. Oh dear, does that make me the oldest here? I suppose it does. He was not as wild as Pryce here, nor as ferocious as our friends Leon or Uvoren. When he fought, it was as though each action was undertaken not to slay the enemy, but to preserve his peers. To be sure, he cut down as many foemen as any other man in battle, but his blows and parries were as frequently in service of the men either side of him, as against those before him. On many occasions, fighting on his left, I knew I was about to die and Reynar's sword preserved me, sometimes at the expense of his own wounds. He appeared to trust me; I did not feel protected or watched by him and yet, on several occasions when I was too tired or my skill was not enough, I was delivered just in time by Reynar. He must always have been aware of me; me, and the man on his right, whoever that happened to be. In him, I thought I had seen the ultimate incarnation of a warrior. One who fights for love of his peers rather than love of glory. You had to watch him closely to know it; he did not speak of such things and most only saw the celebrated warrior. But I believe that by the end I knew him well, and that I was correct in my assessment.

'Well, on my third campaign with Reynar, the Sutherners succeeded in capturing one of our fire-throwers, tank fully charged with sticky-fire. They retreated to the town of Eskanceaster and we followed, determined to recapture it before they had an opportunity to discern the recipe for sticky-fire and make their own. It was a task given specially to four of us: myself, Reynar and another pair of guardsmen. We were to enter the night before the main assault in great secrecy, find the fire-thrower and make sure it could not be used against our forces.

'We made it over the walls and advanced to the keep, where we believed it was being held. The keep is surrounded by a moat and can only be entered by a single bridge; there was one way in, and that was where they had positioned the fire-thrower. We could see it was manned by a pair of soldiers, ready to immolate anyone who tried to cross the bridge and gain entrance.

'We watched them for a time, knowing we would not have time to rush their defences before they turned on the sticky-fire. Then one of our number, who had been an engineer before he was a guardsman, spotted that they had overcharged the tank. They had pumped too much air into it,' he explained in answer to Roper's questioning look. 'He could tell from the way they couldn't push the pump down any more. The pressure was too high, meaning they would not be able to shut off the sticky-fire once they had turned it on. They had one shot, then the tank would be empty.

'We decided to try to panic them into firing early and then wait until they had emptied the tank. We showed ourselves and though they raised an alarm, they did not fire. They were cautious and, try as we might, we could not make them fire before we were within full range of the weapon. We could hear the garrison coming and we were running out of time. Then Reynar,' Gray stopped suddenly, brow furrowed, and drew a deep breath. He shook his head and continued. 'Reynar handed me his sword, bade me take care of it and ran onto the bridge. He was sprinting for the fire-thrower, though he must have known he would never have made it. They turned it on.' Gray stopped again and took a spoonful of hoosh. He looked up at Roper and gave a depleted smile. 'On that bridge, Reynar was finished. There was so much fire that afterwards we saw no trace of his body. Just empty armour and an upturned helmet. All I remember is him running head on into that jet of flame, raising a hand as though to shield himself from its heat.

'Reynar did that for us. He did what he had to, because we

were running out of time. We waited for the thrower to empty, for the flames to die away and then crossed the bridge and tipped it into the moat. We managed that and escaped thanks only to Reynar, who was awarded his fourth Prize for that. When he handed me his sword, I did not realise what he was about to do because I could detect in him no fear. When he laid down his life, I believe Reynar was close then to achieving my dream. Though, of course, I do not know what he was feeling as he ran into the flames. He did raise his hand, so perhaps he felt fear. One day, I will see him again and I will ask him about it. Until that time, I carry his sword as a reminder of his sacrifice.'

Gray drew his blade and balanced it on its tip before them, showing the etched alloy to the engrossed guardsmen. Ramnea, she was called, and she was a beauty. Long, thin and paler than any Unthank blade that Roper had ever beheld. Her handle was engraved whale-bone and she seemed almost to glow in the dying light. She shared her name with the dog-headed angel of divine vengeance, and it had been an act of unusual generosity to bequeath the sword to Gray. The argument could be made that it had not even been Reynar's to give. It was one of the most famous blades in the land, handed down through the Vidarr for centuries and highly coveted by Reynar's own sons. A weapon of such quality was considered the property of the family throughout generations, rather than just one man. The nature of Reynar's death and his surpassing stature had meant that the Vidarr had been generous, however, and had not contested Gray's claim on the weapon. Reynar had started a new path for it; not father to son, but from one exceptional warrior to another.

'There ends my tale; you shall not hear it again,' said Gray. 'Since my lord asks, that is why I believe the state of mind I seek to be possible. Ramnea reminds me of it, every day. She reminds me that by shielding myself from what I knew must be done, I allowed a great man to die for me. To that example, I dedicate my life.'

Gray sheathed the sword in the ensuing silence. Then he shrugged. 'But who cares what I say? This is all irrelevant if I don't live as I talk. Worse than irrelevant.' Two quick spoonfuls and he had finished his hoosh. He stood, face crumpling slightly, and deposited his bowl by the fire. 'I'm going to relieve the sentries. Well fought today, all of you. Especially you, my lord.' The guardsmen thumped their feet again and Gray departed.

Later, Pryce left the fireside and headed for the outer rim of the camp. He collected a thick leather roll of supplies: bleached linen strips, phials of vinegar in which betony had been soaked, spools of silk and catgut thread, curved steel needles, four tweezers (two needle-nosed, two flat-nosed), several leather tourniquets and a sharp knife. He skirted the camp perimeter, raising a hand to the sentries who hailed him, and soon found Gray staring out into an ink-black night. The moon and stars had vanished without trace behind dense cloud.

'Old fool,' Pryce said irritably.

'What?'

'Show me your leg.'

Gray lifted his chain-mail skirt to reveal a jagged wound in his thigh; deep and clotted thickly with blood. 'Sit,' commanded Pryce. Gray sat, stretching out the injured leg before him, and Pryce began to clean it with a linen cloth, soaked in the betony vinegar. 'How did you get this?'

Gray took a deep breath and closed his eyes as the vinegar seeped into the wound. 'Doing what you should be doing now; protecting the Black Lord.'

'He's safe,' said Pryce dismissively.

'Not without you,' said Gray urgently. 'Today's victory has put him in greater danger than ever. Uvoren will hear of this soon and he will know that Roper has become a genuine threat. Gosta and Asger will be looking for an opportunity to kill him; all Uvoren's friends will.'

'Uvoren is safe inside the Hindrunn with thirty thousand soldiers,' said Pryce. 'He has no need for underhand tactics.'

'Even Uvoren would rather avoid the necessity of obliterating half the legions before the walls of the Hindrunn,' insisted Gray. 'He will try to have him killed, and soon. Before he can make any more of a name for himself.'

With the clotting cleaned away, Gray's wound was now bleeding freely again. Pryce looked at it thoughtfully, wiping away the blood, and then bade Gray press a wad of linen against it whilst he threaded one of the needles with silk. He washed his hands in vinegar, removed Gray's palm from the wound and began to stitch it together.

'You needn't worry, Gray. I can stop Gosta,' he said, finishing a stitch and blotting the wound. 'And Asger. I'll even stop them together, if I have to.' He bit his lip as he focused on the work.

'You can only stop them if you're with him. I won't leave unless I have to, but one of us must always remain and it should be you. I won't defeat Gosta one-on-one.'

'Nannying,' said Pryce angrily. 'How long am I to stay diligently by his side?'

'As long as is necessary,' said Gray, simply. 'You are a Sacred Guardsman, are you not? Guard him.'

'Get someone else to do it.'

'There's no one else I trust. Maybe Helmec, but I do not know him well enough for his loyalties to be clear.'

Pryce shook his head, tightening a stitch sharply and causing Gray to take a sudden breath. 'Sorry,' he muttered. He finished the stitching in silence and then began winding a linen strip around the wound, finishing the dressing with a tight knot.

'Thank you, Pryce,' said Gray.

'So I must watch over him now?'

'Now and until we've worked out how to be rid of Gosta and Asger. But you think you could fight the two of them?'

'Perhaps,' said Pryce, frowning.

'Well, then maybe they'll make it simple for us and attack whilst you guard him.'

'I wouldn't do this for anyone else, Gray,' said Pryce, getting to his feet and swinging the leather roll onto his back. He looked angry and clearly wanted to say more. 'I'm certainly not doing it for Roper.'

Gray stood with a little grunt of pain and took Pryce's hand. 'I know,' he said, turning back to the darkness.

10

The Pass Beside the Sea

The first thing the Sacred Guard did before their day began was to pray. They lived lives more intimately connected with their own mortality than almost any other man in the army; only the berserkers died with greater regularity than the guardsmen. The accepted wisdom was therefore that, at all times, each guardsman had to be at peace with the idea that the breaking day might be his last. He must be able to accept his end without complaint or disgrace to his comrades. He must consider every action he took in the knowledge that it might not be long before he had to stand his ground before the Almighty and answer for each one of them.

The clouds in the east were growing lighter and Gray, the rest of the Guard kneeling behind him, led the prayers that morning. Roper had taken to praying with them and found himself kneeling beside Asger. The disgraced guardsman stole belligerent glances at Roper whilst dutifully reciting the prayers. Roper paid no attention, considering Asger broken. Gosta was on Asger's other side and he neither prayed out loud nor shut his eyes. He just stared unblinkingly at the back of the guardsman in front of him.

Other legionaries, particularly the auxiliaries, would

come and watch the Sacred Guard at prayer, fascinated. They did not often get the opportunity to campaign with these heroes. The Sacred Guard were the most glorified echelon of Anakim society and the auxiliaries took every opportunity to observe their alien practices. They would stare greedily at the eye engraved on a guardsman's right shoulder-plate, or the silver-wire wolf embedded in his cuirass, or his steel helmet through which he had threaded his long ponytail. Their eyes would linger on the guardsmen's sword-hilts, which had, embedded in the pommel, a ring particular to the Sacred Guard, gifted by the Black Lord himself to symbolise the mutual obligation between guardsman and lord. If the guardsman had a Prize of Valour, signified by a silver armring, they were more glorified still.

The auxiliaries would watch the way the guardsmen moved in pairs; still bonded, mentor and protégé, to fight together on the battlefield. They would listen anxiously to anything a guardsman might say, seeking to understand some essence of what made these men so special; how they had achieved such contentedness in the face of death and skill before the enemy. They knew each guardsman's name. They knew the name of his sword; what deeds it had performed. They would fight all the harder if they knew they were watched by one of these heroes.

This was another reason for the Sacred Guard's piety; before the Almighty alone could they appear humble. They were so elevated and glorified among other men, it was considered important that they show utter deference to a higher power, to which they were exposed each day through prayer.

'Until we walk with you,' finished Gray, at last. Most of the Guard stood and moved off to prepare breakfast, but some, including Gray, remained kneeling, eyes shut for a while in personal prayer. Roper, inspired by Gray's example, had begun to do this as well. Kynortas had not been a pious man; indeed, he had had little patience for the religious devotion of the Sacred Guard. That was why he had allowed Uvoren so much licence with it; the two of them agreed it was unnecessary.

Roper prayed for his brothers in the northern haskoli. He prayed for the souls of his father and mother. He prayed to become a better man. He prayed for a secure throne from which he might rule the country justly and effectively. But, no matter how much he prayed, he was always finished before Gray, who would stay kneeling towards the east, eyes closed, mouth framing the softest of whispers.

Roper stood. Something was towering in the corner of his eye: a dark silhouette that blocked out the day's grey light. A huge figure was watching over the guardsmen still at prayer: a man who must have been a foot taller than Roper himself. There was nothing unusual about another warrior watching the Guard; a dozen or so were doing it at that moment. But Roper knew this one. He had spotted him several times before, watching the Guard. The plate on his chest bore a dog-headed angel that wielded a sword and his left shoulder was unarmoured, with an iron band affixed around his upper arm instead. These signs marked him out as a lictor in Ramnea's Own Legion but, elevated as that position was, there were many of them. It was his unnatural height and the position of his sword on his right side, showing that he was left-handed, which marked this man apart.

This was Vigtyr the Quick.

He was not as famous as Uvoren the Mighty or Pryce Rubenson or Leon Kaldison or one of those heroes but, to those who knew what they were talking about, Vigtyr was the best of them all. It was said that this left-handed monster had not been beaten in the practice ring for decades: other warriors simply could not match his speed, his reach or his precision.

It was said too that Vigtyr craved the Sacred Guard with a desperate thirst. That was why he watched this morning. He was the most skilled warrior in the country but would not get that recognition until he wore the Almighty Eye over his right arm. Roper paused and watched him for a moment. Vigtyr had not noticed. He had eyes only for the kneeling guardsmen.

'Vigtyr the Quick,' said a voice behind Roper. He turned and found Tekoa standing immediately behind him.

'How quick is he?' said Roper.

Tekoa placed an arm behind Roper's back and steered him towards the fire to join the other legates. 'Not as fast as Pryce,' he said. 'But he looks faster because his movements are so economical. That man has perfected sword-craft. He'd skewer Pryce.'

'So why isn't he a Sacred Guardsman?'

'He isn't a good man. Everyone owes him favours and he knows all their secrets: nobody wants him any more influential than he is already. He could have almost anyone in the kingdom before the Ephors for judgement if he wanted it, and sometimes he does. Many of the darkest events of the past few decades have had the whiff of Vigtyr about them. When you're under the kind of stress that the Guard gets placed under regularly, he is not the person you want at your back.'

Roper wanted to know more but, as they sat, the legates began to demand his attention. He helped himself to a breakfast of boiled oats while they fed him their most recent information. It had been four days since their victory against the Sutherners and, in that time, Roper had given the Suthern horde space. Though it was only the cavalry who had been engaged in strenuous fighting, his men had all marched hard both before and after the attack. Some were still recovering from the wounds they had sustained, while most of the Sutherners had barely exerted themselves in their last encounter. Before the two sides met again, Roper wanted his men as fit as possible. In the time they waited, short rations would drain the Sutherners of energy and make them more vulnerable to disease.

But there was another reason he gave the Sutherners space. Roper had reasoned that in order to negate the enemy's superior numbers, he would need an advantageous position from which to fight, where their flanks were well protected. He knew that Lord Northwic's response to losing his supplies would probably be to retreat to the more reliable harvest provided by the sea. So tethered, that was where they could be destroyed and Roper had asked Tekoa to locate just such a battlefield at the coast.

If the battlefield could be found and the Sutherners persuaded to use it, Roper had dared to feel confident of victory. He had dared to look past the next battle, and forward to how he was to re-enter the Hindrunn afterwards without Uvoren eradicating him and his soldiers. The Hindrunn's Outer Wall was riddled with cannon and crowned with all manner of siege-breaking weapons. The wall itself was solid granite, one hundred and fifty feet in height and fifty feet in depth at the base. It would be guarded and manned by thirty thousand warriors, every bit as ferocious and professional as the ones under Roper's command and, with its full fury unleashed, would atomise Roper's forty thousand.

When Roper had voiced these concerns to Gray, he had not received much sympathy. 'Stop worrying about the Hindrunn, my lord,' Gray had said sternly. 'If you consider anything other than the next battle, it will be the end of you, me and the Black Kingdom as a whole. You have badly wounded the Suthern army; they will be exhausted and malnourished and perhaps even diseased, but never underestimate the danger of the wounded beast. They will have nothing to lose. They will outnumber us by thousands. They will not be conservative. They will try and overwhelm the legions and you *must* be equal to the task, or all we have achieved so far will be for nothing. Forget the bloody Hindrunn.'

'I can't, Gray. I know I should and I try, but all I can think about is that fortress and the man who holds it.'

'You are not thinking about the Hindrunn,' responded Gray. 'Not really.' His expression softened a little. 'I have tried to warn you about this. This is why you must do away with your hatred; it will overwhelm you in the end. What occupies your mind is Uvoren, not the fortress he controls. Why do you want to be the Black Lord?'

'To serve,' said Roper, automatically. Gray waited. 'And perhaps because if I fail, I will die. It is also my purpose; my function in this world.' Gray waited. 'And maybe to defeat Uvoren.'

'If you do not consider what drives you, you will not notice your own flaws. It is clear that you hate Uvoren and with that I have a great deal of sympathy. He is bad for the country, and hatred is the hardest emotion to control,' acknowledged Gray. 'The advantage of acting through hatred is also its greatest disadvantage: there is no goal to achieve. No matter how successful you are in humiliating or perhaps killing Uvoren, your hatred for him will never dissipate. You can ignore fear and it will pass as you grow used to it. Grief will heal. Triumph will fade away, no matter how you try to hold on to it. But hatred will burn undimmed. It is like revulsion: a base reaction to everything you hold most in contempt. You cannot make yourself forgive when it is not in you. You must change who you are, so that those things that make you despise Uvoren are no longer hateful to you. Forget the Hindrunn, my lord. It is what it is.'

There speaks a man preparing for death, thought Roper, though he said no more. He thought Gray was right and his obsession with the fortress was based on his hatred of Uvoren; but he could not forget the Hindrunn. After dark, as the men around him lay still and silent, Roper stared at the sky, his mind dwelling on towers, walls and weapons. It felt like a canker within his mind, swelling and hardening as he explored it. It was invincible. It had been constructed as the foremost bastion of a paranoid race against an overwhelming enemy, and somehow Roper had to take it. His unbreakable home had turned against him and become a malignant presence in his mind.

Tekoa had started speaking, disturbing Roper's reverie. 'My men have discovered a battlefield for you, my lord.'

'Tell me,' said Roper, using his teeth to gouge a sticky clump of oats from the bowl of his bone spoon.

'Thirty leagues from here; a place called Githru. To get there, we must pass through the crossroads of Harstathur, which the poets have been claiming would be auspicious. They tell me Harstathur is the site of some nebulous ancient battle.'

'What ancient battle?' asked Pryce.

'The Battle of Harstathur,' said Tekoa flatly.

'Thank you for being so helpful.'

'I'm not a damned poet, that's all I know.' Tekoa raised his hands to the general assembly, looking about the circle for someone who could shed some light on the Battle of Harstathur.

'Oh, come, come,' said Skallagrim. 'Harstathur was the last and most important battle of the Uprooting, when the Anakim finally defeated the Sutherners to establish the Black Kingdom. They call Harstathur the Altar of Albion.'

'Do you know the poem?' asked Gray, who had finished his prayers and had come to sit with them. 'I should like to hear it some time.'

'I know it well,' said Skallagrim. 'I would be happy to sing it.'

'Perhaps later,' Roper intervened quickly. 'What about the battlefield beyond Harstathur?'

'Githru. It's a pass between the mountains and the sea. Rangers report that it is about two leagues across and falls away abruptly at the eastern side, with a steep cliff bordering the west; perfect for neutralising the enemy numbers. They have produced a map.' Tekoa reached down from the stump on which he sat and picked up two kinked sticks. He laid them parallel on the floor and Roper leaned forward to examine them. They would have meant nothing to a Sutherner, but the Anakim recognised these carved sticks as the outline of the pass being described. Each stick represented a border, with a pair of V-shaped notches signifying a river flowing into the sea, and further knots, bulges and kinks indicating the rise of the terrain, a perilous drop or, Roper was surprised to see, a risk of the sea flooding a portion of it. This map would not be a real representation of the field as it would appear to a circling crow. Rather, the size and distance of certain features would be exaggerated or reduced to reflect areas that the Skiritai who had produced it had thought would be important in the coming battle.

Roper sat back, scraping his wooden bowl clean with a frown. 'Githru,' he said slowly. 'What's happening there?' and he pointed at the swelling that indicated a point where the sea might swamp the pass.

'They found some locals hiding out in the hills,' said Tekoa, 'who said on a spring tide, the sea reclaims that area of the pass. With the moon as it is, probably not something we have to worry about. But luring the Sutherners to Githru might be difficult.'

'I doubt it,' said Roper. 'It is we who can afford to wait, not they. Every day they delay weakens them. We will take up position and send them an invitation.' He knew that before the last battle, these men would have raised objections. Now there was a short silence, broken by Skallagrim.

'There could be no more fateful omen than passing through Harstathur,' he said. There was a murmur of agreement.

'It would be a proper battle,' said Gray, staring down at the map. His tone made Roper blink. 'Two powerful forces crammed into a battlefield that small. The intensity. It will all come down to nerve and endurance.' He looked up at Roper. 'I like it, my lord.' Then, more quietly: 'What a test that shall be.'

'Let's get this over with, then,' said Pryce. 'Our food is running low too.'

'And I'm still hungry,' complained Skallagrim.

'I'll alert the herald,' said Tekoa nastily.

'Githru,' said Roper again. 'Then we have thirty leagues to

march.' He stood abruptly. 'Peers; prepare yourselves. We leave in an hour.'

'That's ambitious,' commented one of the legates.

'But we will do it nonetheless,' said Roper, departing.

The news that they were heading for Githru ran through the legions like a roll of thunder. The soldiers seemed re-energised and Pryce made it his personal mission to ensure they departed within an hour. As a lictor, he was invested with considerable authority and threw every bit of it at the Sacred Guard, strutting through their encampment and roaring the men into a flurry of activity. 'Our lord has ordered our departure for Githru! On your feet, you sacred bastards! We rest not a moment longer; not one more! Put out your fire; pack your cloak and your food! Bring your helmet and put on your armour; we are marching to battle!'

The one guardsman who did not move was Gosta, who remained seated by his fire and stared insolently up at Pryce, stirring a bubbling pot of oats. Pryce took one look at the expression on his face and swung his boot into Gosta's pot of food to send it soaring. Kicking the heavy iron pot must have hurt terribly but Pryce did not show it and next he kicked apart the fire in front of which Gosta still sat, gritting his teeth in rage but powerless. 'There, Gosta, I've got you started,' said Pryce calmly. He stalked off.

'You are Sacred Guardsmen! You are the beating heart of this army! You are our vengeful angels, servants of Ramnea! You are steel, you are oak, you are granite! You are our claws! You have sworn your life to this country; march now for Githru!'

Their route would take them over the mountain crossroads of Harstathur and, as they prepared, the bards sang of the great battle that had taken place there almost fifteen thousand years before. Against this backdrop, the horses were loaded and saddled. The stakes used in fortification were packed into the baggage train. Fires were doused. Food was wolfed down and the pots and utensils stowed without cleaning. Armour was carried by being worn. Helmets were hooked to each legionary's pack by the chinstrap. The horses, ponies and oxen had their hobbles removed. Pryce's energy was contagious and the men set to.

'Prepare yourselves, if you think you can, for a scarlet, bleeding slab of a battlefield! The thirty-league march is your rest! The climb up Harstathur is your sleep! Your only waking moment shall be the battle by the sea! You are the chosen few! When you have memories of that field; you will laugh to hear the word *fury*, shrug when another man says *terror*, and when a peer tells you he is exhausted, you will say you were at Githru! You will understand rage! You will reconsider the word *violence*! *Fortitude* is a pale shadow of what you will need by the sea! Everything you've got, you bastards!'

Githru. The pass by the sea. The legions were ready within the hour and Roper, mounted on Zephyr this time rather than marching with his warriors, led the column north-east; back towards the Suthern army and towards the battlefield. Tekoa and Gray flanked him and Pryce and Helmec marched behind, eyes roaming the landscape. The Skiritai spread forward, scouting the hills surrounding the column. The end was in sight and, tinged with shades of Pryce's manic energy, the legions were hungry. No matter that they were still outnumbered two to one and had not even begun to fight the Suthern elite and heavily armoured knights; they wanted this challenge. Their morale was high and they were assured in their cause.

'I bloody hate horses,' grumbled Tekoa, tugging irritably at his reins as he trotted alongside Roper. 'They're arseholes. They're overly sensitive, they're selfish. They're not attractive or affectionate. I do not find their inability to produce art or music endearing. They're useless unless you've put their shoes on for them. They make a fuss when you try and put their shoes on. What a mediocre animal. So I thought it might make a suitable wedding gift for you, lord,' shot Tekoa, glancing straight-faced at Zephyr, trotting alongside him.

Roper restrained a smile. 'What animals do you favour, Tekoa?'

'Hounds. Loyal, loving, obedient and born useful. You don't have to give a dog shoes, do you?'

'I suppose not,' said Roper. 'I'm pleased with Zephyr, though. He is a warrior as fine as most in the Sacred Guard.' He patted the beast's thick neck.

'I had no idea what I was going to do with that monster,' Tekoa admitted. 'I wasn't going to ride it but I'll be damned if someone like Pryce has a bigger horse than me.' They rode in silence for a while. 'So I doubt you're looking forward to the end of this campaign, Roper, what with the coiled viper that is waiting for you back home.'

'Uvoren?'

'Keturah,' said Tekoa. 'You'll be glad for someone as easy to handle as Uvoren once you've tried being married to my daughter.'

'Oh,' said Roper, smiling. 'That is a challenge I'm looking forward to tackling.'

'Keep your tackle out of this, young man,' growled Tekoa.

Gray burst out laughing and Roper even heard Pryce let out a snort behind them.

'She may have found someone else,' called Pryce. 'My cousin is not short of suitors.'

'Following her around like lapdogs,' snapped Tekoa, frowning suddenly. 'A pack of fools.'

'Worry not, my lord,' said Gray. 'Keturah strikes me as someone who can handle a fool.'

'So, you've had it, I'm afraid, Roper,' put in Tekoa.

Helmec laughed again and Gray was grinning broadly. Roper observed dryly that Tekoa was in fine humour.

'Naturally,' said Tekoa. 'We're on our way to a good fight and, even better, thereafter we're back in the Hindrunn. It is the only comfortable place north of the Abus.'

'You have been south of the Abus?'

'There was a time when we went south regularly,' said

Tekoa, furrowing his brow. 'Your grandfather, Rokkvi, considered it wise to terrorise the Sutherners as a defensive strategy and in those days we would march with impunity. The Sutherners were more or less powerless. They had no standing army, but every town was fortified and when we moved south they would retreat, like an oyster closing its shell.'

'Did you make it as far as Lundenceaster?' Suthdal's sprawling capital.

'We occupied it,' said Tekoa. 'But Rokkvi considered it decadent, infested and corrupted; and besides, he had no wish to rule over the Sutherners. So he returned it to them in exchange for an extremely large quantity of iron.'

'But you liked it?'

'It had something about it,' said Tekoa, shrugging. 'But Rokkvi was right: it was more trouble than it's worth.'

'I never met my grandfather,' said Roper.

'Lucky you,' said Tekoa, grimly.

'Rokkvi was a fine leader, my lord,' said Gray. 'But almost as cantankerous as Tekoa, here.'

Tekoa spared Gray a contemptuous look. Roper wished to know more, so between them Gray and Tekoa told him the stories of their campaigns. The two had shared many battles and had an unexpected fondness for each other. Everyone seemed fond of Gray, but what was more surprising was that Gray had equal regard for Tekoa. They were not natural friends but made good company for the march.

Roper asked to hear about the siege of Lundenceaster, fishing for inspiration on how he could ultimately retake the Hindrunn. The question was followed by a pause which told Roper that both men had understood what he was really asking.

Gray spoke first. 'The thing about assaults, my lord, is that there are always casualties. You cannot attack a well-prepared fortress without losing many, many men. That's just the way of things.'

'They are the very worst of warfare,' said Tekoa. 'There is no glory. Just bodies. Thousands and thousands of them. And fire. And the fear is worse than anything else.' There was silence for a while. 'Gray won us Lundenceaster.'

Gray laughed hollowly. 'So it was said.'

'He did,' said Tekoa. 'Rokkvi focused our forces in too small an area and the Sutherners were fighting fiercely. We were rebuffed again and again, and the ditch before the wall was filling with bodies. Uvoren was knocked out by a bouncing shot from a catapult. He was lucky not to have his head smashed in. Gray took command, seized a couple of ladders and led the rest of the Guard onto another wall, leading them onto the battlements and drawing enough defenders to allow us to gain a foothold. Clever fighting.'

'I didn't want to die in that ditch,' said Gray. 'And Uvoren did very well. He came to in time to bully his way onto a ladder. It was he who gained the Guard the space that we exploited.'

'By all accounts, yes; he did well,' allowed Tekoa. 'That got him the Prize of Valour. But no matter what claptrap Gray tells you about being frightened, Roper,' he continued sternly, 'you will never meet a braver warrior. People say Uvoren is courageous. They say my nephew, Pryce, is courageous. These are lions. It is easy for a lion to fight what's in front of it. Gray thinks. He observes; and then he does what must be done. He has a mind made for battle.'

'So how would you take the Hindrunn?' Roper asked Gray.

'I would not consider it yet, lord. We finish the Sutherners; then we can worry about Uvoren.'

They discussed the remainder of Rokkvi's campaigns, with Gray relenting and telling Roper of how three other sieges had ended in a successful assault. Tekoa mostly left this to Gray, but would interrupt every now and then with his own perspective.

'I was told once,' said Roper, 'that the greatest warriors can fight in any theatre. Do you think that's true?'

'Undoubtedly,' said Gray. 'The warrior's greatest gifts are endurance and courage. There are very, very few who are born natural fighters, and even they will never be more than passable if they don't work at their skill. If you do not flinch from hard work and you have the grit to pick yourself up again and again when you fail, then you will be hard to overcome in any field.'

'So is Uvoren one of those?'

'He is,' said Gray. 'He is in love with his own reputation, but do not underestimate him. He works very, very hard. When he first adopted Marrow-Hunter, he was something of a joke. It was to enhance his own prestige; no more than that. He was one of the very few privileged to use a weapon other than a sword, so he did, just to underline his status. He was not used to the weight, and when he fought, he looked clumsy and childlike. But he trained every day, longer and harder than those who used a sword. And then we all saw him fight at Eoferwic, knocking knights flat left and right to gain access to King Offa. Suddenly, these armoured men looked as vulnerable to him as an upturned limpet. Yes: he can fight in any arena.'

'Damn,' said Roper.

'Indeed,' said Gray. 'Well, my lord, think about this: the greatest warriors can fight in any theatre, but perhaps the greatest leaders do not need to fight at all.'

They rode on. On the first day, the legions covered eleven leagues, four of which they had swarmed across country, between tree trunks and across swollen streams, before joining with the road. It was sheltered by the forests, moving gently in Anakim fashion with the terrain, rather than through it.

That night, over a bowl of boiled, salted mutton, Roper observed that though tired, the legionaries seemed in high spirits. In part their morale had been boosted by the victory they had already won over the Suthern army, but it was Roper's first encounter with the fact that the men under his command were happiest when they had a purpose. They knew where they were going and why, and so served more readily than ever. There was no longer a disconnect between their duties and the ultimate aim of the campaign. Each man could see how every action he performed contributed to defeating the Sutherners.

Roper pushed the legions hard the next day. He dismounted Zephyr, shouldered his own pack and set out fast. Marching along the line, Roper soon came abreast with the Pendeen Legion. He had been apprenticed to them earlier in the year: plucked from his position in the berjasti – the second stage of education in the Black Kingdom – to be given accelerated training in what it meant to be a leader. Some called out to him as he passed, Roper returning the greetings and exchanging a few words. Many of them knew him and this was the only legion that had felt some fondness towards him when he had taken command. Presently, he came across a half-dozen of his particular friends, who hailed him.

'Lord!'

'Young lord!'

Roper gave a genuine smile of some scarcity, falling into step beside them.

'You're walking straight again, lord,' said a short legionary with an irrepressible grin.

'Let's not talk about that,' said Roper. The last time he had seen these men was at the Feast of Avadon in the Pendeen mess; Roper's first warrior feast.

'I think we should talk about it, lord,' said another with a flattened, crooked nose.

The short legionary took pity on him and changed the topic. 'So what's it like, giving the orders now, lord?'

'It is what it is,' said Roper, cautiously. They might be friends of his, but Roper was not prepared to shatter the image he was cultivating by revealing too much to them. 'I get to add the Almighty Eye to my coat of arms, though. That counts for something.'

The short one chuckled. 'What coat of arms would we give the young lord if we could?' It was a favourite marching game.

'An owl, perhaps?' said one of the legionaries.

'He's not as sensible as an owl,' said the legionary with a flattened nose. 'He can be a shrew. For his unhinged solo ride through the Suthern encampment.' That found favour and was met with a hoot of laughter.

Roper looked sour. 'Unwise to say that to the man who genuinely has the power to change your arms, Otar,' he said. 'Yours shall be a thistle.'

They marched on. In front of the Pendeen marched Ramnea's Own Legion and Roper quickened his pace so that he could inspect the elite of the Black Kingdom. He noticed that even when marching, these were trying to differentiate themselves from the ordinary legionary. They walked straighter, talked more, and had an unmistakable swagger even now that was only produced by appointment to this esteemed institution. It was widely said that when appointed to Ramnea's Own, you bade farewell forever to the friends you had made in your old legion, who would henceforth find you unbearable.

Roper frowned as he watched them. One of the legionaries, a particularly tall figure, was walking without a pack while the man next to him carried two, one strapped to his back and one to his front. The tall figure did not appear to be particularly tired: indeed, he was laughing merrily with the figure on his other side. He had simply bequeathed his pack to a neighbour, who appeared to be carrying it willingly enough, though wearing a sombre, strained expression. Drawing level, Roper saw that the legionary without the pack was Vigtyr the Quick, the extremely tall lictor he had seen watching the Sacred Guard at prayer. He observed him thoughtfully as he marched past, wondering if there were any more to this scene than the apparent idleness.

They marched until the sun had passed overhead and sunk again below the horizon. In the afterglow from the west, the men hurried to set up camp before true darkness made their work clumsy. Roper had counted thirty-five mile markers along the road: nearly twelve leagues. Seven to Harstathur.

His reunion with the Pendeen aside, there had been less talk on this march. The men had little energy for anything but the road. And in the evening, Helmec, hands shaking with fatigue, had taken a full ten minutes to strike a fire. Too proud to take a flaming brand from any of those bursting into life around him, he had persisted until at last a spark had caught the fragment of charred linen he used for tinder. Then he waited patiently, drawing several deep breaths and composing himself before adding the smouldering cloth to a bundle of stripped bast and blowing a fire into life. The darkness, nearly complete on a night when the clouds smothered the moon, was insatiable.

They gathered in the fire's shifting light and boiled another pot of salted mutton. Tekoa brooded hopelessly, scarcely bothering to reply to anyone. Even Pryce was largely silent; spent by the day's effort. To Roper's relief, Gray kept talking. With little input from anyone else, he held court with his weary audience.

'Did I ever tell you about the time I got put on grave-digger duty?' Gray began unprompted, looking around the fire. 'Stop me if you've heard it. This was after Prestaburgh. I'd forgotten to hobble some of the baggage ponies the night before and managed to earn myself a flogging and a stint on burial. We were at it all day: the bodies kept arriving and we kept digging them graves. It was raining a bit and the work was slow. Then one of the peers went to fetch water and it was agreed that we should play a joke on him. I'd cover myself in mud and battered armour and lie down with the other bodies, pretending to be dead, and then when he came back to try and hoist me into the grave, I'd grab him.' Some of the men were grinning. 'Seemed like a good idea; I was young and keen so I got ready, lay down in the mud next to one of the other bodies and waited. I was there for a while, waiting for the man to come back. Then the body next to me grabbed my hand and said, "Bit damp down here, isn't it?"'

Laughter rang out across the fire.

'One of the bodies was alive?' asked a guardsman, earnestly.

'The body was the man I'd been waiting for,' said Gray. 'Dressed up while I was digging to terrorise me. It was obviously a joke they did quite a lot but my screams seemed to be of particular satisfaction.'

Roper led the column again the next day, pretending he could not feel the stiffness in his legs or the pain in his wounded thigh as the road began to climb. They were drawing near the ancient crossroads of Harstathur, where they planned to camp the night before advancing to battle at Githru. Roper dispatched Helmec and one of the Rangers on horseback to act as heralds and invite the Sutherners to battle, arranging to rendezvous with the pair of them on top of Harstathur.

As they climbed, the trees began to fall away from the road, growing thinner, slighter and finally disappearing. Two hours before sunset, the road at last levelled and they found themselves at the top of a mighty stone outcrop. Harstathur was shaped like an enormous rectangle, though significantly broader at the end opposite the legions than the one they had entered. The crossroads radiated from each corner of the rectangle and, at its longer edges, the plateau sloped steeply away to provide ample defence for the flanks of any army that might occupy the stage. Its nickname, the Altar of Albion, was well bestowed. It indeed resembled a vast sacrificial table. There was no way of knowing how high they stood but they had been climbing for hours and the air was significantly colder than in the shelter of the valleys. It was easy to imagine that whatever unfolded atop it might be particularly conspicuous to the heavens. It felt weighty. Significant. Gazing across it, Roper took a moment to envisage the ancient battle that had stained this place.

The legionaries were grateful to have arrived and began to set up camp. The sun had fallen beneath the edge of the plateau before Helmec and his companion found them. They had evidently been riding hard and Roper brought them straight to his hearth, presenting them with a bowl of hoosh before asking the results of the errand. 'The Sutherners are coming,' were the first words out of Helmec's mouth.

'Did you speak to Lord Northwic?'

'Yes, lord. He and Bellamus both.' Helmec described how he and his companion had ridden into the Suthern encampment bearing a white flag. 'They're petrified of us, lord!' said Helmec with glee. 'Petrified! Their warriors were trying to look tough but a glance was all it took to make them back down.'

Roper was not surprised they were scared of Helmec. The guardsman stood more than seven feet in height and his face was as scarred as a battlefield. It was one of the reasons Roper had sent him. *Nobody negotiates in negotiations. It's an exercise in intimidation.*

'So they led us into a massive dark tent, tricked out with skins and tables and chairs and servants, and Bellamus was there. He sent for Lord Northwic and offered us wine while we waited.'

'Wine and servants!' said Roper, amused. 'Perhaps I would lead more campaigns if that was how I lived out in the field.' Helmec grinned, and Roper almost shrank away from that smile. 'How was the wine?'

Triumphantly, Helmec took his water-skin off his belt and held it out to Roper, who laughed incredulously and took a sip. He had rarely tried grape-wine and it was intoxicating.

'You don't reject hospitality like that, lord,' said Helmec earnestly. Roper, Helmec and his Skiritai companion shared the wine together in the evening's gentle dark, the cool light of the stars smouldering above. 'So then Lord Northwic arrived and I said we would wait for them tomorrow at Githru to finish this war. And Bellamus started joking and asked whether we would actually fight them this time.'

'You promised we would?'

'I promised, lord. And Lord Northwic said that that was where we were going to die. Then Bellamus said he had something to show us before we left and led us up a little hill. He was chatting away, very friendly.'

Was Helmec friendly back?

'No.'

What had been on top of the hill?

'It was just a vantage point. He wanted us to see the army, spread out over their campsite. There are a lot of them. He pointed us towards a huge patch of tents, which took up more space than our entire encampment, and said it was just their knights. He said he had thirty-seven thousand of them and that they had so many horses they were stripping away the hillsides. He said they'd been resupplied by sea.'

Which was nonsense. Roper would have been prepared to wager the Hindrunn that they could not have got a message to the south and received a response in the time since they had destroyed the wagon park. Thirty-seven thousand also seemed a drastically unlikely number of knights. 'He wants you to spread that rubbish among the legions,' said Roper. 'So what are you not going to do?'

'Spread that rubbish among the legions?' suggested Helmec, sweetly.

'Very good. So they're coming.'

'They're coming, lord.'

The word spread through the camp: tomorrow, they would fight as Pryce had promised; in the narrow pass beside the sea, until their lungs were raw.

11
The Fight by the Fire

The night over Harstathur threatened to disappear altogether. No sooner had the sun set than it looked ready to rise again: an ominous, flickering glow staining the sky from the east, as though dawn quivered just beyond the horizon. The sight was met with dismay by the legionaries, who desired nothing so much as a few hours of soothing dark to sustain them for the crush by the sea. A memory of quiet to set against the smash of weapons and armour.

But the glow was no unnatural dawn. It was the distant blaze of the Suthern campfires; thousands upon thousands of them. A galaxy, spread on the distant plains.

It gave Roper an idea. He commanded each group to build a bonfire, rather than the more practical-sized cooking hearth that they would usually have used, and imagined with satisfaction the immense blaze that the Sutherners would be able to see emanating from the plateau.

That night, they slept in the open; truly close to the heavens and encased in a dome of stars, sliced open every now and then as one of them tumbled from the cosmos. The camp went quiet. The legions brought their equipment to the fireside and began to check it thoroughly, burnishing and oiling the plates of their armour. They patched the holes in their leather and honed swords and axes obsessively. Some talked, usually too loudly. Roper noticed that his own bonfire was quiet: Gray had gone to address the Sacred Guard, reminding them of their duty the following day. They were still outnumbered at least two-to-one, and the expected intensity of the battlefield weighed heavily on the camp.

'Skallagrim,' said Roper, breaking the silence. 'You never told us of the Battle of Harstathur.' Such a tale was delivered in the form of a chant, learned by heart. There were thousands of them; tens of thousands, documenting the history of the Black Kingdom and all safeguarded by the sisterhood of historians who lived in the Academy, the pyramid nearby the Central Keep. It formed a living record of the Black Kingdom's history, of utmost importance to a society which had no writing. The Chief Historian and her deputy attended each council, giving historical precedents when called upon, and forming a narrative of this latest stage of the Black Kingdom's history. They had committed a broad outline of the recent past to memory. For in-depth assessment, or for anything beyond twelve thousand years ago, they would need to visit a cell: a trio of historians who specialised in a particular period of history. There were hundreds of these. Anyone who wished to add the bard's skill to their repertoire could make an appointment with the Chief Historian, who would arrange for a cell to tutor them in as many poems as they wished. The bard could then deliver the poem as entertainment at a great feast. For now it would make a fine distraction before battle.

Skallagrim was an old warrior, and there was not much of him that ran as easily as it had done in his youth. His right shoulder was ruined to the extent that it would dislocate if he moved it suddenly upwards. He would groan as he stood up or sat down, stretching scar-tissue that had formed in both his thighs and calves. Sometimes he would find breathing difficult and have to massage his chest, a legacy of the time it had been splintered by a war hammer. And at that moment, he was winding leather strapping around his weak right knee in preparation for the next day.

'Should you like to hear it, my lord?' he asked, securing the strapping and testing his leg gingerly.

Roper said that he should, and Skallagrim stared into the fire for a moment, took a deep breath and began. The chant was often performed with drums and throat-singers accompanying it, but the only adornment that evening was the location; the sense of significance and anticipation that loaded the air. The men paused in the treatment of their equipment, leaned close, and tried to lose themselves in the tale.

It began fifteen thousand years before, with the arrival of the Sutherners. A small band of them emerged from the deserts to the east. Where from, exactly, and why they had arrived, nobody was sure. Some said that they were the forerunners of Catastrophe, the vast serpent that threatened to overturn the world. Others thought that the thousands of years of cold that had come before had isolated and ruined a band of Anakim, and that they had become these stunted Suthern men. Still others suggested that these creatures had burst from the ground and were the subterranean race of dwarves, forced to the surface by civil strife. Whatever the cause, the small band was followed by another larger one, and then a steady stream of men, women and children, pouring from some distant source. They came with their own language, their own tools, their own ways and their own history. A fully formed people, as shocked to encounter the Anakim as the Anakim were by them.

The first encounters between the two had not been hostile, but cautious. As they learned more, the caution turned to confusion. The Sutherners were restless, voracious and rootless; incomprehensible to an Anakim mind. The confusion was mutual, the Sutherners not understanding the crude Anakim art and their limited symbolism; despising the wilderness in which they delighted; scornful of the tools that they used and scarcely able to communicate with these giants. In those days too, the Anakim were vast; standing nearly nine feet in height and intimidating their smaller Suthern neighbours. Though differences can be overcome, the Sutherners were beginning to understand: theirs was not the only way to be human. The distinct place they occupied on the earth had been disturbed; the narrative of their civilisation had to adapt, and the Sutherner is nothing if not adaptable.

As the Sutherners bred, so did hostility, and through a hundred small clashes that spread and sowed distrust, the fleeting period where the two coexisted peaceably was truncated. So began the Uprooting. With a singular and voracious will, the Sutherners proceeded to strip the Anakim from Erebos. Their lands were taken, their wilderness destroyed and replaced by the order beloved of the Sutherner. The new arrivals were more numerous, they could infest the land more intensely, and their conflict with the Anakim had given an edge to their innovation. They copied the bow from an Anakim weapon, improving the arrows to make them more accurate, and matching their bone-plates with armour made from slate and boiled leather. This new form of man crept north; a tide that never ceases to rise, and the Anakim, who would not retreat, were overwhelmed.

From all sides, the Sutherners attacked as the disparate Anakim families were fragmented and pushed into refuges. Some fled to the very southernmost tip of Iberia. Others were pushed along the coast and into the north-east; to a land of darkness and ice. It was not just the Anakim who suffered. The Mountain Men, known as the Unhieru, were surrounded and destroyed, and now survived only in the hills and valleys in the west of Albion. The Haefingar and the Riktolk, the other two races who had shared Erebos, met the same treatment and were extinguished altogether. They would never again walk this earth.

The last Anakim in the west of Erebos found themselves pinned against the coast, and though their kind had never before taken to the water, they floated across that raging sea, and retreated into Albion. The Sutherners followed them, overrunning their defences, seeking not space but eradication.

For the Anakim, it seemed hopeless. Their options were to unify, or face oblivion. There was a single figure who frightened the Anakim enough to command their respect: Chlodowich, the mighty king of the Jormunrekur. A huge figure, known as 'Roper' to his enemies for his habit of cutting the hair from those he had killed and weaving it into his own, forming a ghastly ponytail that wrapped around him twelve times in all to form a broad plaited belt. This was a leader to terrify the Sutherners, and beneath him the tribes united to name him the first Black Lord.

However, even together, even led by Chlodowich, a warrior so fearsome that the Sutherners began to shave their heads before battle so as not to join his ghastly belt, the Anakim were losing. They were driven further north through the land that would become known as Suthdal, fear hanging low over the hills thick as fog. His forces scattered, Chlodowich and his few remaining warriors stumbled across the Abus, a Suthern horde scenting after them.

It was the end for the Anakim. Chlodowich had just his three hundred household warriors remaining to him; his Sacred Guard. He retreated to Harstathur, climbing onto the Altar of Albion and, sacrificing his own horse, he prayed for the strength to defeat the Sutherners. He offered his own life in a pact with the Almighty, if he would preserve the Anakim.

And the Almighty answered his prayer.

Four hundred horsemen of the Oris tribe appeared on the plateau. Chlodowich sent them out in all directions, seeking reinforcements from his scattered army. They arrived in small groups; all the tribes. The Vidarr, the Baltasar, the Nadoddur, the Lothbroks. Some of the Oris rode north and found the hill people called Alba, who agreed to join them. Last of all, the Algauti were found and joined together with Chlodowich's warriors; the scraps of his alliance.

Atop the plateau, they prepared themselves by placing fresh stone tips on their spears and creating the first shields by splitting wood found nearby and bracing it with rawhide, as defence against the Suthern arrows. It was clear that even together, there were not enough Anakim to defeat the Sutherners. So they also prepared for death, Chlodowich leading his men in prayers atop the Altar.

It was not long until the great tribe of warriors from the south had found them. The two armies formed up, the Anakim resolved not for victory, but to face oblivion on their own terms. Volleys of Suthern arrows made the air hiss and sting, but it became clear they were ineffective against the shielded Anakim. They would fight spear-on-spear: stone tips clashing and cracking. The fanged lines advanced and met one another atop the Altar. With each attack and parry it became clear: the Almighty had not forgotten them. Chlodowich and his Sacred Guard had been invested with holy power. The Sutherners' stone spearheads shattered as they touched them, and Chlodowich and the Guard were insatiable in the middle of the plateau. The battle lasted for hours; the lines drew back and attacked many times, but at last, Chlodowich and the Sacred Guard broke through the centre of the Suthern line and turned on them, tearing their formation apart. The Sutherners broke and retreated, pursued by the horsemen of the Oris, who were able to cut down thousands.

Through faith, victory had been won. In their very darkest hour, the stubborn resolution of the Anakim had been rewarded by the Almighty. But a pact had been made. As the lines split apart for the last time, Chlodowich, his purpose completed, was at last struck down by an axe. The Almighty is just, and cannot be cheated. The great man's bones were buried here, atop Harstathur, an offering to god.

Skallagrim finished his chant. The fire crackled and the silence in the circle was deeper than before. There, at the very site of this holy and primeval triumph, and beneath a clear and beautiful sky, every man had envisaged the ancient heroes. Skallagrim was a fine bard and he had charged the air. At the soft edges of the firelight, Roper thought he could see shadows moving. Gently shifting coagulations of darkness; watching him in return. There was the faintest gleam, as though a dark flint spear tip was moving in the night. What was this? The ghost of one of those giant heroes? Chlodowich himself? Those around the fire saw where he was looking and followed his gaze out into the blackness. The pattern of the night responded. There was something moving away, Roper was certain. He was not sure if he could see it or hear it. Or maybe he was feeling it, the vibration of weighty footsteps exiting via a dark corridor.

Looking around, Roper discovered everyone else had sensed it too. 'Peers, you have heard how holy the place in which we rest is,' he said. 'There could be no more fateful omen. Go now, and address your legions. Let them know that atop this anvil, our country was made.' The legates dispersed into the night, leaving just Roper and Pryce by the fire.

Roper, who had ceased running a whetstone along Cold-Edge to listen to Skallagrim, began sharpening the blade again. Pryce was casting around him, looking into the night and seeming restless. It was quiet but for the fire and Roper became very aware of the fact that this was the first time he and Pryce had been alone together. He found the guardsman's presence uncomfortable.

'Skallagrim is quite the bard, is he not?' ventured Roper.

'In a place like this, such a story tells itself,' said Pryce dismissively. There was a pause. 'Chlodowich is said to have been your ancestor, Roper.' Roper. 'His great achievement was to end the most shameful chapter in Anakim history: the Uprooting. And now here we are, at the same battlefield, with a leader in whose veins the same blood flows, soon to face the same enemy.' He was giving Roper an odd look across the fire. 'I can only conclude that Chlodowich bought us time; no more. His blood is much diluted.'

Roper had stopped sharpening Cold-Edge. 'Make yourself clear, Guardsman.'

Pryce looked at him coldly. 'They all seem to have forgotten your retreat. I haven't.'

Roper's mouth was open. 'I stand by that retreat,' he said, face growing warm.

'As I said: Chlodowich's blood is much diluted.'

'Is this treachery, Guardsman? Have you forgotten your oath?'

'I want to know what you have done to deserve my loyalty. I can't think why I should die for you.'

'Though you kneel each day before the Almighty, you are arrogant, Pryce.'

Pryce did not care. 'I am what I am.'

Silence fell again and Roper returned to sharpening Cold-Edge. His hands were shaking so much that the whetstone chattered against the blade. It was as though a loyal dog had turned on him. At the edge of his vision, Roper could detect the movement as Pryce turned his head towards him, evidently having heard the chattering whetstone. He did not have to look up to know that Pryce's expression would be scornful.

Presently, another guardsman appeared at the edge of the fire. 'My lord? Captain Gray urgently requests your presence at the edge of the encampment.'

Roper stood abruptly, grateful of the chance to escape. He sheathed Cold-Edge carefully and hurried after the guardsman into the darkness. Pryce, evidently assuming he was Gray's problem now, let him go. 'What is the issue?' asked Roper, falling into step with the guardsman.

'I cannot say, lord, but he was most insistent that you should come as soon as possible.'

Roper nodded to himself. The guardsman led Roper past

many bonfires, surrounded by silhouetted and silent warriors. They all stared into the flames, thinking on the next day. The sky still blazed overhead and the path that Roper was being led on was in line with the great river of stars that cut through the sky. The Winter Road, they called it, and they followed it now towards where it began at the horizon. Soon enough, the fires around them had begun to dwindle and finally disappear until Roper could see just one in the distance, which marked an outer sentry. Figures shifted around it, temporarily blotting out the orange pin-prick.

The guardsman he walked with was silent and Roper felt sick. Had he not just had the confrontation with Pryce, he would have recognised his discomfort for what it was: a creeping unease over the way this situation was developing. He was walking further and further into the dark with this guardsman, whom he did not know. They had left the encampment behind and Roper was now quite isolated.

As he drew close enough to make out who was beside this outer fire, he froze.

Or rather, he tried to. The guardsman he walked with gripped the back of his neck and pushed him onwards, steering him into the fire's light and forcibly sitting him down on a log within its glow. Sitting about the fire were three other figures. One was another guardsman Roper did not recognise. The other two were Asger and Gosta.

You idiot, he thought to himself. *You god-damned bloody fool.* There had been no message from Gray. These guardsmen, surely Uvoren's closest allies, had used his trust of Gray to draw him out here. With what purpose, Roper dared not think. Then he thought about the presence he had felt on the edge of the fire. Had it been one of these men, coming to check if he was vulnerable?

'My lord,' said Asger ironically, glancing at Roper. Even on this cold night, his face shone in the firelight. The guardsman who had escorted him went and sat down on Asger's other side, holding his hands out to the fire.

'What am I doing here, Guardsman?' asked Roper. He did his utmost to sound authoritative, rather than aggressive. 'Where is Captain Gray?'

'Captain Gray is where he belongs; a long way from here.'

Roper gathered himself. 'Then I must go. Excuse me.' And he stood.

'Sit down,' said Asger. Roper glanced at Gosta, sitting next to him like a compressed spring, and decided to sit. He licked his lips, staring from one guardsman to the next.

'So what is it that you brave men intend to do with me, all the way out here? Because if you are to kill me, it is the very worst hell that awaits you.'

'We have sworn no oath to you,' said Asger simply. Still seated, he drew his sword very slowly from its sheath and balanced it tip-first on the ground, just as Gray had done with Ramnea. With two fingers atop the hilt, he began to spin it about its tip, looking at Roper with a grin. The blade flashed in the firelight.

'I know the pressure you must be under from Uvoren,' said Roper. 'But you'll be hunted down. You can't possibly get away with this. If you leave me now, I swear I will seek no vengeance. We can just forget this.'

'I don't want to forget this,' said Asger coldly. 'You took the Guard from me.'

'I had to. You were Uvoren's man, but it is not too late to serve a different lord. Chlodowich's blood flows in my veins. I am the rightful Black Lord.'

'Your army is doomed tomorrow, *my lord*.' Asger still twirled his blade. 'But Tekoa will take command if you do not survive the night. He is a practical man. He may see the sense in withdrawing to the Hindrunn, where Uvoren will, of course, welcome him as a loyal servant.'

'More likely he'll unleash the Skiritai on you,' said Roper.

'No member of this army would dare kill a Sacred Guardsman.'

And there, Roper thought, he might be right.

'So there's just one thought going through my mind at the moment, Roper,' said Asger, now standing and hefting his sword. Roper sat back, taking a deep breath.

But there came an unnatural pause. Both Roper and Asger could sense a presence approaching once more. There were footsteps coming from the darkness.

Roper and Asger, one seated, the other standing, stared into each other's eyes for a long while as the footsteps grew louder. Gosta shifted restlessly, turning to strain his eyes into the darkness. Someone was moving towards them.

And, into the glow of the fire, stepped Pryce. He looked from Roper, coiled, hand resting on Cold-Edge's hilt, to Asger standing above him, sword drawn. He chuckled softly to himself and sat down comfortably on the log next to Roper.

Asger let out a breath. 'Oh, Pryce.' He smiled and, after a moment of hesitation, sat back down again. The fireplace was suddenly restless. A new piece had entered the game, and Roper had no idea for which side it fought. 'We've been talking with Roper, here,' said Asger smoothly. 'About how he thinks the battle tomorrow will go.'

'We'll probably lose,' grunted Pryce. He gave Asger a meaningful look.

Shit.

'I must say, that's what we rather thought. Better not to waste a half-call-up on a fool's errand.'

'True, true,' said Pryce. He was sitting back on the log, relaxed and content.

'Well, then,' said Asger, beaming now. 'As I said. There's just one thought going through my mind at the moment, Roper.'

'If there's a thought going through your head, it means somebody else has put it there you obsequious prick,' exploded Roper. Pryce burst out laughing. He glanced at his lord, grinning, but Roper did not meet his eye. He was still staring at Asger. 'And you refer to me as "my lord".' He would not die begging.

Asger looked as though Roper had just struck him about the face. He stood up suddenly. 'I do not kneel to a boy. I have not sworn my allegiance to you.' He raised his sword, but froze as Pryce too got to his feet. He was still smiling, his hand resting on the hilt of his sword.

'Pryce,' Asger said blankly. 'Step aside. I have no wish to kill you.'

'That is just as well,' said Pryce. 'You entirely lack the ability.'

A sneer crossed Asger's face. At his side, Gosta stood abruptly, followed by the two other guardsmen. For his part, Roper stood up as well. 'Sit down,' snapped Pryce. 'You cannot fight these men.'

'You call me "my lord",' snarled Roper, feet planted firmly on the ground.

Asger looked on, smiling unpleasantly. 'For years now, all I've heard is "Never fight Pryce; you're going to die whether you win or not." And yet . . . you are not much of a swordsman, really. You're reasonably quick, but all the speed in the world can't make up for a complete lack of finesse. "Don't fight Pryce." I'm tempted to find out why not.'

'I invite you to do just that. It would be my greatest pleasure to mash your bulging eyeballs into the back of your bastard skull.'

Asger stared for a long while. Very quietly: 'You're going to die for this boy?'

'One day.' Pryce was no longer smiling.

'I know where this order has come from,' said Asger, so quietly now that Roper could hardly hear the words. 'How rich, Pryce, to have mocked me when your real allegiance has always lain with Gray Konrathson. The great Pryce simpering and bowing to that talentless killjoy. You follow him like a wet dog.'

'That is my honour,' said Pryce. 'My loyalty and life are at his disposal. For your man Uvoren, I have no words base enough.'

'You're a headstrong fool, Pryce. A fool. You would take on the four of us single-handed? Uvoren will hear of this treachery when we are done with you. And when he does, you know Gray will die too.' Roper could hardly breathe. The night had solidified about him, holding his limbs fast in sheer blackness. A log on the fire cracked loudly, vomiting sparks into the night and causing Roper to blink.

And so he missed the instant when Pryce's sword leapt from its scabbard and sliced straight through Asger's neck. Asger's eyes opened wide and he dropped his sword, raising his hands to the blade that had pierced his throat. Pryce ripped it away and Asger was dead before he hit the ground, a great fountain of blood spurting from the wound as he sprawled in the dirt. With the speed of a striking serpent, Pryce stepped into Gosta, who had managed to draw his own sword. The blades clashed three times in quick succession, releasing a shower of white sparks on each occasion before Pryce headbutted his opponent to the ground.

By this time, Roper and the other two guardsmen had also drawn swords. The one opposite Roper came to kill him; the other to help his downed comrade defeat Pryce. Roper and the guardsman clashed, causing Roper to retreat and lose sight of what was happening to Pryce. There were screams, roars and the clang of blades smashing together but Roper heard none of it. His entire world was in the slender piece of alloy held before him.

He managed to block a first attack, then a second. The third was a feint but Roper knew it and stepped aside, sliding his opponent's blade past him to release a great curtain of white sparks and bringing the pommel of Cold-Edge forward to smash into the guardsman's face. It connected with a wicked crack but barely seemed to register with the man. He struck Roper a dizzying blow with his gauntleted fist. Roper staggered back and was unable to block the next attack, which slammed into the bone-armour of his chest and hammered him back again. Another attack and Roper could not block this one either, sweeping below his guard and cutting his legs from beneath him. The blade had struck the bones of his ankle and, for the second time in his life, Roper found himself on his back fighting for survival.

The guardsman lunged for his throat and Roper parried desperately, more sparks staining his vision. He wafted a counter-attack in the guardsman's direction but his sword was batted aside dismissively and this time he had to use his gloved left hand to deflect the blade from his throat. It cut deep into the flesh of his hand but he did just enough to avoid having his neck filleted.

The night went black; blood had got in his eyes somehow and all he could see was the blotch of those sparks. Something heavy dropped on top of Roper and he could feel hot blood pouring down his side. He struggled to thrust his sword into the body atop him but the blade was too long and he flailed, unable to plant the tip in the guardsman.

'Enough!' snarled a voice above him. 'He's finished.' Roper obeyed, freezing. The body on top of him was limp and still. It was dead.

His attacker was dead.

Roper drew a few deep breaths and wiped the blood free from his eyes. He wriggled out from beneath the body and sat up to see Pryce standing above him. The lictor was dreadfully cut on both his arms, had a deep gash in one calf and appeared to have lost an ear but he still stood. Around him were sprawled the bodies of four dead Sacred Guardsmen. Roper simply stared.

Pryce stared back with hard eyes. Blood was trickling down his arms and dripping off his hands. He seemed to Roper perfectly like a hawk. A hunter. Something to whom the affairs of men did not matter in the ordinary way; whose thoughts were so instinctive that they bypassed the brain altogether, operating entirely on nerve and synapse. He was an order of magnitude faster in thought and deed than any other man that Roper had met. It was true: he was not much of a swordsman. But his movements were so uncompromisingly fierce, so violently rapid, that Roper could not imagine any skill that could overcome Pryce's speed.

'"Don't fight Pryce",' said Roper, voice trembling. 'Thank you.'

'That was my pleasure.' Roper thought he meant it. 'Back now, and quick.'

He helped Roper to his feet. His left hand was cut deep and he could barely limp on his wounded ankle, but his injuries were nothing compared to Pryce's. Blood was pouring off the lictor and he was ignoring it, even hooking Roper's arm over his shoulders and helping him walk back into camp. 'Quickly,' he urged. They began passing by fires and Pryce roared out instructions, scattering men from their hearths and sending them out in all directions. They needed surgeons, they needed water and, most of all, they needed Gray. 'Somebody find him!'

But he found them. He was at their side in a flash, white-faced and furious. 'What the hell is this? Asger?'

'The bumptious prick is dead,' said Pryce savagely, still supporting Roper back to his own hearth. 'Gosta did almost all of this.'

'Thank god you were there,' said Gray, before taking command. The camp was in uproar; officers clucked and swarmed about the little group and Gray batted them away. 'Search for the bodies! Bring them to me!' he commanded. The surgeons were there and began seeing to Roper's wounds. He lost sight of Pryce but could hear him snarling as he too was attended to.

'Gray?' called Roper.

'Lord?'

'Pryce saved my life. Will he live?'

Gray gave a short laugh. He placed a hand on Roper's

shoulder. 'It'll take more than a pair of Uvoren's finest to kill that man.'

'There were four of them,' muttered Roper. 'Four guardsmen.'

This shocked Gray. 'Forget it, lord. We have you now; you're safe. There is only one important thing to think of: tomorrow's battle.'

12
Open the Gates

Uvoren was not accustomed to being absent during campaign. Ordinarily, he would be shaping the victories on the field rather than waiting anxiously within the Hindrunn for news. It had raised no more than an ironic eyebrow from him when he had seen the crowds cheering Roper as he led the legions out of the fortress. But news of the first victory had been rather harder to accept. Word had reached the Hindrunn of a dawn raid in which Roper had played a tactical master-stroke. The legions had marched and fought like heroes and people were saying that Roper had ridden alone through the Suthern encampment, killing dozens. That could not be true, of course, but it smarted.

Taking the Hindrunn when it was offered to him like a ripe fruit had been the right decision, but Uvoren could hardly bear to wait within its walls. When he had been sure that Roper was leagues away, he had taken some of his remaining cavalry out, looking for a fight, but found nothing. The Suthern army was more cohesive than expected for such a horde. He was restless and infuriated.

But Roper was not the only one who knew how to inspire loyalty, and Uvoren started from a more elevated position than his rival, commanding considerable respect through sheer reputation. He trained alongside the legionaries that had been left to him in the fortress, aware that his mere proximity was enough to please his warriors. He saw the way they behaved around him. These grizzled, battle-hardened men stuttered and stumbled under his gaze. They beamed absurdly if he chose to speak to one of them, offered him their water-skins, flattered him, and asked if he might recount the tale of how King Offa had died. Unlike Roper, Uvoren did not seek to earn loyalty through service, but through insisting on service to him. He knew that if men performed a favour for a gracious lord, it quickly built respect. Uvoren was therefore everywhere, making demands of every soldier and thanking them handsomely when they fulfilled them. He made sure to issue a different compliment to each group of warriors he encountered: admiring the sword-craft of one here; professing to have heard of the deeds of another there.

He held a tournament almost as soon as Roper was gone, with the aim of keeping the fortress occupied. Uvoren did not himself fight (better to keep his fighting prowess the subject of wild speculation than have it confirmed), but watched and applauded as the warriors clashed and wrestled in front of a roaring crowd. He supplied the tournament prizes (an immensely expensive cuirass of Unthank-silver for the First Sword and a fine Unthank-silver blade for the winner of the wrestling), as well as the food and birch wine served for the grateful crowds. Roper's reputation might be growing, but Uvoren made sure his grew faster.

He next staged one of the brutal games of pioba in the streets. The rest of the Hindrunn delighted in watching as two huge teams wrestled for control of the inflated pig's bladder used as a ball, each side throwing punches and seeking to carry the ball into their opponent's district. The ball-carriers weaved down backstreets with cheering subjects looking down at them from the windows; or else joined one of the great presses of men, seeking to build some advantage for their side in a main street by heaving the opposing team backwards.

Finally, and most effective of all the entertainments Uvoren laid on, were the athletics contests. There were sprints with and without armour, contests of strength and, the Hindrunn favourite, a gruelling twelve-lap race around its perimeter. The races had not been so open in years, with lesser athletes emerging from Pryce's shadow for the first time in decades to claim his titles in the sprints.

Uvoren made a great show of riding every day on the back of his finest horse, dressed in full war gear and accompanied by a retinue of esteemed warriors, down to the Outer Gate, where he would stand on top of the gatehouse and survey the horizon, as though seeking some indication of how Roper was doing. He accepted the adulation he received sternly, raising a hand in acknowledgement but neither cracking a smile nor looking at the subjects who saluted him: the gracious ruler, who expected total obedience and received nothing less. Now, if the moment arrived and his soldiers were forced to fight fellow Black legionaries under Roper's command, he was sure they would obey.

But Roper was making things difficult. He had won an overwhelming tactical victory and, for the people of the Black Kingdom, martial achievement trumped all else. So Uvoren used that to his advantage. Subtly, through a dozen sources scattered about the Hindrunn, a new rumour began to circulate. It was being said that after Roper's latest victory, the Sutherners had approached him with a deal to share the eastern lands and that Roper had accepted. It was all the fortress spoke of for days: had you not yet heard that the Black Lord planned to make peace with the Sutherners, in exchange for a fat slice of the east?

But in the end, it was Roper himself who eliminated the need for Uvoren's machinations. On the twenty-third day after Roper had left the fortress, new tidings reached Uvoren. They started faint and unconfirmed, then became a little more persistent. Finally, there could be no doubt. Roper, having marched to Githru and sought to bring the Sutherners to battle there, had suffered a cataclysmic defeat.

It had been tactical incompetence; no more. Reportedly, he had held a strong defensive position and legionaries in good morale but, spooked by something, he had tried to withdraw at the last minute. The Sutherners had unleashed their knights and the narrow battlefield had seen a slaughter.

And now they were retreating. The remnants of Roper's legions were withdrawing to the Hindrunn, hounded by the Suthern army. Roper was fighting a desperate rearguard action with what forces remained to him and a column of wounded men were beginning to draw near to the Hindrunn. Uvoren rode out to meet them himself.

Wagons, stuffed with the injured, were trundling by the dozen along the road back to the Hindrunn. Even to Uvoren, this was a pitiful sight. It seemed they had retreated so fast that the surgeons had not even had time to address their wounds. Shrivelled intestines lay sprawling from several legionaries, who were pale and still. Most were evidently dead already. Blood, both dried and fresh, stained everything and the men groaned and writhed as the wagons jolted over ruts and stones in the track. Some of the men were bandaged in linen strips stained rust-red, many just hunched and unmoving. Few of them would survive much beyond their return to the Hindrunn.

'Not many of them,' observed Uvoren.

'The rest are dead, lord,' responded the wagon-driver. 'These were all we could save.'

'Almighty god,' said Uvoren, mouth twitching. He stared at the driver in incredulity, keeping his horse level with the man. 'How many does Boy-Roper still have?'

'Few enough, lord. Fifteen thousand, I would guess.'

Uvoren coughed and spluttered. 'Fifteen thousand! The Hindrunn will not be pleased.'

So that was that. Roper's nerve had failed him, as Uvoren

had known it would, and he had thrown away his warriors and his chance of ruling the Black Kingdom. Uvoren did feel the glow of triumph that he had expected, but also a wave of hot anger. Incompetence: that was all that had killed those legionaries. Roper had no business being a ruler. He was weak.

'I bet the first victory was Tekoa,' he suggested to Tore, legate of the Greyhazel, as the two rode back to the Hindrunn together. There was a chill on the air and Uvoren, like all good Anakim, was enjoying the cold. That was why there was so little glass in the Hindrunn: to be warm was to be insulated from the wild. The Anakim had a word for this insulation: *fraskala*, the feeling of being cocooned. The opposite, expressed as a positive, was *maskunn*: exposed.

'He would have known that Roper could not be trusted and would have kept him on a short leash.'

'And Tekoa let him off his leash for the second battle,' agreed Tore. 'With the result that Roper spent twenty thousand legionaries.' He spoke bitterly. It was a terrible waste and even if they could still repel the Sutherners from their lands, it would take generations to recover from such a loss.

'Let the legions know!' said Uvoren, glee and rage vying for control of his voice. 'Tell them what Roper has done, Bera,' he addressed Tore by his haskoli nickname. 'Do you know, we might get away without destroying Roper's forces? I doubt they'll fight for him after a second disaster. If we kill Roper, the others will join us.'

'Probably. But kill Roper in front of the gates and we can see how his remaining legionaries react.'

'Very good. A couple of cannon will do nicely.'

'And what about Tekoa? How's he going to react to all this? If he's even alive.'

'He'll have survived,' said Uvoren, confidently. 'He's not one to die in a losing cause. He'll have seen which way the wind was blowing. We'll take him in. Give him a nice position and some influence and he'll be happy. And with his daughter widowed? Maybe I'll take her in too.'

'You have a wife,' observed Tore.

'Yes,' said Uvoren impatiently. 'But think about the authority invested in a child that was half-Lothbrok, half-Vidarr. That'd be a lineage to rival the Jormunrekur.'

'With or without the Vidarr, we can rule for a thousand years.'

The two men returned to the fortress. The wagons of wounded that trundled through the gates and straight into the surgery shortly after them would be the last soldiers allowed in whilst Roper still lived. Behind them, the locking bars clunked into place and the portcullis, lowered only when a hostile army approached, slid down in front of the Great Gate.

The legions were summoned. The two regular legions, the Blackstones and the Greyhazel, assembled on the wall either side of the Great Gate, prepared to receive Roper's men with a show of force. The others, the auxiliaries, formed up closer to the middle of the Hindrunn, ready to be sent to any part of the wall that might face attack.

The great bronze dragon-cannons which studded the Outer Wall were loaded, double-shotted for a devastating first volley. These were so enormous that, when they were fired, their operators had to stand against the wall and scream to prevent their eardrums bursting. Their range was immense but that night Uvoren did not expect them to be used at more than fifty yards. Roper would be declared an outlaw and blown apart.

The fire-throwers' tanks, held deep within the Outer Wall, were charged. When the enemy drew near, pedals would be used to pump air into the tanks and raise the pressure, ready for use. These could drench all those within thirty yards of the wall in sticky-fire, hot enough to melt flesh and unquenchable except when smothered in sand. Certainly, they were the most feared instruments at the Hindrunn's disposal.

Ballistae and siege bows were manoeuvred into position and bolt-caches positioned nearby.

The plate-hurlers – mechanical weapons that could fling sharpened steel disks into the enemy ranks to produce devastating cutting wounds – were shuffled into position and loaded with their heavy projectiles.

Buckets and buckets of arrows were brought to the top of the wall. Next to them, old masonry was piled, ready to be hurled down.

The refugees beyond the Outer Wall could hear these preparations, deduced there must be a hostile army approaching, and fled into the evening. Those within the walls saw the legionaries mustering in the street and the weapons being carried to the outer layers and hurried away. It would not have been unusual to prepare the fortress in this way with a Suthern army nearby, but everybody knew who these weapons would be aimed at. They knew Roper and his ruined army were drawing close. Everyone had heard of the disaster at Githru and that Roper was soon to be declared that worst of things: an enemy of the realm. An outlaw. A creature without loyalty, whose body would be obliterated to prevent it rising to fight with the dead when Catastrophe emerged from the sands in the east. In the conflict between the Wolf and the Wildcat, the only sensible thing to do was to get out of the way.

Shaded figures scurried up the street, too preoccupied to pay attention to the two women who sat in a bordering garden beneath a hawthorn. The taller woman was propped against the wall of the house at her back; the smaller against the trunk of the tree. Even through the gloom, the taller woman's green eyes shone as they tracked the figures before her. They were mostly women, clutching wood, nails, charcoal, axes and sacks of dried fruit; the last items needed to prepare their households for the impending siege. Their men were elsewhere: already waiting armoured at their stations.

There was a long-established and unspoken agreement in

siege warfare. If you forced an opposing army to storm your stronghold, they would make you pay for your resistance once inside. If the Black Lord could somehow force entry, the fury of his soldiers would be terrible. They would almost certainly vent it on their own home, which, after all, had turned against them first with cannon and fire-thrower.

'A lot of fear,' observed the tall woman.

Her smaller companion was the young serving girl, Glamir, who worked in Tekoa's household. She did not turn to face Keturah as she answered. 'We should go inside. What if Uvoren comes for you?'

'The Captain of the Guard has bigger issues on his mind just now. He'll probably come when he's finished with my husband, and a closed door won't stop him.' She rolled her eyes. 'That's going to be a tedious conversation.'

Keturah was not thinking about Uvoren. She was not thinking about her husband. She was not even thinking particularly of her father, trusting him to find his own way through whatever happened beyond the walls.

She was thinking about the friends she had, marching under Roper. Or maybe now marching no longer, but spent by him; left at that feverish battlefield by the sea. But some must have survived: kind men, with whom she had often shared a joke and a snippet of gossip. Who had trained their particular interest on her; tried to charm and impress her; given her little presents they had made; appeared outside her father's house to sing to her when drunk. More than once, Tekoa, his brow thunderous, his manner abrupt but his eyes gleeful, had dressed in his mighty legate's cloak and stormed outside to the gathering circle of onlookers and demanded that, unless they removed this twittering scoundrel at once, he would take a testicle from each one of them to be hammered together for a bar of soap.

How would they behave, those kind men, if they broke past the warriors waiting on the walls, and forced their way into these streets? The most likely possibility, she considered, was that they would come and find her, to protect her from the blooming chaos and others who stalked these passages with less worthy motives. But there was an alternative that she could not quite put from her mind. Perhaps, instead, their thoughts would be contaminated by the violence. She did not fear the appearance of a fierce stranger, crashing through her bolted door, as much as she feared that figure being one of her friends. Or rather, a shell that resembled a friend, but walked more purposefully, each step like a lunge. In the aftermath of great battles, she had seen men rendered unrecognisable by the horrors through which they had passed. Creatures beyond emotion and beyond reason; their consciousness savagely truncated, wide eyes set on her. She pitied them, but she also feared what it would do to her to see those figures prowling the dark streets beyond her door, or worse still, trying to get through it. Whether that was truly what her friends were, when pushed beyond the harsh laws of her country, she did not want to know.

'Do you hear that?' said Glamir, unexpectedly.

Keturah listened. She could not hear anything in particular. The patter of leather-soled slippers hurrying over the cobbles. A pair of wood pigeons sitting in the tree above, cooing into the dusk. The tree's last leaves scratching in the wind. The soft gurgle of the stream that crossed the street.

But she could feel something, she realised. A faint, rhythmic quiver in her guts. It crossed her flesh, prowled through her lungs and up her throat. She glanced at her companion. 'I feel it.'

Before the two women, the figures on the street slowed and came to a halt as they too became aware of the sensation. Heads jerked up to look above the walls, up at the lavender sky, and all fell quiet. The leaves shivered and the stones quaked at the bass tattoo of a distant army, marching in step. Many on the street shared a look; some of them seeming to become aware of Keturah's gaze for the first time and glancing at where she sat in the shadows. The water of the stream began to pulse in regular waves, ordered by the rhythmic thump of boots. Then the spell was broken and the activity in the street redoubled. Doors began to slam left and right from Keturah and, within a few moments, the cobbles were abandoned.

Keturah glanced at her companion with a wry smile and received a look of sympathy in return. 'I hope your father is victorious, 'Turah.'

Keturah looked away. 'So do I,' she said. 'But it seems unlikely. Belligerence will only carry you so far.'

'Your father is a survivor. He will come through.'

'It's possible,' said Keturah. 'The one person who won't survive is Roper, though. So much for my marriage.'

'You're better without him,' said Glamir. 'He struck a deal with the Sutherners!'

Keturah tutted, drawing that conversation to a close. 'Of course he didn't.' She sat unnaturally still, head tilted back against the wall, her countenance almost bored. Beside her, Glamir was agitated; looking down the street and then up at the sky.

'How much of this fortress do you think will be left standing by tomorrow?' said Glamir.

'Swords cannot cut stone,' came Keturah's tart reply. The ensuing silence was tainted by the thump of marching boots. Keturah knew that Glamir was about to speak again, and what she was going to say.

'I am scared,' came the quiet words.

'You'll be fine, my dear,' said Keturah. She grasped Glamir's hand to soften her calloused tone.

'Not only of the assault,' said Glamir. 'I am scared for you. You are a pawn in this game.'

The ground trembled in the pause that followed. Keturah did not move. Then she shrugged. 'Me and everyone else.'

As night began to fall, it felt as though winter had at last draped its cloak over the fortress. The air was sharp and dry.

The breath of the legionaries assembling atop the wall rose as mist. The men gathered, exchanged a brief word by way of greeting, and then waited in silence. No one wanted to speak. The rumbling of marching feet had morphed into something they could sense with their ears. It was like distant applause: an audience of ten thousand clapping in time.

Tramp-tramp-tramp-tramp-tramp.

There was no moon that night; the Blackstones and the Greyhazel could see nothing from behind their high battlements. The lime-lanterns were lit: four enormous lamps on the Great Gatehouse which burnt a combination of lime and pressurised gas with a brilliant white flame. A parabolic mirror behind the flame could be used to focus this intense light before the walls of the Hindrunn and illuminate any approaching army. These were as much weapons as anything else: an enemy advancing into such intensity would be utterly dazzled. Bundles of hay soaked in oil were tossed from the walls, ready to be ignited with flaming arrows. The darkness would offer no shelter to Roper's men.

Uvoren watched atop the Great Gatehouse, leaning against one of the battlements and waiting for the enemy to come into view. He knew the sound of a marching army, and maybe it was something to do with the cold air, or just the contrast with the intense silence that had fallen over the battlements, but this one was louder than he had expected. Deeper. He tried to talk to calm his men, but his voice, like a candle lit in an abyss, merely highlighted the true extent of the dark. He fell silent.

It was no wonder the men were quiet. They had never fought Anakim before, still less their own kin. If it came to hand-to-hand combat, they would meet with friends across steel. It was easier to be brave going into battle against the Sutherners: fellow Anakim were a different proposition entirely. And not just any Anakim. Ramnea's Own Legion. The Sacred Guard itself. No man wanted to fight such warriors.

It was not until the noise of marching feet was powerful enough to rattle the grit on the battlements that Uvoren thought he could discern Roper's army in the darkness beyond the walls. It was barely visible: a shimmering river of reflected starlight, heading straight for the Great Gate. It seemed they bore no torches, allowing themselves to be guided home by the charcoal glow of the Hindrunn.

'Not long now, boys,' declared Uvoren. His words did not even seem to have reached the man next to him. Even Tore, standing to Uvoren's left, was silent and watchful as the head of the column gathered itself from the dark, illuminated by the lime-lanterns. Though it was hard to tell, there was no sign of the pursuing Suthern army. The legions must have out-marched them.

They were in good order, for a broken force. They looked almost ghostly, light drizzling from armour and weapons while their bodies remained dark. It was as though this was nothing more than a column of armour coming to besiege their home, having left their flesh behind. But surely armour could not make the ground tremble with the tramp of feet. It menaced the whole fortress. Those subjects waiting inside their homes could hear it shaking the slates on their roofs, and anticipated the first roar of a dragon-cannon that would tell them their home was being assaulted.

At the front of the column was the Sacred Guard. Now they had drawn closer to the lime-lanterns, they looked magnificent. Brilliant white light radiated from their armour. They were straight-backed and proud; almost angelic in their bright raiment, and far from the whipped dogs Uvoren was expecting.

Among them rode Roper. He looked quite as splendid as he had when he left, mounted on his enormous destrier, a huge presence in his cloak which resisted all attempts at illumination. He and his men marched proudly, showing no signs of trepidation, though they must surely know that Uvoren was not about to open the gates for them.

Roper and the Guard drew closer and closer and still nothing happened. Uvoren did not command the cannon to open fire and Roper did not look as if he was planning to attack. He was simply heading directly for the gate, as though it would open for him as surely as it had always done. Perhaps Roper simply had not understood the deal he had struck with Uvoren. Whatever the cause, he and the Sacred Guard were marching straight for the gate. They were within range of the fire-throwers.

'What is he thinking?' muttered Uvoren. Behind the Sacred Guard, the front of Ramnea's Own Legion was beginning to come into view, their armour looking just as polished as the men who marched with Roper. Uvoren leaned close to Tore. 'Do you think Boy-Roper stopped to polish up his soldiers?'

'That's how it looks,' said Tore. Uvoren appeared convincingly relaxed but Tore, like the men on the wall, seemed edgy.

A trumpet wailed from the column in front of the walls and, in perfect order, the marching legionaries halted. 'Steady lads,' said Uvoren lightly; several of his soldiers had flinched at the trumpet.

A voice, like Roper's but a little deeper and a little harsher, rang out across the night. 'Open the gates! The Black Legions have returned to the Hindrunn!'

Uvoren beamed to himself on the dark battlement. He could hear more soldiers marching in the streets behind him; coming to reinforce the men on the wall now that it was clear Roper's entire column was focused on this point. 'The fool wants to die. He thinks standing among the Sacred Guard is going to save him. How touching!'

'You would fire a cannon into the Sacred Guard?' murmured Tore.

'Ballistae, then,' conceded Uvoren. He nodded at the two ballistae crews that stood either side of the gatehouse and they began to prepare their weapons. They were like enormous crossbows, the crews cranking the bow back and preparing to load. The Black Lord still waited, staring up from beneath his gleaming helmet to where Uvoren stood. Men still marched behind the wall. There was a satisfying snap as the ballista crews finished drawing their weapons and allowed the strings to rest on the triggers.

'Halt!' bawled a voice from behind Uvoren. Irritated, the captain swung around, a remonstration already building in his throat. The only sound he uttered was a slight hiss as the breath escaped his lungs. His mouth fell open.

Five hundred warriors stood behind the Great Gate, swords drawn and armoured in plate and mail. They held three banners at their head, the emblems described in cream on a background of black cloth. On the left, a serpent devouring the roots of a tree. On the right, a rampant unicorn. And in the middle, a snarling wolf. House Vidarr. House Alba. And House Jormunrekur. This force was led by a single warrior, tall and broad, who stood alone at the front of the formation.

It was Gray. His feet were spread wide, his sword was in his hand and he stared up at Uvoren, jaw set.

'What in the name of god?' Every warrior on the battlement had turned to stare, dumbstruck at the sight of these warriors behind them.

'Who are these?' hissed Tore. 'They're already inside!'

Uvoren's mind was racing. 'Those *bloody* wounded. That sneaky, underhanded bastard.' His face resembled the wolf on the Jormunrekur banner. Wave after wave of revelations were washing over him, pummelling him and making him screw up his face against it all.

There had been no defeat. Merely a tale to get him to open his gates to a bunch of Roper's most loyal soldiers, tricked out to look injured. Now they stood, fully armed, armoured and ready for combat. The intent of these warriors was clear: open the gates, or we will kill you and open them anyway. Uvoren's best warriors would be stuck on the wall as the army flooded through the Great Gate. It would be a massacre; one that Uvoren, so close to these five hundred warriors of Roper's, might not even get to witness.

Uvoren stood still for just a moment, staring down at Gray. The silence was broken only by the sound of the bolts being loaded onto the ballistae either side of him. Tore was glancing rapidly from Uvoren to Gray and back again. Gray could have been a statue. Uvoren was not even breathing.

'Open the gates!' shouted Uvoren at last. His grin returned. 'Open the gates! Welcome the Black Lord home!' He turned away from Gray's forces below him and strode to the edge of the gatehouse. He gestured calmly to the ballista crews: *Unload, now!* and made his way down to ground level. The portcullis groaned as it was raised and the bolts of the gate shot back, making Uvoren flinch a little at the noise.

Gray and his five hundred still stood behind the gate and Gray still stared at Uvoren as he strode forward.

'Gray Konrathson,' Uvoren said softly, coming to a halt before the guardsman just as a ticking noise behind told him the gates were opening. 'It seems you serve a new master.'

'My master was always the Black Lord.'

'But you are a Sacred Guardsman,' said Uvoren, taking a finger and prodding it hard into Gray's armoured chest, a little smile on his lips. 'And *I* am the Captain of the Guard.'

'And that's all you are, Captain,' said Gray. Uvoren was very close to him, eyes boring into Gray's. Uvoren was a little taller than the guardsman and looked down at him coldly, stepping a little closer. Gray's sword, still clutched in his right hand, moved very slowly between them, coming to rest just below Uvoren's chin. 'That's all,' he repeated softly. 'That's all.'

'Uvoren!' called a voice behind him. 'I thought you were going to open fire on us!'

Uvoren whirled around, the grin returning to his face in the time it took him to turn. 'My lord!' He and Roper strode towards each other and embraced like brothers. Uvoren broke away first, gripping Roper's shoulders and beaming at him. 'We merely wanted to greet you properly!'

Roper laughed delightedly, looking into Uvoren's face with genuine pleasure. 'Githru was a triumph, Uvoren! The campaigning season is over and the Sutherners have been driven south of the Abus.'

'Oh,' said Uvoren, allowing the grin to slip a little. 'I wonder where the rumours we heard came from.' He stared at Roper for a moment. The boy was bigger than he remembered. Broader, taller and certainly bolder. Roper shrugged. At his back, the legions were re-entering the fortress. Uvoren's forces on the battlement were looking on, nonplussed. 'And I thought these men were your wounded.' Uvoren jerked his head behind him to where Gray and his five hundred stood.

'You are surely overjoyed to be mistaken,' said Roper.

Uvoren re-engaged his smile. 'Naturally, lord. Come!' He turned away from the gate and placed his hand in the small of Roper's back, steering him towards the keep. 'We must prepare a victory feast!'

'Gray.' To Uvoren's fury, Roper slipped his grip and headed instead for the veteran guardsman. He stopped just before Gray, who offered him a smile and a deep bow. Roper raised Gray up and the two embraced tightly. 'Thank you,' said Roper as they broke apart. 'Thank you for everything.'

'"Don't think about the Hindrunn," I believe was my advice to you,' said Gray. 'Where would we be now if you'd listened to that?'

'You also gave me another piece of advice. "The greatest warriors can fight in any theatre, but the greatest leaders do not need to fight at all." And here we stand. We're back, brother.'

Part II
WINTER

13
The Honour Hall

Victory.

The word was nectar to Roper. He and Gray wandered through the streets as though drunk. The cobbles were deserted: the residents had dared not emerge.

'Victory!' Gray would hiss, to Roper's joy.

'Again,' demanded the Black Lord.

'Victory!'

It did not matter how late the hour; they would have a feast. A successful campaign always ends in a feast and this one would take hours to prepare. All the warriors would attend, each at one of the barracks sprinkled throughout the Hindrunn. Cauldrons of birch wine, mead, ale, cider and beor would make the tables bow before the food even arrived. Such food! It was not salted, nor smoked nor dried. Freshly slaughtered pork, beef or poultry, roasted over charcoal and stuffed with ramsons. With it, burdock baked in clay ovens and flagons of buttermilk.

Roper's feast would be the most magnificent of all. Two hundred of the country's most esteemed figures: legates, councillors, historians and warriors, would process up the steps into the Central Keep and cram into the Honour Hall. Those who had fought most bravely on campaign would be rewarded with an invitation and perhaps a place at High Table with Roper and his most honoured guests.

No one had known there would be a feast, so celebrations had to be started from scratch. The clay ovens were packed with wood and brought up to temperature. A small battle was fought between an army of pigs and their drunken herdsmen. After but half an hour, the herdsmen declared themselves triumphant and their vanquished enemies were loaded onto wagons to be sent to the kitchens. The drink was lifted from cool cellars by the jar and barrel, swinging pendulously beneath cranes and dumped onto carts from which they were distributed around the citadel. They were almost ready to begin cooking before anyone realised that the chefs were nowhere to be seen. They were still hiding within their barricaded homes, unable to tell the difference between the noises outside and the sound of an army sacking the fortress.

They were coaxed out and set to with gusto once they realised this was not a sacking but a celebration. Roper issued the summons for those who would attend his feast, with fifty-three Sacred Guardsmen, thirty-two Ramnea's Own legionaries, twenty-one Skiritai, eleven Pendeen legionaries, forty-three auxiliaries and a score of berserkers joining the nobles of the country in the Honour Hall. Roper was not convinced all of the berserkers had earned their invitation but Gray had advised him otherwise. 'Any feast with less than a dozen berserkers won't be worth attending, lord.'

It was hours past midnight when the kitchens finally declared themselves ready and the double-height doors to the Honour Hall (more bog-oak) were opened. Roper sat in the centre of the High Table, raised on a dais and overlooking the other great tables where his subjects sat. The Honour Hall itself was solid granite with a high roof of vaulted stone. Small windows that permitted no light on this moonless night were set just below the roof, with illumination instead provided by two-score blazing braziers which lined the walls. These cast their flickering light on the thousands of carvings that rippled the wall, depicting the outlines of endless scenes of battle, victory, slaughter, treaty, duty, hunting and coronation.

That evening, Roper's right-hand man was Gray and on his left sat a stranger: his wife. On her other side was Uvoren, and next to him was Pryce. On Gray's other side was Tekoa.

First, the drink. Roper noted that Gray, Pryce, Tekoa and Uvoren all took a horn of the buttermilk before helping themselves to anything more potent from the cauldrons. Pryce was especially partial to mead and passed his horn down the table so that another guest could fill it with the sparkling golden brew. Once it was returned to him, he stood and raised his horn. He did not wait for silence in the enormous hall, simply boomed: 'First, the good stuff!' There was a cheer and the others raised their horns. 'My Lord Roper!' he toasted and finished the horn. The others did likewise, with Roper's eyes drawn magnetically to Uvoren, who had drained his own horn with a passable murmur of respect.

'Why the milk?' asked Roper, leaning towards Keturah.

She turned to look at him, her pale green eyes a bright corona around huge dark pupils. 'To line the stomach of course,' she said. 'This will last for hours and I suggest you do the same, if you want still to be conscious by the time the food arrives. Husband,' she added with a smirk.

Roper took the buttermilk and then decided to try the beor, which was closest. It was horrible. He discreetly fed it to Keturah, who pretended to like it so as to tease him, and moved on to the more familiar birch wine.

Gray stood now, raising a horn of ale. 'There were many heroes at Githru!' he called and Roper noticed that the table fell remarkably still for Gray's words. 'None more so than Leon Kaldison, who almost split Lord Northwic in two!' There was a mighty cheer and they raised horns to Leon Kaldison, a powerful guardsman on Pryce's left who acknowledged the toast with a nod. This one had a big reputation,

Roper knew, as one of the Guard's most highly esteemed fighters. Even Uvoren liked to joke that Leon terrified him.

Through fifty toasts, the tale of the battle unfolded. It had hinged, as these battles so often did, on the Sacred Guard. Winds swept across Githru as the battle lines clashed, salty spray flying over the eastern portion of the field. The crash of the two lines striking one another was a punch to the guts; like an immense volley of cannon-fire, or a tremendous rolling wave of thunder. It was the sound of shields cracking and slamming into steel; of men smashing to the ground; of axes reducing wood to splinters. Beneath all that was a deeper, more subtle noise. It was the 'ooph' of five thousand men having the air forced from their lungs.

The battle that had followed was quite as intense as had been reckoned. Roper had anticipated a contest of skill: heroic flourishing of the sword and men fighting one-on-one. But Githru was about muscle. The Anakim line exerted huge pressure onto their Suthern opponents, who were warping and buckling beneath it. Bodies falling backwards as if time had slowed, held between the pressure at their backs and the more powerful, more inexorable force pressing from the front. The Suthern line churning and tumbling like ploughed earth. Swords almost forgotten. A great wheezing escaping from that dynamic arc where the two forces met, as the Sutherners being trampled underfoot fought for air.

The stench was overwhelmingly of metal. The churning mud smelt of metal. The blood smelt of metal. The grinding armour reeked of it.

Three times they fought together and three times the result had been an exhausted standstill. The Sutherners would pull back before rotating their front line and assembling another wave which was hurled against the legions, still fighting for breath. The heavily armoured knights joined the battle line on foot for the fourth and final wave, going toe-to-toe in the centre with the Sacred Guard. There the brawling had reached a new pitch. They lost thirty-one guardsmen dead, another fifty or so injured. The knights well outnumbered the Guard, the legions were growing tired and being forced back from their positions. It had been Gray, Pryce and Leon who had saved the day.

First, Pryce had lost his mind and charged shrieking into a dense formation of knights, knocking them flat rather than trying to kill them. His savagery was enough to create a gap and Gray had been the quickest to react to it. He piled in with his protégé, creating a spearhead which the rest of the Guard used to drive through the formation of knights, tearing it asunder. Lord Northwic had been behind, roaring his men on and, when they had broken through, Pryce, Gray and Leon had charged his bodyguards. Protégé and mentor had defended Leon as he carved through the household warriors to cut off the head of the army.

That had been enough.

But there was one tale Roper still wanted to hear. He leaned towards Gray. 'So the plan came off without a hitch?'

'It was just as we discussed, lord,' replied Gray. He did not attempt to keep his voice down, though Roper noticed that Uvoren had frozen a couple of places away. 'We had enough corpses in the wagons for them not to bother inspecting those of us still moving. They let us right through to the surgery. Things got a bit sticky for a moment when the surgeons came poking around, but we managed to capture them all and hide in the surgery until we could hear you approaching. Getting to the Great Gate was just a case of looking like we belonged. Easy. The Hindrunn captured without a life lost.' Gray beamed at Roper, who thought that he might be Black Lord for another century and never again win such a victory.

The meat arrived, with the centre-piece a magnificent boar roasted in honey and crisped with salt, borne by six serving girls who received the biggest cheer of the night. It was accompanied by the Goose Legion, the Duck Legion and the Chicken Legion, a pig per table that oozed butter and the intoxicating waft of ramsons and two hundred loaves of thick-crusted bread.

Roper stood now (a little unsteadily) and raised his horn. Silence fell in the vaulted stone hall, the warriors absent-mindedly helping themselves to meat as they gazed up at Roper. He looked sternly around at them all. 'First: to fallen peers!'

'To fallen peers!' echoed the hall, getting to their feet in a great rumble and crack as at least three benches were knocked over. They drank deep and a slight chill ran through the hall. There was a soft hiss as, under their breath, the warriors recited the names of recently fallen friends. Roper bowed his head, horn still outstretched before him, and repeated one name of his own.

'Kynortas.' He looked up. 'We will see them again. Second: the awards of valour!'

This elicited a murmur of interest rather than the raucous cheer that had greeted almost everything else this night, and the silence intensified. 'This campaign has not been two battles, but three, and on the first, we left the field before the Sutherners did.' Roper paused and held up his hands, as if to keep the good-natured jeer with which these words were received at a distance. They were laughing about what for so long had been his deepest shame, and he let out a breath that he had seemed to hold since that rain-soaked day. 'It is not as glorious, but valour in a losing cause is surely the most heroic of all, and there would undoubtedly be fewer men celebrating tonight without the actions of Pryce Rubenson. Perhaps we would not be celebrating at all. For putting down Earl William when other men were looking to the hills, I award him the Prize of Valour!'

Another roar.

Roper turned to Pryce and beckoned him forward. Pryce stood to another great bellow of raucous joy and approached Roper. He bore the adulation of the other warriors lightly, wearing no discernible expression on his face. He dropped to a knee before the Black Lord and leaned his head forward, raising his hands. Roper laid his left hand on Pryce's head and with his right produced a silver arm-ring. Pryce already wore one on each wrist and Roper added a third, bending it around his right wrist. 'A rare reward, for rare courage.' He regarded Pryce, who looked up to meet his eyes. 'I'd have given you two if I could.'

'I am honoured with one, my lord.'

That was Pryce's third.

The record, awarded to Reynar the Tall, was four. Gray had imparted to them the story of how Reynar had died eighty years before, in the act of winning his final prize. It had taken him until the age of one hundred and twenty to win his four prizes. Pryce was barely forty.

Gray, at over one hundred and forty, had two.

Uvoren, almost one hundred, had two.

Roper pulled Pryce to his feet and they embraced, Pryce returning to his seat to the sound of thunderous applause.

'I have one more to give,' declared Roper. 'Its recipient shall come as no surprise to those who were at Githru, but here I must honour Pryce once again, as well as Gray Konrathson.' At the mention of Gray's name, the warriors began to beat their hands upon the table in support. Roper raised a hand and silence fell after a time. 'Both showed mighty heroism and, if heroes were scarcer, would each be collecting a prize of their own.' He waited for the hubbub to subside. 'But the final Prize is for Leon Kaldison, who ended the battle by the sea for us by slaying a true leader: Cedric of Northwic.' Through the din, Roper turned to Leon and beckoned him forward, affixing his ring as he had done Pryce's and embracing him. Leon stood humbly before Roper and asked that he might be allowed to speak.

'By all means,' said Roper, standing aside and gesturing to the guardsman. The cheering fell away.

'This is my greatest honour: my first Prize of Valour.' Leon's voice was deep and slow, and he frowned as he addressed those below him. 'But I merely finished Lord Northwic. As my Lord Roper has said already, the work was done by Gray Konrathson and Pryce Rubenson. This ring,' he gestured at his adorned wrist, 'is as much theirs as mine.' The hall clapped appreciatively and Leon bowed to Roper and returned to his seat.

Without waiting for silence, Roper hollered: 'Peers, have at the meat!' and sat down to help himself to some of the splendid boar before him.

'Well spoke, Husband,' said Keturah, leaning close. 'For your first time, at any rate. It's a shame you can't win the Prize of Valour. I'm told you'd have had one for charging single-handedly into the Suthern encampment.'

'Miss Keturah,' said Roper. 'They exaggerate. The truth is that I lost control of the horse your father gave me.'

'Apparently, it took you rather a long time to regain control of it.' She played along, straight-faced.

'I am a poor rider,' confirmed Roper. 'But I wasn't single-handed. Gray was with me.'

Keturah looked past Roper to the guardsman on his right, who at that moment was weeping tears of laughter. Tekoa was looking on, amused, and every time it looked as though Gray was about to compose himself, Tekoa would mutter something else to him and Gray would almost collapse into the boar before him. 'I think he will be with you as long as you need him.'

'He is the best man I know,' said Roper, sincerely.

'Have you met his wife?'

'No.'

'Sigrid Jureksdottir. You should know her, she's Jormunrekur.'

'Is she?'

'And perhaps the most beautiful woman in the Black Kingdom.'

'How is it that I've never heard of her?'

'Not your generation,' said Keturah wryly. 'But I'm told it was a scandal at the time. The beautiful daughter of the Jormunrekur, marrying a mere Pendeen legionary from House Alba. His esteem has risen considerably since those days.'

'The devil,' said Roper, grinning. 'Good for Gray. And good for Sigrid, that her seeds have flourished.'

'As have mine,' said Keturah. 'I married a boy who rode off to war and whom I never thought I'd see again. And now here I sit, at a victory feast with the Black Lord.'

'You didn't trust me?'

'I didn't know you. But I didn't believe it when I heard you'd been defeated.'

'You knew I'd win?' said Roper hopefully. She laughed raucously at that, placing a hand on his arm.

'I knew my father wouldn't have let you lose.'

Roper scowled. 'Next time, I'll leave your daddy at home and you'll see I don't need him.'

She rolled her eyes. 'Please don't: he'd be unbearable.'

'My lord!' boomed Uvoren over Keturah's shoulder. Lord. 'I trust you aren't going to spend this entire night talking to a woman!'

Roper looked frostily at Uvoren but it was Keturah who spoke next. 'Don't worry, Husband,' she said, switching her hand on Roper's arm so that she could turn to face Uvoren. 'This is rather a new attitude from the captain. He was so keen to keep me company while you were away.'

'Is that so?' said Roper, leaning forward to look at Uvoren, who regarded Keturah with that familiar curl on his lips.

'Just making certain I didn't feel your absence too keenly, I'm sure,' said Keturah sweetly. For the first time that Roper could remember, Uvoren had nothing to say. He looked away with a sneer, refilled his horn with ale and then changed the topic.

'I note that the Lieutenant of the Guard is not among us. Quite a departure from tradition.'

'He's here,' said Roper, gesturing to Gray sitting at his right. 'Oh, what? You didn't hear? Asger fell at Githru. Gosta too.'

Uvoren froze, evidently considering Roper's words, but before he could reply, Pryce had started speaking. 'And Guardsman Hilmar, and Guardsman Skapti. They were all friends of yours, I believe.'

'What a shame that one battle claimed so many fine men,' said Uvoren carefully.

Pryce shrugged. 'It was actually a little before Githru, Uvoren: those four were dead before the battle had begun.'

'Pryce,' said Roper, warningly. He was trying to make peace with Uvoren. He had learned that this did not mean letting him say whatever he pleased, but neither did it mean antagonising him unnecessarily.

Pryce seemed deaf to Roper's warning. 'That's right,' he said as Uvoren turned to look at him with his eyes unnaturally wide. Pryce leaned a little closer to the captain and met his gaze unblinkingly. 'They tried to attack my Lord Roper, so I killed them all. First, I tore out Asger's neck. He was no guardsman; he died easily. Then, when I'd knocked Gosta to the ground, I rammed my sword into Skapti's armpit. It sounded painful; his screaming was rather extravagant. He got me though,' Pryce added, indicating a deep, stitched cut on his forearm below his freshly minted arm-ring.

Uvoren was entirely tensed. It looked as though he was shrinking in his seat as his muscles contracted and rage pulsed from him almost as a physical aura.

'Unfortunately, I couldn't kill Gosta right away. He was tough and my Lord Roper needed help with Hilmar, so I cut some tendons to immobilise him before I nicked a vein in his neck to bleed him out. I didn't do it very well; he was still breathing when they collected the bodies half an hour later. But he got me a couple of times too.' Pryce held back his black hair to indicate his missing ear and several more slashes on his arms. Roper was watching in horrified fascination. It was fortunate that there were no weapons allowed in the Honour Hall, otherwise he was certain Uvoren and Pryce would be hacking each other to pieces. 'I put down Hilmar last. I confess his back was turned; the Black Lord was keeping him busy so I went for his armpit again to see if it hurt as much as it had Skapti. He didn't make any noise at all: just crumpled. I must've got him in the heart.'

Uvoren was breathing deeply, staring back into Pryce's eyes and neither one was moving away from the other. Uvoren's right hand twitched a little.

'Cousin, you do exaggerate,' said Keturah waspishly. 'And your ear is horrible. What will the women of the Hindrunn say when they see? You may have to find a wife.'

That made Pryce blink and glance at Keturah. 'What?' He felt the ear again. The tension began to dissipate as he and Uvoren broke eye contact. 'Marks of combat. They don't matter to a female.'

'They do if you want a human female.'

Roper thought that was masterful from Keturah. Her assault on Pryce's pride had distracted him enough to prevent what would almost certainly have been a fight between two of the foremost warriors of the realm. At any rate, Pryce no longer seemed intent on winding up Uvoren, his hand flying frequently to his savaged ear and a frown on his face.

After a month on campaign rations, the boar was exquisite. The legionaries had been dreaming of this feast throughout the endless mornings of boiled oats and evenings of boiled salt-mutton and, now that it had arrived, they attacked the food with savage pleasure. The mood was jubilant, with the enormous tension that had been built on their bold march to the Great Gate dissipated without bloodshed.

As they had approached, Roper had no way of knowing whether his ruse had worked. He simply had to trust that his concealed soldiers had made it inside undetected and stayed loyal to him. He had been waiting for the clunk that would have meant the fire-throwers had been unleashed, and for the jet of sticky-fire that would have consumed the entire Sacred Guard.

It was the berserkers who took fullest advantage of the

feast. Ordinarily, they lived entirely separate lives from the rest of society. Nobody outside their ranks was quite sure what their training involved, that flipped them from normal men into individuals of disproportionate and frightening violence. Some were spat out of the training system, apparently unsuited to be berserkers. Some died. Those who survived the ordeal were tattooed with the angel of madness and carried around phials of vinegar that had been infused with the fly agaric mushroom. Once it was consumed, usually directly before battle, they entered a state of hyper-arousal where they were unable to tell friend from foe and attacked on almost any stimulus. Use of this vinegar was governed by strict rules and they were forbidden to take it when they would be fighting in close proximity with their comrades. That evening, deprived of their phials, they still hurled brute fists at one another at the slightest provocation. Roper saw one pair just headbutting again and again until one of them fell aside feebly, trying to crawl on hands and knees but finally sprawling onto his face. Another stood and punched the victor in the stomach, unleashing such a spectacular jet of vomit that it was enough to douse a candle and make even a berserker back off.

'They don't seem to be selected for their intelligence,' Roper observed to Gray.

'Quite the contrary, lord,' Gray agreed.

Beside Roper, Keturah seemed to be regretting breaking the tension between Uvoren and her cousin and had started harrying the captain. She needled him over his age, over Pryce's third Prize of Valour, over having been so content to wait in the fortress while other men did the fighting, over his use of a war hammer which she declared 'clumsy'.

'And what would a woman know of this matter?' growled Uvoren.

'Oh I'm sorry, Captain, have I upset you? I do apologise, but there's really no need to take it so seriously. I am, as you say, a woman. All I know is what other warriors have told me. Admittedly, there is something close to a consensus that your use of Marrow-Hunter is impractical and nothing more than a move to enhance your own prestige, but I'm sure you have your own reasons.'

Uvoren was looking more and more displeased, but even he would not retaliate physically. He tried to fire some shots back at her, but they fell well wide of the mark and were merely greeted by her delighted laugh.

Uvoren stood abruptly and raised his horn. 'Warriors!' he called. 'Warriors!' The men were too drunk for silence to fall swiftly and, even once most of the noise had died away, there was still the loud squabbling of several berserkers. They were hushed impatiently by those around them. They resisted until Roper thumped a fist on the High Table, when at last they fell still.

Uvoren inclined his head in Roper's direction by way of thanks. 'I thank my Lord Roper for a magnificent feast!' There was a roar directed at the Black Lord who acknowledged it with a graceful nod before training his attention back to Uvoren, keen to hear what he was to say. 'Truly, it is a worthy celebration of a campaign which we may proudly add to our noble history. To have dug such a hole,' more good-natured laughter, 'and extracted himself quite so masterfully is testament to this young lord. He has spirit.' And Uvoren raised his horn to Roper, taking a drink. There was something in that last sentence that made Roper think they were the first words that Uvoren had truly meant. It was a salute to a worthy adversary. 'But as he has already said, this campaign was three battles and not two. On our first, we did retreat from the battlefield for the first time in centuries. Our full strength was not enough to defeat the Sutherners and we left many, many brave legionaries in those flood waters. For the first time, the Sutherners tasted blood. They sensed our weakness and it emboldened them.

'My warriors, I don't know about you, but that fills me with rage. How dare those low creatures presume they could defeat the Black Legions! Don't they know who they're dealing with?' There was a cheer and shouts of anger from those who had lost friends. Roper had started frowning. 'Warriors, we must exact revenge! We must make it clear once and for all who the dominant force in Albion is. Why, we have not raided beyond our borders since the days of Rokkvi! The Sutherner grows bold and we cower in the north!'

Uvoren was forced to wait while the fervent noise subsided.

'You all know me. You know what I and my war hammer have done. By my hand, King Offa lies in his long grave!' He held up his left arm and indicated the silver ring that gleamed there, his Prize of Valour. He indicated his right. 'I took Lundenceaster!'

By this time the men were baying. Roper glanced at Gray and saw for the first time base contempt in the guardsman's face as he watched Uvoren speak. 'You *do* hate him,' prodded Roper with a reproachful smile. Gray glanced at Roper and composed his face.

Uvoren was still speaking: 'I would do anything for this country. And if it needed it of me, I would remain in the Hindrunn and guard it through Catastrophe itself. Even whilst heroes like Pryce and Leon win prizes in glorious open combat, I am content so long as I serve my country. But I still thirst for Suthern blood. Marrow-Hunter is restless and I would do anything for my chance against our enemy. You know me, and I am not done yet. I implore you all, may I have the honour to lead you against the Sutherners?'

'Yes!' roared the hall.

'Will you come south with me and do as honour demands?'

'Yes!'

'Remember this moment! If you ever need a warrior to take you south and to war; remember that Uvoren Ymerson still lives. Remember that Marrow-Hunter always thirsts for Suthern blood! And if my Lord Roper forgets, remind him!' He grinned and winked at the crowd who burst into applause.

Someone started thumping a table and the rest of the hall took it up, chanting 'U-vor-en! U-vor-en!'

Now Roper stood and Gray, Pryce and Tekoa began to bay for silence, which came after a time. 'How fortunate we are to live in an age of such warriors,' said Roper, more calmly than Uvoren. He nodded at the captain. 'Peers; rest assured your swords will not lie idle for long. Winter is upon us and the campaign season has ended. Rest, eat well, grow close with your family and, by spring, we shall be ready to march again.' He raised his horn and there was polite applause. Uvoren sank into his chair a fraction after Roper, beaming as though reluctant to surrender their attention.

Chatter broke out again and Gray leaned close to Roper. 'Well done, my lord. It was important that you spoke. But this is the problem with keeping Uvoren close. As he said, he's not done yet.'

'What else can we do? It seems we have kept the civil war in the shadows for now, but he is too powerful for us to truly disgrace him, or to have him killed. It would fracture the country. We must just wait until his threat subsides.'

'I'm not sure he'll give you that chance,' said Gray, watching Uvoren who had turned back to Keturah with a broad smile and begun speaking to her again. She was looking coldly back at him.

Roper's head was hazy and he was too happy for Uvoren's words to bother him unduly. There were no more speeches and the warriors feasted until the sun began to slip through the small windows of the Honour Hall, when they stumbled back to their homes. Roper and Keturah had been last to leave, she leading him from the hall by his hand, picking their way over the wreckage and out to the Central Keep.

14
The Barn

'Wooden houses,' said the big man. 'Bloody hell, they're beautiful.'

There was nothing especially beautiful about the buildings: a stooped cluster of raggedly thatched timber and daub homesteads, barely discernible through the thick flakes of floating snow. Such poor villages studded every part of Suthdal, but were not to be found north of the Abus, hence their beauty in the eyes of Bellamus's men.

The upstart could hear cheers and cries of relief echo from his small column as the men behind sighted the village too. He turned and saw that some of them had dropped to their knees at the sight, arms held up at the sky in thanksgiving. Many others were embracing with tears in their eyes or raising fists into the air. He turned away, neither responding to the comment from Stepan, nor the reaction at his back.

The village looked like failure to him.

He had gone north beneath a fluttering stream of banners, leading a column clanking and tinkling with the panoply of war and truly believing his would be the invasion which at last subdued their ancient enemy. As far as he knew, his filthy, truncated band were the only remnant of that proud force to have stumbled back across the Abus. There were barely four hundred of them: all reeking, bearded and dressed in tatters. The others lay still beside the sea.

'God grant this dung heap an inn,' said Stepan. The towering, amber-bearded knight had been Bellamus's most constant companion on the retreat from Githru, though the two had never spoken before the calamitous battle. He combined easy company with the stoic endurance Bellamus valued so highly in his soldiers. Unusually for a noble, he also seemed more than happy to take instructions from Bellamus, who had come to rely very much on his humour and consistency.

'There'll be an inn,' replied Bellamus. 'Which will prove too much for some of our men.'

'I'll keep them in line, Captain,' said Stepan. He glanced sidelong at Bellamus, his gaze lingering thoughtfully on the upstart's face. 'You haven't failed, you know,' he said. 'When you've been over there,' he cast a thick finger into the swirling snow on their left, through which lay the far bank of the Abus, 'just coming back is an achievement.'

'I haven't failed,' agreed Bellamus. 'Not until I've given up.'

'Good lord, sir!' Stepan burst out laughing. 'You're planning to go back?'

Bellamus smiled. 'You and I together, Stepan. Why do you think we're heading south?'

'Our terrible experiences in the north?'

'To ask the king for more men,' said Bellamus, patiently.

Stepan just laughed again. 'Find me an inn, then try putting that to me again.'

The village did indeed have an inn: barely larger than the surrounding houses and with a roof so laden with thatch that it extended down to the level of Bellamus's shoulders. An enclosure in front contained a dozen chickens sorting through the snow, which they shared with three enormous, shaven-headed men. These last sat with their backs against the inn, a clay jug between them emitting potent fumes which Bellamus could smell from ten yards away.

'Good afternoon, friends!' boomed Stepan, striding forward and holding out a spade-like hand to the nearest of the three. The sitting man made no attempt to take it, merely looking up at the knight. Stepan withdrew his hand abruptly. The eyes raised to meet him were yellow: a shocking, feverish sulphur which caused the knight to take a pace back. Before he could say any more, Bellamus laid a hand on his arm. The upstart gestured down at the men's ankles, which were bonded with dark iron shackles. All three of them had now looked up: three pairs of yellow eyes scouring Bellamus. All were extraordinarily lean, with twisted, knuckle-busted hands protruding from beneath the mangy furs that collected snow about their shoulders.

Bellamus nodded at the three of them and held the door of the inn open, gesturing Stepan inside and stooping beneath the thatch to follow him into the pungent gloom. He had to crouch low to accommodate the huge war-blade strapped to his back: one of his few possessions to survive the retreat.

'What was that?' said Stepan, as soon as they were inside, the rest of their men crowding the door behind them.

'Anakim–Sutherner hybrids,' said Bellamus. Stepan fell still and Bellamus gestured him onward. 'They're common slaves here, but dangerous. Be careful with them.'

'Dangerous?' Stepan enquired, looking around the tavern's interior. 'This place smells like parsnip.'

A dozen villagers already sat drinking inside, the convivial atmosphere falling away as they turned to stare at the new arrivals. Though it was clear from the villagers' stature and expressive faces that all were Sutherners, they looked nearly as alien as the hybrids outside. All of them, men and women alike, had the sides and backs of their heads shaven; with the hair above twisted into long, brightly coloured braids. The braids were embedded with brass, copper, iron and stone ornaments, and rattled as each head swung round to examine Bellamus and Stepan. The villagers also wore vibrant necklaces and bracelets, similar in style to their hair-braids, which contrasted starkly with their dark, threadbare clothes.

One of the braided men stood at the sight of them, a skin of drink clutched at his side, and strode over to Bellamus. 'Welcome, strangers,' he said. 'You look like you've been travelling for a spell. Is it ale brings you here? Or food?'

There was a short pause while Bellamus tried to decipher the thick accent. The words the innkeeper had used for 'travelling' and 'spell' had both been Anakim, to Bellamus's ears. 'Both,' he said eventually. 'But food first.' He produced a golden bracelet from his pocket and dangled it in front of the innkeeper. 'Is there enough food in this village to feed four hundred? And five barrels of ale.'

The innkeeper blinked at the gold before him. 'I might have to get some supplies from a neighbouring town. No more than an hour away.'

'We've waited a long time,' said Bellamus, giving him a tight smile. 'We can wait a little longer.'

The innkeeper rubbed his hands together and glanced at the vagabonds clustered in the door behind Bellamus. 'I've got the ale now, if you want it.'

Bellamus hesitated, turning to look at the beaming soldiers behind. 'That would be welcome,' he said, eventually.

The innkeeper recruited help from the table of regulars and departed to fetch the ale.

Bellamus went outside to address the column, informing them that the first thirty could enter to share the inn's warmth for an hour, and the rest would have to wait their turn. 'No trouble, boys,' he warned them, and then gestured at the shackled hybrids sitting in the snow. 'Don't bother the slaves. Or the chickens.' Back inside, Stepan had saved a seat for him at one of the long tables.

'Why are they dressed like that?' demanded the knight as Bellamus settled next to him. He was glaring suspiciously at the heavily adorned villagers, who were staring back with equal curiosity.

'These people use Anakim words in everyday language,' said Bellamus. 'They tell each other translated Anakim poetry, and are separated from their enemy by no more than a narrow strip of water. They are more alike than they would care to admit, so they separate themselves with their appearance. The Anakim wear no adornment and do not value colour. People dress like this throughout northern Suthdal to create a barrier more resilient than the Abus. Stop staring, my friend,' he added.

Stepan looked back towards Bellamus. 'And what did you mean those boys outside are "hybrids"?'

'Cross-breeds of Anakim and Sutherner,' said Bellamus. 'The yellow eyes always turn up in the hybrids. They're livestock here, as common as oxen. The villagers breed them, and enslave them with chains and drink.'

Stepan raised an eyebrow. 'Dangerous, eh? I'd be dangerous too if they kept me in drink and chains.'

Bellamus smiled briefly. 'Not dangerous like them, I think,' he said. 'They're dangerous because they're unpredictable. Hybrids are unstable.'

A braided woman arrived, placing leather beakers of ale down in front of Bellamus and Stepan. 'What?' asked Stepan bluntly, reaching for a cup. 'Ah! That's not bad.'

Bellamus left his own cup where it was. 'The Anakim can be reasoned with,' he said. 'Our kind can be reasoned with. For whatever reason, hybrids cannot. Whatever decision-making process they go through, I've yet to meet anyone who can interpret it. The most unexpected stimulus can evoke a feral rage.'

'Strange though, to keep a farm animal capable of plotting against you,' said Stepan.

'Using them is an art,' acknowledged Bellamus. 'For these folk, one that pays off more often than not. If you can't work out how they'll react, then don't give them anything to react to. Keep their conditions exactly the same and, through trial and error, you can find a way to keep them calm.'

Stepan stared into his cup for a while. 'And they breed them?'

'Captured female Anakim are used to breed,' said Bellamus. 'But the hybrids are infertile, and most don't survive childhood.' Bellamus had intended to leave it there, but Stepan had lowered his heavy brow. He went on. 'The males have trouble breathing and, more often than not, both sexes succumb to unbearable headaches.' He shrugged at Stepan's expression. 'It is their way, up here. They have a hard life, and the hatred of the Anakim runs deeper than we can possibly appreciate.'

'It sounds a grim practice,' declared Stepan. 'I wouldn't breed a horse that had only an evens chance of making it to adulthood.'

'Neither would I,' said Bellamus, 'but the Anakim are not just an animal they feel neutral towards.' He gestured over at the table of villagers, who were now sitting in silence as they continued to stare at the new arrivals. 'All of these people will have lost family to them. Their lands are terrorised every year and their livelihoods destroyed.' Bellamus was silent for a moment. 'Though I'd like to think otherwise, I cannot say with any certainty that if I were in their position, I wouldn't do the same. Many of them must be good folk, and yet I have heard no common objections to the use of hybrid slaves. If I were born in this village, what are the chances that I'd be the only one of them to renounce the practice?'

'You could say the same to excuse any behaviour,' said Stepan, mildly.

'You're right,' said Bellamus. 'Were I here in a different capacity, perhaps I would judge them for it. But my role in these lands is as a student, as it is north of the Abus. If I judge them, I might miss something important.' Bellamus reached for his cup at last and toasted Stepan. 'But let us not talk of this, my friend. To survival.'

'To ale,' replied Stepan, knocking his cup against Bellamus's.

They drank together, and before long the lucky few who had made it inside the inn had been supplied with drink as well. All manner of receptacles, from livestock bowls to boots, were filled with foaming ale and passed to those outside, where they were received with muffled cheers that came through the walls and made Bellamus smile. The warmth of a grubby hearth that crackled at one end of the room began to reach through his damp clothes and even Bellamus found himself on the verge of a glowing euphoria. For now, survival would do. His score with the Black Kingdom could wait.

Next to him, Stepan was on the defensive from good-natured jeers. It transpired that in their first victorious battle on the flood plain, he had swung his sword so wildly against the Black Cavalry that he had cut into the neck of his own horse, fatally wounding it. 'Hilarious, hilarious,' said Stepan, as the men around him rested their heads on their arms, tears of mirth leaking down their cheeks. 'I promise, it's easier than you're imagining,' he said. 'And it saved me! I hit the horse and it toppled, ducking me beneath a blade being swung at my head.'

The innkeeper returned, still clutching his skin of drink, and declared the food was on its way from a larger village nearby. Bellamus thanked him, which seemed to be taken as an invitation to join their company. The innkeeper, whose braids were slowly ceding ground to his forehead, and whose cheeks would have drooped below his jaw had the folds of skin there not been equally pendulous, squeezed in between Stepan and the man next to him. 'It's been a long while since we had travellers here,' he said. 'And I wasn't expecting anyone this winter, let alone four hundred of you. Where are you from, lord?' Several Anakim words had once again squeezed their way into his speech, and Bellamus could see Stepan frowning thunderously as he tried to decipher what the innkeeper was saying.

Bellamus smiled wryly. 'I'm not a lord, friend. We've come from beyond the Abus.'

The innkeeper nodded as though he was not surprised. 'I thought you must have.' He leaned close to Bellamus. 'There was an army, headed up there recently, under that Earl William. You haven't heard tell what happened to it?'

Stepan sat up straight, clearly delighted to have understood this last sentence, and spread his arms as wide as the crowded table would permit. 'You're looking at it!' he boomed.

The innkeeper nodded again, as though he had suspected this too. 'I'm only surprised there's as many of you as this,' he said. 'Not many who go beyond the river end up coming back.'

'Well, not many are led by our captain, here,' said Stepan, gesturing at Bellamus. The knight's ears seemed to have attuned themselves to the innkeeper's dialect.

'You must have a tale or two from past the river,' said the innkeeper, looking shrewdly at Bellamus. 'How is it that you survived out of the thousands who crossed into the Black Kingdom? Last I heard, your victory was assured. Earl William had banished them in battle and had the devils on the run.'

'That's almost true,' said Bellamus. He glanced at Stepan. 'It is a fine tale, but my noble friend is a better storyteller than I.'

Stepan needed no second invitation. 'A mighty tale it is, my friend,' he said, wrapping an arm around the innkeeper's shoulders. 'As you say, things did not seem to be going so badly until the battle beside the sea. After that, we discovered the Anakim to be the warriors of legend that we'd been promised.'

'I could've told you that,' said the innkeeper.

'I don't doubt you could have,' said Stepan, winking at Bellamus. 'A ferocious clash it was,' continued the knight, now placing his palms flat against the table. 'A tight pass beside the thrashing ocean, the warriors obliterating each other as wave upon rock. Our side fought bravely and we were holding them. I even dared believe we might exhaust and break them with our superior numbers. But there was no room for manoeuvre and their flanks were secured by the sea on one side, and the mountains on the other. Our captain, here,' Stepan gestured at Bellamus once more, 'came up with a plan. We'd built a couple of hundred crude boats to help us forage from the sea, and Bellamus bade us fill them. "We'll row around behind their lines," says he, "and crush them on two sides!" We got a good few thousand into the boats, the best we could find. Bellamus took his own soldiers: a frightening bunch, a fair few of whom sit listening to me now.' Stepan raised a hand to indicate the assembled company. 'Not nobly born, but experienced Anakim-slayers from across Erebos, loyal only to the captain. We supplemented these with as many knights as we could find, and loaded up the boats.

'It was a good plan and we put to sea, hopeful of seizing a second victory against our old enemy. We began to row and were nearly behind the Anakim lines when we saw a change occur in the battle on the shore. Our line was collapsing, right in the centre. We understood later, when we heard that our brave leader, Lord Northwic, had been cut down by some Anakim hero.' Stepan paused here and raised his cup. 'I will not simply let his name pass by. To Lord Northwic. May God take him!'

This was met with a murmur and a toast. Bellamus held his own cup aloft a moment longer than everyone else, bowing his head as he took a drink.

Stepan went on: 'Without Lord Northwic's stout presence, and with the elite troops of the enemy on the rampage, our centre lost its nerve. All this we heard later, but it looked inexplicable to those of us riding the sea. As we watched, the whole line crumbled and was overthrown by pursuing Anakim. Bobbing among the waves, we saw nothing less than a massacre unfold. Every man who turned to run was cut down and Bellamus, here, said the battle was done, and ordered us to row south.

'Through luck, we alone had survived. The Anakim cannot swim, and had no boats, and so we were safe as long as we stayed at sea.' Stepan sobered a little, the theatrical glint extinguished from his eye. 'We floated south, Bellamus commanding us to throw our armour into the sea. "Strength of arms is no longer our primary weapon," he told us, "and if you fall overboard you will drown. Keep your weapons only." We did as he bade, saving only a few breastplates to bail out our leaking tubs.

'We wanted to put ashore: dark clouds were gathering on the horizon and a strong wind was building up the swell, but bands of Anakim scouts were shadowing us along the coast. We had to wait until night fell, but fortune was against us that day, and an early winter storm overtook our company. Lightning cracked the sky and the waves towered above us. Every last boat was overturned and we had to swim for land. Though it was not far, thousands drowned in the rough waters, unable to see the shore beyond the waves which crowded them. Every last one of us would have joined them if our armour had not already been committed to the sea, and we crawled back onto the shores of the Black Kingdom. Quite rightly, our captain left us barely a moment to rest on the sands. We were too exposed on the open beach, and though it was the last thing any of us wanted, the flash of lightning lit our path as we retreated into the dark forests.

'They are places of unnatural evil, my friend. The trees are like mighty towers, and make those here in Suthdal look like shrubs. Little light makes it from the canopy above to the floor below, which is haunted by nightmare creatures and strange phantoms. The howl of the wolf is a constant ringing in your ears. Woven eyes and carved hands have turned the trees into barbaric totems of worship. Suthdal seems like a pleasant dream to me now. Over there, beyond the river, is reality.'

Bellamus, listening intently, smiled as he heard that. He felt a small thrill run through his fingers, and picked up his beaker again to hide the wistful expression he could not keep from his face.

Stepan had not noticed. 'We struggled south under cover of dark, Bellamus here navigating through such subtleties as the growing places of lichen and the stars glimpsed through the canopy on rare cloudless nights. Among the trees we lost dozens more: poor souls who fell victim to bears and wolves, or simply disappeared on the march, never to be seen again. I pity any man wandering alone among those forests.

'We were the lucky few. By avoiding campfires and through no small fortune, we were not discovered by the enemy. We made it to the northern bank of the Abus, and there waited three days for a moonless night, constructing rafts so we could steal across that cursed water and back into the south. That was last night, and I can barely believe that here we now sit, in a comfortable inn with good ale.' Stepan raised his cup to Bellamus. 'One more toast, I think. To our captain. Every one of us owes him their life.' The table toasted Bellamus lustily, Bellamus raising his cup with them.

'I've always said they couldn't swim,' said the innkeeper. 'Demons cannot stand water. We've lost a good few of the hybrids to the river.'

'Probably because their legs were shackled together,' said Stepan, from behind his cup.

The braided innkeeper did not seem to have heard. Instead, Bellamus could see his eyes lingering on the inhuman sword he had strapped to his back. The innkeeper opened his mouth to comment on it, but was intercepted by a roar from outside. Bellamus was on his feet at once and running for the door, the innkeeper staggering up behind him and Stepan on their heels. Bellamus burst into the blue snow glare outside, to find one of his men, a red-haired knight, flat on his back just beyond the door. One of the hybrids, spitting and swearing, was in the process of being dragged off the red-headed man's chest by another three soldiers. The snow all about was adulterated with specks of blood and clumps of cream feathers, drifting gently over the spoilt surface. Another soldier with hollowed cheeks stood nearby, a limp chicken hanging from each hand.

The hybrid, still swearing and at one point managing to flatten one of the soldiers with an open-palmed slap, was forced onto his back and pinned there, just as the innkeeper ducked beneath the thatch, a heavy cudgel in his hands. 'Your men have killed my chickens!' he shouted at once, pointing accusingly at the hollow-cheeked man who stood clutching the birds. There was uproar as the men replied to the accusation, most appealing to Bellamus.

Bellamus held up a hand, and his men fell quiet at once. Only the hybrid continued moving, struggling to free himself of the soldiers who held him down, until the innkeeper cracked him on the head with the cudgel. It seemed to stun the wretch, whose movements became gentle and uncoordinated.

'What happened?' asked Bellamus, looking at the red-headed knight who had been pinned by the hybrid, and was now getting to his feet.

'The monster threw itself on me!' he said. 'We left them alone, like you said, Master.'

'He attacked you because you were killing my chickens!' accused the innkeeper.

Bellamus looked at the man clutching the two ruined birds. 'Is this true?'

The man said nothing. He blinked twice, and then laid the chickens down in the snow.

'I'm sorry, Master,' said the other, again.

'Those weren't your chickens!' said the innkeeper, hefting his cudgel. He began to advance on the red-headed man, but Bellamus held up a hand to still him.

'You will not lay a hand on one of my men,' he said. 'Every

last one is under my protection.' Before the innkeeper could reply, Bellamus went on. 'But nor do I expect any man of mine to steal.'

'I'm sorry, Master,' said the man who had been holding the chickens.

'Too late,' said Bellamus. 'Arrest them.' He gestured to the watching throng, and half a dozen men stepped forward to take hold of the thieves, who offered no resistance. Bellamus stooped down and unlaced his tattered boots, throwing the laces to his men and instructing them to bind the prisoners' hands. He turned to the innkeeper. 'You have a barn behind the inn. Will it hang a couple of ropes?'

The watching crowd stirred suddenly, and from the corner of his eye, Bellamus detected a spastic jerk from the prisoners. The innkeeper looked hesitant. 'It will,' he said warily.

'To the barn,' said Bellamus, waving the prisoners onward.

'Sir?' shouted one of them, his voice quaking. A murmur went up from the crowd and Bellamus repeated his gesture. 'Move.'

The stupefied prisoners were pushed forward by their captors, the crowd following behind in a daze.

The barn behind the inn was low, but still the brace between two crucks would serve as a gallows, being some twelve feet off the ground. There was a coil of manky rope beside the door which Bellamus took and cut in half. The prisoners, hands now tied behind their backs, had been pushed immediately inside the building and the crowd was gathering in the doorway, more men hurrying to join the back as word spread of what was happening. Stepan pushed his way to the front to stand with Bellamus.

An echoing, cavernous silence filled the barn as the upstart knotted the end of each piece of rope and flung it over one of the wooden braces, securing the free end on a lower brace. With his own hands, Bellamus then tied two nooses. The sight of them at last spurred the prisoners into speech.

'What?'

'Master!'

'They were just chickens, Master, we can pay!'

Bellamus paid no attention, fetching a pair of milking stools and positioning one beneath each noose. 'On the stools,' he said. Haltingly, the prisoners were moved forward, each one of them jerking like a cogwheel as they were lifted into place. Bellamus had an idea that his men were only obeying so willingly because they thought that he would not go through with the threatened punishment.

As the red-headed man felt the noose tighten around his neck, tears spilt suddenly into his beard. 'I'm sorry, Master,' he moaned. 'We were hungry. I'm sorry!' he called at the innkeeper, who stirred, taking a pace forward.

'I will take compensation for the chickens,' said the innkeeper, as Stepan, by Bellamus's side, tightened the second noose around the man with the hollowed cheeks. 'There is no need to hang your men.'

'You will have compensation,' said Bellamus. 'But my men have not just stolen from you. They have disobeyed me.'

Someone from the crowd objected that one of the prisoners was a knight, and Bellamus had no authority to hang him. Abruptly, Bellamus turned on the muttering crowd. 'Listen to me now!' be bellowed. 'Not a single one of you would have made it back south of the Abus if you weren't with me. Do you deny it?'

Silence.

'You are now my men, until I've discharged you. If we steal from these communities, word will travel ahead of us that a band of marauding villains approaches, and we will be hounded until those scraps of us who made it back from the Black Kingdom are finished too. I do not give instructions lightly. I do not give them without reason. These fools,' and he pointed a resolute finger at the crying men, standing yet upon their stools and held in place by the ropes around their necks, 'have disobeyed me. Trust in me: I will secure you food and warmth on our road back to Lundenceaster. But if any of you steals, there will be no exceptions.' He turned back to the prisoners, who began to beg once more.

'It was a mistake, Master!'

'Please! We marched with you like all the rest. We fought for you! I'll serve you, my lord!'

Bellamus shrugged. 'You have proven to me that you can't maintain your discipline. If you can't maintain your discipline, you cannot be trusted to fight in the north. You are no good to me.'

And he kicked away the first stool.

The red-headed prisoner toppled, and then was caught by the rope. He bounced a little, swinging as his feet kicked wildly.

Bellamus advanced to the second stool. The hollow-cheeked prisoner gave a scream and shook his head frantically, eyes bulging white and mad as Bellamus hacked at the stool with his foot. The second man dropped.

Bellamus turned away, back towards the aghast crowd.

'Out. All of you.' He stood before them, his eyes cold and feet rooted to the floor. There was a tense silence, broken only by the squeaking of the rope against the wooden brace above as the two men flailed and kicked behind him. After a long while, some at the back of the crowd turned away. Others followed in drips until, finally, it was just three men left, particular friends of the prisoners, staring confrontationally at Bellamus.

'Off you go, brother,' said Stepan, shoving one of them away. The man sprang back towards Stepan, assessed his towering form, and then retreated, his eyes swivelling between the knight and the upstart. The innkeeper followed in silence, leaving Bellamus, Stepan and the suspended prisoners behind them.

'This is my fault,' said Bellamus. 'I knew we should have waited for ale after the food.'

'It was they who made the mistake,' said Stepan, simply.

'And I doubt there'll be any more mistakes this evening. Even so,' he turned around to face the prisoners, 'you could cut these two down now and they'd probably recover.' He glanced sidelong at Bellamus, who still had his back to the scene. 'I'm not sure the men will like this.'

'My men have seen worse. They would never have disobeyed an order of mine. The new ones needed to learn.' Bellamus scuffed a line through the hay that covered the floor. 'And they're angry now; that will fade with time, but the lesson won't.' He stared bitterly through the open door of the barn, still facing away from the men swinging at his back. Their coarse flailing had ceased, and been replaced by a rattling tremor. 'What a bloody shame,' he murmured. 'Let's get out of here as soon as we can. I need to see the king.'

15
The Giant Elk

Roper awoke cold in the narrow bed in his quarters. The rough woollen blankets had mostly slipped off him and he pulled them back about his shoulders, eliciting a groan from Keturah next to him. She shuffled irritably to release some blanket for him and draped an arm over his chest, burying her face in the horsehair pillow.

My head, thought Roper, screwing up his eyes and grimacing. He could not remember leaving the Honour Hall yesterday, nor much beyond Uvoren's speech. There had been wrestling; that he remembered. He had an idea that Uvoren had won it, and that Pryce had been surly because he had lost his second bout.

He glanced at the window above his table a little too quickly and the room span. He shut his eyes and after a time, when the world seemed to have stabilised, opened them again. Snow was resting lightly against the panes of glass and more appeared to be drifting down past the window. No wonder he was cold. *I must find a bigger bed,* he thought absently to himself.

It was too cold for inactivity. He dragged himself out from beneath Keturah and stood to another wave of nausea. Gingerly, he pulled on a cotton tunic which he belted before extracting a heavy wolfskin cloak from an iron-clad chest and draping it about his shoulders. Opening the door to his quarters, he found one of the young women serving her time as a maid and requested wood, water and dried dandelion roots. These were brought, with the woman insisting on building the fire for him in the hearth at the back of the room, pulling across a small lever with a clunk to allow air to flow up through the grate and feed the flames. She set a blackened copper pot above it to heat the water before bowing herself out of the room. Roper waited for the water to come to the boil before tipping the dried, ground roots into the tumbling liquid and leaving it to brew.

While he waited, he stared out of the window. He could not see far as the air was thick with snowflakes but the roofs all around him were six inches deep in the crystals. The snow covered the leaded gutters, collected on the sills and leading of windows and rested gently on the slate tiles. The fire was roaring now and its warmth was beginning to permeate the room, along with the burnt-earth smell of the simmering roots.

Roper stood and poured some of the steaming brew into a birch cup, straining out the roots with a cotton gauze. He sipped it and sat back at his table, staring glassy-eyed out of the window. 'Yes please,' mumbled Keturah into the pillow and Roper stood again to supply her with her own cup. She sat up, black hair hanging loose over her shoulders as she sipped the brew and wrinkled her nose. Roper stared at her, half in fascination, half through sheer vacancy.

'Who won the wrestling last night?' he asked at last.

'That berserker, Tarben,' she said. 'It was him and Uvoren for the final bout. Uvoren nearly had him, but he was too strong.' Vague images flickered through Roper's head of an individual so vast and hairy that it had assumed the form of a bear in his memory. Keturah's eyes raked his face and she offered him a smile of such sweetness that he returned it entirely involuntarily. 'So what will you do about him?' She meant Uvoren.

'I don't know,' said Roper. 'I can't kill him. Not yet. It would split the country and his allies would declare war. And he has strong sons who would take up his mantle. Last night I thought to bring him close and offer peace, but I see now that he came too near to ruling this land to be happy with his old role. I think I shall have to finish him, one way or another.'

'Yes, you will. He's certainly not going to have a quiet winter.'

'He'll spend it plotting against me,' Roper agreed.

It was a holiday. There was always a holiday after a feast. They could do what they wished for the rest of the day.

Keturah glanced out of the window. 'Poor devils,' she said, taking another sip of the brew.

'Who?'

'Half our country,' she said. 'So many of the eastern subjects lost their homes and granaries to the Suthern invasion. You know better than I, you've seen it. But they must be facing a bleak winter.'

Roper paused. 'You're right. Those without homes and stores can't possibly survive. We can't just leave them.'

'We can,' said Keturah. 'Your father would have. As would mine, if he ruled. The Black Lord is not supposed to bother himself with concerns like that. He is a warrior ruler.'

'And because I withdrew on the battlefield, they suffered. We should take them into the fortress.' Since the return of Roper's army, the refugees had begun to herd in front of the Hindrunn walls once more.

'Do you think that wise?' asked Keturah. 'Thousands of refugees cramming the streets?'

Roper was silent again. Keturah's warrior-ruler comment fitted with everything he knew about his role, but he had also been taught that the Black Lord was the ultimate servant of the realm. And if the realm suffered, surely he should allay that suffering.

But at that moment, there came a knock at the door. 'Come!'

A Vidarr legionary entered and Roper recognised him as

the one who had waited on Tekoa when they had first met. Harald, he thought he was called. 'My lord? Tekoa is leading a party hunting in the Trawden forests and said it would be his great honour if you would join him.'

'That wasn't how he phrased the invitation.'

'No, lord,' admitted Harald with a bemused smile. 'It wasn't.'

The Trawden forests were where the delicious boar from the night before had been hunted. They were part of the Vidarr estate and jealously guarded. The trees teemed with deer, aurochs and, it was claimed, giant elk with each antler as long as a man is tall. Tekoa was a keen huntsman and an invitation to the Trawden forests was worth having, even to the Black Lord.

Roper licked his lips and looked solemnly at Keturah. 'Go,' she said shortly.

'Are you coming?'

'Almighty, no.'

It was a holiday, after all.

For Roper, the day was breathless. He had hunted before, of course. In the berjasti, the young apprentices were encouraged to hunt and fish to supplement their meagre rations. But it was for food alone. They would tickle trout from the brooks that ran nearby, floating their fingers beneath the bellies of the fish that sheltered beneath the overhanging bank and drawing them into their chests before throwing them, flapping, onto the bank. They would snare hares and grouse, dispatching them gleefully and roasting them right away. They would create little gallows for squirrels, wait for badgers to emerge at dusk and pin the snarling beasts to the earth with a spear. Little fishing lines with hawthorn or antler hooks would be set out, or else used by hand to tempt crayfish out from the shelter of the stream bed. Roper had set deadfalls that had caught foxes (tough, dry, not pleasant), hedgehogs (fatty and delicious) and marten (like fox, but a slightly sweeter taste). Sometimes, if they had time, they might find the tracks of a deer and pursue it with bow and arrow, but that was rare and successes were rarer still.

Hunting with Tekoa was nothing like this. They were after the giant elk, with the legate declaring that nothing else would do. 'The stags aren't in the best state this time of year. We should have more of a challenge if we went after them in the summer, but they still have their antlers. Look for the antlers, lord.' They rode out on coursers; a trio of enormous shaggy hounds loping behind them. It was Tekoa and Roper, a couple of Vidarr legionaries including Harald for assistance, and two other senior officers of the country whose names Roper did not know. They carried lances, and each had a bow and a quiver of arrows strapped on to their horse.

The snow was still falling, thick and soft, and the forests were a delight to Roper. They were somewhere between broadleaf and evergreen, with the skeletons of immense beech and oak standing out stark against the snow, their leaves long gone. Alongside them grew pine, spruce, larch and cedar, needles gleaming dark green beneath a white dusting. Thrushes squeaked and chirruped from the branches as they passed, cantering up a winding path, the noise of their horses' hooves softened by the snow. They had barely entered the forest when they stopped at Roper's insistence to listen. In the distance, a pack of wolves was howling, voices weaving in and out of one another as they claimed ownership over this stretch of the wild. It made Roper think of his time in the haskoli. Often in the evenings, they had been able to hear the wolves in the surrounding mountains. They rode on, Roper already beaming to himself.

'Quiet now,' said Tekoa after a time. 'And look there!' Roper followed his finger and saw something immense and dark stealing away into the undergrowth. He waited some more but all was still. It was gone, leaving just the memory of its grace and power. 'Bear,' said Tekoa. They were still for a time longer, though it was not coming back.

They would usually have taken a huntsman with them,

but Tekoa insisted on directing everything himself. They rode on, passing trees with the familiar Anakim handprint carved into their trunk; people who had been to this place before them and declared their love for it. Each would be invested with memories, but only to the right people. Even beneath the snow, this forest smelt damp and intoxicating. Roper could feel eyes watching their progress as they moved through and he observed Tekoa, for whom this place must crawl with memories, stare distractedly at a particular spot every now and then, a slight smile coming to his face. No Sutherner would understand what this wilderness meant to the Anakim or their attachment to the land through which they moved. They were *maskunn*: exposed.

After an hour's riding, they reached an immense central clearing. 'Watch here; the elk come for the fresh shoots and shrubs that grow out of the shade of the trees. When we see one, we will drive it against the trees. We'll trap it somewhere where its antlers are too big for it to fit through. Then we have a fight.'

They skirted the edge of the clearing. A herd of aurochs grazed in the centre, their breath rising as a mist above them. The hounds whined at the sight of the beasts, but Tekoa snapped his fingers and they went silent. Nothing but giant elk would do.

They followed the treeline for another half-hour, keeping a constant eye on the direction of the wind, which had begun to swirl somewhat. Finally, Tekoa spotted something up ahead. He was more than a hundred and sixty, but his eyes were keen and he held out a hand that stopped both Roper and the hounds. 'There,' he whispered. Against the snow up ahead was a powerful silhouette. Roper caught a flash of cream as the mighty beast raised its head and swivelled it towards them, its great antlers swinging round to face them. 'We've been spotted,' said Tekoa with a grin. He whistled and the hounds streaked out before them, rushing silently for the elk. 'After them!'

The hunt was on.

The elk, still three hundred yards distant, turned and lunged away, building up speed until it was in full flight. It was extraordinarily powerful, but not as swift as the hounds who pursued it. Before long, they were upon the mighty beast which swung its head this way and that on the run, trying to catch a hound with its colossal bone branches. The hounds were equal to that and danced out of its range, shepherding it towards the trees. 'I've got the finest dogs in the country,' called Tekoa over his shoulder. They certainly impressed Roper.

Dogs and elk disappeared into the trees, still sufficiently broadly spaced for the beast to slip its antlers through the gap. Tekoa tore after it, followed closely by the rest of the party, lances at the ready.

And suddenly, the moment was upon them.

There was a mighty crack from up ahead and Roper saw that the elk had misjudged a gap between two trees and stopped dead, antlers quivering. Snow showered from the shaken trees before it. The elk shook its head and swung round, antlers sweeping too fast for one of the hounds which was caught in the chest and hurled backwards with a yelp. It crashed against a tree and dropped to the ground where it stirred weakly. Tekoa roared his fury and spurred faster. The other two hounds had been driven back by the swinging antlers and the elk was trying to break away, dodging past Tekoa's horse and charging, head lowered, straight for Roper behind. 'It's yours, Roper!'

Roper had a fleeting impression of an antlered head hurtling towards him, of the rippling of the elk's muscles as it charged. He stood in his stirrups, lance swaying before him, and lunged.

He had no idea what happened. One moment he was on his stirrups, aiming for the base of the neck that thundered with raging blood, the next he was crashing to the floor, his horse collapsing on top of him. Head ringing, face half-buried in the snow, Roper could see the hounds streak past him again and then the hooves of Tekoa's horse.

He stirred groggily, laying his hands on the horse and trying to push it off him. It was not moving. He looked at it. 'My god.' It was dead, neck evidently broken by one of the elk's antlers. Tekoa was roaring somewhere behind him, the hounds were barking and the elk was bellowing in rage. Roper extracted himself from beneath the horse. Bits of him felt jarred and it took several stunned moments to judge that he was unharmed.

Just then, Tekoa came trotting back. 'All right, my lord?' he asked, beaming. 'That was brave of you.'

'Was it?'

'Sort of. Very unwise really, but you got it.'

'I did?'

'You did. It's down, come see.' Tekoa glanced at Roper's broken courser. 'Ah.'

They followed the sounds of celebrating hounds, Roper on foot and Tekoa mounted, back almost to the clearing again. There, just before the end of the treeline, the beast lay fallen on its side, head twisted extravagantly to accommodate the huge antlers. The rest of the party was gathered around it, still mounted and chattering raucously. At the sight of Roper, there came hearty laughter and an ironic cheer. 'Impressive commitment, lord!'

'I'll wager that was a surprise.'

The elk was truly enormous. At the shoulder it had stood taller than Roper and its antlers must have spanned fourteen feet from tip to tip. The hounds were lapping greedily at the puddle of blood accumulating beneath its neck.

'That's where you hit it,' said Tekoa, swinging himself out of the saddle and pointing at the base of the neck. 'Not quite deep enough, but you slowed it. I had to lance the heart from behind. Tricky manoeuvre,' he said modestly.

'Masterful strike, sir.'

'Be quiet, Harald.'

They left the elk to the attentions of Harald and the other legionary. They would prepare the carcass for transportation and then drag it behind the horses to a cart waiting on the road to the forest. It could then be taken back to the Hindrunn.

The rest of them would ride back ahead, with Roper borrowing a horse and the other two officers riding together. One was the Councillor for Trade, the other was the Treasurer. Both were Vidarr and appeared to be old friends of Tekoa. They were middle-aged. Only after one hundred years' service in a legion were subjects of the Black Kingdom permitted to apply for an administrative or councillor's position. There they would specialise in their chosen field and then be able to advise the Black Lord, or oversee the enacting of his will across the country. It was an option seldom exercised by regular legionaries, who preferred the status of the battlefield, but they were desirable posts for members of the auxiliary legions.

Roper fell to talking with them on the road back. The snow fell more and more thickly, though fortunately there was no wind. He hunched into his wolfskin cloak as they followed a line of withies that marked the way back to the Hindrunn. The paving of the road had long since been assimilated into the whiteness around it.

He realised almost at once that these were the men who would be able to tell him what he could do for the eastern refugees. However, broaching the topic with them, they seemed surprised that he was bothering himself with it.

'The eastern subjects are tough, my lord. This is not the first time their homes have been torched by invading Sutherners.'

'It is the first time in centuries that the torching has been so comprehensive,' suggested Roper.

'Even less could we afford to help,' said the Treasurer. 'Your father was a strong ruler, lord, but strong rulers are often as much a problem for their own nation as they are for other nations.'

'A great ruler,' agreed the Councillor for Trade. 'But he would not be counselled. He rejected a trade agreement with the Hanoverians over a perceived slight, cancelled existing agreements with the Yawlish and the Svear and refused to accept emissaries from Iberia whilst they supplied ships to the Sutherners. He also stopped raiding south, to avoid antagonising the Sutherners, so that source of revenue dried up.'

'As a consequence, lord, our coffers are almost empty. It was only the timely intervention of the Vidarr that enabled us to mount your campaign without forgoing the legionaries' Out-of-Fortress Pay,' finished the Treasurer.

Roper glanced at Tekoa, for this was the first he had heard of Vidarr fiscal intervention, but Tekoa was fiddling with a pair of gloves and did not appear to be taking any notice of the conversation.

'So what would it cost us to relieve the suffering of the eastern subjects?'

Both officers let out a breath, the plump Treasurer shifting uncomfortably in his saddle.

'In depth, my lord? Surely you don't need to concern yourself with such numbers . . .'

'Itemise it,' insisted Roper.

'Well . . . Out-of-Fortress Pay for the legions. To meaningfully impact the crisis in the east, lord, we'd need all nine auxiliary legions. Then building materials; it would take weeks of work and therefore more Out-of-Fortress Pay for the auxiliaries to source the wood, the stone, the withies . . . The water-reed will not be ready yet, so we'd need heather from the north, which is more money. Then, of course, the grain. We don't have anything like the reserves to supply to the eastern subjects; in fact, we're looking at a shortfall for the Hindrunn itself. So we'd need to buy grain from the continent . . .'

'Iberia might trade with us, though relations are frosty,' put in the Councillor for Trade. 'Bavaria and Alemannia are not out of the question, but neither has a coastline, so getting the grain here will be expensive. In short, lord, we have no hope of affording anything meaningful. The country is broke. If you want to do anything for the eastern subjects, you will need to rely on charity. And if you want your reign to amount to anything meaningful, we will need to find an additional source of income.'

'Such as invading Suthdal,' said Roper.

The Treasurer and Councillor for Trade exchanged a glance. 'Exactly, my lord.'

'But it isn't just the finances,' said Tekoa, who appeared to have been listening after all. 'Vengeance, Lord Roper. As you said in your speech, the Sutherners must be taught to fear us once more. They cannot invade us with impunity and expect to return to safe, intact homes. Vengeance.'

16
One by One

Tekoa sent the giant elk's head, boiled and scraped to spotless white bone, to Roper complete with its immense antlers. Roper had it mounted on a beech board as a memento of the day and displayed it above the hearth in his quarters. In the following days, Keturah twice awoke screaming at the alien form of the giant moonlit skull now hovering opposite their bed.

Roper had taken his father's skull, stripped equally bare of flesh, into the Trawden forests during the hunt and, riding off quietly for a moment, buried it between the roots of a vast oak, carefully pointing the empty eye-sockets east before filling in the hole. Above it, he whittled a rough outline of his own hand. That would be good enough for Kynortas, he thought.

The snow had proved as relentless as the rain that preceded it. Some of the subjects, those who cared less about the light and feeling the moving air, attempted to raise the temperature inside their houses by putting up in their window-frames translucent shutters of greased paper with a wooden lattice behind. Most preferred open exposure to the elements, and left their houses with the feel of a hand-made cave. The ground around the Hindrunn grew smooth and white, the branches of the forests began to bow and crack under their fresh burden and the legions sweated to keep the streets clear. That was where most of the refugees were now to be found. Roper had decided to open the gates and admit them to the Hindrunn's granite embrace. In hours, the cobbled streets were thronged with the homeless, who gratefully sheltered from the winds that swirled beyond the Outer Wall. But their life was still far from comfortable, with most sheltering beneath crude tents made from old cloaks and begging food from passers-by.

Roper thought about the Treasurer's words and the only solution he could think of to help the refugees further was to appeal to the generosity of the people. To that end, he appeared on the steps of the Central Keep to make a plea to the subjects of the fortress to receive the refugees into their homes. They responded in magnificent fashion. Just three days after his speech, Roper had made the ride from Central Keep to Great Gate and seen not a single tent. The homeless had been taken into the citadel's sturdy stone houses, hosted by a generous populace.

To attempt to refill their coffers, Roper sent the Councillor for Trade, whose name was Thorri, to Hanover to attempt to barter a fresh agreement. He was not expected back for another three weeks, during which time Uvoren was a constant thorn in Roper's side. He was seeking to rebuild his influence and began with constant displays of altruism towards the subjects.

When the snows had fallen, the great warrior had received a cheer for stopping his horse by a mother and her freezing child and, dragging the two into the saddle behind him, had taken them into the Honour Hall with him for a fine meal at his own expense. He took no one into his home, but received the adulation of the crowds nonetheless for the freshly baked rye bread that his household produced each evening and handed out to those on the street. He even donated a small herd of the pigs bred on his northern estate to the people of the Hindrunn, having them slaughtered before the Central Keep where cups of their hot blood were passed out to those who came to watch. Lothbrok legionaries roasted the carcasses all day in the open air, so that by the time night fell and more snow was descending on the citadel, a great crowd had gathered to be rewarded with bread pockets of glistening pork.

But that did not seem to be the limit of Uvoren's machinations. Roper had also come to wonder whether the captain was having him followed. Twice now, when he and Keturah had been at the mess, he had caught the eye of a couple of legionaries whom he had spotted regularly during the day, always nearby, always seemingly otherwise engaged. They had looked away swiftly, and Roper wondered what their intentions could be. Were they just reporting his movements? Or were they waiting for a moment when he was unguarded? Roper did not know, but his was a devious enemy and, as he and Keturah had discussed, the captain must be destroyed soon.

Roper and Keturah had taken to walking the streets of the Hindrunn together in the mornings. Keturah had lived in the citadel for longer than Roper, having returned to her father's household at the age of sixteen when she had completed her time in the freyi (the female equivalent of the haskoli). She seemed to know everybody, while Roper had only recently returned from an extended apprenticeship with the Pendeen Legion and thus had an extremely small pool of acquaintances. He thought it might do his support base good if he could build on Keturah's already impressive networks, and so they toured the streets together. When Keturah was not introducing him to someone or other, Roper liked to bounce ideas off her, with the level of her derision a good yardstick for whether he might be able to propose it at one of the afternoon councils. The standard for rejection was if she laughed raucously at the suggestion. If she only tutted impatiently, then Roper considered it a good idea.

'They're following us again,' said Roper one morning. Keturah did not react for a moment, then she glanced behind her and gave an apathetic wave at the two legionaries who were once again stalking them. They did a devoted impression of being in deep conversation with one another, as though Roper's affairs were none of their business, but they had been spotted nearby once too often for that to be convincing. Roper wondered again what they had planned, though he did not greatly care any more. 'They're not very subtle, are they?'

'Uvoren needs better spies,' said Keturah scornfully. 'Perhaps we should just spend the entire day walking in circles around the outer track and amuse ourselves by seeing when they give up.' Roper deliberately did not laugh: he had an idea that it might be bad for Keturah to have too much positive feedback. She smiled and threaded her arm through one of his. 'You don't have to laugh, Husband. I know you find me funny.'

'You're quite funny,' said Roper. 'I don't want you collapsing under the weight of your own head.'

That was exactly Keturah's kind of joke and she shrieked uncontrollably, startling two women picking crab apples from a nearby garden. Keturah waved her free hand apologetically at them.

'Perhaps I should hold a march through the streets?' pondered Roper. 'In celebration of the victory over the Sutherners. We missed it on our return because everyone thought we were going to sack the fortress.'

Keturah had recovered herself. She frowned at him with total bafflement. 'Why?'

Roper did not bother to develop the half-formed idea. She would just laugh at him. He changed the subject. 'Do you smell that?' There was something bitter on the air.

Keturah sniffed. 'It's like the homecoming smell.' She meant the scent of herbs being crushed underfoot which accompanied the legions on their return to the Hindrunn.

'Harsher than that,' said Roper. There was something threatening about it. It grew thicker as they walked until it was completely overpowering. After a time they could even see it: a gentle grey blurring that hung over the streets. 'Smoke,' said Roper. 'They're burning herbs.' The street was deserted. Each of the glassless windows had its shutters sealed and, unusually, all doors were shut.

'Look there,' said Keturah. She was pointing at one of the doorways. Beneath the lintel, something dark was turning in a gentle breeze. It was a tuft of hay. As Roper looked, the streets seemed to him like a gallows. Dozens of doorways had hay hanging above them. Roper and Keturah both fell still, looking across the deserted road.

'A tuft of hay,' said Roper. 'Isn't that the sign of plague?'

'There hasn't been a serious plague here for fifty years,' said Keturah, dubiously.

'Away from here,' said Roper. They turned back from the deserted street, filled with the smoke of herbs burnt against the poisonous smells that led to infection, and hurried for the Central Keep. The direct route was blocked: more tufts of hay, more of that bitter smoke. They skirted around it, following the smell of fresh air and the more familiar trace of charcoal smoke. The two legionaries who had been following them had gone: perhaps they had recognised the scent earlier.

'Why now?' said Roper, once they were back within the reassuring form of the Central Keep. 'If it's been fifty years since a plague, why has it reappeared now?' They took the stairs up to Roper's quarters to find Helmec, as usual, standing guard over the door, and Tekoa standing with him. The legate turned to look at Roper, scowling as he caught sight of him.

'I don't believe I've ever been allied to such a bloody fool.' He jerked his head inside Roper's quarters, indicating they should speak within.

Roper did not immediately respond to the accusation,

instead producing a key which he fitted to the lock. 'You're well, Helmec?'

'So well, lord,' said Helmec, with indecent cheer.

Roper, Tekoa and Keturah entered, leaving Helmec on guard outside. Within, Tekoa unfastened his cloak and threw it over Roper's bed, before proceeding to the hearth and opening the vent to reignite the charcoal in the grate. 'Make yourself at home,' said Roper.

Tekoa turned back to him. 'You are a god-damned fool. A vapid, half-baked clod.'

'Why?'

'There is a plague.'

'Which is my fault?'

'*Of course* it's your fault!' exploded Tekoa. 'You think you can just shelter thousands of people in squalor in the streets without building additional latrines or ensuring they are properly fed or warmed? You think you can then cram those people into the homes of others without infection? Plague is not a coincidence. It is not a bloody curse from the Almighty or something cooked up by the whims of chance. We have not had one for fifty years because we have not had a damned oaf like you in charge. This is what happens to rulers with a soft heart. Calamity!'

Roper blinked. He was caught off-guard by the tirade, and could think of no obvious defence of his actions. 'Your counsel would have been welcome long before this stage, Tekoa,' he said, at last.

'The extent of your lunacy has only just been made clear to me,' snarled Tekoa. 'You must move fast, or this fortress will be overwhelmed. We cannot lose a large proportion of our population to plague. There must be a quarantine, and it must be now.'

'What do you propose?' Roper took a seat, staring at the legate who was prowling back and forth across the room. Keturah had fallen quiet and sat on the bed beside her father's cloak.

'Legionaries to cordon off any street where there is infection: nobody goes in or out.'

'The people won't like it,' said Roper. Tekoa looked incredulous at that. He stalked to the chair in which Roper sat and leaned close.

'Have you not yet understood, my Lord Roper?' he said, lips barely moving. 'When the piles of suppurating corpses are building up in the streets, and you cannot breathe without wanting to retch through the smell of burning flesh, and whole neighbourhoods vanish within days, you see how much the people like that.'

Instinctively, Roper wanted to resist Tekoa's advice for the tone that it carried; for the fact that he had been made to feel like a child again. But the decision was as blatant as sand in the mouth. Within an hour, legionaries had flooded from their barracks to seal off all streets with a tuft of hay hanging in a doorway. The soldiers built barricades of barrels and carts and tables which they guarded night and day, turning away the subjects within who were at first furious, but before long had retreated silently into their own homes. The legionaries supplied them with food which they traded over the barricades to those caged inside; taking care to soak any metal they received in return in bowls of vinegar to destroy the contagion. They also provided bundles of wood, propped against the inside of the barricades for use after dark had fallen. And everywhere, pervading the fortress like the cold, was that bitter smoke, emanating from braziers of herbs.

Each day, the death toll grew faster. With every new dawn, corpses were ejected into the street by their families, beginning a pile in the middle of the cobbles that grew until dusk brought a measure of peace to the fortress. Then those bundles of wood were collected from the barricades and propped over the bodies, which were arranged with their heads facing towards the east. Nobody but the families would touch the corpses, so they were burned in the streets in which they had died. The pyres smoked and smouldered terribly, so that what remained by morning was often a pile of white ash, surrounded by charred limbs. They were scraped together and reserved for that evening's conflagration.

Roper watched the fires. He stood with the legionaries after dark, watching from behind the barricades as flames stuttered into life further down the street and trying not to retch at the sense of responsibility that made his limbs weak. He was not sure that the connection between his treatment of the refugees and the plague was yet widely known, but he had an enemy who would ensure that it soon was.

Despite the swift implementation of Tekoa's suggestions, the plague was already widespread. It had developed on the snow-laden streets among the refugees and spread before it had become clear what they were dealing with. Beneath locked doors, between sealed shutters: through the air or carried by the flesh or in the water or however it spread, it suffused the fortress. There was little worse that Roper could have unleashed upon his subjects. Plague was a Suthern problem: very rarely one which bothered the Anakim with their superior standards of hygiene.

The streets were deserted but for the legionaries who guarded the barricades. The markets fell quiet. The smoke invaded everything. The sickly orange glow of the corpse-fires crept beneath Roper's shutters at night. One morning, after a night of dead-calm, Roper awoke to discover the smoke from the corpses hanging as a fog above the fortress, so that only the rooftops were visible from his elevated quarters.

He toured abandoned streets, being sure he was seen sharing in the danger of the legionaries. He felt like a fool and was desperate to regain the trust of the subjects. He had seen the way Earl William and Lord Northwic had interacted with their knightly bodyguards. He had heard from his father, from Tekoa, from Gray, how King Osbert, ruling from his throne in the south, treated his subjects. They were his servants. At all times they stood in deference to him: bowing, flattering and fearful of his vengeance. King Osbert led through fear. Tekoa did the same; people were motivated by his displeasure. That was not a leader, as Roper knew it. A leader shares in every bit of danger that he asks from his subjects. A leader commands from the front, not the back. He shows how it should be done and invites others to take their turn with him. A leader's character is the most potent weapon in his arsenal: sharpened and honed to be the presence his followers need at all times. That was the Black Lord, as Roper saw the role. That was the difference between him and a king.

So he spent his days at the snowy barricades with his legionaries, doing no more than sharing in their danger and discomfort; showing he was not scared. Keturah, against Tekoa's fervent insistence, accompanied him. More than accompanied him. Barred by the quarantine from stepping foot inside the affected streets, she went to the markets at the request of those within the barricade, trading for whatever it was they particularly desired. In this capacity, she encountered Gray's wife Sigrid, who, as well as trading for the subjects caged by the quarantine, sat at one end of the barricade and told stories to those on the other side.

It was Roper's first encounter with Sigrid, who was quite as stupefyingly beautiful as Keturah had described; almost intimidatingly so, with silver-blonde hair, high cheekbones and eyes of such a light grey that Roper found them abrasive to look into. She did not have Keturah's sense of humour, coming across as kind but unyielding. 'So here's the lord who had my husband travel home in a wagon of corpses,' she had said when first meeting Roper, referring to the deception that had gained him entry to the Hindrunn.

'That is I, my lady,' confirmed Roper, taking her hand and not quite clear whether she was joking.

She surveyed him for a moment. 'Well, I shall forgive you for your bravery in coming onto the streets now, lord.' She looked stern until she greeted Keturah, the two embracing like old friends. 'Thank you for the last time, my love. How are you?'

'Thriving, blooming, inspired, fulfilled,' said Keturah carelessly, making Sigrid laugh.

Keturah had begun to follow Sigrid's example and sat on the barricade with her; the two women taking it in turns to tell stories. Keturah told those which came from the Hindrunn and which her mother had taught her when she was younger. There were many of the chivalric deeds of legendary warriors; a few on the race of dwarves which emerged after dark to snatch newborn children from their cribs and the subsequent adventure in recovering the infants; some which told of talking livestock, mistreated by their owners who then spilt their secrets about the fortress.

Sigrid was a child of the east, like the refugees, and the stories she had learned as a girl featured mighty storms after which nothing was the same; strange happenings when watching over the flock at night, or miraculous objects discovered in the iron mines.

Though the subjects who gathered around to listen covered their mouths and noses with cloth, Roper still felt his heart quicken at the sight of them. It seemed that the two women were inviting infection, but he knew how Keturah would react if he suggested she should take more care.

Roper left Keturah with Sigrid and toured further afield. His presence was most valuable spread as far as possible; theirs in individual communities.

'I'm running out of stories for them,' said Keturah one evening to Sigrid. It was dusk, the sun now hidden behind the walls of the Hindrunn but an orange glow capping the snow-blanketed roofs around them. The two women were walking to a new barricade, one they had visited two days before, to attempt to lift the spirits of the people trapped there. The snow squeaked beneath their feet and was hard going for Keturah, who felt weary.

'Then maybe you should go home and get some rest,' said Sigrid. 'The plague will still be here tomorrow.'

'I can rest later, I must just think up another story.'

'You look tired,' said Sigrid, examining her. 'These people will die with or without our help. All we're doing now is leaving behind an example to those who survive.'

'You're staying though,' said Keturah.

Sigrid gave her distinctive smile: a slight narrowing of the eyes and twitching of the corners of her mouth. 'I'm older than you. I've had my children, I've done my service, and I have had enough happiness for several lifetimes. You've got all that to come.'

Keturah raised her eyebrows at that. 'Worthy of a Sacred Guardsman.'

Sigrid smiled. 'Who would want to be a Sacred Guardsman? It seems an unrewarding lifestyle to me: all the prestige in the world can't make up for a complete lack of freedom.'

'It offers recognition,' said Keturah, who quietly coveted the extreme prestige of those three hundred men.

'That's true,' said Sigrid thoughtfully. 'Though what sort of person spends their life seeking recognition? A discontented one, I suggest.'

Keturah frowned. 'Why does Gray do it?'

'The same reason we are doing this,' said Sigrid. 'To serve.'

A left turn and they reached the street they had been aiming for. But it was deserted. Four cold legionaries stood guard over the barricade, with nobody in sight beyond them.

'Those bodies were there when we last were,' said Sigrid.

Keturah looked and saw six corpses, lying facing east, further down the street. They lay on a bed of ash, where several fires had evidently already burned themselves out and which had melted a crater in the snow. She turned to the guards at the end of the barricade. 'There's been much death in this street?'

'A lot,' confirmed the legionary. 'Dozens have died here.'

'When did you last see a subject alive inside the barricade?'

'Two days ago. A man laid out the final body and then went back inside.'

There was a long pause. Sigrid was gazing out over the

street. 'Then they're all dead,' she said. 'There's no one left to burn those bodies.'

'An entire community destroyed,' said Keturah. She stared across the empty street, mouth slightly open. The buildings were covered in a fine layer of ash, picked up by the wind and dusted over the stone. A few of the wooden shutters were half-open, like the eyes of the dead. There was nothing left to animate the houses.

Sigrid gave Keturah her steady look. 'Then there's nothing else we can do for them. Come, my love.' She held out her hand, which the younger woman took. 'There're people all over this fortress who could do with our help.'

On the other side of the fortress, Roper too was touring the streets, accompanied once again by the resolute presence of Helmec. He glanced at his companion, who did not seem to have been fazed by the devastation unfolding around them and still walked with a bounce in his step. 'What are you doing here, Helmec? Go home, I'm in no danger. Uvoren's best hope at the moment is that the plague strikes me down. I can't lose you to disease as well. Go home.'

'I'm going nowhere, lord.'

'It's an order, Helmec. Off you go.'

'I have no interest in your orders, lord,' said Helmec cheerfully.

Roper tutted. 'I have no idea how a legionary as mad as you has survived so long.'

'I too am mystified, lord.'

Roper was touched by Helmec's loyalty, but did not want the responsibility of yet another soul hanging over him. Particularly one so close. Generosity had begun to make him feel guilty; that he had erred so badly and still enjoyed such dedication from those closest to him.

The corpse-smoke hung on his shoulders like a leaden cloak, making him sick to his heart. He had never really considered why he wanted to rule. He supposed, looking back, that it was because this was what his life had been spent in preparation for, and that because the alternative was death. Uvoren had tried to take it away from him and so, naturally, he had fought back. He had not really thought beyond that. But now, standing at night behind a barricade as he watched frail, trembling figures further down the street ignite the piled bodies of their loved ones; or saw the pale faces of his soldiers, who were being forced to contain their friends and acquaintances with a silent, inglorious threat; he was not sure he had wanted it after all. He did not admit this to anyone. Not Keturah. Not Gray. Certainly not Tekoa. There was only one way through this: onwards. Confessing that he was not sure he was the man for this job was a certain way to have others agree.

Perhaps they already did. Returning to his quarters that evening, Keturah had seemed uncharacteristically muted and irritable, just as she had the day before. Was she appalled by what she was seeing and by the man she had married? That thought was better than the alternative. That the invisible infection had crossed the air and infiltrated her lungs.

There was no one so expert at making Roper regret his actions as Uvoren, who challenged him in every council meeting. 'You tried to provide justice for the displaced eastern subjects. How can they have justice now that they are being ripped apart by plague? Where is the justice for those already within the fortress, who were unaffected by war and now find their loved ones dying in a manner more ignoble and drawn out than that offered by any battlefield? Ever the man for the grand gesture, Roper, but you didn't think this one through, did you?'

No, was the honest answer. Roper, overwhelmed for an instant, stood furiously to say they were doing all they could; that they had acted as fast as they were able, and found even his allies shaking their heads at his excuses. One by one, Uvoren's closest supporters stood to make speeches against Roper, driving home the catastrophe as hard as they were able.

First came the dark, brooding form of Baldwin Dufgurson, the Legion Tribune. 'Let us examine the facts of this boy's rule so far. He has overseen the first ever retreat of a full call-up from the battlefield.' There came a rumbling jeer. 'And now, just months later, we have our first serious plague in fifty years as a direct consequence of his policies. The streets are choked with bodies! Our people cannot move for the soldiers that force them to stay and die! Is this what leadership in the Black Kingdom has come to?' He sat to raucous affirmation. The Vidarr and Jormunrekur, perhaps complacent, perhaps tired of this struggle, were quiet and it was the Lothbroks who dominated.

Next up, Vinjar: the rotund, sarcastic Councillor for Agriculture. 'Tell me! One of you please, tell me, where is the Hindrunn's food to come from? It is not merely that we live in such squalid, cramped conditions. This fortress is overpopulated and now that the eastern subjects have been accommodated so generously at Lord Roper's invitation, the supplies from the east have dried up. At a time when our population is largest and most in need of nourishment, Lord Roper has helped ensure that we have as little food as possible. You must tell us all, Lord Roper, what was going through your mind!' This speech seemed to be particularly effective and was met with a mighty jeer.

Roper tried to stand and retort but was drowned out by the Lothbroks, who were instead insisting that Randolph, legate of the Blackstone Legion, who had also stood, should be heard instead. Randolph was one of the swaggering rogues who did so well under Uvoren, a handsome warrior with a reputation for recklessness. He was grinning as Roper was forced to give way to him under pressure from the table. 'It becomes yet harder, Lord Roper, to see where your true talents in fact lie.' The Lothbroks hooted. 'While we've got you here, perhaps you could respond to the rumours that you only secured a Suthern withdrawal by promising them a large part of the east, and that this is why you keep the eastern subjects from returning to their homes: because you have set the land aside for Suthern cultivation?' There was a low boo and a hiss and even Uvoren broke into a laugh at this accusation, winking at Randolph across the table. The legate was grinning. He went on, extracting laughs from the council with his ever more absurd descriptions of Roper. Among other honorifics, he referred to him as 'calamity's happy servant' and 'the high priest of total catastrophe'. By the end, some of the table had tears of mirth in their eyes and Roper himself had almost been driven to unwilling laughter.

More of Uvoren's supporters stood and added their weight to Roper's humiliation, though Roper noticed that the captain's two sons, Unndor and Urthr, were not among them. Both sat scowling at the table but neither stood to speak, nor lent their voices to the Lothbrok cause. Had Uvoren's casual choice of bride for the two proud men alienated them? It was common knowledge that neither was satisfied with the arrangement, particularly as the houses they had brought close, Nadoddur and Oris, were of almost unrivalled irrelevance.

Under cover of another hoot aimed at Roper, Gray leaned across the table. 'He must be broken soon, lord,' he muttered. A disquieting episode lay heavily on both their minds. On their way to the council that day, Uvoren had fallen into line with them. The sight of the Black Lord had initiated no more than stares and resentful silences. Then the crowds had spotted Uvoren, which had prompted a great and raucous cheer. The captain had acknowledged it sternly, raising a leather-gloved fist in response to the crowds as he rode past. The glory of Roper's last campaign had faded quickly and while the subjects of the Hindrunn had not sent their eastern cousins back onto the streets, Roper was once again staggeringly unpopular. He was such a recent lord that people only seemed to remember the last thing he had done and base their opinion of him on that.

'How?' Roper asked, watching Uvoren laugh uproariously

at another blow aimed at his leadership. *I thought I had you.* He had the energy of an ocean current.

Across the polished bog-oak, Roper could see the Chief Historian looking at him wearily. *The greatest warriors can fight in any theatre.*

'Smother him,' said Gray. 'You always need to be a step ahead. Make sure he has not a single opportunity to further advance his reputation. He has earned himself huge adulation simply through minor gestures about the fortress. Remove his opportunities for glory. Send him on a fool's errand to keep him occupied, while you raid south. Dismantle his allies, one by one, until he has nothing left. And then, when he is small enough, force him to disgrace himself.'

One by one.

The room seemed to change before Roper. He was no longer sitting at the Stone Throne. His perspective, duller, less vivid but somehow starker, had shifted to one of the obscure chairs about the table. The other occupants had changed too, and the light had faded.

On his right sat Pryce, but not as Roper now knew him. He was a colder, more intimidating version.

Opposite Pryce was the Sacred Guardsman, Hartvig Uxison. He sat next to Baldwin, the Legion Tribune. Next to him were Unndor and Urthr Uvorenson; they were opposite their father. Vinjar, the Councillor for Agriculture, Legate Randolph, and Legate Tore. Also sitting at the table were two darker figures: Gosta and Asger. They did not matter any more.

Roper remembered every one of them. They had all sat at this table months before, in the aftermath of the battle that had claimed his father. Two were dead. One now served him. He would have the rest.

He leaned over to Gray, eyes always on Uvoren, who was regarding the two of them with something like triumph. 'My understanding is that Vigtyr the Quick would be able to break Uvoren's allies for us.'

Gray went very still. 'Who told you that?'

'Tekoa. You know him?'

'I know him,' said Gray. Vigtyr was widely regarded as the finest swordsman in the country but had never been appointed to the Sacred Guard because of questions over his temperament. Instead he was a lictor in Ramnea's Own Legion. He had a dark reputation. It was said that Vigtyr cultivated favours as other men bred sheep. This in turn gave this wildly ambitious man influence and access to a great array of secrets. It was he whom Roper had seen observing the Sacred Guard so intently at prayer whilst they were on campaign.

'I cannot make your decisions for you, lord. All I can say is no matter how desperate I was, nor how terrible Uvoren seemed, I would never turn to Vigtyr. Do you hear me? Using a man like that would cost you more than you can possibly afford.'

'If you say so, but how else am I to break Uvoren's allies?'

'We wait for them to make a mistake.'

Roper was not sure that he had that long. Gray seemed sincere, so he put Vigtyr from his mind for the moment. He weathered the storm of the council, standing at the end to address the concerns raised in more measured tones, though he could tell he had not been convincing and left the chamber with the feeling that this situation was escalating beyond his control. He bade goodbye to Gray and disappeared into the obscurity of one of the spiral staircases that surrounded the Central Keep, rising several storeys to his quarters.

Roper wished that he lived in a different building from that which housed the Chamber of State, so that he could feel that the day's business was left in the keep and his time in his quarters was his own. Or that, just for a few moments, he could feel cool air that moved rather than the still, stifling atmosphere that surrounded him now. He might ask Keturah whether she wanted to walk on top of the battlements, above the smoke. If she were well.

He found her sitting in a chair by the fire in their quarters, some half-finished weaving lying unattended in her lap and that impatient expression on her face. The giant elk's skull looked down over her. She glanced up as he entered and he was shocked to see how tired she looked. Her face was lined, her eyes were terribly bloodshot and her lips even had a bluish hue to them. He stopped at the sight of her. 'Are you all right, Wife?'

'Of course,' she said. She was evidently trying to keep her voice light; Roper knew that she would not admit her troubles to him. 'How was the council?'

Roper pulled a chair up next to her and sat down. 'Bad. Uvoren had hold of the plague like a rabid dog; he wouldn't let go.'

She appraised him. 'Not the most unjustified criticism you've received.'

'Certainly more justified than the claims that I beat the Sutherners by trading half the east in exchange for their withdrawal.'

Keturah laughed briefly. 'Is that still being said? If that were the case, why do they now think the Sutherners have retreated behind the Abus?'

'They say they couldn't weather the winter in a hostile land, so have gone south for now and have my word that they can return in the spring.' He thought that might amuse Keturah, but she had turned towards the fire and was staring into it vacantly. 'That's Randolph's theory anyway.'

'I like Randolph,' she said, still staring at the fire.

'I like him too. It's a shame he's on the wrong side.'

'It is. But if you kill the others, perhaps you can let him live to show your mercy.'

'Maybe. I want to kill Baldwin first. Then Vinjar. Pompous prick.'

Keturah shuddered a little. 'Baldwin sucks the energy from a room. He's so dark.'

Roper thought for a moment. 'What about Unndor and Urthr? They look so disillusioned with their father that perhaps they would join us?'

Keturah tried to smile but merely looked strained. 'I don't think so. They're still family. They may hate their father but, if anyone else threatens him, you can be sure they'll be at his side.' She tucked a stray lock of hair behind her ear. The gesture was so familiar to Roper but it seemed odd. It took him a moment to register why.

'Keturah,' he said.

She glanced at him and saw that he was looking down at her left hand. She followed his gaze and saw that the lock of hair had come away in her fingers: a thick, dark ribbon that rested on the back of her hand. She jerked it up to her eyes, staring at it with disbelief. Then she dropped it in her lap and both hands flew up to her head. Both came away with thick locks of hair between the fingers, leaving behind embarrassed, fallow skin.

Keturah stared at the hair in her hands for a moment. Then she let it fall to the floor. She looked up at Roper. His mouth was open and his face like chalk.

'What's happening to me?' Her voice was like the whistle as air escapes a bellows and, for the first time ever, Roper heard a tremor of fear. They shared a look, and Roper could do no more than shake his head. Her gaze brightened as he watched. A single tear heaved over her eyelid and splashed onto her cheek and Roper stood abruptly, taking her still outstretched hands.

'Come, Wife. Lie down and I'll fetch the physician.' She stood, allowing her weaving to fall to the floor, and let him guide her to the bed. He kissed her cheek before turning away. She would not want him to see her cry.

17

Vengeance Is for Now

The physician, the same wire-haired man who had stripped Kynortas's skull for Roper, examined Keturah where she lay on the bed. Roper left him to it, waiting outside to spare his wife her dignity. When the physician emerged, Roper, sitting with his back against the corridor wall outside, stood abruptly. 'Is it the plague?'

'This isn't plague, my lord,' said the physician. 'Plague does not make you lose your hair.'

'What is it, then?'

'Your wife has been poisoned, lord.'

Roper stared, silent for a moment. 'Poisoned?'

'I believe so. She says she has felt unwell for two days: we must begin purging her at once if we are to have any hope of avoiding permanent damage.'

'As fast as you can,' said Roper. The physician bowed and hurried away to fetch his tonics. Roper hesitated. Those men of Uvoren's whom he had thought were following him: could they have been for Keturah instead? He opened the latch to his quarters and found Keturah inside, lying on the bed. She looked at him, eyes quite dry now, and offered him the shattered fragments of a smile.

'I think this may be my fault, Husband.'

Roper sat down on the bed. 'Why would you think that?'

'This is Uvoren's doing. He wants to kill me so that I have time to know I'm dying.'

'Why?'

'Just a conversation we had while you were on campaign. Then I goaded him at the feast when you were back because I thought we'd won.' She rolled her eyes wearily. 'Stupid.'

'No,' said Roper. 'Nobody can allow that man to act as powerful as he thinks he is. And you couldn't have known this would happen. We had no idea he was so underhanded.'

She smiled, looking ironically amused again, and placed a hand on his knee. 'What about when he tried to assassinate you?'

'Even that is in a different league to poisoning your enemy's wife.'

'So what are you going to do about it?' asked Keturah, who seemed to be trying to enjoy herself.

'First, we're going to get you well,' said Roper. 'Then we're going to see how much vengeance Uvoren has brought down upon himself.'

'Getting well is going to involve a lot of purging, isn't it?'

'That's what the physician says.'

'I propose we don't bother, then.'

Roper did not laugh. 'No joking, Wife. I imagine you won't look back at the next few days with much fondness, but at least it may give you the chance to look back on them from some distance. And I don't think Uvoren intended to kill you.'

'Why?'

'I will tell you when you're well.' He took her hand from his knee and kissed it. He no longer sensed that tremor of fear in her voice.

The physician re-entered, holding an armful of phials. 'Distillation of foxglove first,' said the physician. 'This will make you vomit for a few hours. Then wood sorrel solution, and as much water as you can drink.'

Roper stood. 'I'm going to send word to your father. I'll be back for the performance.' He departed to find Helmec, requesting that he pass news of what had happened on to Tekoa, and then returned to assist Keturah.

The foxglove solution, once administered, took effect in moments. The physician had supplied two pails for Keturah to vomit into and at first Roper held her hair out of the way as she purged the poison. After a time that ceased to be necessary: Keturah's hair was coming away in great tufts with the force of her exertion. He could tell she had noticed but was pretending that she had not. Roper looked up at the physician in dismay.

'She will lose all her hair, lord,' he said quietly. 'Maybe the outer half of her eyebrows as well.'

'Will it grow back?'

The physician shook his head. 'That depends on how much of the poison she is able to expel. Everything depends on that. She has already lost feeling in her hands and feet.' This was news to Roper. Then he remembered Keturah's weaving lying unattended in her lap as he had entered and how she had not noticed the hair come away in her hands. 'That may be permanent. The effects of the poison may progress further. Her one hope is to purge, and then we can only wait.'

So effective was the emetic that had been administered, it was all Keturah could do to lean on her knees and haul in shuddering breaths in the brief moments of respite she was afforded. When her retching became dry, the physician gave her water so that she could keep going, an act that was met with a brief moan of resistance from Keturah. That was the last voluntary noise she could utter. Soon she was barely conscious, lying white against the bed's woollen blankets and retching pathetically over the edge.

The physician departed at Roper's request soon afterwards, leaving them the wood sorrel solution to be administered when the vomiting had ceased. As Roper thanked him, he noticed that tremor again. Then he and Keturah were left alone. Roper wondered what words might comfort her and though he was not sure she could hear him, he began talking. First he told her about the insults Randolph had rained down upon him. '"The cheerful warrior of misadventure", was another one. I don't know whether he comes up with them on the spot, or prepares them in advance.' Then he told her about the revenge he was going to wreak on Uvoren. 'When Pryce defended me on Harstathur, he told Asger he'd *mash his bulging eyeballs into the back of his bastard skull.* That's how it'll finish for Uvoren. But we'll leave him all alone first. Tear down his allies and his family, his reputation, his past, his prospects and his friends. He'll know he's all that's left. He'll know he's going to die, and he'll face it alone. And we'll see how brave Uvoren the Mighty is.'

Once he had run out of imaginative things to do to Uvoren, he returned to reality and told her about his favourite wild places. 'There was a spot I found in the forests near the berjasti which was where I'd go whenever there was time. Next to a forty-foot waterfall, where the bed of the stream disappeared and the water dropped into nothing. You could sit with your legs dangling over the edge, listening to the roar. You could smell the ferns and the resin from the pine trees overhead and feel the spray on your skin. The cold air used to tumble down the valley sometimes and you could feel it hit you. It's the only place I've ever seen a lynx. Just a flash of it, moving through the trees on the other side of the stream.'

Helmec was back within the hour. He stood in the doorway for a moment, staring at Keturah, his face sombre for once. 'You'll be all right soon, Miss Keturah,' he said after a time. 'You're in the best of hands.' If Keturah had heard that, she did not appear capable of acknowledging it, but Roper looked up and nodded gratefully.

'Where's Tekoa?'

'He's coming, lord.' Helmec bowed and smiled consolingly, backing out of the room. 'It looks like you've got this under control, lord, but you summon me if I'm needed.'

The legate arrived not long afterwards. Roper himself had just returned from emptying a pail into the gutter when Tekoa hurled the door open, leaving an indignant Helmec in his wake. The legate, who never looked anything short of purposeful, walked as though he would not be troubled by a company of berserkers barring his path. He strode in and stopped before his daughter, who still lay on the bed, drawing shallow breaths. She was very pale and at first Roper did not think she was awake. Then she opened a poisonous, bloodshot eye and fixed it on her father. She panted for a moment longer before expelling something dark from her mouth, missing the pail it had been aimed for. She stared at Tekoa a moment longer and then moved her head a fraction in acknowledgement, shuttering the eye again. Her lips were a dark, faded green, her body wracked by spasms and her hair was almost completely gone, leaving an inflamed scalp and some fine wisps on the back of her neck. It occurred to Roper that had Tekoa seen his daughter just two hours before, she would have appeared almost well.

'Hello, Daughter,' said Tekoa. Keturah did not respond. 'Glad to see you looking so well.' Keturah spluttered a little, which Roper thought was an attempt at a laugh. 'I'm going to speak to your husband for a moment.' He gestured for Roper to come outside with him. Roper followed him out and shut the door, leaving Keturah alone. Tekoa turned on him, jaw set and eyes narrowed.

'Lord Roper Kynortasson.' His voice was very low. 'The man who would protect the country but who cannot even protect his wife. Our alliance is finished. Do you hear me, Lord Roper? Finished! I will take my daughter back under my own roof this very night and with her the debts that you owe me.'

Roper retreated slightly from Tekoa's anger, placing a hand on his shoulder. He could feel the heat coming off the legate and Tekoa knocked his hand away and pushed him hard in the chest.

'Get your hand off me!'

Roper staggered back but did not react. He was the bigger man and he took the blow, once again stepping forward and placing his hand at Tekoa's shoulder. This time the legate left it there. 'You can try collecting your debts,' Roper said. 'I can't pay them now. As for your daughter, I should imagine this confrontation is exactly what Uvoren wanted when he poisoned her. If this shows you anything, it's that you have chosen the right side.' Tekoa did not look mollified. 'We will have revenge and we will have it together. I'm going to break him, Tekoa. Him, and anyone else connected to what happened to your daughter.'

'Yes, you bloody are,' said Tekoa. 'Revenge is for now, Lord Roper. Now. Now, this moment. Uvoren must understand stimulus and reaction. He poisons the daughter of the Vidarr, the entire bloody universe comes down on top of him. Him, and whoever did this at his order.'

Roper hesitated, remembering Gray's warning. 'I will summon Vigtyr the Quick.'

Tekoa raised his arms. 'Anyone. Just kill that bastard and all who follow him.'

'We will. Uvoren doesn't want your daughter dead, Tekoa.' The legate bared his teeth, apparently furious that what Uvoren wanted was even being discussed. 'Killing her would only gain sympathy for our cause. He wants to make Keturah look weak, so that it looks as though my followers are weak. He wants to divide our alliance and my marriage. He is destroying my image and making me harder to follow. And to achieve a goal as feeble as that, he has poisoned your daughter. We have made him desperate together and now we need to beat him together.'

'I wish to sit with my daughter,' said Tekoa abruptly. Roper stood aside and Tekoa Urielson seemed to steel himself for a moment before he reached for the door handle.

Keturah vomited through the night. Both Roper and Tekoa remained at her side, taking it in turns to empty the pails and feed her water to sustain her. By the time dawn pierced the windows, the retching had stopped, though whether the foxglove distillation had worn off or she simply no longer had the strength to persist, Roper could not tell. They responded by giving her more water and the wood sorrel solution, a diuretic that would help expel the poison she had already absorbed. She was desperately weak and Roper could not help but wonder whether the treatment was killing her.

A few hours after dawn, Harald, the legionary who had spent so much time in Tekoa's service, appeared hesitantly at Roper's door with a pot of honey. Tekoa turned to bark at whoever had disturbed them, but seeing Harald so timid, holding the honey, he froze. It was a large earthenware vessel: a week's pay for a humble legionary. 'A gift for Miss Keturah,' Harald said, half dropping the pot clumsily onto Roper's table. 'Sorry for disturbing you, my lord.' He turned to leave, hurrying from the room.

'Harald,' said Tekoa abruptly at the legionary's back. 'I'll tell her when she wakes up. That's kind of you. Uncommonly kind.' Harald turned on his way out of the door, offered a smile and then shuffled awkwardly out. 'Well, I'll be damned,' said Tekoa, glancing at Roper with something like his old humour. 'The man has a heart.'

Roper had other thoughts. 'Can we be sure it hasn't been poisoned too?'

Tekoa jerked his head dismissively. 'He watched her grow up. If we can't trust him, there's nobody we can.'

When Keturah awoke, they fed her spoonfuls of honey along with the water and sorrel solution. It seemed to strengthen her somewhat and her moments of consciousness grew longer and more lucid. By the evening, Roper thought she might be strong enough to be moved to Tekoa's household. He had matters to attend to here and no sooner had she been carried down the spiral staircase by Helmec and into a waiting litter, than Roper summoned Vigtyr the Quick.

Roper knew Vigtyr was tall, but had not realised just how immense the figure who arrived at his quarters would be. When Helmec showed him in, Vigtyr had to stoop beneath the lintel of the door, straightening up just enough to make perceptible the bow he offered Roper. 'Lictor,' Roper acknowledged. 'Will you drink birch wine with me?'

That would be Vigtyr's honour.

He was gigantic: perhaps the tallest man Roper had ever seen. He was a full foot taller than Roper himself; taller too than the berserker, Tarben, who had won the wrestling at Roper's feast (though leaner as well). His hands were massive; each finger as thick as a baby's arm, with chestnut-knuckles and forearms corded with muscle. Roper watched the way Vigtyr moved as he handed him a full goblet; noting his balance, how he took the goblet with his left hand, the way his eyes seemed to look through Roper to the wall behind, rather than at him. His hair was long and black, his high boots a dark-brown leather and, instead of the usual woollen tunic, he wore a split-leather jerkin with a carved ivory brooch bearing the crest of House Baltasar over the heart. He had several thick gold rings stretched around his fingers and his belt-buckle was intricate silver. That was a demonstration of personal wealth that would have raised even Uvoren's eyebrows. It was almost disturbing. Anakim status is built on memories and deeds, not embellishments.

At Roper's invitation, Vigtyr settled himself in a yew chair that squeaked beneath his weight and stretched out his legs before him, looking lazy and content. Roper began to partition his mind. He forgot Keturah. He forgot the plague stalking the streets. He forgot Uvoren, he forgot Tekoa's displeasure. Almost most painful of all, he forgot Gray, and the look of disappointment in his eyes when he had suggested meeting with Vigtyr. This encounter would require a clear head.

Dutifully, he began the work of charming Vigtyr. He saw that Vigtyr's grey eyes lingered on the elk skull. There was quite a story behind that. Did Vigtyr hunt? Had he had the pleasure of visiting the Trawden forests? A shame. Oh, but he had been to Pendle? Magnificent, by all accounts. Roper hoped to go there himself when the winter was over.

Word had it that Vigtyr had faced the knights at Githru? Easier than expected, eh?

Where were his farmsteads?

Did he have hounds?

Vigtyr was exceedingly good company. He laughed in all the right places, told eloquent stories of his own in his deep voice and Roper found himself unexpectedly warming to this character, in spite of his Suthern ostentation. It was surprisingly easy to devote himself to this encounter, and Roper began to wonder whether the dark rumours that surrounded Vigtyr were just that: rumours. They had refilled their goblets before the topic turned to Uvoren.

'Now it is a great surprise to me, Vigtyr, that the rank of Guardsman eludes a warrior of your renown.' Vigtyr seemed to stop looking through Roper for the first time and looked at him instead, straightening perceptibly in his seat. 'And as I'm sure you know, there are currently thirty-five vacancies in the Sacred Guard. We have a whole scroll of potential warriors, of course, and naturally you're on there but competition has never been fiercer. I am afraid that I am finding Uvoren difficult as well.' Roper allowed himself a little shake of the head. 'He thinks it is his unit, you see, and does his best to turn the other guardsmen against appointments that he does not agree with. It is getting increasingly difficult to overrule him, and, as you know, he has many influential supporters.'

'I'm not sure they'll be influential for long, my lord,' said Vigtyr, reading Roper perfectly.

'How interesting. Do you really think so?' asked Roper, smiling now.

'I'm certain, lord. I like to stay well informed and hear that the Ephors are developing a keen interest in many of Uvoren's friends.' The Ephors were the five supreme arbiters of justice in the Black Kingdom.

In response, Roper slid a sheet of parchment across the table, scrawled with coats of arms. 'Well,' he said, 'I wonder if they have an interest in any of these peers.'

Vigtyr took the parchment delicately and cast his eye over it, muttering the odd name to himself and frowning as he wracked his memory. 'Yes,' he said at last. 'Yes, yes, yes, yes.' He rolled the parchment carefully, stowed it in a leather pouch at his belt and drained his birch wine. His light grey eyes flashed over Roper. 'They're taken care of, lord. Will that be all?'

'One more thing,' said Roper. He allowed his smile to slip. 'My wife has been poisoned.'

'I'm shocked to hear it, lord.'

'If you can find out who is responsible then I will be especially grateful. Who gave the orders and who carried them out. That is all, Vigtyr,' said Roper, standing and watching Vigtyr climb to his full height opposite him. 'Please let me know if you need any assistance.'

'Very good, my lord.' He bowed, more deeply this time, and strode from the room.

He left Roper standing, staring after him, his brow gathered into a frown. It was the first time he had tried using the subtlety which Kynortas had so often employed, and so subtle had he been, that he had no idea whether Vigtyr had understood what he had been asked to do.

But Vigtyr had understood every last word.

When on campaign, discipline was handled by the Black Lord himself. By strict Anakim law, an army could only have one head and that must include the ability to discipline his soldiers. When at home, however, matters of disgrace, justice and vengeance were handled by the Ephors. It was the most prestigious non-military position that the Black Kingdom offered and immensely powerful. To even be considered for appointment, which was by unanimous verdict from the existing Ephors, you had to have served a century as a legionary. You were then the ultimate judge in all cases of indiscipline, with the mandate to hand out death, disgrace, or any manner of imaginative punishment to anyone else in the Black Kingdom. Even the Black Lord was not immune from the Ephors, who were wholly independent.

In a vindictive twist, Uvoren's sons were the first to fall.

At the first hint of dawn in the east, just three days after Roper had spoken with Vigtyr, six Pendeen legionaries arrived at Unndor's house with an Ephorian mandate for his arrest. 'What charge?' Unndor, the younger son, had growled.

'Cowardice,' said a captain with barely disguised contempt in his face. He was dragged to the prisons beneath the Central Keep.

Urthr, the elder son, followed the next day. Rape, this time.

The two were Ramnea's Own legionaries: men second in martial reputation only to Sacred Guardsmen and individuals from whom the very highest levels of discipline and honour were expected. Their arrest set the fortress abuzz and they were tried less than a week later in a windowless granite chamber beneath the Central Keep. People could come and watch, of course, to ensure that due process was followed, and Uvoren's own supporters bullied their way into the room, roaring with rage each time an allegation was made and greeting Unndor and Urthr's defences with cheers and applause.

They lost that battle.

The presiding Ephor, draped in an immense cloak of eagle feathers that flashed and rippled every time he shifted in his seat, was not swayed by the noise of the hall. There were witnesses who spoke out against the two brothers. Three quivering women, teary-eyed but unwavering, insisted that Urthr had forced himself upon them. 'Lies!' Urthr screamed at each in turn. 'Where did they find these wretches? Every word, a lie!' He was found guilty, though, and trussed up to be sent to one of the prison-ships in the North Sea.

'There you will labour,' decreed the Ephor, voice well trained to carry over the baying crowd, 'for twenty years for each woman you have wronged. Once free, you will start afresh as a nemandi and re-earn your status as a subject.' Urthr had been demoted to an apprentice rank, a rung below the full peers and subjects of the Black Kingdom. Stricken, Urthr appealed to his father, but Uvoren had turned away and strode from the room as soon as the sentence was read out.

Unndor was next to be dragged down, falling victim to a dozen tales of cowardice. On three separate occasions, it was said, he had shuffled back from the front rank when it was his turn, and sheltered behind the flesh of worthier subjects. Four times, it was alleged, he had attacked warriors already engaged in a fight and slain them from behind. One legionary testified that he had seen Unndor turn away from the battlefield earlier in the autumn before the Black Lord had signalled the retreat.

'How convenient that every witness so far has been either Vidarr or Jormunrekur!' howled Uvoren.

'Yes,' said the Ephor cuttingly. 'What a surprise that none of the Lothbroks have testified against these men.' Cowardice, in its most extreme form, was punishable by sticky-fire. But this was not one of those: Unndor had twice been close to receiving a Prize of Valour and had something of a reputation of his own. Nevertheless, the evidence could not be ignored and, though he avoided the prison-ships and even retained his status as subject, he was reduced to an auxiliary legionary.

Roper had been at both trials. At first Uvoren had ignored

him, but after Unndor was reduced to an auxiliary, the captain had looked across the chamber to Roper and raised a trembling finger to point in his direction, his jaw set, his nostrils flared and his eyes shining with spite. Roper had responded with a cold nod, holding Uvoren's eye for a time before turning away from the scene.

Two gone from the table. Six remain.

18
The Hybrid

It was a still morning when Bellamus and his ragged band at last snaked through Lundenceaster's main gate. As they travelled south, the influence the Anakim exerted on the locals had lessened. A hundred miles after the barn in which Bellamus had left two of his soldiers hanging, the locals started to lose their hair-braids and bright bracelets. Many of the Anakim words remained in use but the land was less sparsely populated and less wary. They knew of the Anakim there, of course, but nobody had seen one in a decade, there were no hybrid slaves, and they had no fear of mentioning the name of that race out loud. Even so, the folk there still stopped their work to stare uneasily at the whipped Suthern force, turning to look back to the north as though they might see pursuing and vengeful Anakim darkening the hills.

Further south, the Anakim had drifted into the supernatural. The people there knew of the race of fallen angels that inhabited the north, but were unclear how they might tell them apart from any other man. Bellamus heard that sometimes individuals were accused of being Anakim and put on trial to determine their innocence. Unusual height was enough to place you under suspicion; but so was having a good harvest when everyone else's had failed, or being a recluse, or having particularly bright eyes, or giving birth to twins.

At last they had come to Lundenceaster: a city where the nobles were taught Anakim along with Frankish, Samnian, Iberian and Frisian as they grew up; a legacy of the days when the Anakim had swarmed over the walls and invaded the streets. To the folk here, the Anakim were almost totally mystical, and were kept at bay with crosses, ceremonial braziers that burned herbs and feathers, and, by royal decree, symbols inscribed in chalk onto the streets at night.

There were no symbols now. Just snow. Everywhere he looked, Bellamus could see signs of the damage wrought by this turbulent year. Skeletal houses stripped bare by the wind crowded those haggard few that had resisted the elements. He could feel from the way his horse walked that beneath its hooves were not snow-covered cobbles but a smooth sheet of ice. A bell was tolling in a nearby church and the sound was enough to make Bellamus smile. He had not heard one since before he had crossed the Abus and it made him realise for the first time that the Anakim had no bells. How could he have missed that?

People stepped aside as they saw the little column enter the streets, watching suspiciously from doorways or upstairs windows as they progressed. They stared particularly at Bellamus, eyes lingering on the enormous war-blade that he carried, strapped over his shoulder.

Bellamus's household was one of the sturdy stone buildings left behind by the empire that had stretched over these lands long ago. Its tiled roof had resisted the autumnal storms much better than the thatch around it, though dozens of the tiles had evidently slipped and, towards the left-hand side, there was a hole through which a wild boar could have escaped. 'My poor home,' said Bellamus.

Stepan, sitting on a pony next to Bellamus, stopped to inspect the dwelling. 'This is yours?' he asked. 'I was always told these old ones are haunted.'

'Not to my knowledge,' said Bellamus. He dismounted, handed his reins to one of the warriors who followed, and lifted the latch on the front door, opening it a few inches to call inside. 'Hilda?' He kicked aside some of the snow in the doorway and dragged the door wide enough to slip through. 'Hilda?' he called again, as Stepan squeezed in after him. The room was bright. Light poured in from a central aperture, below which was a pool of water now covered in snow and probably, Bellamus thought, frozen solid. It was the snow which was providing the illumination, reflecting the daylight into the corners of the atrium.

In answer to Bellamus's call, a stout old woman came shuffling into view. First her head appeared from a door to the side of the atrium, her face framed in grey curls, broad and perplexed. Then she moved further into the atrium to reveal fine leather slippers below a loose-fitting brown robe. 'Master?' she said suspiciously. 'Good God, that isn't Master Bellamus?'

'It is,' said Bellamus, embracing the woman who was suddenly beaming. They broke apart and Bellamus gestured at his companion. 'This is Stepan, a knightly friend of mine.' The stout woman gave a flustered curtsey and Stepan bowed in return. 'Are you well, Hilda?'

'We all thought you were dead!' said she. 'Word came that your forces had been defeated and there were precious few survivors!'

'Well, as luck would have it, I was among them,' said Bellamus. 'I and four hundred others who are now waiting outside. They'll need feeding, Hilda. I appreciate it will take some time, but I would be most grateful if you could see to it.'

'Of course, Master,' she said, a little confused. 'The stores are low but we'll do our best. Nobody expected you back at all. The cook is seeing to his house, the servants are gone. It's just me here. It will take time.'

'We have time,' said Stepan, breezily. He gestured at the snow and gave her a wink.

'We do indeed,' agreed Bellamus. 'Fetch the cook and, if there aren't any servants, hire some. There must be thousands in need of employment in this city. See to it for me, Hilda.'

'Yes, certainly, Master.' Hilda knotted her fingers. 'A message arrived from His Majesty in your absence. Delivered by his royal guards.' Bellamus smiled, inviting her to continue. 'It was a summons to court. They said if you ever came back, you had one day to present yourself. I tried to tell them that you would come in your own time but they were extremely rude.'

Bellamus laughed out loud at that, placing a fond hand on her shoulder. 'Nobody could have done more, Hilda. I'll go first thing tomorrow, then. His Majesty would not be pleased if I reappeared alone of the forces he sent north, looking like a beggar and smelling like a stable.' Bellamus gestured down at his clothes, dark with moisture and spattered with mud from the trail. The gold that had been hung at his neck and wrists was gone: bartered away for food or billets for his men on the long journey back. His hair was loose and ragged, and he had a month's beard-growth on his face. But there was something about him all the same. For all their tattered appearance, his clothes had evidently once been fine and he did not carry himself like a commoner. This was the sort of man whose rough appearance did not make him less respected: it merely made him more noble.

Hilda departed to organise sustenance for the soldiers and Stepan settled himself to sleep on the floor of the hall, wrapped in a musky cloak he had acquired on the march south. Bellamus, meanwhile, began seeing to a bath. First he struck a fire with the very last of the tinder which he had carried with him on the march, striking iron and flint onto a piece of charred cloth. Adding this to some hay that he had kept close to his chest, he was able to blow it into a small flame that he fed with twigs until it was large enough to add some of the seasoned logs stored at the rear of the house. He left the fire to establish and next wiped the snow off the icy surface of the pool in the atrium. With the help of a cobble uprooted from the road outside, he discovered that the ice was only a few inches thick, with liquid water below. The snow must have insulated it from the worst of the cold. He smashed a hole large enough to allow him to fill a kettle with freezing water and hung it on a hook above the fire. It would take a long time to heat enough to fill the wooden half-barrel that he used to bathe and so he began searching for his razor. He was not surprised to find it undisturbed upstairs, along with his other possessions. Hilda was known throughout the community and would have kept the house safe. And besides, most people feared to step foot in the ancient stone houses.

As he shaved, inspecting his handiwork in a dull brass mirror, Bellamus thought. The first thing he needed to do was get a message to the queen. King Osbert would likely be in a fear-driven rage at having lost so many soldiers north of the Abus and Bellamus did not doubt that, without Queen Aramilla's intervention, he was at serious risk of this shave being his last.

But contacting her would be difficult. In court, they affected barely to know one another. Any message he sent for her would look exceedingly suspicious, and news of it would no doubt be relayed to her jealous husband. He must rely on her to contact him, if she still felt enough affection to play this game. In the many years of their acquaintance, she had not yet let him down and she would certainly have heard of his arrival in the city. Bellamus could not slip unnoticed into Lundenceaster with four hundred soldiers in tow.

They had met when the queen was on a pilgrimage to Iberia. Bellamus had already garnered a considerable reputation as a man who could deal with the Anakim and had thus been summoned to assist the royal train as it passed near the blurred Anakim border. The queen had been on foot, as ever the least elaborately decorated of her handmaidens, who sweated and flapped at themselves with fans as they trotted along behind her. Bellamus ignored the royal men-at-arms who gestured to him as he approached, riding straight past them and to the queen, at that moment in stern conversation with a handmaiden. He dismounted and offered a bow, receiving an indifferent glance in response. 'You are safe to cross, Majesty. The band that lives here is nomadic and our scouts report they are some days away.'

She narrowed her eyes, assessing him from dust-caked boots to unshaven face. 'You are not Iberian, sir,' she said, as though he had tried to deceive her. 'Your Saxon is excellent.' She waved off the guards in front who had turned towards Bellamus, furious at being ignored.

'My mother was Saxon, Majesty,' he said, hands finding his pockets and smiling breezily at her. 'I am from Safinim but Saxon was the language we spoke in my house as I grew up.'

So unflustered was Bellamus, so cool in the face of such vaunted royalty, that the queen made a slight exclamation. It was an 'Ah' of disbelief, accompanied by a look of astonishment. Then her eyes narrowed a little and she smiled. 'Your mother *was* Saxon? Is she dead?'

'I'm afraid I don't know, Majesty,' said Bellamus. 'I have not seen her these past eighteen years.'

'Family feud?'

'I had a feud, and I left to preserve my family.'

The queen tilted her head back, exposing her neck a little, then glanced at her handmaiden. 'I am going to quiz Master . . .?'

'Bellamus.'

'Bellamus, here.' The handmaiden curtseyed and shuffled back through the retinue, the queen gesturing that Bellamus should fall into step beside her. Dutifully, he took the bridle of his horse and led it down the road with her. 'What was your feud?'

He glanced at her, assessing her reaction to his words. 'I was accused of taking a white stag from some neighbouring forests, which regrettably belonged to a prince.'

She snorted. 'And did you?'

'Certainly not,' said Bellamus. 'I shot it and lost it.'

'So, not a glorious cause.'

'Venison is always a glorious cause,' said Bellamus. Then he shrugged. 'I have no regrets. Had I not tried to take that stag, I would not be walking down this sunny road, talking to a queen.'

The compliment bounced off the queen. 'And I hear that road has led you to know more about the Anakim than any man in the land.'

'I'm flattered you've heard my reputation.'

She looked ahead, wearing a slight frown. 'Just recently.'

'The Anakim fascinate me. As a naïve runaway, I reached the Alps and took a job keeping an eye on the Anakim there for the local villages. My first day cost me two fingers, but I still went back. Have you ever seen one, Majesty?'

'Never. I am kept well away from such dangers.'

Bellamus gave her a sympathetic face. 'What's life without a little danger?'

She surveyed him from the corner of a narrowed eye. 'Exactly, Master Bellamus.'

'I have a spare sword and a spare horse. I promise life won't be boring.'

For the first time, she looked at him directly, rather than out of the corner of her eye. 'I don't ride.'

'Well, our standards aren't high,' confessed Bellamus.

That drew her laugh like a magpie's rattle. 'Perhaps you would accompany us? I daresay we will need further protection and the road is long and dull . . . Much like my retinue,' she added under her breath.

Bellamus shrugged. 'I am your servant, Majesty.'

The road was indeed long, and in between stops to pay homage to each church or shrine or sacred relic, the queen delighted to interrogate Bellamus, who was rather surprised to find that he enjoyed himself. Over the following weeks, he entertained her; at first on the road, then after dark in the sturdy tent that was pitched for her. In each other's arms, they were both less guarded. 'A man with no name must have a valuable trade. Mine is the Anakim,' Bellamus said.

'There is no place that trade is more valuable than Albion. My husband fears them with his every waking breath. A man like you could rise far in my country.' After the queen had said that, Bellamus knew he had given too much away. For the first time, something other than relaxed humour crossed his face and he could see that she had noticed it. Perhaps she had liked it. On her departure, Queen Aramilla left him a letter, suggesting he cross the channel and come seek his fortune in Albion. It was a greater opportunity than Bellamus would find in Iberia and he took the chance, bringing his loyal band north. From that day forth, the queen's invisible hand had helped guide his rise.

Queen Aramilla usually had months to act on his behalf: time during which she could ensure her favour for the upstart went unnoticed. If she were to intervene on his behalf now, it would have to be fast. They could not afford the subtlety with which she usually worked.

The queen sent word that night, carried by one of the few handmaidens that Bellamus recognised: one of the young, pretty women who rarely left Aramilla's side at court. He was to meet the queen at a hall behind Ludgate Hill; one that he knew belonged to Earl Seaton, Aramilla's father. Bellamus did not move for a moment when he heard this.

'Is everything all right, sir?'

'Of course,' he said lightly. 'Thank you.' He beamed at her and bade her goodnight, his smile collapsing as the door shut behind her. It was a peculiarly conspicuous location for such a secret meeting. But Bellamus had learned two things above all about his patron. The first was to trust her. The second was not to bore her.

Hilda had soon returned with the cook and two servants, who set about thawing the house. More fires were lit, food was fetched from the stores and they began to prepare a meal for the soldiers who had started to dissolve into the ragged buildings on either side of the road. They were now Bellamus's men, all with valuable experience of fighting against the Anakim. An experienced warrior was worth two or three callow recruits, and every man here would be returning north with him when the time came. Bellamus walked past them as he headed for the hall that night, exchanging a few words as they received hot food from his kitchen. They were cheerful, a calm night in a ruined house with a warm meal representing a significant upturn in their recent fortunes.

'Where are you off to, Captain?' asked Stepan, abandoning a game of dice with three companions and getting to his feet, evidently intending to accompany Bellamus.

'Going to meet a friend,' said Bellamus. 'Alone this time, Stepan.'

The knight raised his eyebrows. 'These are dangerous streets,' he insisted.

'A female friend,' said Bellamus. 'She's not far.'

Stepan's smile shone through the darkness. 'Say no more,' he said, sitting back down.

Bellamus walked to the hall alone, the streets near empty. He supposed that even the roughest of Lundenceaster's residents preferred to be huddled by a fire that night. Then he reflected that perhaps he and his band were the roughest of Lundenceaster's residents, and it was from them that the others were hiding.

He found the hall, raising a fist to bang on the double-leaved doors. He was shocked when they were opened by two more handmaidens, both new to him. Was there to be nothing secret about this meeting?

Within, the hall was extravagantly lit by candles and a central hearth; to the extent that Bellamus had to shield his eyes for a moment. The first figure he was able to discern was the queen, who stood before him, dressed in black. Stars were embroidered into her neckline like a chain of silver, and there was a delicate crown resting on her golden hair. Beside her waited another two handmaidens. Though she was his anchor against the coming storm, he cursed himself at the sight of her.

This was a game to her. It had always been a game. He could see from the way she wore a crown to this most covert of meetings; how she had slowly begun to let her most intimate handmaidens in on the secret. Even the way she smiled as he approached. She was courting with peril. Each new partner to their secret fractionally increased the chance that the king discovered. She would grow bored and try a little more danger, liking the taste. But Bellamus had known that. And here he was, relying on her more than ever. She was affectionate enough but he could feel the fickle nature of her admiration. Every moment that he did not entertain her, she drifted away from him.

She wanted the excitement and the unknown in which Bellamus was so expert; he needed her influence at court. But his need was greater. The king doted on Aramilla who, whatever else, had a keen mind. Her hold over King Osbert was suffocating and he feared her loss almost as much as he feared the Anakim. The moment that Bellamus ceased to excite her, he would be cast aside. Or worse. A whisper would find its way into the king's ear: allegations that Bellamus had touched her, or behaved inappropriately, and it would be over for the upstart.

This was a game to the queen, but not to Bellamus. But he had known that from the beginning, and panic would bore her. Calm, now.

The handmaidens curtseyed and left without a word, retreating discreetly into a room at the back of the hall. Bellamus walked close to her and looked down at her upturned face, overcoming his desire to ask about whether her companions could be trusted.

'I was sure you were dead,' she said softly.

He kissed her. 'Without your help, my head will leave my shoulders tomorrow anyway. The king is angry?'

'Not angry, really. Horrified. He moans and he shakes and he quivers at the thought of what happened in the north,' she said, wearily. 'But we'll get to that. Tell me your stories.'

There was a couch at one side of the hall and the upstart and the queen sat together. Bellamus began to talk. He told her about his deception which had won the first battle and forced the Anakim from the field. About the tangled wilderness through which they had marched, torching and killing, looking to bleed the legions from the Hindrunn. About the wild animals that had made life so cheap and sleep so dangerous. How they had then been tricked by the new Black Lord and stripped so contemptuously of their supplies. How the army had begun to fall apart and spill men over the wilderness before they had at last faced the Anakim in a narrow pass by the sea. Here, he went into detail, knowing that the tale of how the Sacred Guard had finally seemed to lose patience with the rest of the army, and simply ripped the Suthern line apart before slaughtering Lord Northwic, would excite her. 'They're coming south, Aramilla,' he finished. 'The Black Lord himself told me. They want to take this city in revenge for our invasion.'

'And what would they do?' Her pupils were very wide. He knew she was not scared, but thrilled. This woman had known nothing but oppressive safety her entire life. She was barely on the side of the Sutherners: she just wanted to roll the dice and, if the island burned as a result, that would do for her. He must shock her.

'I cannot say. Wholesale slaughter? Simply kill the nobility and force the people into serfdom? Maybe just raze the city and sow the earth with salt. We cannot have them here: Suthdal would not survive. We must fight them in the north. If we take the war back to them as soon as the roads reopen, they will not be prepared and we can subdue them. Then you can come north and tour their conquered kingdom.' He took her hand, interlinking their fingers. 'I cannot rest from that place. It is haunting me. Since I came back, I have felt like I am in a dream. It is as though I am living in a faint reflection of the world beyond the Abus. Everything is so soft, so easy. So flat. Up there, I felt awake for the first time in my life. Every tree; every hill and stream and word and footstep seemed more significant. I have to go back.' Bellamus stopped abruptly and glanced at Aramilla, taking a moment to compose himself. 'And you must see. It's worth subduing them simply to explore that land unopposed.'

'So not only do you propose to keep your head tomorrow, you want him to give you another army?' She raised an eyebrow at him.

'Why not? You have him on your leash. He must believe I am the only man who can stop them.'

'And are you?'

For a heartbeat, his smile slipped, and she was confronted with the upstart's face at rest. 'You tell me.' She feasted on him for a moment and then looked down at his hand, beginning to play with his fingers.

'I will struggle to convince him. He doesn't trust you because you're lowborn. He doesn't believe you should command an army of nobles.'

'Look what happened when I was only an advisor.' He beamed at her and she exhaled with a slight hum, leaning into him.

'There will be concessions, my upstart.'

'If I survive and I have the army, that's more than I need.'

'Perhaps more than a man with no name has ever had before,' she said. She gave his cheek a light smack. 'Do your ambitions have no limits?'

Bellamus let out a slow breath. 'I am always hungry.'

'Even if you vanquish the Anakim? If you become protector of the north?'

'Why just the north?' asked Bellamus. 'You are a queen, are you not? You have no children with the king. You can rule if your husband dies.' She had gone quite still in his arms. 'We could have Albion.' He had never before revealed that monstrous objective, and waited to see whether he would regret it.

She was silent a long time. 'Some day.' Her tone made Bellamus think it was not the first time that thought had occurred to her. 'I'll do my best for you, but I don't know what he'll say and we must not arouse his suspicion. You will have to play your part well.'

'I trust you.'

The next morning, Bellamus rode for the court of King Osbert. The king's hall was by the river, which had solidified into a vast white highway, stretching hundreds of miles inland. Dark figures walked upon the river and a few souls were fishing through the ice. Bellamus wondered if they were having any success; there were precious few sources of food in a winter like this.

If the river was a giant's roadway, King Osbert's hall could have been the giant's house. The king had constructed it himself after burning down his father's hall when he took the throne. A plinth of stone raised it above the flooding, with broad stone steps leading up to the door. Its thatched roof, as mangy and ragged as any of the others in Lundenceaster, was meadow-like in its scale. Enormous wooden pillars of hornbeam, so broad that three men linking hands would have struggled to encircle them, supported the overhang of the roof. The dark, weather-battered wood of the front was carved and patterned: sunken patches and engravings coloured in reds, blues and golds, and a great yellow sun engraved above the doors.

Bellamus paused briefly at the bottom of the steps that led to the hall's doors, but, seeing no one to take his horse and only four weary retainers standing by the door above, clicked his tongue to encourage the horse to climb to the hall. The retainers, armed with halberds and their faces exposed by open helmets, stared stunned as Bellamus rode right up to the door before dismounting. 'Would you take care of that for me?' he asked one, proffering the reins. Bellamus was shaved and had trimmed his long hair. He had no more gold but wore fresh, well-made clothes and his easy, confident manner was that of a man born to high status, rather than an upstart. Most remarkable of all, however, was the immense war-blade strapped to his back, the handle of which protruded above his shoulder. So one of the retainers took the reins of his horse with a little bow and a muttered, 'Lord.'

'What are you doing here, lord?' asked another.

'No need to call me lord,' said Bellamus. 'I am here to see the king. Please tell His Majesty that Bellamus of Safinim has arrived.'

The guard complied, turning to the door behind him, lifting the latch and sliding through. It did not take long for him to return.

'His Majesty will see you at once, lord.'

'You're most kind,' said Bellamus. The door was held open for him and he advanced into the hall.

The interior was dark and cavernous. Shadows flickered on the walls, cast from a large central hearth in which a fire squirmed and wriggled; the smoke it gave off escaping through a hole in the roof above. The floor was some kind of mortar embedded with crushed tiles, and a dozen more retainers lined the walls, scrutinising Bellamus as he walked by. At the far end of the hall was a platform surrounded by a small cluster of nobles and bishops who also stared at him as he approached, each face wearing a look of disdain and, Bellamus noted, months of uncontrolled beard-growth. He knew why they had all gathered: they had heard of his return and wanted to see how the king punished him. They were hoping to witness his downfall that day. One earl in particular stepped forward as Bellamus approached, a smile of withering insincerity on his face.

'Bellamus of Safinim,' he said, savouring the words. 'I

thought you might survive. The universe is a perverse place.' This was Earl Seaton: father of Queen Aramilla and thus uniquely elevated among King Osbert's courtiers. The earl was tall and extremely lean, with a narrow face and a slightly effeminate stance, as though his joints moved more freely than those of most men. His clothes were black, his eyes were black, his hair was jet-black and great clusters of gold had congealed about his extremities.

Bellamus stopped before the earl. 'A feat in itself,' he said. 'Not many return from the Black Kingdom.'

'Which still stands,' observed Earl Seaton. 'Though I'm sure you did your best.'

Bellamus laughed. 'I look forward to seeing you lead our next campaign, my lord.'

'I cannot deny I feel more at home here in the south, Bellamus. And what have we here?' The earl hauled a gold-weighted hand over Bellamus's shoulder and tapped the handle of the great war-blade that hung there.

'A trump card,' said Bellamus. 'His Majesty is through there?' Bellamus pointed to a door at the back of the hall, beside which two royal guards waited.

'He certainly is,' said Earl Seaton. 'His mood is fickle at present, Bellamus; watch your head as you leave.' Bellamus walked past the earl, staring fixedly at the door to avoid the gazes of the other courtiers, who watched him pass in silence. Standing a little way beyond the noble cluster was Queen Aramilla, who appraised him coldly as he approached. He caught her eye and winked, a gesture invisible to the courtiers at his back. She did not respond, but as he passed she turned to watch him go.

'I did what I could,' she murmured at his back.

Then he was past, lifting the latch of the door and slipping into the dark beyond. This room was much smaller, with the floor covered in deerskins and a hearth set into the wall on Bellamus's left. Between this and a single window, located high on the other side of the room, illumination was provided. The air quivered with the soft tones of an unseen harpist. Directly opposite Bellamus was a platform, on either side of which stood a retainer. One of them was uncommonly tall; so tall that Bellamus blinked and stared at his shadowed form for a moment. It could not possibly be a Sutherner.

On the platform was a throne of oak, ornately carved and stained like dried blood. A plump bishop, purple of face and robe, was stooped next to the throne, and on the throne sat King Osbert.

The king was fat and bearded (which explained the hirsute state of his courtiers). His nose was broad and flattened, his cheeks so pink as to be almost cherubic, and he stared at Bellamus from beneath a pair of spectacular eyebrows: black, and ending in a mighty upward flourish. They gave him the appearance of an owl and Bellamus often privately considered that the king's eyebrows did more to rule the kingdom than the rest of him combined. Though it had been decades since he had swung a sword in anger, King Osbert retained many of the affectations of a warrior. Bellamus had never seen him without the gilt-circleted helmet he wore on his head, and against his throne was propped a polished, unsheathed sword. A gold chain rested upon his shoulders and he wore a robe of dark shaggy bear-fur, which must have been feverish in the warm room.

Bellamus ignored the retainers on either side and knelt before King Osbert, who was now leaning back in his throne, eyes closed. 'Your Majesty,' he said.

'A new one,' the king rumbled, voice so deep as to be almost ludicrous. The harp paused briefly and then began a fresh tune. 'This is wonderful,' he said with a sigh, eyes still closed.

'This music, Your Majesty?' enquired the bishop, sympathetically.

'I know it's music,' snapped the king. Bellamus grinned down at the floor. 'Wonderful,' repeated the king. He hummed lightly with the harp for a few moments, plucking imperceptible strings with a thumb and forefinger. 'We should send harpists out onto the streets: I should say that'll brighten the city a bit. My dear people can forget the floods, the storms, and that menace to the north as long as they have good music. I have always believed in its restorative power.' Bellamus wondered how many people's homes would be restored by the sound of the harps. Thc king kept ignoring him and kept talking, his voice melodic, as though he were telling a story. 'It is my great ambition to some day rule a country in which harpists outnumber swordsmen.'

'Amen, Majesty,' said the bishop.

'Where harpists outnumber swordsmen. A gift from Heaven,' said the king. Then he opened his eyes, resting them on Bellamus. 'Bellamus of Safinim,' he said, leaning forward and licking his lips as though the upstart was a particularly plump mouse that he intended to devour. He cocked his head a little and gave a smile of indulgent benevolence. 'Has God granted the Anakim the gift of music?'

'Of a kind, Majesty,' said Bellamus, raising his head a little. 'They sing, they chant and they drum. They play with wind as well, using flutes and trumpets of bone; but they have no harps.'

'No harps? I am ever astonished by their crudity.' He inspected Bellamus a while longer. 'Here you kneel,' he said softly, his voice an earth tremor. 'I thought you must be dead.'

'By the grace of God I survive, Your Majesty,' said Bellamus piously.

'When Earl William and Lord Northwic did not,' said the mighty voice.

'Yes, Your Majesty. Many men died: more than survived. Through great fortune and some skill of my own, I was preserved.'

'Fortune has ever been yours, Master Bellamus,' King Osbert said with a mighty heave of his furred shoulders. 'But I do wish it extended to the men around you. It sometimes seems to me that you strip their luck from them and spend it yourself. Hum, hum.' The king shook his head and tutted softly. 'It should not be so, Master Bellamus. It is not natural that a commoner should be favoured above a noble. I think there is a touch of sorcery in you,' and he prodded a ringed finger at Bellamus. His voice was still low and whimsical, but the king was puffing out his feathers. He was swelling on his throne until it could no longer hold him and he rose slowly, suddenly filling the entire platform and forcing the bishop to retreat onto lower ground. The harp faded discreetly into silence. The king still looked down on Bellamus with that air of kindly interest, but it was now joined by a tinge of regret. He opened his mouth to say more and Bellamus intercepted him from where he knelt.

'The only sorcery at my disposal, Majesty, is my skill with the men I lead. I brought four hundred of them home from beyond the Abus and your kingdom will need that experience more than ever in the days to come. The Anakim have sworn vengeance on us.' The king closed his mouth abruptly. *I recognise that look, Majesty,* thought Bellamus. *I am not another servant of yours to be brushed aside.* This king's affable manner, his indulgent tone and his soft appearance disguised a monster. Very few people were of true value to him, and certainly not a foreign upstart. Bellamus had to make himself valuable, at least enough to give the king pause to remember the words that Bellamus hoped Aramilla had planted in his ear. Osbert was still frozen, his eyebrows raised. 'They are coming south, Majesty.' Bellamus kept his voice low. 'I heard the Anakim king swear it with my own ears.'

Colour and expression were abandoning Osbert's face. This was the most valuable piece of information that Aramilla had given Bellamus: above all things, the king feared the Anakim. He had watched his father slain by one at the Battle of Eoferwic, and had had nightmares about them from that moment. The Sacred Guard had caught his father's bodyguard and, like a fire licking at a thatch roof, consumed it.

One warrior in particular, immense in its steel and rage, had stepped forth and flattened Suthdal's best knights with an inexorable hammer. This horrifying weapon had then been turned on the king's horse, slamming down on its back and oddly denting the beast, which fell with a scream. King Osbert's father, King Offa, had rolled to the feet of the anti-hero. He had stirred, trying to raise himself from the ground under the weight of his armour, and the war hammer had come down on his head.

King Osbert had seen it all. He had watched, little more than a boy, as this formation of the noblest men in the land was ripped apart, and their forces overwhelmed. And then, as his father was killed before his eyes, the figure responsible, that monster with the war hammer, had raised a gloved hand at the young prince being ushered away and pointed directly at him.

I'll come for you, the gesture had said.

The king still felt the shock of that moment. In the fertile flesh of his brain, a seed had been planted. Something vigorous and unyielding, whose roots had sunk deep and resisted all attempts at extraction. For him, the Anakim were at the heart of everything. At the lowest level of his mind, of every action he undertook, was that image of his father's head being crushed within its own helmet; that gloved finger pointing at him. So great was his fear of the Anakim that his other courtiers dared not even mention them. Only Bellamus spoke of them to the king, and he could do so because he was so knowledgeable on the subject. Only he could provide the balm that soothed the king once he was agitated. He did so now.

'But my tidings are not all ill, Majesty.' Bellamus fumbled at a belt over his chest, unbuckling the enormous sword that was strapped to his back. He pulled it forward and, shuffling a little closer to the dais, laid it before the king. 'I bring you the sword of Kynortas Rokkvison. The Black Lord who defeated your father at Eoferwic and who is now dead.' The king gazed down at the weapon before him and sank slowly back into his throne. 'It is yours, Majesty. It is one of the great weapons of their race and I give it to you as tribute. Long may you reign.' Bellamus had not laid a tribute so much as an ace. He knew what the sight of a sword on that scale would do to the king. That was why he had thought better of giving Kynortas's skull to the king: this was equally magnificent, but more intimidating by far.

'You believe the Black Lord will carry out his threat?' King Osbert asked, his voice a touch quieter.

'Undoubtedly, Majesty, if we allow him.' Bellamus stayed calm. 'But we also have an opportunity to destroy them for ever, if we take the right actions at once. But it must be now, and we must have help. I counselled that this might happen when I last saw you, but Earl William was quite insistent. Now we have broken the peace. They plan to take Lundenceaster by way of vengeance. They are coming, Majesty, and the only way we can stop them is by resuming the fight north of the Abus before it infects our lands. We must keep the war there, with help from our allies on the continent, before they can reach us here and before they are ready to fight again.'

The king's head was shaking fractionally to each side, gaping eyes accented by his brow. 'We are not ready for another invasion, my dear Bellamus. We shan't be for a year.'

'The longer we leave them, the graver this threat becomes. Please, Majesty,' Bellamus shuffled closer, still on his knees which were now shaking slightly. 'Hear me now. The Anakim live more than two centuries, but their numbers are kept under control by war. If we leave them, if we allow them to multiply unchecked, then it will not be long before they are quite as numerous as us. Now that we have started this war, we must finish it. Every season that we delay makes our task more difficult. Though they were victorious, they have been weakened. Do not give them the opportunity to gather their full strength and unleash it on us. Attack; as soon as the roads reopen. Let us assemble an army.'

'You are a man of action, Master Bellamus,' said the king. 'But to reinforce failure would be the worst we could do.' Bellamus almost rolled his eyes at that. 'We cannot defeat them.'

'We can, Majesty. I can.'

King Osbert gazed sympathetically at Bellamus for a moment and then picked up his own sword which leaned against his throne. He heaved onto his feet and hefted the weapon in his hands, beginning a shuffle back and forth across the dais, taking care always to step high over Bright-Shock, which still lay where Bellamus had presented it.

The king paused, looking down at Bellamus still kneeling beneath him. 'Rise,' he ordered. Bellamus stood slowly, his knees cracking as they straightened. 'My dear queen,' said the king, 'counsels that you are our best hope against the Anakim. She is a wonderful woman. Blessed with a great many virtues and graces. An example to us all.' He nodded humbly at Bellamus. 'But I cannot place an army of nobles under the command of an upstart. You are a sudden blaze, Master Bellamus. You have no name to protect and so I have no assurances of your conduct. I need assurances.'

'You have my word, Majesty.'

'Your word, your word . . .' The king flapped the phrase away with his free hand. 'I need more, as you very well know. You are cleverer than you allow, I think, but you shan't wriggle your way out of this. Garrett?' The enormous shadow on the king's left stirred and then stepped up onto the platform. It was the huge retainer; the one Bellamus had stared at as he approached the dais, who now knelt before the king. King Osbert motioned him up quickly. 'Rise, Garrett. Will you watch Bellamus for me, as he returns north?'

Garrett stood and Bellamus's eyes followed as he straightened up, his form towering above the upstart. This man would have looked down on most Anakim, Bellamus was sure. He had a breadth and solidity about him that lent his flesh the cold nature of stone. His hair was a bright-blond shock and his countenance dominated by the skull-like cross-section of a severed nose, which left two tall nostrils stranded in the middle of his face. But of his shocking appearance, it was the eyes which disturbed Bellamus most.

A febrile, sulphurous yellow.

Garrett nodded at the words of the king, who turned back to Bellamus. 'There, Bellamus. You shall go north again, this time with the Eoten-Draefend as my representative. He will guide your conduct.' Osbert gave Bellamus a satisfied nod, the matter settled.

Bellamus was dumbstruck for a moment, appalled at the proposition of campaigning with Garrett at his back. He could hardly believe that anyone had allowed a hybrid to become a warrior, let alone one with such close access to the king. But this was not just any warrior: Garrett Eoten-Draefend was famous across Erebos, though Bellamus had thought he was a Sutherner. He had faced the Unhieru: the savage and giant race of men that inhabited the hills in the west of Albion. There he was said to have lost his nose in the process of killing Fathochta, an Unhieru warrior-prince. He had hunted Anakim in the borderlands below the Abus, and was famed as a warrior of surpassing skill and uncontrollable violence. 'Majesty,' said Bellamus carefully, 'perhaps I have been unwise. I would accept—'

The king interrupted Bellamus with a jocular laugh, causing the upstart to take a breath and almost a pace backwards. 'No, Bellamus, it is I who have been unwise and you who have been correct. You warned us before our last invasion. You said that Earl William was not up to the job. I should have listened to you.' The king smiled down at him. 'You want to go north and finish this war? Very well. My kingdom will gather what forces remain to her; we will seek help from the continent and raise another *heregeld*. You will gather the army together in the north, and be ready to go beyond the Abus as soon as the snows have melted. But, when you pass into the Black Kingdom, you will be watched by my Eoten-Draefend. And should you fail, your luck will have at last run out.'

You mean you'll tell him to cut my head off. 'I won't fail, Majesty,' insisted Bellamus. 'There is no need for supervision. I have the measure of the Anakim.'

The king shrugged sadly. 'If you won't fail, then there is nothing to worry about. And you have gained a valuable warrior.'

Bellamus cast around, speechless for a moment. But he thought he would rather risk the wrath of the king than a campaign with Garrett at his back. 'I won't return with him, Majesty,' he said at last, indicating the huge man.

The king, still standing above Bellamus on the dais, gently brought the tip of his sword down to rest on the crown of the upstart's head. 'Go back, Bellamus. With the Eoten-Draefend. If he doesn't come back, you die. Finish this war, or you shall not leave this hall. That is my royal command.'

19

The Stump

Roper and Helmec walked together to Tekoa's household. When he saw the faces of the Lothbrok legionaries that they passed, Roper was glad of his grizzled companion. All fell silent and stared at him, evidently certain that he had been behind the disgrace of Unndor and Urthr. Roper ignored them, though he could not help but feel this war was beginning to slip out into the open.

He hammered at the door to Tekoa's household and it was opened by the familiar face of Harald, who ushered them inside. Within the room in which Roper and Keturah had agreed their engagement just a few months before, Roper found his wife sitting up in a chair by the fire, covered in a blanket. The sight of her heartened him: she had been improving steadily under the physician's care and now glanced up at him with something close to her old energy. Her eyes were still bloodshot, her face still sunken and the skin dry, but colour was returning to her lips. Roper thought he could even detect a faint fuzz of new hair growing on her bare scalp. She raised an ironic eyebrow at him. 'Husband. Hello, Helmec.'

'Good morning, Miss Keturah,' said Helmec, offering a bow before he and Harald retreated into a neighbouring room.

Roper dragged a seat close to Keturah and sat. 'How do you feel?'

'Tired. And I still can't feel with my hands and feet. No more weaving for me, Uvoren's done me a favour.'

Roper smiled. 'You look better. What does the physician say?'

'He says that the feeling may never come back. He thinks my hair might, though.'

'It looks that way,' agreed Roper, surveying her scalp. She looked hopeful and raised her hand to her head but, unable to feel anything, she tutted and dropped the hand again, frustrated.

She and Roper talked, Roper telling her about Vigtyr; about the trials of Unndor and Urthr. He was describing the surly reactions of the Lothbrok legionaries they had encountered on the way, when the door to the street outside opened. Roper blinked, the flow of his story interrupted, and Keturah leaned forward in her chair to try and see who was coming in. To enter a house without first knocking and waiting to be let in could scarcely have been ruder.

The face that appeared around the side of the door was a new one to Roper. It was a pale woman, dark-haired and dressed in well-made, well-fitted clothes. He supposed she might have been beautiful if she had not looked so fraught. She was looking directly at Keturah and managed a tremulous smile. 'May I come in?'

'Hafdis?' said Keturah, evidently baffled. 'Yes, do.'

Hafdis scurried inside and shut the door behind her, casting a glance out onto the street before she latched the oak into place.

'Hafdis, wife of Uvoren?' said Roper, eyes unblinking. 'What are you doing here?'

'Don't be rude, Husband,' said Keturah. 'Come join us, Hafdis.'

Hafdis moved closer and, once her eyes had adjusted a little to the gloom and she was able to see Keturah properly, she clapped her hands to her mouth. She stared at Keturah for a few moments, her eyes shining. Then she began to weep, her face filling with colour. She dropped to her knees and shuffled forward, clutching the arm of Keturah's chair and drawing in a shuddering gasp every few moments to fuel her silent tears. She bowed her head and rested it on the backs of her hands that still clasped the chair, quivering with grief. Keturah took the opportunity to throw a look of astonishment and amusement at Roper, before patting the other woman's head. 'Pull yourself together, now, Hafdis,' said Keturah. 'I was feeling rather good about my condition before you appeared.'

Hafdis spoke in a tiny voice, her head still bowed. 'I know who put you in this condition.'

Roper and Keturah glanced at one another.

'Who?' asked Roper, leaning forward.

Hafdis looked up at Keturah. 'It was Baldwin's idea. Baldwin Dufgurson, the Legion Tribune. I heard him suggest it to my husband.'

'How did you hear?' Roper's voice was full of suspicion.

'He came to our house,' said Hafdis. 'Uvoren sent me away so they could talk. But I stayed outside the door and listened.' Keturah rolled her eyes. Even Roper knew Hafdis had a reputation as a terrible gossip and on this occasion she seemed to have heard more than she wanted to.

'And Uvoren agreed to the plan?' Keturah pressed Hafdis.

Hafdis nodded miserably. 'But it was Baldwin's men who did it. Baldwin gave them the poison. I'm so sorry, Keturah.' A fresh tear ran down her cheek. 'I'm so sorry.'

'Sorry for what?' said Roper, a bite in his voice.

'For not coming to warn you, and coming—'

Keturah flapped for Hafdis to be quiet. 'You're sorry, you're sorry, I know. Too late for that now, Hafdis. It's done. Dry your tears and leave at once, before you're seen by anybody. Uvoren must not know you came to me, understand?'

Hafdis nodded, hands at her throat. Keturah pulled her

close and gave her a kiss. 'Go on. Off you go.' Hafdis flashed a glance at Roper, then stood and scuttled from the room. The door slid gently closed behind her.

'We can't take that to the Ephors,' said Keturah at once. 'Uvoren would know she helped us and it would only be her word against both of theirs.'

'You believe her?' said Roper, staring at the door through which Hafdis had departed. 'She's probably just trying to save her husband.'

'She hates her husband,' said Keturah, staring into the fire. 'I believe her.'

Roper gazed at her for a moment, then nodded. 'Helmec!' The guardsman entered, eyebrows raised expectantly. 'I want you to take a message to Vigtyr the Quick for me. Tell him: Baldwin next.'

'Baldwin next,' repeated Helmec.

'And tell him to make sure the punishment fits the crime.'

'And he'll know what all this means, lord?'

'He will.' Helmec bowed and was gone.

Stimulus and reaction.

Just two days later, the Hindrunn was set abuzz. Word was travelling from household to household and scattering between tables at the officers' mess that the Legion Tribune, Baldwin Dufgurson, had been placed under house-arrest amid allegations of deliberate military sabotage. Farriers and fletchers both reported that he had deliberately withheld vital supplies from the Black Lord's army as it had set out on campaign, seeking to bolster the chances of his friend Uvoren maintaining his grip over the Hindrunn.

Those charges proved to be baseless. Baldwin fought hard and could bring enough witnesses of his own to make it clear that the lack of horseshoes and arrows had not been his fault. But a closer look at the meticulous tally-systems that he supplied in evidence revealed that they did not match up with those of the Hindrunn armourers. For years he claimed to have been sending iron and steel to the armourers that had never arrived, instead siphoning it off for his own household.

'I suspected embezzlement,' Vigtyr had reported to Roper, late one evening. 'But it's hard to prove without close access to his records. So I found men to accuse him of sabotage so we could get the evidence we needed. He'll pay for what happened to your wife.'

'What's the punishment for embezzlement?' asked Roper.

'That will be up to the Ephors, lord. But it will be exceedingly harsh.'

This latest move shocked the Hindrunn more than what had happened to Uvoren's sons. Baldwin was a powerful and influential figure, and had been Legion Tribune for many years: it was a scandal right at the heart of the Black Kingdom. It was also the first time people who were not affiliated with Uvoren began to suspect Roper's involvement. The rapid disintegration of Uvoren's power block no longer looked like a coincidence. There must be a powerful hand guiding the demise of Uvoren's allies and he had no more powerful enemy than Roper.

Baldwin did not do well. His crime had been going on for decades and had deprived the Black Kingdom of resources desperately needed for defence. Two days after his trial, he was led to one of the 'honeypots' situated around the Central Keep: enclosed courtyards with intentionally fragile doors, designed to attract the interest of invading armies who would then flood the space. The walls were mounted with fire-throwers and Baldwin was locked in the centre of the courtyard.

Roper watched from atop one of the walls in his wolfskin cloak, the Ephor who had sentenced him nearby with his mighty eagle's wings enfolding him. Keturah, making her first foray outside since having been carried into her father's house on a litter, stood at Roper's side, bundled in a long cloak with a cowl up over her head, covering her baldness. Legionaries were pedalling on the fire-throwers to pressurise their tanks. They exhaled clouds of mist into the freezing air, blurring the view of the watchful score that lined the walls. The bubbling noise elicited by the pedalling caused Baldwin to drop to his knees in the snow that dusted the courtyard and hold up his hands towards the Ephor.

'Lord, please . . .' His voice came at first as a tiny cheep. He glanced at the silent watchers surrounding him and then back at the Ephor, eyes two enormous white jewels. 'Please, my lord. Please!' Suddenly he was wailing. 'I will do anything! Don't, my lord! My family can repay all costs to the fortress double! If you spare me, I will dedicate my life to duty! Anything, Lord Ephor, anything!' The Ephor looked on, expressionless.

The pedalling stopped.

'Please! Please! Please!' The tanks gurgled themselves quiet and everything fell still. Even Baldwin seemed to be breathing too hard to beg any more. He threw a glance at Roper and then his gaze flicked left, resting on Keturah. He shook his head a fraction.

Then one of the legionaries seized a lever, hauled it back with a clunk and, almost simultaneously, boiling sticky-fire spewed from the bronze-mouthed fire-throwers. Baldwin was engulfed at once; Roper could not even see him beneath the molten waves being sprayed over the courtyard. It seemed to him that the very snow was burning and black smoke billowed into the sky. The hurlers operated, grinding and shrieking, for just a few heartbeats, and then they dribbled themselves quiet. Down in the courtyard, Baldwin's flesh had almost fallen apart. What was left protruding from the blazing ocean, just a stump, was not easily recognisable as a man.

Roper turned away before the remains had stopped moving.

Three gone from the table. Five remain.

He and Keturah moved away from the swirling courtyard and Roper was rather surprised when the elderly Ephor fell into step beside them. 'Not a good sight, Lord Ephor,' said Roper. 'He'd have done better not to have begged.'

'Indeed, Lord Roper,' said the Ephor before seizing Roper's arm with a bony talon. 'The speed with which Uvoren's closest supporters are falling may be a coincidence, Lord Roper,' he hissed vehemently. 'I do not know: I shall judge each case by its merits. But if I discover that your people are fabricating evidence against these men, I will bring down vengeance upon you.'

'Baldwin's own records condemned him,' said Roper, unflustered. 'I hardly think I can be blamed for that.'

'But the claims of sabotage were baseless. They only served to make him present his tally in evidence, which, conveniently, condemned him of a further crime. I will be keeping a very close eye on you.'

'As are the Kryptea. Who do you think I fear more?'

'That depends on whether you have any sense,' fired the Ephor.

'These are guilty men, my lord,' said Roper stubbornly. 'You have found that yourself.'

'The question, Lord Roper,' said the Ephor in a voice like grinding metal, 'is whether they are guilty of any more than having been your enemy.'

Roper could hardly explain that the man whose earthly remains had just been atomised was responsible for the poisoning of his wife. He feared Uvoren's retribution, though, and from then on, kept Keturah close, giving both her and Tekoa their own escort of trusted guardsmen.

But men were beginning to fear acting on Uvoren's behalf.

Next to fall was another Sacred Guardsman, Hartvig Uxison. This one had two Prizes of Valour to his name and a big reputation. But three witnesses said that they had seen him strike a woman in the aftermath of the post-campaign feast, when he had been slighted by not being invited to the Honour Hall to dine with the Black Lord.

Hartvig went down with more honour than those before him. He quietly admitted that it was possible he had done such a thing; he had, after all, been blind drunk. But he had no memory of the incident and professed never to have met the woman he was accused of striking.

Guilty.

He was stripped of his place in the Guard, but allowed to remain a subject, with the Greyhazel agreeing to take him in as a legionary. The Ephor also left it in Roper's hands whether he should be stripped of his Prizes of Valour; it was the Black Lord's power alone to remove or bestow those. Roper considered the legionary. 'Hartvig earned those prizes,' he spoke at last. 'And in my view, a single drunken error does not change that. Keep your prizes, Hartvig. I hope that one day you earn the right to wear the Almighty Eye again.' Hartvig inclined his head in genuine gratitude. He was disgraced, but it was not over for him.

That had been on Gray's advice: Hartvig was already taken care of and, in the future, Roper might want to welcome him back. There was no sense in making enemies unnecessarily, especially as there might be a time after Uvoren when he would need men like Hartvig. Roper also considered that Hartvig, though he had been with the army at the time, had not been one of those who had attacked him beside the fire atop Harstathur, when Pryce had intervened. Perhaps Uvoren had not truly believed that Hartvig was enough of a friend of his to slay the Black Lord. Perhaps he had been ordered to, and refused.

Empty chairs were appearing at the ancient oak table in the Chamber of State and Roper filled them with men beholden to him. Sturla Karson, legate of Ramnea's Own Legion, took one. Skallagrim took another. Those of Uvoren's supporters who remained were much quieter. Uvoren spoke out, as ever, against Roper but his proclamations were now followed by a tense silence. Vinjar, the Councillor for Agriculture, had ceased to come to the councils at all. Perhaps he hoped that Roper would consider he had renounced his alliance with Uvoren. His place was duly filled, but as far as Roper was concerned he had not escaped.

It was after Hartvig's disgrace that Uvoren struck back. Helmec had reported as usual to train with the Sacred Guard whilst Gray had been advising Roper. Uvoren took full advantage of the Lieutenant of the Guard's absence, commanding Pryce to beat Helmec.

'Why, sir?' Pryce demanded coldly. 'He isn't late.'

'I have found him insolent, Lictor. Do as I tell you,' said Uvoren, fixing Pryce with his narrowed glare and taking a pace towards him.

'When was he insolent, sir?' Pryce had no choice but to be respectful in front of the rest of the Guard, many of whom owed their stations to Uvoren.

'Yesterday, Lictor. Beat him.'

Pryce was still for a moment. 'No, sir.'

Uvoren took another pace towards Pryce and reached forward to seize his long black ponytail. He bent Pryce's head back and pressed his own into the lictor's face. 'Are you disobeying my orders, Lictor? Beat him, or the others will beat you.'

'No, sir,' said Pryce through gritted teeth, holding eye contact.

Uvoren burst out laughing and let go of Pryce's hair, letting him straighten up. He placed his hands on Pryce's shoulders affectionately, chuckling in Pryce's raging face. 'It's a joke, Pryce, calm down!' He patted Pryce's hollow cheek and then glanced at Helmec. 'But seriously, Helmec, get out of here or I'll have you torn apart.' Helmec stood his ground for a moment, face expressionless, and then turned and walked away across the training hall. 'Don't even think about coming back. You are no guardsman!' roared Uvoren after him. He glanced at Pryce. 'And you're not a lictor. Lictors obey their commanding officer's orders.'

Pryce was breathing hard but did not respond.

Roper was with Gray when Helmec arrived to break the news of what had happened to him and Pryce. 'Helmec? What are you doing here?'

'I've just been dismissed as a guardsman, lord,' said Helmec. 'And Pryce is no longer a lictor: Uvoren forced him to disobey an order and demoted him.'

Roper watched Gray's face fill with rage at the story of what had befallen his protégé and quickly suggested that they should take the air on the roof of the keep. 'Come, you two. We've been inside too long.'

He led the pair up the broad staircase of spiralled stone outside his quarters, climbing thirty or so steps to a locked oak door at the top. Roper produced a key from a leather pouch at his belt and the lock clunked open. Behind the door, the leading of the roof was almost entirely hidden beneath a pristine white cape. A broad fire step protected by a crenellated wall ran the whole circumference of the roof, tracing the outline of the Central Keep and the towers which studded it. From above, it would look like a giant, round-toothed cog. Inside the fire step, the slate roof rose towards the centre of the keep like a mountainside.

These were the materials of the Hindrunn: slate, lead and granite. Everything was made of unyielding stone to prevent fire spreading within the tight walls of the fortress. Roper, Gray and Helmec broke a fresh path through the snow and walked on the fire step around the roof, Helmec gazing intermittently through the crenellations at the fortress sprawling beneath them. 'Uvoren was never going to go quietly,' said Roper, tugging his cloak tight about his shoulders.

'He has just sent out a powerful message though, lord,' said Gray. 'The Sacred Guard is the most esteemed institution in this country. Every ambitious man dreams of the Almighty Eye on his right arm. If he's saying that friends of yours cannot serve in the Guard; that is a compelling argument for not siding with you.'

'It is,' agreed Roper.

'There's also a rumour going around, my lord,' put in Helmec. He hesitated.

Roper glanced over at him. 'Tell me,' he said, shrugging.

'The rumour is that you have been unfaithful to Keturah on several occasions. People think you are now revolted by her appearance so have started inviting other women into your bed. If I've heard this rumour, lord, so has everyone else. People know I'm your man: I will have been one of the last to hear.'

Roper nodded. 'That rumour has Uvoren written all over it. Do people believe it?'

'Some do,' said Helmec.

'Then we must finish him before he can do us too much damage,' said Roper.

Roper's two companions were silent a moment. 'What have you offered Vigtyr for his services, my lord?' said Gray at last. 'He is a man even you do not want to be in debt to. I cannot think what you can offer him that has made him so willing to act.'

'He thinks he's going to be a Sacred Guardsman,' murmured Helmec. Gray stiffened.

'He thinks what?'

'I didn't tell him that,' said Roper, carefully.

'But if you led him to believe it, you may regret disappointing him.'

'Why couldn't he be in the Guard? He is the best swordsman in the country.'

'He is not a guardsman,' said Gray without hesitation. 'Yes, one-on-one, Vigtyr would probably kill Uvoren, Leon, Pryce; any comer. He is exceptional. For the Guard, fighting skill comes into it, but only insofar as it is not possible to survive acts of extreme valour without it. I promise you, however bad you think Uvoren is, Vigtyr is so much worse. He scares me.'

'And Uvoren doesn't?'

'And Uvoren doesn't,' Gray confirmed. 'He's a bastard, but a straight warrior-bastard. Vigtyr is something else.'

'He is my cousin, lord,' volunteered Helmec. 'I knew him well growing up. We were at the haskoli together.'

'And what was he like as a boy?'

'Frightened, my lord,' said Helmec. 'His father, Forraeder, was . . . a monster.'

'A monster how?'

Helmec shrugged. 'Violent. And a drinker. I hear he used to be a good man, but he had his spirit broken on the battlefield. Then Vigtyr's mother died giving birth to him, and Forraeder blamed Vigtyr for that. I remember when he first arrived at the haskoli,' Helmec's voice held nothing but pity, 'he was the quietest boy there. I don't even think he was shy: he just hadn't developed a personality beyond fear and obsession. He had nothing to say. I think that is why he worked so hard at the sword; it was a way of gaining control and protecting himself from his father's shadow.'

'So why does he want the Guard so much?' asked Roper.

Helmec shrugged. 'I don't know. All I saw was that, as he grew up, his need for recognition became more and more overwhelming. Perhaps, for him, it fills the gap that ought to have been taken by affection.'

'And he had no siblings?' asked Roper.

'None, lord,' said Helmec. 'But he's certainly had enough wives and none of them ever lasted long. Divorced,' he added with a small smile at Roper's sidelong glance. 'Not vanished.'

'He sounds damaged,' said Roper.

'Oh, lord; beyond repair,' said Helmec. 'But I would never want to be his enemy.'

Roper felt a trickle of guilt, that he might be abusing Vigtyr's need for recognition to his own political ends, but those few drops disappeared into the dark pool that was the plague he had caused. 'I will deal with him when I must,' said Roper. 'I will reward him, but if you say he is not a Sacred Guardsman, Gray, then he is not a Sacred Guardsman.'

Gray was not mollified. 'There is nothing you can give that man that will equal the prestige of a guardsman. If you do not deliver that to him, I can promise you that you will make an infinitely devious enemy.'

'Well, he's our devious servant for now. Vinjar Kristvinson is next to fall.'

Gray, evidently uncomfortable, was silent a little longer. 'Are these men guilty as charged, lord?'

Roper shared his discomfort. At first the speed with which Vigtyr had hauled down these mighty men had made him gleeful. He had laughed out loud at the malice of targeting Uvoren's sons first and when he had seen the fear that had been sown in his enemy. That glee had soon turned into a strange sort of horror. Men were falling everywhere and Roper had no idea whether or not they deserved the punishments they received. Hartvig had seemed to be a genuinely good man and when he had been disgraced, and taken it so graciously, Roper became aware of a growing sense of unease. He remembered the fear in Baldwin's eyes as he stood in the honeypot: the look of a man who knew things were out of his control. In retrospect, Roper recognised it. 'I don't know, Gray,' he said honestly. 'Baldwin was. And he was guilty of more than the charge which killed him. The others . . . That is what the Ephors are there to determine, is it not?'

'Our vengeance system was not created to deal with conspiracy,' said Gray. 'There's nothing the Ephors can do about enough paid witnesses. We must defeat Uvoren, but is that at any price?'

'We've come a long way down this road, brother,' said Roper. 'I'm not sure there's any turning back. One way or another, this country must have a clear leader. And it cannot be Uvoren.'

They walked along the battlements in silence for a time, Helmec distracted by the view of the Hindrunn below and Roper loosening his cloak a little so he could feel the cold. 'The pair of you should come and dine at my house tonight,' said Gray, at last. 'Uvoren still holds court in the mess and Sigrid would like to see you both. Bring Keturah and Gullbra?' The latter was Helmec's diminutive wife. Both Roper and Helmec said they would be very pleased, and that evening attended Gray's house for a supper of goose with lingon berries, prepared by Gray's wife Sigrid. She was warmer with Roper than she had been last time, giving him her odd half-smile and a decorous kiss. 'Welcome, lord, welcome.' She steered Roper into a chair, thrust a goblet of mead into his hands and began to interview him. 'The plague looks to be relenting, lord, have there been any new outbreaks?'

'We have not had to close off a new street for weeks now. The quarantine seems to be doing the trick.'

'It is lucky you acted so fast,' said Sigrid steadily.

Roper's mouth twisted and he was close to saying that had he not been such a fool in the first place, none of this would have been necessary. But the moment passed and he smiled instead. 'I am grateful for everyone's discipline in this matter.' Her expression showed she had seen and understood the momentary warping of his mouth. 'Your efforts were well beyond the call of duty. I am amazed that you did not contract it yourself.'

That half-smile. 'Something has been taking care of me. And of this one,' she added, putting an arm around Keturah who had finished saying hello to Gray and had come to join them. 'Your hair is regrowing fast.'

'Not before time,' said Keturah tartly. 'This is not a winter to be walking around with a bald head.'

'Is there ever a time to be walking around with a bald head?' asked Roper. 'You look like an earthworm.'

Keturah laughed, giving an accidental snort as she inhaled.

Sigrid looked flatly at the pair of them. 'An easy audience,' she observed. 'You've married the right woman, lord.'

'Sigrid here is just jealous, Husband,' said Keturah. 'Unfortunately, she has no sense of humour.'

'I hear Pryce has also lost his sense of humour,' said Sigrid, as Gray came to join them.

'He is in a fearsome temper,' confirmed Keturah. 'I've just been to see him.'

'Poor Pryce,' said Sigrid. 'He is a lictor to his marrow.'

'I am surprised he didn't break Uvoren's jaw for demoting him,' said Roper.

Gray laughed sourly. 'He knows Uvoren was looking for an excuse to get rid of him entirely. But he won't forget. He will have his revenge, one way or another.'

Roper had his revenge first.

Legionaries called on the house of Vinjar Kristvinson, the Councillor for Agriculture, the next morning. He had not been seen in public since Baldwin had been eviscerated by sticky-fire and answered the door pale but straight-backed.

'Councillor Vinjar Kristvinson?'

'I am Vinjar.'

'You're under arrest for adultery. You will come with us now to the dungeons beneath the Central Keep to await trial.'

Vinjar threw a helpless look behind him to where his wife Sigurasta stood, white-faced and with her hand covering her mouth, as his wrists were bound in leather. The evidence was compelling and the trial, three days later, did not take long. Uvoren had stopped coming to defend his accused allies and Roper, the words of the Ephor ringing in his ears, did not want him or any of his men associated with the trial. It was just Vinjar's family and that of his wife who watched on.

Guilty. Three left at the table.

20
The Kryptea Do Not Knock

'What happened to Vinjar?' asked Keturah. They sat in Roper's quarters together, the door held shut by bolts of iron in an effort to keep out the sense of unease that pervaded the rest of the fortress. It was late, snowing again, and charcoal burned white-hot in the ventilated hearth.

'Nothing too serious,' said Roper. 'He's avoided the prison-ships at any rate, but he's lost his status as a subject. He's a nemandi again.'

'I know his wife,' said Keturah.

'Sigurasta?'

'She's devastated. Did he do it?'

'No idea,' snapped Roper. The bolts were evidently not working.

'Very early in our marriage to be getting tetchy, Husband,' she reproved him.

'Don't make me think about it. The Ephors released Tore and Randolph without charge today.'

'Why?'

'They voted unanimously to suspend the courts. They're certain I'm behind the purge but they can't work out how much of the evidence is fabricated. No doubt they're looking for something to pin on me. If they find it . . . sticky-fire.' He remembered Baldwin's begging in the honeypot. He remembered his eyes, almost comically wide. He remembered his supplicatory hands quivering as he held them up to the Ephor.

And then that stump.

That was all that had been left, after the waves had swamped him. It was still moving, but surely it could not possibly have been alive. When his time came, maybe Roper would beg as well.

Only one man knew the truth of whether or not these men were guilty: Vigtyr. Roper feared very much that he was about to disappoint him. If he had brought down the others, it would be no harder to get to Roper. Not when the Ephors were looking for any excuse.

'Don't worry, Husband,' said Keturah with surprising tenderness. She put an arm behind his neck and a hand on his knee. 'This storm will pass. And whether or not the courts have been suspended, most of Uvoren's supporters are now too scared to show their faces in public.'

'I wish Vigtyr had gone for Tore and Randolph first,' said Roper. 'The legions are loyal to their legates, and while Uvoren still has legionaries, he has power.'

'His influence is a shadow of what it was.'

'I worry . . .' Roper stopped himself. Self-doubt was not Anakim.

'You worry about what?'

He shook his head and Keturah tutted.

'You worry that you are not the man you thought you would be.'

He looked at her. 'Yes,' he said, his voice a dim reflection of its usual self. 'I regret this. I truly, truly regret this. If I am to fall short of holding the Stone Throne unopposed, I wish I had done it on my terms. I wish I had never spoken to Vigtyr. If my body is to be destroyed by sticky-fire, I wish that I'd fought this war against Uvoren with more honour than he. I want to be able to die without regret.'

'We must all do things we would rather not for the sake of the country.'

Roper was too preoccupied to give proper attention to that line. He dismissed it. 'I have told myself that so often I don't believe it any more. I can't believe Uvoren would have been any more terrible a lord than I have been. This fortress is like the underworld; plague still stalks the streets and nobody speaks their mind for fear of hard legionaries hammering on their door the following dawn. People are terrified.'

'Roper the Ruthless,' mocked Keturah. 'Roper the Tyrant?'

'I prefer the first.'

She laughed.

In Roper's tangled mind, the alleviation of the plague had enmeshed with his own salvation. If he could return the fortress to something approaching normality, it would be a balm for the raw guilt on his mind, first at causing it, and second at the way he was tearing down Uvoren's allies. Perhaps, too, it would show the Ephors and the Kryptea that he was fit to rule.

'Well, you've frightened Uvoren,' said Keturah after a while. Roper made a sceptical noise. 'You have,' she said confidently. 'He sleeps with Marrow-Hunter by his bed now. He has nightmares about the Ephors.'

'How do you know?'

'How do you think? We are a partnership now, Husband. If there's ever a time when a warrior doesn't stand behind you, you'll find me there instead. For instance,' she tucked her legs beneath her and leaned into him. 'It was I who passed Vigtyr the information that condemned the Councillor for Agriculture.' Roper stared at her, disbelieving. 'He was guilty. It's been going on for years.'

'You should have told me before.'

'I'd meant to keep it a secret, but I have been very clever. I had to tell someone.'

Roper laughed in spite of himself and put an arm around her. 'Strange wife.'

'You are not a bad lord. You must believe me, Uvoren would be worse. Hafdis has not a single good word to say about him. But I think beneath all the hatred she loves him still.'

'She does?'

Keturah nodded. 'Or at least, the idea of him. She is still waiting for him to reform: that's why she delayed telling me about the poisoning. She was hoping Uvoren wouldn't go through with it. But he is rotted through by love for himself. There is so little man left at his core that I am amazed the wrestling did not break him in half.' She was silent for a moment. 'And don't worry about sticky-fire. If you have gone too far, the Kryptea will let you know before the Ephors do.'

'I don't know how far the Kryptea can be pushed,' said Roper. 'Or what they consider acceptable. How can I rule when it is not even clear what I am permitted to do?'

'I could go to the Academy,' suggested Keturah. 'Find out more about them. They'll know what has caused the Kryptea to intervene before.'

There came a knock at the door and Roper flinched. A matt-black blade cut across his memory and left in its wake the flash of a cuckoo with outstretched wings.

'The Kryptea do not knock,' said Keturah impatiently. Roper stood and unbolted the door, pulling it back to reveal Helmec leaning idly against a wall and, next to him, Thorri, the Councillor for Trade.

'You left a message that I was to come as soon as I returned, lord,' said Thorri, who was fresh off a ship from Hanover, where he had been acting as a trade envoy. 'I trust I have not disturbed you?'

'Of course not, Councillor, thank you for coming.' Roper stood back and showed Thorri in. Keturah, still sitting on their bed, gave Thorri a little smile.

'Good evening, Councillor. How are your daughters?' Thorri's wife had given birth to twins just four months before.

'Teething, thank you, Miss Keturah,' said Thorri, taking the yew chair that Roper steered him towards. 'A trip to Hanover was a welcome distraction. What has happened, lord?' Thorri asked, turning to Roper.

'What do you mean?' Roper furnished Thorri and Keturah with birch wine and took some for himself.

'Thank you. The atmosphere, it's . . . it feels like there's been a tragedy. Begging your lordship's pardon, I've never seen this fortress so quiet.'

'Who knows?' said Roper, knowing perfectly well. 'What of your mission?'

'Successful, lord,' said Thorri, cautiously. 'The agreement is a tenuous one and limited for now to wool and copper in return for grain and iron, but I am hopeful it will provide a limited source of revenue. In time, as relations improve, it may expand into more as well. But it was a wise move, lord, because it sends out the message that the Black Kingdom is once again prepared to do business with the outside world.'

'Well done, Councillor, it's a good start. I take it the agreement takes effect after winter?'

'Quite, lord; the seas are too rough to start now but in the spring we can begin.'

The Councillor stayed for a time and told them about Hanover. It was one Anakim in ten thousand who wanted to travel outside their own country, so the picture he composed of alien ways and lands was of special fascination, however disturbing it might be. He told them about the strange Hanoverian dialect; how it was barely comprehensible to ears tuned in the Black Kingdom. How the Hanoverian princes had adopted the confusing Suthern love for gold (though they seemed to have little answer when asked exactly why it was valuable), and lived in mighty palaces that towered above the steep-roofed hovels of their subjects. How they had no regular legions; just a warband, bonded to the princes and a citizen militia that was roused when the

Sutherners were restless. Their food was strange: though they had bread, it tasted rough and the stones they used to grind it deposited dust in the flour, making it gritty. Their customs were strange. The land even smelt strange: dust and mortar pervaded the air from the ever-expanding palaces, raw effluent flowed through open gutters beside the streets and, as their brewers were not restricted to a single district, a ripe miasma of barley, honey and yeast hung over the streets. Even the smoke smelt different: it was not the rich, smooth scent of blazing charcoal that was dominant in the Hindrunn. It was a harsher, thinner trace of ash- and oak-smoke. Roper shuddered and Keturah declared she felt sick.

To an Anakim, a home was something that grew with time. They sank their roots into the earth slowly, as memories and loved ones became associated with the place. They became familiar with the orientation of the surrounding hills, mountains, forests and rivers. They knew so exactly where the stars would be at which point in the night that they had no need of timekeeping devices. They knew from which peak the sun would emerge on the winter solstice, how the earth would smell when the spring rains arrived, and all the oldest trees of the forest. The world around them was inhabited by spirits, formed from the powerful memories they had of the area and the people who had moved through it. To be uprooted from all this was bitter indeed and initiated the feeling of *fraskala*; being cocooned, as you were not connected to the land around you.

Of course, the Anakim had to travel abroad sometimes. They had invaded Suthdal regularly over the centuries, and when it had no longer seemed wise to use that training ground, they had sent the legionaries to help in conflicts over the sea, to renew the perishable skills of war. But this was all accomplished with a wretched heartsickness, which most thought to be the explanation for why Anakim armies seemed to be a more fearsome prospect at home than they were abroad.

When Thorri had departed, Roper bolted the door behind him and sealed the shutters, for the clouds had lifted and the moon was shining off the snow. His last thought before sleep took him was to wonder whether Keturah knew that Cold-Edge lay beneath their bed. Perhaps that was why Uvoren had armed himself: each night the two famous weapons clashed in Roper's captive mind. He allowed himself to descend into dark combat.

Resurrected once again the following morning, the dreadful depressions created by Marrow-Hunter filled in and his limbs untwisted, Roper dressed to tour the streets once more. It was the coldest day yet of the winter and he wore two woollen tunics: one finely woven and close-fitting, worn next to the skin; one loose and thick which he pulled on over it and which he then belted about the waist. Goatskin gloves, elk-skin leggings, high oxhide boots with woollen socks, and his wolfskin cloak. As he pulled it on, something needled his back. Reaching a hand round, Roper discovered a little patch of cotton pinned to the inside of the fur. He inspected it briefly once and then glanced at it more intensely a second time, his gaze lingering on the image printed thereon.

'What is it?' asked Keturah. She was half out of the door, already dressed, and her short hair covered by a cowl. She still had no feeling in her hands, making her unable to weave. Instead, she was going to the Academy to discover what she could about the Kryptea.

'Nothing,' said Roper, balling up the cotton scrap and casting it on the fire. 'Keep your enquiries subtle, won't you?' She nodded. 'I'll see you this evening, Wife.' He kissed her and she departed, leaving Roper a little pile of food on his table: cakes of dried salmon and lingon berries. Roper put them in a large pouch at his belt, to which he attached Cold-Edge.

On his way out, he cast one more glance at his hearth, beneath the great elk-head mounted on the wall. The piece of cotton was blossoming slowly as the heat of the charcoal caught it. It opened just wide enough for Roper to catch sight once again of the image printed on it: a spread-winged cuckoo. The cuckoo discoloured, the cotton turned grey and a small flame burst from the cloth. Roper did not wait to see it consumed; he was gone.

He and Helmec walked the streets together. It should have been a cheering sight, for half a dozen communities were reopened that day, all trace of the plague gone. The area it affected had grown smaller and smaller and Helmec chattered happily about how it would soon be over.

But Roper's mind dwelt instead on the linen cuckoo in his cloak. Watch your back, that meant, he was sure. It was the Kryptea letting him know that what he had done to Uvoren's friends, full subjects of the Black Kingdom and thus protected by its ancient customs, had been noted. A ruler had to rule, the Kryptea knew that. Sometimes he must discipline and make examples, so they would allow him some freedom. If he were to abuse it, however, he would be reintroduced to the matt-black blade, this time wielded by a skilled assassin. He hoped Keturah was safe, asking questions about that organisation.

The linen cuckoo was their idea of a dialogue. If Roper wanted to survive the winter, he would need to come up with a riposte.

The Academy had always been Keturah's favourite building within the Hindrunn. Its position within the innermost wall of the fortress – a status awarded only to the Central Keep and the Holy Temple besides – marked it out as one of the Black Kingdom's buildings beyond price. It took the form of a broad, stepped pyramid; the top echelon of which was a tower that rivalled the Central Keep in its reach towards the heavens. The lower levels were like desiccated honeycomb: more window than wall and more space than structure, eased into the island on which they stood by a slight meniscus. A deep defensive lake surrounded it, crossed by a solitary strand of stone. From the vines that scaled its earthenmost twenty feet, to its ancient alignment with the star Thuban, to the water that surrounded it, so clear that some evenings it was not easy to tell where the dry winter air ended and the lake began, it was perfect to Keturah. It was a better marriage of wilderness and refuge than she had seen anywhere else in their rugged country: the edge on which function and form combined. And at the apogee of this building was a great metal structure that burnt in bright sunlight and hardened before clouds: a cold silver eye.

Keturah crossed the bridge (scarcely necessary at this time of year as the lake on either side was clouded ice), delivering a patronising smile to the berserkers who watched over the doors. These were the guardsmen of the Academy, trained to recognise the robes of the historians even when at their maddest, though Keturah remained scornful of the decision to entrust the security of the Academy to these most unstable warriors.

She passed them, passed through the open stone arch behind, beneath a carving of a spread-winged angel with giant, spidery hands, and through the gaping jaws of the Academy. The hall within was fresh and cavernous, with the inner edges again lined with vines. Corridors led off on three sides and in the middle of this hall was a woman in the thick cream robes of an acolyte, kneeling next to a small fire set in a depression in the floor. The smoke was escaping through a hole in the roof and a blackened copper pot was sitting beside it, half-filled with tumbling water.

Though her head was covered by a hood, there was something familiar about the acolyte's posture. 'Sigrid?'

The acolyte looked up and Keturah saw the two light grey eyes of Gray's wife shining like daylight beneath the hood. 'Keturah.' Sigrid stood and gave Keturah her strange smile: a narrowing of the eyes and a slight raise at the corners of her mouth. The two women embraced over the fire. 'You're here to see the Chief Historian?'

'I am. She knows I'm coming, where can I find her?' asked Keturah.

'You wait here for her, but she'll be some time. Share the fire with me.'

Sigrid gestured at the empty stone floor and the two knelt together, Keturah a little too close so that her knees became uncomfortably hot and she had to retreat slightly. Sigrid gave the smile that was not really a smile and took up the copper pot, pouring some of the steaming water over a sprig of pine set in a wooden bowl. She offered the bowl to Keturah, who accepted with an inclination of her head and set it aside for a time, waiting for the brew to cool. The Academy was famously cold, hence the thick robes of both acolytes and historians and, in spite of the fire, Keturah found herself cooling swiftly on the damp day.

'I heard you were coming,' said Sigrid, pouring a second bowl of hot water and pine needles which she took herself and set aside as Keturah had done. 'I asked to be gatewoman today. Why do you want to see the Chief?'

'There's a chant I want to hear. And I have an interest in the acolyte's robes. Have you settled on a cell yet?' A cell was a trio of historians, led by a senior academic, that specialised in the total recollection of four hundred and thirty-one years of history.

'For now I am happy as an acolyte, but one day, perhaps the robes of a Deep Historian will appeal to me.' Sigrid paused for a moment. 'Though I'm not sure I shall ever be ready to renounce my marriage. Unworthy a motive as it may be, I may end up joining a cell as my refuge.' To become a full cell member and thus be entrusted with the identity of the Black Kingdom, a woman had to renounce her marriage and live within the walls of the Academy itself. She became part of the country: something too precious to be chanced elsewhere, and too important to risk corruption through marriage and alliances to those outside the Academy. Sigrid meant that she was only likely to take this harsh and disciplined way of life when Gray was killed in battle: close to an inevitability for a man serving in the Sacred Guard.

Keturah thought of herself as an astute judge of character. The motivations and temperament of others were there to see if she only looked, and she could not imagine a time when Sigrid would be unhappy. The older woman, though serious, had a serenity about her that made her company restful even though she barely talked. But that silence just seemed to make the words she did utter weightier. If Keturah was in awe of one person in the Black Kingdom, it was this woman. She was quiet, so Keturah was quiet too. Just being in the presence of her tranquil companion, beneath the sheltered stone of the antechamber and with the frozen lake stretching out before them, Keturah felt peace descending over her. The Academy offered clarity. Sitting here, the appeal of joining this institution was obvious.

They were silent for a time. From a pouch at her belt, Sigrid produced a couple of handfuls of hazelnuts which she split with Keturah. The hazelnuts were slightly dry so both women roasted theirs next to the fire and Keturah began to sip at her pine-needle tea. It was resinous, aromatic and refreshing.

'Which is the chant you wish to hear?' asked Sigrid.

Keturah was aware of only the faintest reluctance to share what she knew she should not. 'Whichever one details the formation of the Kryptea. Do you know where it is?'

'I know where,' said Sigrid, 'though I cannot remember which cell has it. It is a famous chant: the Chief will be able to help you. Be careful how much you learn about those men, though. They have many ears, even in here, and if you want to know about their foundation, someone will report that to them.'

'Not you, though?' said Keturah.

'What do you think?' said Sigrid, staring out at the bridge. She put more wood on the fire. 'But someone will.'

'I doubt it matters. I'm no threat to them or the stability of the country,' observed Keturah.

'It does matter,' said Sigrid. 'They are an organisation of almost unlimited power and jealousy, entirely separate from the law. Sometimes I think the Academy is too reserved. Nobody asks about the Kryptea because nobody knows to ask. We don't volunteer information unless people come to seek it.'

'The only threat they pose is to my husband.'

'And yet they murdered those two legionaries,' said Sigrid, referring to those who had been killed in retribution for Uvoren's foiled attempt on Roper's life. She took a sip of her own tea. 'Everyone knew the Kryptea were not behind the assassination and so their name was unsullied, but they took vengeance anyway. That was an action of spite. Do not disregard the Kryptea.

'You see those berserkers? We have thousands of them here, living below the pyramid. In full battle-madness, they would tear apart every bit of the Hindrunn beyond the lake. They could protect us from a legion, but they could not protect us from a Kryptean. We don't know who they are, we don't know how many they number. We don't know how they are recruited, how they are trained, or if they have women in their ranks.'

'They must,' said Keturah, 'or they're brainless. The women of this fortress are far freer in their movements than the men, and much less likely to be suspected of murder.'

'No one has ever caught a Kryptean agent,' said Sigrid. 'So we don't know. The Kryptea is not the safeguard from tyranny that everyone thinks it is. The Ephors protect us from over-ambitious Black Lords. The Kryptea has no function beyond the long shadow that it casts. It is a toxic fungus whose roots go too deep to ever be cut out. I have learned what I can of them and, as far as can be told, no one has ever caught one of them. How do you stop them when you don't even know how they act? Were those men killed beneath the cuckoo truly guilty? Everyone has just assumed they were.'

Keturah considered this. 'I suppose I never questioned it.'

Sigrid touched her hand briefly. 'Just take care.'

'Everyone's been saying that to me.'

'You should heed their advice.' Sigrid glanced pointedly at Keturah's newly sprouted hair.

'I think you may be the first person who's told me to take care where I may indeed heed it,' said Keturah.

Sigrid thought about that for a moment. 'Why?'

'Usually, I'm told to take care by people who would be too scared to do what I'm doing. They tell me to take care because they wish they had the confidence to try it themselves and don't want to be made to feel inadequate by someone doing what they would like to.'

Sigrid was watching Keturah steadily. 'Well, it's true, I don't have the faith in my own abilities that you have,' she said. 'I think you're right, a lot of the time, envy makes people react strangely. It bursts out of them before they know it. It is good to live bravely, but remember that inexperience can make you naïve. And with the Kryptea, you won't get two chances to make a mistake. One will kill you.'

The light was failing and there was a pink tinge to the sky in the west before the Chief Historian arrived, but Keturah had been prepared to wait on such an important woman and besides, she had Sigrid's company. It was Keturah's first encounter with the Chief Historian. She was almost as tall as Keturah herself, with a sheet of steel hair, white-blue eyes and heavily lined skin hanging from the startlingly prominent architecture of her face. 'Keturah Tekoasdottir?' She stared down at the still-kneeling Keturah.

'That is I, my lady,' said Keturah, getting to her feet and giving a polite smile.

'Good. My name is Frathi Akisdottir.' The Chief Historian's eyes had settled heavily on Keturah's. 'What can I do for you, miss?'

'I have an interest in one particular chant and hoped that you might be able to take me around the Academy as well,' said Keturah. 'I've had a long-standing interest in being an acolyte.'

'You are very young to have had a long-standing interest,' observed the Chief Historian. 'Which chant do you wish to hear?'

'Whichever details the assassination of Lelex,' said Keturah.

The Chief Historian did not react at all for a moment. Then she said: 'The formation of the Kryptea?'

Keturah shrugged. 'Indeed.'

'You will need to be swift,' said the historian. 'The cells are nearly leaving for the evening run. Come.' She turned on her heel and started back through the corridor through which she had arrived: that on the right. Keturah waved at Sigrid, who semi-smiled in return and watched her leave.

The corridor down which Keturah was being led skirted the outside of the Academy: an open colonnade that almost kissed the hard waters of the lake. It appeared, despite the rallying darkness and though it stretched in a broad arc that made it possible to see fifty yards ahead, that they were completely alone in the passage. Every five yards or so on their left was a door of flat, greyish-white wood that looked like it might be hornbeam: a wood that showed little mercy to its carpenters, both in its fiendish difficulty to work and its tendency to warp and crack. On the wall surrounding the doors were carvings: animal-headed angels; forges powered by lightning, churning out supernatural weapons; highly stylised, goblet-stemmed human figures that appeared to be giving direction to smaller people below them; disturbingly lean figures with narrow heads ranging across the walls. As Keturah advanced, the content and tone of the carvings began to change: a baby being plucked from a prone stone figure; serried ranks of soldiers; more figures that appeared to be spinning rivers in their laps that flowed over the walls. In many of the depicted scenes, Keturah noticed a figure in the background with giant, spidery hands; observing but not intervening.

'The Academy is built to resemble the passage of time,' said the Chief, still striding several paces ahead of Keturah. 'The cells use it as a memory aid, with each room used for a different chant. As with time, it can only be approached from one direction so that just by living in this space, my historians become intimately familiar with the period for which each is responsible. That also means we shall have to hurry to catch the cell you want.'

'And which cell is that?' Keturah was tall and usually strong but she could feel the lingering weight in her legs from the poison, and the older woman was almost pulling away from her. The disciplined running regime built into life as a historian, thought to clarify the senses and improve the all-important memory, was said to make them the fittest women in the Black Kingdom.

'Forty-seven thousand eight hundred from the Deep,' said the Chief Historian. 'A time three thousand years ago.'

As they walked, the curve of the corridor became tighter and when the lake disappeared from their right-hand side and was replaced by stone walls, Keturah realised they were spiralling into the centre of the Academy. There were doors on both sides now, seemingly still made of hornbeam, and a humming was beginning to fill the air, as though they drew close to the core of a bee-hive. But instead of a choir of workers, she found that at the centre of this spiral was a flight of steps that led upwards on to the second floor. They were at the centre of another stone spiral, and without breaking stride, the Chief led her onwards. This time the doors on either side were made of a wood with a dark stripe of heartwood running up the centre of each board that Keturah could not place.

'What wood are these doors?' she asked.

'Rowan,' came the reply from ahead.

They spiralled outwards, carvings still flashing past Keturah (a vast serpent covered in chain mail erupting from beneath the earth; enormous butterflies that snatched up racing figures; people without eyes, crawling through tunnels to piles of treasure within; always that spider-handed angel lurking behind, carved less deeply into the stone so that its presence was faint), the humming persisting and at times reverberating powerfully enough to make the doors rattle. After a rather shorter time than it had taken to navigate the first spiral, they came to the outside of this one. It was another colonnade that looked out onto the lake, but this one more elevated. Keturah reflected that the entire purpose of their journey so far had simply been to get to the first floor of the building. Apparently, this was not the end, however, for the Chief was leading her up another flight of stairs to another spiral corridor, this one with honeyed doors of beech.

Keturah understood. By making the passageway of the Academy a multi-layered spiral, its builders had produced a single immense corridor some miles in length, with each storey demarcated by a different kind of wood, fresh carvings and a tally that helped distinguish it from its fellows. It was a parsimonious model of the river of time and, as each Historian remembered the period for which she was responsible, she would envisage the walk through this immense spiral. Each door was a different episode and, if they chose to enter it, they could perform an in-depth chant regarding the events of that particular period. That was the humming which Keturah could discern: the chanting of each cell, performing one of the hundreds of historic episodes they could recall. The entire structure was a memory aid.

On the fourth floor (this with doors of walnut), they at last stopped outside a room bearing a 'III' carved into the wood. The humming was still reverberating through the door and the Chief raised a knotted fist, battering at the boards. The humming stopped abruptly and there was a pause before the door opened to reveal a cream-robed acolyte on the other side. 'My lady,' said the acolyte, a little surprised. She stepped aside and the Chief Historian swept inside, Keturah on her heels. Within the room was bare, grey stone, adorned only with a fragrant oily scent which Keturah could not place. Another acolyte sat in a corner and three historians knelt on thick rush mats. Unlike the acolytes, their robes were black, with a system of cream bands representing the time period in which each cell specialised.

'Peers, this is Keturah Tekoasdottir,' announced the Chief. 'Perhaps you can help her. She wishes to hear the chant that details the formation of the Kryptea.'

A look of swift surprise passed between the two acolytes, and the two peripheral historians glanced at their central colleague. She was older than they, perhaps a hundred and eighty years, her black hair heavily lined with grey and her face the spider's web of lines that denotes someone who has lived a life outside. 'Certainly we could sing it, take a seat, Miss Keturah,' she said and she gestured at the bare stone floor before her.

Keturah folded graciously at the waist and knelt. 'Good,' said the Chief Historian. Her eyes rested on Keturah once more, and then she left without another word. To Keturah's surprise, the acolytes stood and scurried after her in silence. She was left alone with the three kneeling historians.

The two peripheral women shuffled around so that they were facing inwards, towards their senior colleague in the middle. She herself faced Keturah, but was staring at the floor just before her. She cleared her throat, sat up straight and gave a low, soft opening note. It drew what Keturah at first took for a surprised gasp from one of the peripheral women, before her opposite number blew the same sound back at her. It was like an involuntary expulsion: the sound made when someone has struck you in the back while you are talking. The two outside women exchanged this sound again and again, forming a rapid dialogue before the noise changed. It became a breathless gasp, like nothing so much as the sound of shock. The two women grew faster and faster, the sound becoming more and more percussive until it seemed to fill the room and Keturah could feel her own breath growing short and her heartbeat quicken. She was assaulted by it, surrounded by it, and when it had almost become too much it changed again, becoming something sweeter. The two women exchanged gasps of pleasure and surprise, as though they were old friends caught up in a cycle of delighted recognition.

These sounds and more interweaved, providing a throbbing, unearthly background tune to the central historian, who had begun to sing. Her words were growled over the top; almost choked on in the very back of the throat.

Near forty-eight thousand years after the Deep,
Lelex, mighty Black Lord, sat on the Stone Throne.
His hair was dark as clotted blood, his judgement
Measured and calm; slow to come, and sweet to hear.
Steel is sooner etched with a fingernail,
Than fear was drawn from his swift, rain-grey eyes.
The Black Lord's allies were the wolf; the wind;
The mighty river and the ragged sky.

When Mighty Lelex took the throne, his duty
Was clear to all. The folk of the north wearied
Of bones and steel. The warrior yearned to lay
Down his armour, and take saddle and barding
From his horse; and the fletcher make his arrows
For hunting alone. So was it hoped that
Mighty Lelex might nurture a wilted peace,
Shrivelled by a sea of blood and endless war.

For three full years, through summer and winter both,
Mighty Lelex did all his people desired.
The Black Kingdom knew the order it had craved,
Scarce and consoling as a still, iron sea.
But peace, precious as a newborn, and fragile
As one too, was dashed at last by Suthern band

Striking north. The legions marched, their swords still sharp,
And met them on the field, at Gusanarghe.

The fight was quick, the Sutherner defeated,
But at conflict's dawn, Mighty Lelex's son,
Brave Amundi, was cut down by Suthern band.
Mighty Lelex saw him die: watched immobile,
Aghast and accountable as his firstborn
Was drowned beneath a sea of Suthern bodies.
Mighty Lelex's heart, once so sure and so hard,
Crumbled like a rock in the fire's blazing teeth.

The fragments of once-mighty Lelex were left
With his son's, and he, who came home from battle,
Could not remember the man he had once been.
His eyes were frozen and his voice was muted.
His council's words sank slowly through his ears,
And his wife, Cleocharia, did not know him.
Mighty Lelex, once so bright, began to twist
The Black Kingdom into an ugly thing.

Anguished and confused on a hunt soon after,
Mighty Lelex quarried his dear friend Agnarr.
His many companions, even he himself,
Grew still among the trees when he'd hurled his spear,
Silent as his dear comrade crashed to the earth.
After, two councillors were hung as earrings
From the gate; testament to unwise comment.
The people were muted, songs no longer sung,
Of Mighty Lelex, bereft of his mind and his son.

The Sacred Guard, who had once been so holy,
Became poisonous fume at their lord's command,
Spreading through the streets so both man and woman,
Were disquieted at the tread of their boots.

One Ephor dared object, summoning Lelex
To court, to match crime with its retribution.
Five guardsmen came instead, breaking down the door
And flinging the Ephor from off his own roof.

Lord by birth, father by love, hero by war,
And tyrant now, to his blasted heart,
Mighty Lelex was beaten at last by war,
The drug that had consumed him and exacted
A fate far crueller than death and long lament,
That waits for the unswerving warrior.
That man was gone, and it was proved beyond doubt
When he drew a knife on his crying daughter.

Cleocharia now suffered the same fate
Which had discharged her husband's mind. She watched
With no whisper of shelter from the screaming
As her own dear child was slain before her. Yet,
Unlike Mighty Lelex, she was not finished
By the ordeal. Her form realigned; her task
Was clear. The watchword was vengeance, she would see
That her husband got all that his actions deserved.

One night, when darkness consumed both stars and
moon,
When the hearth had burned low and a bitter wind
Mourned through the north, Cleocharia summoned
A band that came forth in greatest secrecy.
'By this way or that, our lord must die,' she said.
'But though his mind is gone and his tongue directs
Evil deeds alone, the Almighty's chosen
He remains. The Almighty must bless our plan
Before we can still that hateful tyrant's heart.'

So she spoke, exposing a pale silver coin,
The captured moon, flattened to bright reflection.

'By Suthern silver was our lord's mind discharged,
Suthern silver now decides his fate once more.
When our lord unjustly kills an innocent,
By the fall of this coin shall god's will be known.
By this side he lives, to chance against the fates
Once more. By this side has the cuckoo flown,
And my second son shall occupy the throne.'

The bright coin was laid in bronze eagle feathers
To yield Almighty blessing; and the true men
That Cleocharia had summoned scattered
To their homes, their purpose now to train through night,
Cold and blue, in the sacred craft of death;
Achieved with the knife, with poison and with wire,
That lacks the honour of the face and the chest,
And seeks instead the inky sufficiency
Of the back, and of the slowly pulsing neck.

Each day that Mighty Lelex or his Sacred Guard,
Killed an innocent without cause, Cleocharia
Cast her silver token. Seven times it flew,
Seven times it fell, delivering fate's judgement,
Seven times it said Mighty Lelex should live;
That his soul should not yet walk the Winter Road.
Finally, Mighty Lelex killed an Ephor
With his own hands, nailing his flesh to a tree.
The Almighty felt the nails hammered into place.

Once more, Cleocharia threw the blessed coin,
And now, it came down on the side of vengeance.
'At last!' she said. 'The Almighty delayed
The consent of chance so that now my soldiers
Are fully trained and cannot fail in their task.'
Word went out to her warriors: that night,
Mighty Lelex would die. Three suffused his house,
Their route unperceived and their footsteps unheard.

When dawn broke, Mighty Lelex did not awake.
He was found where he slept, life strangled from him
And the cuckoo burnt into his troubled brow.
'My men disquieted his sleep,' said Cleocharia,
'As they shall for each tyrant from now, until
The overturning of the earth.' It was she
Who took the throne, ruling with gracc for four years
Until her son by Mighty Lelex, young Rurik,
Had learned to use seasoned eye and studied ear.

The Ephors saw the wisdom of Cleocharia's
Deeds, and that she had acted in full deference
To Almighty will. They blessed those who worked
Beneath the cuckoo, and decreed that if the pull
Of tyranny once more gripped a Black Lord,
Then retribution would be dealt between them
And the Almighty. So formed the Kryptea,
To protect these lands when the Ephors could not.
By the cuckoo shall their dusky work be known.

For the final two lines, the peripheral historians had fallen silent and it was only the senior cell member who kept chanting. It finished, leaving only a fading echo off the cold stone. Keturah beamed at them in gratitude.

'That was wonderful,' she said.

'A sad one to sing,' said the middle historian, clearing her throat.

'Why so?'

'I believe it to detail the greatest mistake our country has ever made. Forming a band of killers with unlimited power was a drastic overreaction to the reign of Lelex. And who has killed more people since? Black Lords who felt "the pull of tyranny", or the Kryptea? It is the Kryptea, I tell you. The Ephors were frightened; they felt reverence for their office had been lost when two of their number were killed. They acted out of un-Anakim vengeance and nobody has questioned their ruling since.'

'That is a novel take to me,' said Keturah. 'And though I have been in the Academy only a few hours, it is not the first time I have heard it.'

'That's because we're the people who know,' said the old historian. 'Go and tell your husband what you've learned here. Tell him the Kryptea have proved again and again that they have no code. Whether they still use that silver token to gain Almighty approval for their killing is doubtful. Tell the Black Lord to watch his back.'

The plague had finally surrendered, providing Roper with the response he needed to placate the Kryptea, albeit temporarily. But he had to do more. In an effort to consolidate his power and prevent the captain from making trouble, he sent Uvoren north to 'act as an inspiration' to the young lads of the haskoli and berjasti. It was a nothing job and all knew it, but he no longer had the voice to resist.

Keturah, her strength returning and her hair regrowing steadily, was spending more and more time at the Academy, trying to discern a pattern in what had caused the Kryptea to act in the past and therefore how Roper might avoid its wrath. She was besotted with the ancient sisterhood and spent so much time there that Roper had had to visit twice to ask for her, only to be told she was witnessing a chant and he would have to wait. There were no further sinister warnings from the Kryptea and Roper assumed that stamping out the plague had placated Jokul. That, and Uvoren's declining influence.

To be sure of their favour, Roper needed to rebuild his popularity with the subjects. To that end, he took another loan from Tekoa and used it to purchase livestock. Twice a month, he held a feast on the streets just as Uvoren had done, staying for long enough to ensure he was connected with the genuine pleasure which this gesture created. He was gratified to discover that, when he returned to the fortress from observing an early spring exercise for the Skiritai, his reception had been almost as positive as that which greeted Uvoren whenever he walked the streets.

Though it remained a lonely post, Roper was becoming used to the responsibility he had for these people and even developing a deep satisfaction at their growing relationship. He found that leadership suited him well. He had always known about people: how to read them and how to motivate them. Now he learned the importance of small gestures and self-sacrifice in cultivating a willing populace. He was absorbing some of Uvoren's most effective techniques and began to understand what Gray had meant about hatred clouding his ability to fight the captain.

It was during one of the feasts that a ranger came to find Roper. He was engaged in handing out rye bread at the time and had been reluctant to follow the legionary, but something in his manner told Roper that he should obey. They were in the courtyard before the Central Keep and he followed the man up its broad stone steps and inside, heading for the Chamber of State. There, they found Tekoa, Gray, several Skiritai officers and Sturla Karson, legate of Ramnea's Own. A forest-floor of maps had been laid out on the ancient oak table and the men were engaged in heated discussion. Tekoa looked up as he entered the room. 'How do you feel about another test, Lord Roper?' he asked.

'What's happened?'

'Bellamus has happened.'

A party of Dunoon legionaries had been ambushed as they undertook a spring exercise near the bank of the Abus. 'It was Bellamus. He's got the whole army this time. A bunch of knights rode our men down and cut them to pieces. They weren't armed, they weren't armoured and they weren't prepared. It was a massacre.'

'How?' demanded Roper. 'The snows are barely melted, it isn't even properly spring yet. How was he ready to march?'

'I don't care,' snarled Tekoa. 'Let's just put an end to this.'

'Recall the legions,' said Roper. 'At once.'

'The Skiritai are already riding; we are to muster here. And I've recalled Uvoren as well.'

Roper froze and Tekoa, seeing his resistance, waved a hand impatiently. 'We shall need him.'

Part III
SPRING

21
Garrett Eoten-Draefend

As though the Hindrunn were the drain of Albion, the legions streamed towards it. Every day for two weeks, men flooded through the Great Gate, swelling the barracks and withering the granaries. Some of the legions were in good order and had not even encountered this fresh Suthern menace marshalled by Bellamus. Other legions came in already battle-weary; injured, exhausted and demoralised. One, the Hetton Legion, had been broken so completely that it merely dripped through the Great Gate over the course of a week. Individual centuries of men, or sometimes even fewer – a score, a dozen – found their way to the fortress never having received the order to withdraw; just knowing that if there was one safe place to which they could retreat, it would be here.

In private, Roper and Tekoa had argued extensively over Uvoren's recall. Roper did not want him anywhere near the Hindrunn. They could break the Sutherners without his help, Roper insisted, and bringing him back sent out the terrible message that they relied on him. Tekoa had said that was childish; that men fought better when they knew Uvoren was with them or watching over them and Roper had to consider the wellbeing of the country above his own leadership.

On this point at last, Roper conceded and grudgingly had allowed the Captain of the Guard to be recalled.

Roper nevertheless afforded himself a passive-aggressive glare at Tekoa when they saw the welcome Uvoren received as he marched through the Great Gate. The fortress had chattered about his impending arrival for days and when finally he appeared, there was a crowd waiting for him on the other side of the gate. He came in on horseback, accompanied by half a dozen stern Lothbrok warriors and dressed in the full finery of a master of war. He was cheered lustily by the crowds. They mobbed him so intently that Uvoren could scarcely advance up the street. He held out his hands to them, assured them everything would be well now that he was here, and told them that they had driven back the Sutherners many times and would do it again.

'This is the worst of it,' said Tekoa in answer to Roper's deepening scowl. 'We'll need him in the battle, but there you might get lucky. Sacred Guardsmen die like newborns.'

'We can dream,' said Roper, turning away from the sight in disgust.

Where this invasion was different from all those that had preceded it was that Bellamus had caught them unawares. They had had no idea that the Sutherners, who had seemed whipped, could be ready to march as soon as the roads had reopened. The legions Bellamus faced did not even have their swords and plate armour with them. They fought with axes, hunting bows and billhooks as they retreated from the hordes. Bellamus had broken one legion entirely and scattered several others, killing thousands. There were already almost as many Anakim dead from this invasion as there had been in all the battles of the previous campaign put together. Roper had to strike the Hetton Legion from the rolls: there were simply not enough men to fill it.

Fear.

It seeped through the fortress, infinitely more contagious than the potent miasma that had caused the plague. It crept between door and doorstep, through open windows, and hung heavy over the cobbled streets. You could perceive it in the way the legionaries now walked in clusters, talking urgently and quietly with one another as they hurried between barracks and keep. Or in the way that the Metal District now clanged and hissed through the night, as the arms and armour were prepared. Or in the frenzied bartering of the markets, as subjects brought up as much food as their modest household assets would allow in preparation for an impending siege. Or in the muted officers' mess, which was almost silent whenever Roper sat down to eat.

The refugees had begun to reappear at the Hindrunn. Roper admitted the first of them at once and then, once the legions were back, sealed the gates. This was met with guilty approval from the subjects within, glad that Roper was the one taking such difficult decisions. Tekoa, as ever the best-informed man in the Chamber of State through the thousands of Skiritai eyes that roamed the country, said the relatively small number of refugees was not due to excessive slaughter; it was simply that the Sutherners had raided this land so recently. They had torched some of the refugee camps that Roper had assembled, but most they had left un-harried as they marched north. As the Sutherners saw it, the canvas and hazel tents were not even worth destroying.

It took more than a week for all the warriors (barring one legion, which had sent word that it was stranded further north) to assemble within the Hindrunn. They mustered at sixty-seven thousand warriors, including the new year's crop of nemandi apprentices. It was a drastically reduced number compared to the ninety thousand who had marched out under Kynortas just last year.

The forges and smiths had worked through the night, churning out Unthank-silver swords, steel arrowheads, iron horseshoes, chain mail, greaves, gauntlets and the steel plating that would be sent to the armourers to be assembled into full cuirasses. The houses were expected to equip their own legionaries, and the poorer ones whose resources were more limited (House Alba, perhaps, or House Nadoddur) would arm only their most esteemed warriors with arms and armour bearing their house crest. Those whom they could not afford to arm would borrow armour decorated with the crest of the Jormunrekur, the Lothbroks or the Vidarr. The more legionaries who went into battle bearing your house crest, the higher the esteem of your house. However, the treasury still had to pay and feed these legions and tumbled further into debt with the Vidarr under the strain of yet another campaign.

There was no debate over staying in the fortress this time. Uvoren no longer had the influence to block Roper and besides, knew that his most likely source of redemption was the battlefield. The legions were almost ready to march when a message arrived.

It was from Bellamus.

A cannon fired on the Outer Wall. It boomed, flat and desolate, around the citadel and disturbed the councillors assembled in the Chamber of State.

'Enemy sighted?' queried Gray.

'It must be,' said Tekoa, glancing towards the window behind the Stone Throne. 'From the south. The Great Gate.'

'Thank you for today, peers, I suspect the cannon has terminated our council,' said Roper. 'Legates, please make certain your legionaries are ready to depart at two hours' notice.' Roper turned to Gray and Tekoa. 'Shall we?'

They were already out of their seats and an agitated humming had filled the room as the rest of the council packed up. Surely an enemy sighting could only mean they were about to be besieged. Pryce was also in the room, begging Roper with a look for permission to come to the Outer Wall. Roper assented with his eyebrows and issued an invitation in kind to Helmec.

The five of them hurried down the stairs that connected the Chamber of State directly with the stables of the Central

Keep. They mounted coursers, usually kept for messengers to speed between the Outer Wall and the Central Keep, and flew up the ramp and onto the packed streets. The girth-straps of their saddles were fitted with great clanking iron rattles that jangled as they rode, warning the subjects to make way. Everyone had heard the cannon-shot and had cleared a path long before Roper and his companions were within earshot, gazing anxiously after the party charging for the Great Gate.

Roper leapt off his saddle, handed the reins to a legionary to tether and then noticed that the Great Gate was already open and a cluster of Suthern horsemen was waiting beneath the arch of the gatehouse. One of them held a huge, long-bladed spear, attached to which was a limp square of white linen. If the gates had opened, that would mean that the sentries above the gate could see no more than these soldiers on the plains that had been cleared around the Hindrunn.

Aware of the rest of his retinue dismounting around him, Roper beckoned the Suthern party come closer. He thought the man in the centre looked as if he might possess unusual height for a Sutherner but did not realise quite how tall he was until the man had swung himself out of his saddle, removed his helmet and looked Roper in the eye. This Sutherner was enormous. He was taller than Tekoa, Pryce and Helmec and was able to match Roper and Gray inch for inch. He and the rest of his party were clad in strange raiment: plates of some rough, ceramic-looking material that overlapped in a flexible suit of armour. It covered their shoulders, their torsos and their thighs, with metal greaves, gauntlets and helmets with horsehair tails completing their defence. They moved easily in it, suggesting that the plates, whatever they were made of, were lightweight.

'Well?' said Roper in Anakim, for the benefit of his companions. 'Who are you?'

'We are the men who have come to take your country from you,' said the tall Sutherner in a faltering, heavily accented version of the same tongue. He was dreadfully scarred, this man. Amid other marks on his face, the front half of his nose was missing, with a skull-like cross-section of his nostrils dominating his features. He had a shock of bright-blond hair and his eyes were a fevered, wolf-like yellow.

'Do you have a name?' pressed Roper, ignoring the tedious reply.

'Garrett Eoten-Draefend, of Eskanceaster.' His demeanour suggested that Roper should have heard of him, though he had not. Roper knew the Saxon word 'draefend'. 'Hunter', that meant, though he could not translate 'eoten'. 'I lead Bellamus's household warriors.'

'And what is this pottery that you armour yourselves in?' Roper posed a dutiful insult.

Out of the corner of his eye, Roper saw Gray look at him abruptly and Garrett gave an unexpected laugh. It was a maniacal, out-of-control kind of laugh that made Roper's hair stand on end. 'You should know,' he said in his heavy Anakim. Roper scrutinised the overlapping plates that were coloured like cream mixed with rust. They were reminiscent of something and his mind was on the verge of grasping it when Garrett spoke again. 'I have a message from Bellamus.'

'Go on.'

'He travels to Harstathur, your sacred mountain crossroads. He says you should join him there and fight for the Black Kingdom.'

'Harstathur?' said Roper, disbelieving. 'Why would he fight there?'

'He will fight you anywhere,' said Garrett. 'Even where you think you are strongest.' Garrett smiled to reveal bleached white teeth before turning away. He and his companions hauled themselves back into the saddle, leaving Roper mystified behind them. Garrett reached out to one of his companions and took the long-bladed spear, which had been held for him. 'I think you know this blade,' said Garrett, lowering it carefully towards Roper, trying to make it clear that he was not threatening the Black Lord.

Roper glanced down at it and felt a jolt run up his back.

It was Bright-Shock.

His father's sword. Roper could tell by the outline and the way its Unthank-silver blade glittered. It had been embedded in a powerful ash-shaft with some sort of steel and lacquer socket. Bastardised into a huge long-bladed spear and here it was, wielded by this immense Sutherner. Roper looked up into Garrett's face to see that white grin bared at him again. With his wide, febrile eyes and severed nose, the smile made his face irresistibly skull-like.

'You called it Bright-Shock,' said Garrett. 'Now it is Heofonfyr.'

'It is your weapon?' asked Roper, switching to Saxon.

'Yes.'

'I hope we meet at Harstathur,' he said.

Garrett laughed. 'Me too.' He rammed his helmet back on his head, gave a mocking bow with a flourish of his hand and turned away, spurring his horse out through the Great Gate. His retinue followed.

'That was bait, my lord,' said Gray at once. 'That man, his weapon, his armour. They were all to entice you to Harstathur.'

'Why wouldn't we go?' Roper asked distractedly. His mind was grasping after that armour. It was so familiar.

'Because that's what Bellamus has asked us to do?' suggested Gray.

'Bugger that,' said Tekoa. 'If he wants to meet us at Harstathur, let him. We'll carve him and his hermit crabs apart.'

Roper looked sharply at Tekoa. 'The armour!' he blurted.

'Anakim bone-plates,' said Gray grimly. 'Extracted from our dead.'

That shocked Roper. It made a grim sort of sense: the bone-plates were lighter and harder than steel and would have a ghoulish impact on the Anakim they faced. But somehow it seemed beyond the pale. To wear the bones of dead, honourable legionaries as armour! That was bitter.

'I agree with Tekoa,' said Roper, vengefully. 'Bugger that. We're going to Harstathur.'

The legions would leave the next day. They had a destination, they had an enemy and Bellamus seemed interested in little other than their destruction, so Roper gave the warriors a final night to prepare themselves and say goodbye to their homes and families.

The fortress went deathly still the day before a march-out. Weighing heavily on the minds of all was the knowledge that, win or lose, not everyone would come back through the Great Gate. Some of the wives now preparing their husbands' equipment would hear a knock at the door in the coming weeks. A messenger, telling them that their husband, the father of their children, had given his life in service of the country. Just as the men were expected to accept their fate with an unwavering heart, so their wives must take the news like a subject of the Black Kingdom. 'Were we victorious?' was the accepted response. And if the answer was 'yes', as it so often was, then the woman might respond: 'Then I am glad', or perhaps, if her resolve was close to failing, 'Good.'

Then the door would slam shut.

Keturah assembled Roper's equipment, just as thousands of other wives were putting together their husbands' arms and armour. She laid it out on one of the deerskins on the floor: first, Cold-Edge. It seemed that she had known where it was all along. Next to that, a long dagger that Roper could use if he lost his battle-sword. Then a task-knife, single-edged for cutting food, cloth, wood. His axe; a saw blade; an entrenching-tool; the oxhide medical roll; two water-skins. His steel cuirass, the patch he had sustained in the battle on the flood plains visible as a faint outline, was laid out next to these. It gleamed. Roper took care of his own equipment, but Keturah had dismissed his efforts and polished the steel herself with fine sand until it shone, then sealed it with oil. Next to the cuirass: a padded leather sark with a chain-mail skirt attached, that he would wear beneath the steel. Then his gauntlets and the leather gloves he wore beneath them. His oxhide boots with steel strips inlaid in the shin and calf; a felt cap to be worn beneath his helmet, with a slit at the back so that it fitted around his high ponytail. Finally, the Unthank-silver helmet that had belonged to Kynortas, the axe-shaped blade at its front so sharp that the eye shrank from it.

Most wives added several small tokens that were not required for the march or the battle line and Keturah would not be outdone. She had included a bundle, wrapped in comfrey leaves, of dried fruits threaded onto a string and dried fungi too, which could be added to stews for flavour. In a separate package she had pressed strips of dried elk and boar, seasoned to make the mouth water. On top of the packages of food was a small silver mail snake on a chain. Catastrophe: the serpent that would end the world.

When Roper entered his quarters and saw his equipment laid out so tenderly for him, with the keepsake and the packages of food, he stopped suddenly. Keturah was sitting on their bed, trying to weave with her numbed fingers. 'Your equipment is ready, Husband,' she said, glancing up at him.

'Thank you,' said Roper, quietly. This did not feel like the last time he had gone to war. Then, his situation had been so desperate that it had seemed an escape from the torment of the Hindrunn. To die trying to undo the retreat that had been his first command would not have been a bad outcome.

This was different. Now, he had something to lose. He was partaking in the customs that warriors of his land had observed for thousands of years. He was connected to that history: through his ancient sword, his father's helmet, the honour of the legionaries under his command and now this farewell from his wife. Pride threatened to overwhelm Roper, that he could be so much a part of the mighty warrior tradition of the Black Kingdom. He was also beginning to feel fear. He might never come back here, to this room and to this woman.

'What?' said Keturah. Roper shook his head; she knew exactly what. She smirked. 'I hear Bellamus sent a big message.'

'Certainly a big messenger.'

'Garrett Eoten-Draefend,' she probed him. 'Garrett the Giant-Hunter.'

Roper did not care about his name. 'He has Bright-Shock.'

'May it bring the same kind of luck to him that it brought to your father.'

'Bad luck didn't kill Kynortas. Men die on the battlefield.' Roper shrugged. 'And I shall make sure that Garrett is among them.'

'Garrett has killed Anakim warriors with many years' more experience than you,' she said. 'He made his name fighting the Unhieru. He killed Gogmagoc's eldest son, Fathochta. That's how he lost his nose. Garrett is famous across Erebos!'

Roper looked at her sceptically. 'How could you possibly know that?'

'You have one great source of Suthern information, it is beyond me why you do not use it. The Academy,' she added as Roper continued to look baffled. 'Everything we know passes through there.'

'You researched Garrett?'

'We are a partnership. I do the things that you do not, and the most recent cell has plenty of information on Garrett.'

Roper sat down next to her. 'But that can't be true. How could a Sutherner possibly kill a creature like Fathochta?' He stared out of the leaded window a while and Keturah shrugged. 'All the same, I want Bright-Shock.'

'Maybe Pryce or Leon or one of those other heroes will kill Garrett. You could let it be known that you want his spear.'

'Yes, perhaps.' There was a pause and Roper's eyes turned

themselves moth-like to the gently stirring hearth. 'How was it last time that I left?'

'Conflicting,' she said. 'We were married then but I didn't know you. If you had not come back . . . I would have been more sorry about the loss of a half-call-up. So many brave men, marching out under this untested lord and against such a large number of enemies. I think most of the fortress said goodbye for ever to your forces the day you left. Nobody expected so many of you to come back. Even if you did, nobody expected Uvoren to allow you through the gates.'

'But you trusted your father.'

'Yes, I trusted him. I thought he would know when to use you and when not to. But he says he never intended to contain you and that you commanded the whole campaign.'

'I did. What do people think this time?'

'This time they expect victory again. Nobody believes that a full call-up will be defeated. And they have all their heroes in this army. Leon is the talk of the fortress after his Prize of Valour; and Pryce, as usual. They love and trust Gray. Uvoren as well: people say his influence is worth an extra legion on the battlefield. There are questions over Vigtyr but people say they are glad he is on our side. And you: people say this new Black Lord is a good one. He has a talent for the business of war, he is brave and he inspires his men.'

Roper grunted. He struggled with that idea. There was a part of him that did not believe that those victories had been earned. Two successful battles were few enough that he could have been riding his luck. And he had never fought against Bellamus, who seemed to be a rare talent and who was already dictating the terms of this campaign. 'Failure is so much easier to accept when people don't expect anything of you,' he said.

She placed her familiar hand on his arm. 'You're not allowed to fail this time.'

Roper looked at her and saw that her other hand lay lightly on her stomach. 'A child,' he said, detached. Absurdly, he wanted to laugh but he controlled himself. He was fairly certain this should be a solemn moment.

She nodded carefully. 'Yes.' Then she smiled.

Roper capitulated to the laughter. 'You're going to be a subject!'

'A thrilling thought,' she said dryly. 'But not as thrilling as the thought of meeting the babe I carry.'

'I should like to meet it too.'

'Then come back to me. And if you can leave Uvoren at Harstathur, so much the better. Go and kill our country's enemies, Husband.'

They marched out.

The streets were thronged with people. They watched solemnly as the legions marched past. There were no herbs and no cheers; those would be saved for a successful return. Roper rode at the front on Zephyr, with Uvoren on horseback behind him. The Guard followed them. Gray's house was on the route out of the fortress and, leaning out of the upstairs window, Roper saw Sigrid, Gray's wife. She was startlingly beautiful even from this distance and supplied Roper with her distinctive smile, as if to say she was thinking kind thoughts about him. Then her gaze had moved on to her husband, marching in the ranks behind Roper.

Eyes followed Roper down the cobbled streets. A few from the crowd called out as Roper passed; just noises of respect. They rode on to the Great Gate, where Roper spotted Hafdis, Uvoren's wife, waiting dutifully on top of the gatehouse. It was a display to complete his warrior image. The fortress must know that she and Uvoren remained united. But even from here, Roper could see her disdain for her husband. She could barely keep the sneer from her face as he rode forward, managing an apathetic wave of her hand in recognition before turning away from the column. Keturah too was on top of the gate, short hair scraped into the ponytail that denoted a married woman with no children. She stared down at Roper with a half-smile on her face and Roper could not resist staring back. He could see her green eyes from here. She was taller than every figure around her, even the stern legionaries who guarded the gate. She was not even a full subject, but looked like a queen.

Roper kept his eyes on her until the moment he rode through the gate and the stone of the gatehouse obscured her from his view. Then he looked down. Before him, the gates were open and the clear acres south of the Hindrunn stretched ahead. The melting snows had revealed a broad road that snaked over the grassland, forking east and west. Easy marching. They would take the eastern road. It led through the ruined Eastern Country and into the hills. There, on the Altar of Albion, a horde waited for them.

Roper had decided (and Tekoa had agreed) that there was a good chance Bellamus was luring them into an ambush. It could of course be that he was so confident in his own abilities as a general that he was sure that he could beat them anywhere and wanted to inflict the greatest possible hammer-blow on the psyche of the country. However, his trick with the caltrops had been noted, as had his canny escape from the Black Kingdom after the Battle of Githru. He appeared to be an imaginative leader and it seemed all too likely that the battle would not be fought at Harstathur, but on the road there. The Skiritai were therefore on high alarum, scanning the land ahead of the army for miles before they marched into it. They were swift, skilled scouts but it still slowed the army's progress considerably.

Unlike the previous invasion, on this occasion they knew nothing about the forces they opposed. Not where they were, not how many, not what those numbers were composed of. They only knew who led them, and where he had said they would be.

Clouds gathered above them on the road. The closer they marched to Harstathur, the more oppressive the atmosphere became. The humidity built irrepressibly and the clouds became an impenetrable smog. It looked as though this wretched, drowned winter might have one last storm left in it. Roper could not decide whether this would favour them or not.

Twenty leagues short of Harstathur, they managed to rendezvous with the final auxiliary legion. They had been separated by rivers swollen by melt-water but a few Skiritai had managed to cross and pass messages between the two forces. They converged at a ford that crossed the river Ouse. The Fair Island Legion were unarmed and unarmoured, still dressed in their labouring fatigues, but Roper was prepared for that and carried spare weapons and plate with the army. The Fair Islanders had been harried and battered by Bellamus's forces and there were now no more than three and a half thousand of them, but they still took Roper's forces beyond seventy thousand soldiers.

Every day they marched closer to the Altar and every day the Skiritai reported no sign of the Sutherners. They scoured every hill and valley surrounding the road and even made several long-distance forays in case the Sutherners intended to come down on them from afar during the night. Roper would not believe that the invitation to Harstathur was a genuine one until the seventh day after they left the Hindrunn. Finally, the Skiritai outriders were within range of the Altar and returned with the news that there, indeed, was where the Sutherners waited for them.

The final night, they stopped just two leagues short of Harstathur, already on the climb up to the plateau. The air felt heavier than ever and there was a definite tingle of electricity around them. 'This will break soon,' said Gray, squinting into the ash heavens. 'Tomorrow will be a horror.'

'We'll be right in the thick of the action on top of Harstathur,' said Roper. 'We'll get the thunder and the lightning up close.'

Tekoa approached the pair of them, riding his grey mare. 'I have something to show you two.'

'How far?'

'Two hundred yards that way,' said Tekoa, casting his hand towards the north.

'I'll leave Zephyr,' said Roper. He and Gray walked together behind Tekoa's mare, crossing to the edge of the track and heading into the close-cropped grass next to it. Roper studied the grass as they walked, frowning to himself while Gray and Tekoa talked about the march. The first observed that he had blisters for the first time in years; the second that Gray should have ridden, rather than walked.

'Here,' said Tekoa, a moment later. 'Look at this.' He had led them to a field where the grass was regularly intersected by long bare strips of naked earth. They looked like pathways, where the movement of thousands of men had worn through the grass to the mud below. There were boot prints visible in the rain-softened paths, which had obviously been formed by infantry of some sort. 'The Rangers have been finding these marks all over the surrounding land. They are strange.'

'Very strange,' agreed Roper. He bent to examine one of the paths and the grass that lined it. There was a gap of around six feet between each strip in which the grass had survived. 'Cavalry,' he said quietly.

'Boot prints,' said Tekoa, who had not bothered to dismount. 'Not hoof prints.'

'Cavalry,' said Roper again. 'This grass has been cropped by horses.'

'Where's the dung?' said Tekoa impatiently. 'Where are the hoof prints?'

'Removed,' said Roper. 'This pattern is Bellamus trying to hide how much cavalry he has. The horses graze along these paths so that they do not leave hoof prints elsewhere, then the infantry march the path afterwards to cover up the tracks. Any dung is cleared away. Look at the grass; the shredded tips are not yet white. They're fresh. This field has been grazed by a large number of horses but they have gone to considerable trouble to hide that from us. So he has a lot of cavalry, but doesn't want us to know.'

Gray inspected the grass. 'You're right; it has been grazed.'

'Your mind is working quickly, Lord Roper,' said Tekoa suspiciously.

'No,' said Roper. 'I just understand my enemy. Remember how we removed our dead after raiding their supplies? We've inspired him to try something similar; Bellamus would have understood what we did. I've been waiting for something like this. He's got cavalry and doesn't want us to know about it, which means he has plans for it.'

'What plans?' mused Gray.

'On Harstathur? Hard to say. He surely can't be intending to flank us; that detour around the plateau would be twenty leagues. All the same, Tekoa, have your men scout far this evening. I don't want to be fighting tomorrow and find that a horde of cavalry has suddenly appeared behind us.'

Tekoa rode to give the orders, and Roper and Gray headed off to find a place to set up camp. As ever, they were joined by Helmec and together they located an area surrounded by a cluster of Ramnea's Own. Roper set the fire and Helmec began adding ingredients to a blackened copper cooking pot. Gray prepared a tripod of greenwood, held together with a withy which also doubled as a pot-suspender. From this, Helmec hung the pot which contained the last of the day's water (saved for exactly this purpose), butter and crumbled marching biscuits. Roper contributed the dried mushrooms given to him by Keturah, and Gray, a chunk of salt-mutton and some lingon berries. They allowed the stew to simmer, Roper able to smell the contents from the pack on which he sat. It was a little better than the evening meal they would usually have prepared. It seemed appropriate on the eve of battle; there was no need to save food you might never get to eat.

After the meal, when the dark amber sunset in the west had faded completely, they would head off into the darkness to circle among the campfires. As Kynortas had said to Roper just six months before, they had no battle plan. They could merely reassure the legionaries, exhorting them to their most honourable duty and their bravest conduct the following day.

The nature of the huge altar that lay between the Anakim and the Sutherners was such that neither side could tell much about the enemy they faced. If they sent scouts forward over Harstathur, they would find the front of their enemy's encampment but be unable to estimate numbers or composition. Two prizefighters had agreed to a fight to the death without ever having seen each other.

'So what can we tell the men, Gray?' began Roper, over his stew. 'Are there any comparable battles you know of, where the armies were so unfamiliar?'

Gray considered this. 'I suppose this makes our position more like that of an invader, rather than a defensive force,' he said. 'As a defending army, it isn't hard to gather information on your enemies. You know the land, the locals are on your side and there are good opportunities to know your foe before you fight them. It is much easier to be a defender than an invader and that is why I believe Bellamus has erred by bringing his forces here. Remind our warriors that this is our ground they fight on. Remind them that we have defended it again and again over thousands of years, and on this battlefield especially, we have broken one of the gravest Suthern threats we have ever faced. Connect them to this land and make sure the Sutherners pay for each foot they take in more blood than they can afford.

'If we are to fight the unknown tomorrow, we cannot feel our way into the battle. If we stand off and allow Suthern aggression to shade the opening exchanges, we may find quickly that it is too late to recover.'

'If we lose tomorrow,' said Roper, then trailed off. He shook his head. 'This is the weakest full call-up that I can remember.'

'Perhaps in numbers,' said Gray. 'In the years that my

memory covers, this is the first time we have had less than eighty thousand soldiers at the Black Kingdom's disposal. But we are more battle-hardened than ever. Not only are there true heroes in this army, but most of the legionaries here have fought more battles than a Sutherner could squeeze into a lifetime. We may be a mere seventy thousand, but these are the seventy thousand hardest, most cussed legionaries ever to walk these lands. They are the descendants of the greatest heroes of our culture. Take our friend here,' and Gray gestured at Helmec, who was licking his bone spoon carefully, 'how many battles have you been through, Helmec?'

'I don't know,' said Helmec, a smile splitting his ruined face. 'Many.'

'Too many to count?'

'Yes.'

'And how many times have you lost?'

Helmec thought about that. 'We've lost small skirmishes. We lost that day in the flood waters.' He glanced apologetically at Roper. 'That's all I can remember. There've been victories which felt like losses, though, because so many died. Lundenceaster was one.'

'Yes, it was,' said Gray. 'Lundenceaster was ten times worse than the defeat on the flood plain.'

'That's where I said goodbye to my face,' said Helmec. 'But it's probably better this way. I was never very pretty, and now Gullbra can imagine that I was once.' The reference to his tiny wife caused Helmec to grin again. 'Better it happens to me than someone like Pryce. He did make a fuss when he lost his ear.'

'It suits you,' said Roper, who then broached the question he had long wanted to ask. 'How did it happen?'

'A morning star,' said Helmec. 'Just caught me lengthways,' he covered the right half of his face with a hand, 'as I was climbing a ladder. The infection nearly killed me, which is why I think it never healed properly.'

Both Roper and Gray had put down their stew. 'You are a

man of remarkably little self-pity,' commented Gray, admiring Helmec across the glow of the fire.

Helmec blushed. 'That is praise from you, sir,' he said, looking down at his stew again.

Above them, a chasm had opened in the mountainous clouds that hung overhead; the sky behind painted with starlight. Just as the last time he had been at Harstathur, Roper could see the Winter Road: the band of stars that marked the route they would all one day take to the underworld. It was a place of cold wonder: illuminated only by moonlight, surrounded by endless forests composed of giant ice crystals and many of the paths blocked by hard, frozen fog. Wolves with spines of frost instead of fur watched your progress and would act as guides for the brave and the well prepared; for the rest, they were a more insidious presence. Some wandered the Winter Road for ever, never finding the underworld on the other side, and watched all the while by the only mortal animals that could travel to this realm: raptors. They sat atop the ice crystals and watched the souls who drifted beneath them. It was the great test. Deeds performed in life were nothing more than practice for that long traverse.

Roper looked down and saw that Helmec and Gray had both paused their eating to gaze upwards. They stared fixedly until the clouds shifted and the stars disappeared again behind their dark bulk. 'I hope you're confident about tomorrow, lord,' said Helmec, still looking up at the sky.

'Confident?'

'In yourself, lord. You didn't get this far by accident. Trust yourself.'

'Thank you, Helmec,' said Roper, quietly.

As they spoke, Roper spotted Uvoren moving from fireside to fireside, clapping peers on the shoulder and patting their heads. He wore a snarl as he discussed the Sutherners and Roper observed how he energised the fires. He had a wake, which lifted the introspective silence a little as he passed.

Then, to the Black Lord's great surprise, he approached the hearth at which he, Helmec and Gray sat. He stopped where the light of the fire and the darkness merged and stared vacantly into the flames for a moment.

'Captain,' said Roper quietly.

'My lord,' responded he. Lord.

'Are you ready for tomorrow, sir?' enquired Gray. 'We will need Marrow-Hunter at her best.'

'She will be, Lieutenant,' said Uvoren sternly. He and Gray had been extremely distant since the latter had replaced Uvoren's childhood friend Asger as the Guard's second-in-command. He ignored Helmec completely. 'And you? Will you be ready?'

'I will, sir.'

Uvoren studied Gray. 'I know you like to be prepared for death. You will need to be prepared for more than that. Tomorrow, you are not allowed to die before your blade is blunt and clotted with blood. Do you hear me, Lieutenant? Only when you are utterly spent do you have my permission to fall.'

At those words, Gray smiled into the fire. 'Thank you, sir, but my death still waits for my wife's permission. Until she grants it, I will do my best to survive.'

'And what about my permission?' asked Roper. 'You do not have that.'

Gray inclined his head to Roper but said no more.

There was a pause, during which Uvoren regarded the Black Lord, that familiar curl on his lips. 'You know what the difference is between you and me, Lord Roper? The difference is that I wasn't foolish enough to let Vigtyr off his leash. Whatever you think you can give that man, you will *never* satisfy him. Sooner or later, he will be the end of you.'

'There are many differences between you and me, Captain,' said Roper. 'Be gone. Other firesides need your company more than this one.'

Uvoren gave an ironic bow and turned away, Roper and

Helmec watching him leave. Gray paid no attention, simply staring into the fire.

'When I was young,' said Gray, a moment later, 'I always thought about death.' He brooded. 'I was *obsessed* with it. When my peers were practising their battle-craft or hunting, I think I was preoccupied with the inevitability that this would all come to an end. Does it hurt? What happens afterwards? Is it better than life, or worse? How will I feel when I face it?' He was perfectly still as he spoke and Helmec and Roper listened closely. 'It is the ultimate unknown. There was only one thing that I really feared about death: how I would respond to it. I used to dream about the moment of my dying, and in my dreams, before the final blow fell, I was always a coward. I would beg my enemy for quarter. Or run away like an animal.

'I wasn't a bad swordsman. I appeared to grasp tactics easily, but when I was named a full legionary, I thought there had been a mistake. I was terrified of what would happen when I knew I was about to die. I must surely disgrace myself. My peers looked so comfortable and so at ease, and I knew I was a coward . . . That began to change in my first battle. My greatest friend from the haskoli, a lad my own age, was pierced by a spear in his chest and fell next to me. You know how that feels, my lord. You watched your father slain by an arrow and were compelled to ride after him into a great mass of the enemy. I can only assume you felt then what I felt as my friend Kolbeinn was felled beside me.

'I just remember rage . . . pure rage. I have never been so overwhelmed. I was utterly, utterly possessed. I cut the head off the Sutherner responsible, and then dragged my dying friend back through the ranks.' Gray fell quiet for a moment. Roper knew he did not need prompting and waited patiently for the story to resume. Helmec had finished his stew and put the bowl aside, listening as he stared into the flames. 'He knew he was dying, and I didn't tell him otherwise. Frothing blood was coming from the wound and from his mouth.

There was nothing we could do. So I just knelt next to him and told him I was there and that he was dying with honour.' Gray made a face. 'And my friend; Kolbeinn . . . he was calm. He knew he was dying and he didn't care. He just looked at me and he managed a smile. He said that now he knew: when you reach death, you can accept it. He said it felt easy.' Gray took a deep breath and let it out, still staring at the fire but sitting up a little straighter now. 'That memory has been my comfort and my strength for more than a hundred years. Kolbeinn was a hero, so perhaps he was terrified and just told me what I needed to know. In which case, his example inspires me. Or maybe, as I believe, he was telling the truth. And there is nothing to fear about death, because when you reach it – when you have no choice – you can accept it.'

He looked up at Roper for the first time and smiled. 'I believe that. Do you two remember my dream? My quest? Reynar the Tall taught me that self-disregard can make you face death willingly, Kolbeinn that you can accept the ordeal itself. On my last day, I should like to show Reynar's willingness and Kolbeinn's acceptance. Do that, and I believe I will have succeeded in my life's work.

'Come, my lord,' he said, rather suddenly. 'We must follow Uvoren's example.' He and Roper dispersed into the dusk like the grey smoke of their hearth, drifting through the ranks and offering reassurance to the legionaries. It got easier for Roper as the men came to know him better. Those who had campaigned with him before now fell still the instant he was by their fire, hoping he would come and share some words with them. Even those who were new under his command were eager to hear what he had to say; they had heard a lot about this Black Lord.

Roper came to one hearth of Blackstones. 'May I join you?'

'Of course, lord.'

Roper shrugged his pack off his shoulders and sat on it. 'Tomorrow's going to be something special,' he ventured into the expectant silence. 'This storm,' he gestured above at the oppressive clouds that had trapped a sticky warmth close to the ground, 'will break some time during our fight. It's going to be a deluge and one hell of a brawl on top of the Altar. It's a narrow battlefield; our lines will clash many times and we're going to batter them into submission each time, till they crawl away from the fight begging for quarter. We'll stand toe to toe in the sand of the arena and trade shuddering blows and, by the end, we'll be bloody but straight-backed. They'll lie broken in the dust.

'I expect the Sutherners to find the Blackstones' company the least bearable.' The men around the fire chuckled darkly. Roper smiled with them. 'Every man here waited through that storm of arrows in the flooding. Many of you still limp from where the caltrops pierced your feet. You watched those treacherous bastards kill your brothers without ever daring to fight you hand to hand.' Roper smiled in grim anticipation. 'The Sutherners are going to see the very best of you tomorrow. And when finally they dare to step inside the reach of your sword, they're going to know about it.'

This was met with an appreciative murmur. 'What is the battle plan, my lord?' asked one on the other side of the fire.

'Why would I need a plan? I have you. There aren't as many Blackstones as there were, but there are enough for this fight.'

Roper could not stay long; the more hearths he could visit, the better. He told them about the last time they had fought, about Leon Kaldison's courage in slaying Lord Northwic and how that had been facilitated by a demented Pryce, whose latest performance had seen him christened Pryce the Wild. Roper had bade them goodnight and turned away before his attention flickered back to the circle. 'There is one Sutherner whose death I very much desire tomorrow. His name is Garrett Eoten-Draefend. Garrett the Giant Hunter. He's a big man, with a lot of blond hair and a cloven nose. Anyone who can kill him and return his spear to me shall have my very great gratitude.'

'You shall have the spear if he comes my way, lord,' promised one.

'I don't doubt that,' said Roper, fading into the darkness.

Some of the veterans at other fires probed Roper suspiciously. To them, he was a callow youth; still green and with little knowledge of battle. Roper did not mind: his legionaries were brave and his aim, as much as anything else, was to reassure them that they were well led.

'Are you scared, my lord?' asked one scarred Greyhazel legionary.

'Of course I'm scared. I may die tomorrow.' Roper shrugged. 'That is a frightening thought. But it has to happen some day, and to die for my loved ones and my peers in the battle line is the best way it could possibly happen. The thought of that doesn't scare me nearly as much as the idea of my nerve failing. Or of defeat, at the hands of these Sutherners. So yes, I am scared. I'm scared I won't do my duty. But I do not think that will be a problem.

'We don't know much about what we're facing, but we know that Bellamus's household warriors will be there. Do you know what they have done? They've carved out the boneplates of our dead peers and wear them as their own armour.' The shocked murmur that greeted this news satisfied Roper. 'I am scared. But I have no doubt that if I come face to face with one of those hermit crabs, my duty will coincide with my greatest pleasure.' Roper stood and had to conceal his surprise when the Greyhazel legionaries stood around him. 'We're going to march in at dawn tomorrow, lads. See you on the Altar.'

22
The Lightning Bolt

Dawn was a barely perceptible shift in the light on Harstathur. Roper could not have said where east was, so deep was the layer of cloud overhead. It seemed to magnify the sound of the drums that thundered oppressively as the legions formed up on the plateau. Trumpets blasted out across the line, dressing it to the narrow width of the field. Opposite them, perhaps a mile and a half distant, the Suthern army was assembling. Roper could not judge their numbers on the field but he could see pikemen: thousands of them.

He was riding Zephyr. To walk would have set an example to his men. To use a courser would have been more practical. But nothing gave him more of a presence on the battlefield than the monstrous destrier. Before Roper had mounted, Zephyr had been dressed in barding: a thick sark of armour plate and chain mail that covered the immense beast from ear to knee. The champron, the thick steel plate that covered Zephyr's head, gave the horse a ghostly appearance, with barely any flesh visible beneath his steel skin. On another horse, the barding might have slowed it significantly. Zephyr barely noticed the weight.

No other general would so prepare their steed for close combat, but this was how Roper's men had come to know him. This was the Black Lord, wiser than his years and with an unexpected flair for command. He had killed an elite legionary in single combat when the man had tried to assassinate him. He had marauded alone into a mist-smothered enemy encampment with little more than a horse and an iron nerve. He had devastated the Suthern forces by the sea. This was their leader, Roper Kynortasson.

At his back was a full legion of heroes. Pryce the Wild. Hartvig Uxison. Gray Konrathson. Uvoren the Mighty. Leon Kaldison. Vigtyr the Quick. Legionaries who, in any other age, would have stood peerless in the recognition of their skill-at-arms and their courage. And, as Gray had said, the hardest, most cussed army that had ever been at the Black Kingdom's disposal. Most were veterans of dozens of battles: the distilled few who had outlived their brothers through skill and serendipity. Those who were new to the battle line were products of a system of duty and education that commanded their allegiance from birth.

The drummers pounded relentlessly as they marshalled on the Altar. They seemed to draw a response from the clouds overhead as the first peal of thunder rolled across the field. Roper was at the centre of the line beneath a fluttering Wolf. The legates, winged and brooding, were gathered around him on horseback along with Uvoren, Gray and several aides. Helmec, having been banished from the Guard and therefore unattached to any fighting unit, stayed with Roper as well. The Black Lord squinted at the Suthern ranks, suspicious that his eyes were not as good as some of the others' there.

'It looks as though they're almost entirely pikemen,' he said. 'With a core of dismounted knights in the centre.'

'Skirmishers in front. Longbowmen behind,' observed Tekoa.

'That's why Bellamus wanted us here,' said Gray. 'We'll have to take on these pikemen head on: we can't possibly out-flank them.' Gray paused. 'So what's he done with that cavalry?' he murmured, almost to himself.

Roper shook his head and gestured to an aide. 'Have all our arrows brought up from the baggage train, as fast as you are able. Ensure an equal number is distributed to each legion.' The aide tore off. 'We're going to stand off for as long as possible,' Roper told the assembled legates. 'Bombard them with arrows to thin out the pikes. We do not want to engage pikemen head on unless we've softened them up first.'

Something tinkled off Roper's armour. Looking down, he saw a hailstone the size of a pea cradled in the gap between his greave and his arm. 'We're about to lose visibility, lord,' advised Tekoa.

Roper nodded. 'Peers, if you cannot hear the trumpeter, then command of your legion is purely yours until you hear from me. Hold the line; on this battlefield, much will depend on maintaining a disciplined formation. Skallagrim? Your lads to stay in reserve until they're required.'

'Yes, lord,' said Skallagrim, a touch irritable at being held back.

'Tekoa? The Skiritai are to make a bloody nuisance of themselves out front as best you see fit. Make sure their skirmishers don't bother us, enrage their pikemen and then withdraw between Ramnea's Own and the Saltcoats in the centre before the battle line joins.'

'I will, my lord,' Tekoa promised.

'I will be in the centre, with the Guard and Ramnea's Own. After the bombardment, we're going to take it to the knights and will need your support on the flanks.' *Tap. Tap. Tap-tap.* Hail was beginning to bounce off Roper's helmet. 'Peers; to your legions. Godspeed.'

'Godspeed, my Lord Roper!' boomed Tekoa. He dragged his horse around and raised a clenched fist in salute to the other legates. They cheered and turned for their own legions. A peal rang out from the trumpets; each made from a human femur and calculated to appal their Suthern opponents. The call aggravated the drumming and a shocking flash of light illuminated the battlefield, followed a second later by a crack so mighty that Roper could feel it as a physical change in air pressure. The hail intensified and a grey haze began to obscure the Suthern forces.

'This is like fighting in heaven,' murmured Roper. As he spoke, a forked bolt struck the ground between the two armies. 'Uvoren,' he said, staring hard at the captain. He would be staying nearby as the Guard were in the centre with Roper. 'I'm looking forward very much to seeing Marrow-Hunter in action.'

Uvoren rode close to Roper and held out his hand. Roper, a little surprised, grasped it. 'Today, Lord Roper, you'll see how much it hurt to stay in the Hindrunn. Those knights are mine.'

'Let's get started,' said Gray. Roper gestured behind him to the trumpeter who blew out three long notes: *Advance!*

The drumming changed, unifying into a single beat that rippled along the line. The legionaries, usually so silent and professional, cheered as they began to advance. The visibility decreased drastically as the freezing hail intensified, so that now they could barely see twenty yards. Roper was grateful for his armour; the deluge felt like a physical weight pressing down on his head and shoulders, and he had to work hard to keep Zephyr under control as the destrier snorted and bucked irritably. He beckoned to one of the aides behind him. 'Go after Tekoa,' he shouted over the roar of the hail and another rumble of thunder. 'Tell him that I'll need the Skiritai to tell us how far away the enemy are.'

The aide nodded and spurred away, using the battle line as a handrail to navigate through the downpour.

'Is this really your idea of heaven, lord?' called Gray through the din.

Roper laughed. 'Strangely enough,' he called back. To Roper, heaven should be dynamic and awe-inspiring. His idea of being close to god was not to feel peace, but fear. The lightning was splintering the clouds and wave after wave of thunder was crashing over them. So ever-present were the bolts from the clouds that it looked as though they were the pillars supporting the sky. The legions appeared to freeze as the white light splashed over them, jerking forward again as it dissipated.

They continued their advance and it was not long before an aide returned to Roper, though not the one he had sent out. 'Lord! Legate Tekoa says your portion of the battle line is five hundred yards from the knights in the Suthern centre. They are advancing as well.'

'How long ago did he tell you this?'

'Three minutes, lord?' hazarded the legionary. 'The Skiritai have cleared away the Suthern skirmishers and they're now withdrawing.'

'Sound the halt!' Roper bawled at the trumpeter who sent three notes soaring out. How far they made it through the hail, Roper could not tell, but the drums around him changed beat as the line ground to a standstill. A faint, mournful blast sounded from his right, then his left, echoing his orders down the line. 'Bows!' A staccato burst from the trumpet, and Ramnea's Own in front of Roper unslung their enormous yew bows. The drumming was not supposed to respond to orders like that and Roper could not hear any other horns echoing the order. But he trusted the legates: they knew the plan, even if they had not heard the order.

Without a word, Uvoren spurred away into the hail in the direction of the Sacred Guard. Gray glanced at Roper. 'I'm going with him, lord.'

'Carry on, Lieutenant.' He left, leaving Roper with Helmec; Sturla, the legate of Ramnea's Own, and a gaggle of aides. He considered giving the order to open fire into the haze, but in the downpour the arrows would quickly lose their force. 'We hold until they are in view,' he said to Sturla. The legate, a man of singular calm, said nothing. He was bareheaded, with the hail collecting in his hair. It must have hurt, but he was expressionless.

'You!' Roper gestured at six of the aides. 'Three go left,

three go right. I want to know what is happening to the rest of the line. Are we firing on the pikemen? Can we even see them? Have some of the legions engaged? Bring that information to me as fast as you are able.' They scattered. Roper sent another two forward to wait before the front rank of Ramnea's Own, with instructions to inform him as soon as they could see the enemy. He did not have to wait long; barely a minute later, one of them came tearing back.

'Men-at-arms, my lord! Advancing fast!'

'Volley!' roared Roper, for he could now see their hazy outline solidifying in the hail. Another staccato burst from the trumpet and the legionaries fitted arrows to their bows. In one immense movement, the entire block of men drew and loosed, spitting a volley at the knights who were now clearly visible, charging through the hail. It had no obvious effect and they were closing fast.

'Bows down, charge! Charge!' Three more notes from the horn and Ramnea's Own Legion had thrown their bows aside and drawn swords. The horn insisted and the legionaries flooded forward.

Men-at-arms: the only soldiers the Sutherners had who could meet the legionaries on equal terms. They were armoured from head to foot in a suit of steel plate, and came from the wealthiest Suthern families. Their lives, while not as harsh or as disciplined, had been spent training for war as surely as the Anakim's and they were truly skilled warriors. Their weapons were of their own choosing: the mace, the war hammer, the halberd or the great two-handed sword. The Anakim were more mobile in their lighter armour but, thanks to their bone-plates, just as well defended. An Unthank-silver blade was equal to puncturing the steel plate worn by the knights, but it would still take a thrust of considerable accuracy and power to break through.

They were well matched, the Suthern elites and the legionaries of the Black Kingdom and they charged now across Harstathur, through the pounding hail and the flashes of lightning. The two sides met in a great clang of steel on steel, and in the moment of impact it was the superior Anakim muscle that told, hammering the knights back.

Roper heard a second wave of thunder and knew that, to his right, the Sacred Guard had engaged with the enemy. 'Drive them back, Legate!' he called to Sturla, turning Zephyr away and towards where he knew the Guard were fighting.

As he rode, an aide galloped alongside him. 'I went as far as the Greyhazel, my lord,' he reported. 'They have engaged the pikemen in volley fire but will soon have to fight hand to hand.'

'Thank you, Reifnir.'

The Sacred Guard were not far along the line and Roper arrived to find that they had carved out an alcove in the formation of knights, which was bowing in the centre to try and alleviate the pressure that the Guard was exerting. Roper could see Uvoren, who had dismounted and joined the fray in the front rank, duelling with a knight who wielded a bloody-edged great-sword. They twisted this way and that until finally Uvoren took Marrow-Hunter in his right hand, used it to deflect a blow aimed at his neck and then seized his opponent's sword-arm, holding it still as he brought his hammer crashing down on top of the man's head. His helmet crumpled, busted open, and the man dropped like a stone.

Right next to Uvoren was Gray. He was on the defensive, blocking thrust after thrust of a halberd that was being aimed for his chest. One lunge almost made it through, but Gray twisted aside just in time and the tip of the halberd caught the shoulder-plates of his armour, ripping them backwards and making Gray slide in the mud beneath him. He reacted by spinning round, allowing the halberd to dislodge from his plate and bringing Ramnea down in a great two-handed slash onto the man's elbow, still extended from his lunge. There was no steel plate on the inside of the elbow and the sword took his forearm clean off, allowing his halberd to drop to the ground. The knight backed away from Gray, knees bent and intact left arm raised in quarter. Gray pushed the man away with a firm hand on his chest-plate and engaged another.

Roper wanted to see Pryce fight but he was nowhere to be seen. He briefly spotted Leon trying to tug his sword free from the helmet of a knight at the same time as ducking beneath a war hammer being aimed at his head, but then he lost sight of him in a crush of bodies. The entire line was writhing with violence, the battering hail seeming to make the warriors more aggressive than ever. Sparks and sometimes chips of steel flew off the weapons as they clashed. Everything was grey on the Altar, and the din of battle assaulted Roper's ears. He saw one guardsman break through the guard of a knight and thrust his sword through the gleaming breastplate and into the stomach behind. His blade got stuck and the knight, pierced through by the guardsman's sword, raised his own and swung it heavily at his enemy's head. The guardsman was knocked flat, his helmet splitting open like an eggshell and blood blossoming from the fissure. The knight collapsed to his knees, helmeted head turned down to the sword in his belly. A guardsman decapitated him, pushed over his kneeling corpse and stepped forward to engage another knight.

This fight was so much that Roper could hardly watch. The noise felt as if it was forcing him backwards, and his eyes shrank away from the mighty collision of weapons as they smashed together. The ground was being churned to mud and several of the warriors had simply fought themselves to exhaustion. They no longer swung their weapons; just pushed against each other, trying to drive the other backwards through the mud. Roper saw one guardsman without a sword fall upon a similarly exhausted Sutherner. He held his hand so that the Suthern knight could not swing his mace at him and used his other hand to wrench back the knight's helmet. He bent forward and Roper realised that the guardsman had sunk his teeth into the knight's freshly exposed neck. The knight flailed weakly but was pushed to the floor and did not rise.

Through the haze, Roper could see some change occurring in the mass of knights. Some were falling back and a relief unit appeared to be forcing their way through to the front line. As they drew closer, Roper spotted a single figure that towered above those around him: Garrett. He held Heofonfyr, his bastardised spear, and was leading Bellamus's household warriors into direct combat with the Sacred Guard.

Roper unclasped his cloak, threw himself out of Zephyr's saddle and advanced without a backwards glance. He forced his way through the exhausted and bloodied guardsmen who had already taken their turn in the front rank and were now recovering at the back. They stared at him as he passed, observing his clenched jaw and Cold-Edge held by his side as he used his size to bully his way to the front. There were bodies in his path. He stepped over eleven knights, their bright armour wrecked and smeared with blood and mud, and two Sacred Guardsmen. He did not look at these. He did not hear the guardsmen at the back begin to call his name in a chant that was slowly taken up by the rest of the Guard until they were all roaring: 'Rop-er! Rop-er!' He did not even notice Helmec barging another path behind him, staying with his lord. He reached the front just as the first of Bellamus's household warriors did, clad in their stolen bone-armour and all armed with the two-handed spear.

To fight well, you must first forget.

A single mistake, a single lapse in concentration, and you could end the day as a cooling corpse. You could bleed inexorably into the dirt. Your windpipe could be severed and wheeze and hiss as life escaped you. Your tangled guts exposed to the air. You could lose a limb, an eye, your hand; the feeble flesh carved open by steel. Fearful, mortal wounds; but what happens then? Pain engulfs you; death comes for you. You know you must hold your nerve, and meet it with honour and courage. But in spite of yourself, you wonder if this final, terrible ordeal is the one that you cannot sustain. Perhaps, as you have seen some among your comrades do, you will weep openly for your mother's face, or because your day was about to go so dark, so soon. The façade would crack and all would know that in your heart, at your core, you were never so sure as you looked; that you were fearful all along and never truly the man you tried so hard to be.

All this, you must forget. You cannot defeat a man hand to hand if terror has made your limbs weak and slow. You must forget what you have to lose: your wife, your children, your mother, your father, your peers. You must forget the pleasure of frondescent sunlight bathing your face; or sitting by a hearth with hot food after a hard day; or the dark, warm embrace of your beloved. You must forget those noises around you: the pain, the retching cries, the clanging, the coughing. Forget the smells ramming the top of your nose, all of them metallic. Forget the frenetic movement to either side; the cold grey flashes, the expression of the warrior opposite you, the restrictive metal girdling your body, the pain in your numb and blistered hands. You must close your mind to all thought and emotion, and open the door that is kept locked at all times but during combat. You must be able to summon immense violence in the time it takes to draw a sword. In the sacred clash of the battlefield, you must be equal to the aggression of every man whom you face. More than equal. Your sword must swing faster and harder, your movements more certain than those of the hero opposite you. You do not have time to consider either attack or defence. Every action must be performed with utmost assurance on reflex, nerve and synapse. To fight must become instinctive. You must develop a self that knows these things, shuts out noisy thought and lives right at that instant, with no delay between stimulus and reaction.

First and foremost; you must forget yourself.

Roper's first twisting lunge went through a man's mouth,

killing him instantly and robbing the thrust that he had aimed at Roper of any strength. He dropped to the floor and Roper dragged Cold-Edge free of his lips. The next spearman stepped off his right foot to confuse Roper and aimed a thrust at his stomach. Roper twisted aside, taking a swing at the man's waist which clattered harmlessly off the bone-plates. He ducked beneath the spear that swung over his head, lunging forward where Cold-Edge was again stopped by the bone-plates. However, the blow was enough to stagger his opponent and drive him backwards where he lost his footing in the mud, dropping to one knee. The spearman reacted fast, smashing his spear into Roper's helmet. Roper staggered, dazed, and the man was up again, ramming the spear at him whilst evading Roper's frenzied parry. It hit Roper in the chest, grating against his plate armour but stopping before it breached the steel. Another lunge and Roper tried to twist aside but it caught the chain mail that protected his thighs, piercing his leg by an inch or so. Roper seized the spearman's wrist and dragged him unwillingly close, bringing Cold-Edge up to his throat. The man pulled back desperately but he was not as strong as Roper and his spear was too long to be used now that he and Roper were chest-to-chest. Cold-Edge cut the man's throat, spraying Roper's mouth and neck in his blood and dropping the spearman to the ground at once.

Two enemies dead and Roper's lungs were already heaving. The air seemed so thick with hail that he could barely breathe, but another spearman was lunging at him over the bodies of his two dead comrades. Roper parried and countered but found himself blocked. They clashed three times, each deflecting the lethal blows aimed at them by the other until Roper slipped suddenly in the mud, crashing to his knees. He sucked in air but it was not enough and his limbs were growing heavy with fatigue. The spear came at him again and he batted it aside. He tried to grab its shaft but it was pulled back too quickly and thrust at him again. This time it caught him in the shoulder and rammed him back against the mud. The hail pelted down on his face as he was forced to look into the grey skies. Roper had felt no pain, merely the impact as it smashed him backwards. His free left hand went instinctively to the shaft of the spear where it joined his shoulder and he seized it. The spearman was trying to drag it free but Roper held it fast in his own flesh, using its bearer's own force to drag himself back to his feet. He blundered forward, the spearman trying to pull back and get away from Roper, but he would not let go. He slashed Cold-Edge down the shaft of the spear and the man had to snatch his fingers away or lose them. He let go of the spear and Roper pulled it from his shoulder, feeling pain at last as the blade came free. He tossed it aside and the warrior flew at him, a long dagger in his hand. In a single backhand swipe, Roper cut his throat.

There was senseless noise around him and Roper could feel the pressure from the men that they opposed lifting. The Sutherners were pulling back and the exhausted guardsmen were letting them go in one of those odd, mutually agreed breaks in the battle. 'Garrett!' Roper roared, casting around for the huge Sutherner, but he could not see him and hands were dragging him backwards and away from the fight. He turned in fury to find Pryce's implacable face behind him, ignoring Roper's protestations completely and hauling him away. He pulled against Pryce's hands and struggled to advance into the no-man's land between the forces, seeking to call Garrett out. But his limbs were heavy. His lungs were straining and Pryce's grip was strong.

'Let him go!' said another voice behind Roper and he turned to see that it was Uvoren who had given the order, looking at him hungrily. This sobered Roper at once. He stopped resisting Pryce and turned his back on the Sutherners, stalking back through the ranks of the Sacred Guard. Gray was after him.

'What the hell are you doing?' he demanded of Roper,

spraying his ear with blood from a split lip. 'Fight if you must, but almighty god, withdraw when we do! Uvoren would like nothing more than for Garrett to cut you down in front of the legions.'

Roper snarled for Gray to get away, and headed back for Zephyr, being held for him by one of the aides. Once he had mounted again, Roper turned to see that the two battle lines were peeling apart. From the point of the Guard outwards, the warriors were disentangling themselves, throwing one last savage attack and pulling back in thin and ragged ranks. 'What news?' demanded Roper, head still fuzzy from the spear that had slammed into his helmet. His thigh ached and his shoulder ached where he had been wounded, but neither seemed serious.

'The lines are pulling apart,' advised an aide. 'We've taken heavy casualties against the pikemen, but they're pulling back too.' A tideline of bodies was becoming evident as the legions and the Sutherners withdrew, both sides stooped with exhaustion and fighting for breath.

'Tekoa!' Roper shouted. 'Find me Tekoa!' But he was there already, at Roper's side in moments. 'Skiritai forward, Tekoa: do not give them one moment's respite.'

'Exactly, my lord,' said Tekoa, who seemed to have come seeking an invitation to undertake just such a manoeuvre. He rode off, and Roper could hear the higher-pitched horn that gave signals just for the skirmishers blow to send the Skiritai swarming forward between ranks. They would pepper the Sutherners with arrows and try to tempt them out of formation to where they could be slaughtered as individuals.

Meanwhile, Roper spurred Zephyr forward and in front of the legions. He raised his bloody sword and cantered along the line. 'Again!' he boomed as he passed them. 'Again! Again! Again! Cut them down, cut them down, cut them down, cut them down!' A cheer built and began to travel along the line with Roper as the exhausted legionaries stood up straight. The Skiritai flooded out past him and another great rumble of thunder rolled over the legions. The hail had abated a little and visibility lifted above a hundred yards.

Roper turned Zephyr back in behind the legions and began to ride back towards the centre of the line. The legionaries were gulping down water, field-dressing wounds and washing and drying their hands so that they did not lose grip of their weapons in the melee. Nobody could eat; even drinking was difficult. The break would last no more than another few minutes and then the lines would clash once again.

Roper dispatched more aides to the legates, requesting an update on how the fighting had gone, and reminded them that, above all, they should hold the line. He heard from left and right how the hail had been too thick to release more than a few volleys before the pikemen were upon them, and how the legions had then been forced to fight their way through a thicket of pikes before they could even strike back at their enemy. Casualties had indeed been heavy. It also seemed that he had been fighting just a few yards from where Garrett wielded Bright-Shock's blade, and that the Suthern champion had killed two Sacred Guardsmen.

Another rider arrived from Tekoa, informing Roper that the Sutherners had begun to advance again and the Skiritai were pulling back. 'Legate Tekoa says that the harvest was good,' said the aide at last.

The legions readied themselves once again, trying to recover their bows from where they had been dropped so that they could release another few volleys into the Sutherners before they engaged once again. Roper heard horns blasting from up and down the line as legions began to charge once again and he reached Ramnea's Own at the centre just in time to see them thrown into battle against the knights. This time, Bellamus's household guard, the 'Hermit Crabs', as they were becoming known, started arrayed against the Sacred Guard. Bellamus was obviously trying to negate the impact of the Guard by pitting his own crack troops against them.

Tekoa was on horseback next to Roper, and the two

watched the battle lines clash amid the constant rattle of hail bouncing off armour. A bolt of lightning pulverised the ground perilously close to where the two sides met. Above the seething horror of armoured flesh, a single figure towered at the front rank of Ramnea's Own.

Vigtyr the Quick.

Roper rode forward, wanting to see this most feared warrior at work. A knight was assaulting him: a plumed noble magnetised by Vigtyr's immense size and the esteem he would gain by killing him. He lunged at Vigtyr's chest with a halberd, teeth gritted and fingers white about the shaft. Vigtyr gave a parsimonious side-step, raising his sword and letting its edge slice deep into the knight's exposed wrist. The knight sprang back, drawing a curtain of scarlet drops that fell with the hail. The cut was deep and blood dribbled from the knight's wrist, which seemed to have been weakened, for his next lunge was a gentle prod compared with the heave he had unleashed a moment before. It came unexpectedly close to landing, Vigtyr leaving the parry late. The same thing happened again; and again, Vigtyr content to defend as the knight's blood drained onto Harstathur and he slowed and weakened. The knight was growing clumsy and on his next lunge he stumbled forward, Vigtyr raising his sword once again and skewering the man's throat just above the breastplate. The knight toppled aside, fading from actor to stage. Vigtyr did not advance into the space left behind. He lowered his blade and beckoned for the next warrior to come and try his luck.

Roper dragged his eyes back to the Sacred Guard, where he spotted another towering figure in the thick of the action, his shocking blond hair plastered to his head: Garrett, who at that moment cut down a guardsman with Heofonfyr, slicing the inside of his knee to drop him to the ground and then killing him cleanly with a thrust to the neck, eliciting a gush of bright blood.

'I'm going back in,' declared Roper, kicking Zephyr

forward. The horse snorted and tossed but did not move. Roper realised that Tekoa was holding on to its bridle.

'Leave the horse,' Tekoa said. 'Those spearmen will bring it down in a heartbeat, even with the barding, and you'll be killed. You fight toe to toe.'

Roper nodded. 'Command is yours.' He dismounted once again to force his way into the Guard, Helmec following loyally behind. He could see where Garrett fought bareheaded at the front and pressed his way towards the giant Sutherner, observing Heofonfyr's long blade greedily. Many guardsmen tried to stop his advance but Roper snarled at them until they let him go and, through sheer force of will, made it into the second rank. To have pushed any further would have been dangerous for those guardsmen who fought at the front; he might distract them from the task at hand. Instead, he had to wait until a gap opened in front of him. The guardsman before him was engaged in combat with Garrett and giving a heroic account of himself. Garrett was snarling and twisting, lunging again and again at the nameless guardsman who batted his thrusts aside and launched blistering ripostes. White sparks were pouring off the two Unthank-silver weapons as they clashed, and twice the guardsman made it through Garrett's defences but had his sword stopped by the bone-plates. Roper was itching to move forward but his mouth opened in shock when, before his eyes, Garrett unleashed a lunge of immense power, catching the guardsman in the stomach hard enough to puncture steel and bone-plate both, pick him off the ground and drive him into the mud at Roper's feet.

Garrett pulled Heofonfyr free and stepped back, wolf-like eyes flicking at Roper, who, he knew, was next in line. He unleashed his wide grin as he saw who his opponent was and hefted his mighty spear, stepping back to give Roper space to advance. Roper raised Cold-Edge, opened his mouth to speak, but another figure stepped out in front of him. It was a guardsman, his ponytail exceptionally long, evidently determined to fight Garrett.

Pryce the Wild.

'No!' shouted Roper. 'The Eoten-Draefend is mine!'

Pryce did not even turn to face Roper. Instead he launched a lunge at Garrett that almost took out the Sutherner's eye. It would have done, but Garrett was just equal to deflecting it so that it grazed the side of his face and sliced into his ear. The force of his lunge had sent Pryce sliding forward through the mud and he danced backwards, parrying Heofonfyr twice before the two warriors separated. There was a tense pause. That first lunge alone had made Garrett cautious, and the two warriors appraised each other across the space that was forming around them as each side gave their champion room.

'What is your name?' called Garrett in his accented Anakim. 'I wish to know who this is that I am about to kill.'

'My name? I am Pryce Rubenson. I cut off Earl William's head. I hold more Prizes of Valour than any man living. I am the fastest warrior in the north. I facilitated the death of Lord Northwic, and when I am done with you I will kill your master too.'

Garrett nodded slowly. 'Lovely accolades,' he said. 'I am the Eoten-Draefend, of Eskanceaster. I have duelled with the Unhieru and killed Gogmagoc's eldest son, Fathochta, in single combat. I have killed one of your winged legates and half a dozen Sacred Guardsmen. Tonight, I shall boast that I brought to justice Earl William's killer.' With that, Garrett attacked. Heofonfyr surged forward, blade silver-white in the hail and streaking for Pryce's chest. But it found only empty air: the guardsman was gone. He had stepped aside as though he had known for days where that spear would be at that moment, and delivered a backhand slice that Garrett had to duck beneath. Pryce bounced off the ball of one foot and struck right, then left, forcing Garrett to parry with a shower of white sparks. He was frighteningly quick and when Garrett returned some thrusts of his own, they seemed to bounce off an impenetrable shield of flashing alloy. Pryce lunged forward and Garrett was forced to react to that snake-like speed, swinging Heofonfyr across his body in a parry. But Pryce had been feinting. His sword, instead of being deflected by Garrett's spear, surged into his chest and sent the huge Sutherner backwards. His bone-plates held the powerful blow but he almost lost his footing in the mud and had to flail his arm to remain upright. Pryce took advantage and lunged for his thigh but Heofonfyr came at the guardsman in a slashing arc that cut across his jaw and sent him reeling back. Pryce stood off for a moment, raising his hand to his jaw and taking it away to observe the fresh blood that beaded there. Garrett's slip had been faked to draw a wild lunge from Pryce and it was the Sutherner who had drawn blood.

The battle raged on around them, less exalted heroes clashing and dying in their thousands, but Roper was entranced by the combat before him.

Heofonfyr surged forward once more, going for Pryce's unarmoured knee. Pryce did not move except to lift one leg so that the spear slid harmlessly past. Garrett swept it to the side, hoping to cut Pryce's other leg from beneath him whilst all his weight was on one limb, but somehow Pryce catapulted himself over the arc of Heofonfyr, escaping quite unharmed and bringing his own blade round in a savage overhead attack. Garrett ducked away and he and Pryce clashed four, five, six, seven times to produce a curtain of white sparks, blades moving so fast that Roper could not tell the difference between lunge and parry. Chips of Unthank-silver were flying off Pryce's weapon where it came into contact with Heofonfyr's diamond-dust edge. The two warriors were almost dancing with one another, feet twisting this way and that in the mud in a series of moves so skilled that they looked pre-ordained. But it was Garrett who was retreating. Pryce was too fast and Garrett had to move backwards to give himself more time to react. Pryce crowded him and launched an enormous swing at Garrett's neck. It was easy to block but so hard that it was clearly aimed to intimidate Garrett. The Sutherner responded with all the force he had, and when the two blades met, there was a dull clunk. Pryce reeled away and half his sword-blade fell to the ground next to Garrett. Heofonfyr was too strong and had broken Pryce's sword. In his right hand, the guardsman now clutched a shard, barely two feet in length and cut jaggedly across its width.

Pryce barely hesitated. It was he who attacked next, slicing the remaining half of his sword at Garrett, feinting and then driving into his chest. It was a hard lunge but again, stopped at the bone-plates, the metal shard with which Pryce fought was not sharp enough to penetrate Garrett's armour.

The battle around them was changing; the lines were peeling apart again and the warriors around Pryce and Garrett began to disengage. Garrett's chest was heaving with effort and he stole glances to his left and right as more and more fighters pulled away. They were left as the only two warriors still fighting in the no-man's land opening up between the two armies. One of the Hermit Crabs appeared on each side of Garrett and threatened Pryce with their spears, lunging at him and forcing him away from their champion. 'No!' shouted Garrett, smashing one of them over the head with the shaft of Heofonfyr, but another two were pulling him backwards and more were pressing forward against Pryce, trying to drive him back.

'You're going to allow this?' roared Pryce, contemptuously cutting down one of the spearmen with his broken sword. 'Garrett Eoten-Draefend is a coward!'

But Garrett was being dragged backwards. He raised Heofonfyr in one last salute. 'I will find you again!' he called in Saxon.

Pryce looked disgusted. Though there were spearmen within five yards of him, he showed total disdain by turning his back on the Sutherners and walking back to the Guard. Roper had been waiting, and Pryce caught sight of him. 'Do not fight the Eoten-Draefend,' he said with a touch of restraint in his voice. 'He would have killed you. Come, lord.'

Roper had been prepared to be furious with Pryce for preventing him fighting Garrett, but the guardsman's uncharacteristic patience drained his fury in an instant. The two of them began to jog back to where the Guard had retreated.

The Skiritai were streaming forward again to an audible groan from the retreating Sutherners. The legionaries were exhausted. Most just crashed into the mud, numbed by cold hail and brutal combat. The stones of ice melted to trickle down forearms covered with dried blood, washing purified veins into the grime. They cleaned their hands numbly; took water-skins pressed forward from the rear ranks and sucked on them. The water tasted good, but swallowing it was almost too much. Some of the younger nemandi, lads of seventeen and eighteen who were not yet expected to stand in the battle line, hurried through the ranks with their medical rolls, attending to the most crippling wounds. The captains, lictors and other junior officers stayed on their feet, prowling through the warriors and telling them that they would break the enemy next time; that they must think of their brothers next to them and that if they did not fight as hard as they were physically able, it would be their peers who paid the price.

None of the Sacred Guard had sat down. They were fitter than any other warrior, and had their wounds staunched and their thirst quenched with an air of necessity, as though their one purpose in life was this next fight. Uvoren had gathered many of the guardsmen into a circle and was addressing them fervently. Snatches of what he was saying carried to Roper's ears: 'Leon, you're fighting like an ancient hero. Stay at the front as long as you can; no man, no matter how well rested, will equal you when you have fallen back. Leikr, we will need your fitness now: you must fight for two men. Salbjorn, there is an aura around you this day. Use it to intimidate the bastards, and we'll break them here.' Gray was doing the same with another group, and Pryce, furious to have missed the chance to kill Garrett, strutted in front of the rest of the Guard. He was no longer lictor; that post had been filled by a friend of Uvoren's, but the friend now stood quiet as Pryce howled at the Guard, blood dripping from the cut in his jaw. 'Their lungs are burning, their limbs are quaking and their fingers are weak about their weapons. They cannot sustain this! They live a soft, plump lifestyle in their neutered country. These bastards have invaded our home again and again and now wear our brothers' bones as armour! Don't just kill them: make them feel pain before they die. I want each Sutherner to know a moment of pure despair before they fall beneath your sword. Kill them! You are a tireless fist! You are a thundering heart! You are lightning! You are relentless as this bloody hail, my Sacred Guardsmen!'

Roper returned to Zephyr to find that Tekoa was still mounted next to the destrier. 'The Skiritai are commanded by their junior officers. They can handle themselves,' he said in response to Roper's questioning glance. The Black Lord hauled himself into the saddle, utterly exhausted by the unremitting hail and chilled so that his fingers had become slow. The lightning, having paused for the last half an hour or so, had begun to flash more regularly again.

'Bellamus has played a good hand,' said Roper thickly. His lips were going numb. 'Pikemen on the fringes and knights in the centre means he can match us for quality throughout the line. That's why he wanted to fight here; so that his pikemen would have secure flanks.'

'This is a bloody tough nut to crack,' confirmed Tekoa. 'We're losing a lot of men and I can't see them breaking any time soon.'

'The knights are their weak point,' said Roper. 'We won't break apart disciplined pikemen, but we can break these knights in the centre and then it's over.'

'Use the Guard as a spearhead, form a wedge and push through?' suggested Tekoa.

'They're matching the Guard with their Hermit Crabs and they're bloody good. And I'm sure they've got cavalry, Tekoa. Bellamus will be holding them as a counter-punch in case we break through. That's why we *must* hold the line.'

Tekoa raised his eyebrows and seemed about to speak again when one of the Skiritai horns sounded through the haze. 'That's the retreat,' he said. 'Round three.'

Roper took a deep breath. The lives of the men around him weighed heavily on his shoulders and he did not know what to do. Bellamus had chosen his soldiers well so that they matched the Anakim for quality and he had an ace: his cavalry, which he must use at some point. Visibility was so low, Roper could have no idea where they were stationed. He might not find out until it was too late.

The knights were advancing rapidly through the haze towards them now. Uvoren, Pryce and Gray all still strode in front of the Sacred Guard, disdaining the proximity of the enemy and pumping their arms to raise cheers that fell in crashing waves upon the field. Both the Sutherners and the legions were dull with mud as the knights splashed towards them. The legionaries jerked into life, staggering upright and finding swords. Nobody bothered with the bows any more; they barely had time to form ranks before the order to charge blurted through the ranks. The lines clashed once more, not aggressive but numbly inexorable. They thudded together, bounced apart, and then began their exhausting work. The Hermit Crabs were arrayed against the Guard again, and now the hail had lifted enough for Roper to be able to see, along the line, the pikemen who fought the Greyhazel. The twenty-foot ash pikes created an impenetrable thicket when approached from the front, but from the side the formation was hopelessly vulnerable. On this battlefield, however, all sides were protected and would remain so until they could dismantle the Suthern line.

Or perhaps not. Roper squinted at where the Hermit Crabs and the pikemen joined, and saw that a gap appeared to be developing there. It was twenty yards across and growing wider as the natural rhythm of thrusting a pike right-handed shuffled the formation slowly to the left. Perhaps the casualties that the Sutherners were taking had shortened their line, thus creating the gap. Or, Roper thought, more likely this gap was of Bellamus's creation and the cavalry was waiting to destroy any unit that went through.

'You've seen the gap?' pressed Tekoa.

'It's bait. We hold the line,' said Roper.

Tekoa glanced at him. 'You fear the cavalry?'

'Yes I do.'

'Your instincts are good,' said Tekoa dubiously.

Uvoren was running towards them. Marrow-Hunter was held low by his side and he was gesturing furiously at the developing gap, which was now forty yards across. 'Send the reserves through!' he demanded. 'Get Skallagrim, tell him we can break them here!'

'It's bait!' shouted Roper. 'I'm certain they have cavalry.'

'So? They'll be miles away! It's shuffling left, that's what pikelines do!'

'I know, Bellamus; I understand that man and this is no mistake. Return to combat, Captain.'

Uvoren opened his mouth and screamed incoherently. His face filled with colour and he quaked as he released sheer rage in Roper's direction. He turned away and sprinted instead for the edge of the Greyhazel.

'He's going to get Tore to advance his soldiers,' said Tekoa. 'Tore will do whatever he says.'

'Stop him!' commanded Roper, and Tekoa spurred after the captain. Roper turned to an aide. 'Tell Skallagrim to bring his men here at once! We're going to need them.' The aide tore away and Roper turned back to see that Uvoren had found Tore. The two were talking animatedly, Uvoren gesturing at the gap.

As Roper watched, Tekoa cantered up to the pair of them. He was clearly shouting and pointed Uvoren back towards the Sacred Guard. Uvoren shouted back briefly and then, quite suddenly, he seized Tekoa's leg and dragged him from the saddle. Tekoa crashed into the mud, causing Roper to utter a single swear word. He spurred Zephyr forward just as Tekoa rose to his feet, a sword flashing in his hand. Roper swore again as Tekoa raised the blade high and hacked at Uvoren. He was an exceptional legate and a brilliant soldier, but as a warrior, Tekoa Urielson was not in the same league as Uvoren. The Captain of the Guard deflected Tekoa's blade easily and rammed a gauntleted fist into his face, stunning Tekoa enough to wrest his sword from his grip and hurl it away. Uvoren punched again, knocking Tekoa flat. Tore pulled his horse away, signalling to the trumpeter who sounded the advance.

The Greyhazel began to move. A large section of their ranks, which had been facing the growing vacancy in the Suthern line, was unoccupied and began to advance. They evidently intended to charge through the gap and then turn on the pikemen, exposed from behind and the flank. Roper knew that right here, in this place and moment, the battle and possibly the Black Kingdom hung in the balance. Uvoren was wrong, and Roper knew that there would be horsemen waiting just out of sight. Somewhere, Bellamus's watchful eyes would be waiting for them to take his bait. Any forces that went through that Suthern line would be obliterated and, once the Anakim line had broken, the vengeful Suthern cavalry would be free to sweep in behind the legions and rampage there. That would be the battle. It had to be the battle. Tens of thousands of legionaries would die under his command.

It was too late to stop the Greyhazel advancing, but Roper galloped towards Uvoren, Helmec as ever by his side. He drew up beside the Captain of the Guard, who was watching the Greyhazel legionaries pour through the gap but glanced up as Roper approached. 'Go to hell, you little shit,' he advised. 'I'll be damned if you're going to cost us this battle.'

'If it were not too late to stop your ill-advised plan, I'd kill you right here,' said Roper.

'Ha!' Uvoren turned to face Roper fully, hefting Marrow-Hunter in his hands. He took a step towards Roper, but was given pause for thought by Helmec jumping from the saddle and pulling his sword free from its scabbard.

'You're going nowhere near my lord,' warned Helmec. Uvoren considered him for a moment but was again distracted by a trumpet that sounded from behind Roper. Creaking round in his saddle, Roper could see Skallagrim's legion beginning to draw near in the hail. On Roper's other side, the Greyhazel legionaries had flooded through the gap in the Sutherners' line and were now in the open. Many were turning on the flank of the pikemen, who could not swing their unwieldy weapons around and had to drop them and draw the short swords they carried instead. The legionaries ate away at the pikemen, pulling the gap further apart so that more and more Greyhazel poured through and began to attack the flank of the Hermit Crabs as well.

Skallagrim rode up behind Roper. 'You called for us, my lord?' he asked eagerly.

'Hold there for the moment, Legate,' Roper said. 'We will need your soldiers very soon. Prepare them to take the place of the Greyhazel Legion.' Skallagrim looked askance at Roper, who had even begun to question himself. Perhaps he was wrong. Perhaps this was a genuine mistake. There might not be any cavalry after all.

The Greyhazel were doing sterling work. They trusted their legate implicitly and had seized on this opening, hacking into the flank of the pikeline as though it were heather. Uvoren was baying, screaming them on, and it truly looked as though here was where they would splinter the Suthern line. Even the Hermit Crabs were being forced to wheel, faced by the ferocity of the legions on two sides. Roper stood in his stirrups, surveying the brawl uncertainly. He had been so sure there would be cavalry.

But at that moment, distant thunder began to rumble and did not stop. Roper strained his ears and looked out into the haze as the thunder rolled on, becoming louder and closer. Uvoren took a couple of paces towards the Greyhazel, hesitating. He could hear it too. From his vantage point on Zephyr's broad back, Roper could see shapes moving through the hail.

Cavalry.

The thunder was the pounding of ten thousand hooves. A dense swarm of plate-armoured knights, their horses grotesquely caparisoned, came careening into view. Almost all carried shields and lances, armed for a shocking charge that would sweep away all before them. Through the haze, skirts swirling about their knees, the riders looked ghostly and formidable. The Greyhazel were not in ranks, they were disordered and most did not even face the enemy that solidified by the heartbeat. They would be obliterated and then? Then the knights would sweep through the gap and behind the legions, attacking at will.

'Form the Greyhazel up!' shouted Roper desperately, looking to his trumpeter who dutifully sent out the notes for *Dress Ranks* but it was not fast enough. The Greyhazel merely looked confused at such an order, and most had not even noticed the cavalry bearing down on them. Those who had seen the cavalry were beginning to edge back, seeing their doom thundering towards them.

Just one figure was fighting against the retreating legionaries, pushing his way into the front rank and stepping forward, in front of his peers. It was Gray.

What he was doing there, Roper had no idea. Perhaps the tides of war had spat him out of the side of the Sacred Guard. Or maybe he had been resting at the back, had seen where the Greyhazel fought and had known that was where the battle would be won or lost and that it was therefore where he was needed. Whatever the cause, the guardsman now stood alone before his peers as the hail thundered down, sword raised to meet the oncoming knights. Roper could hear him faintly, calling as the other legionaries backed away. 'With me, my friends! With me or I die here alone! Will you help me? Will you die with me?'

There was an immediate reaction. Half a dozen Greyhazel legionaries jumped to Gray like iron-filings to magnetised rock. First among them was Hartvig, the disgraced former guardsman who had been one of Uvoren's war council. He was at Gray's side in an instant, with several others joining the two famous warriors. And then, as though the retreating line had the surface-tension of a puddle of water, that half-dozen sucked a score with them. A chain-reaction spread, warriors being dragged forward on the immovable figure of Gray and inter-linking. Swords were raised and there was a sudden jolt as the line lunged forward a little, reinforced by more and more warriors that joined them, like a blood-clot forming in the face of an arterial surge. Something brushed past Roper's thigh and, looking right, he saw Helmec sprint past him, hoping to pile in with Gray, who was still shouting, growling over the top of the clash of battle that surrounded him. 'Yes, my friends, come! Let's end this together! To serve! To serve!' He was screaming now, galvanising the line which solidified and braced itself. They began chanting with Gray.

'Serve! Serve! Serve! Serve!'

It was evident madness. Disordered foot soldiers versus a shocking charge of heavily armoured knights could have only one winner. But there was something dog-like about the legionaries. Unshakeable unity and commitment to a cause had been drilled into them from their earliest years, so that now they were prepared to die for the sheer sake of it. Because they were not used to defeat and could not countenance retreat. Because they trusted Gray implicitly. Because the will to resist had passed all logic or reason. Because.

'Serve! Serve! Serve! Serve!'

The knights were roaring too as they charged at this hastily assembled line, sensing victory. They were forty, thirty, twenty yards away. Roper saw Helmec reach the back of the line and plunge into it, pushing for the front rank. The knights lowered their lances and struck home.

It was like a gate being splintered by a ram. The front two ranks of legionaries were hurled backwards: bowled off their feet by the momentum of the cavalry charge. Gray had vanished beneath a press of falling bodies and the knights plunged onwards, fragmenting the Greyhazel. The line of knights was rearing up, as a wave rolls onto a beach, as they climbed the barricade of bodies thrown down before them. But still the legionaries pressed forward, laying down their flesh just to slow the momentum of the charge. Roper saw Helmec go down, smashed off his feet by a careening horse, only to rise again and continue pushing forward, obviously casting around for Gray. The sheer mass of bodies hitting the ground was horrifying, with warrior after warrior being buried in a pile of his fellows.

The knights were slowing. They had to keep moving or they would be dragged down and hacked apart but this disordered legion was resisting beyond any expectation; resisting like mud, clinging onto the horses and sucking at the riders' boots. Some of the knights were falling now; as the momentum from their charge began to fade so they turned, riding back the way they had come. They rode clear, leaving behind a flattened, writhing mass of the living and the dead. Legionaries still pressed forward after them, still infected by that bloody-minded will to resist, but the ranks were thinner now. Many had fallen, dead or injured by the Suthern cavalry, and those bodies impeded their peers who stumbled and slipped as they pursued.

It was a horrifying achievement: the most impressive example of what it meant to be a warrior that Roper had yet seen. With little hope, order or expectation, the Greyhazel had resisted and somehow managed to rebuff a fully armoured charge. But they would not beat a second. The knights were regrouping beyond the battle line and preparing another charge. Gray was down: he had been in the overwhelmed front rank and was now nowhere to be seen. Helmec had vanished again. The Greyhazel were scattered and stumbling and the knights were beginning to surge forward once more. A Suthern trumpet blew out, inviting the knights on to finish the Greyhazel.

'Skallagrim, advance!' shouted Roper. 'We must stop this charge!' Skallagrim signalled for his legionaries to advance but it was all too late: they were too far away and the dazed Greyhazel would be obliterated. That Suthern trumpet called again and some of the pikemen were cheering as they sensed their side's victory. The knights were thundering forward; fifty, forty, thirty yards away.

The heavens burst.

There was a crack so loud that Roper did not hear it apart from the ringing noise that reverberated in his ears afterwards. A flash like ten million stars burst into life before Roper's eyes. Some fissure in the matter of which the world was made was blown open and a bolt of pure energy escaped. It scarred his vision, so that all he could see was the stain of that unbelievable burst of power. Besides it, the rain-drenched world was dim and diluted. A violent tingling surged through Roper's torso and out to his fingers, as though a thousand-thousand strings running through his body had been plucked simultaneously.

Roper could not think. He could see, but what he could see was of no consequence. Something stirred in his vacant brain. *But the cavalry,* said his mind. *The cavalry, the Greyhazel: what's happening?* He looked for the horses that had been bearing down on the Greyhazel but the formation had atomised. It took Roper stunned heartbeats that felt like minutes to work out what had happened.

A bolt of lightning.

The lightning that had been flashing upon the battlefield for hours had finally struck something and had blown out the heart of the Suthern cavalry charge. A few dozen had been blasted away from the point of impact and now lay smoking and stirring feebly on the ground. The horses that still stood had bolted in all directions, away from the lightning. Some of the knights were reeling drunkenly away from the scene, their momentum suddenly disturbed. Perhaps forty knights who had been in front of the lightning did not seem to realise what had happened to their comrades and had hit the Greyhazel, but they were drastically outnumbered. Behind them, the charge had faltered. Silence seemed to have fallen. Most of the surrounding infantry had simply stopped to look on in awe.

There was only one thing to do.

Roper spurred forward and tore his helmet backwards so that his face was exposed. 'Well?' he roared with all the force of his lungs. 'What are you waiting for? Do you want more proof that god is on our side? Charge! Charge!'

The trumpet sounded again and, with a roar, Skallagrim's men streamed forward, heading for the gap through which the Greyhazel were already pouring. They rushed the disorientated Suthern knights and began to butcher them, dragging them from their saddles, cutting their reins and bringing down their horses. Roper knew that now was the time to gamble and was driving Zephyr forward into the press of legionaries who were pulling apart this gap in the Suthern battle line. 'Gray!' he called. 'Helmec! Where are you?' If they were still on the ground, they would surely be crushed by this swarm of legionaries that now assaulted the knights. 'Gray! Helmec!' Roper swore to himself again and again. Then one last time: he could not worry about two of his soldiers at the expense of so many others. He spurred Zephyr forward, screaming like a madman so that the legionaries made room for him. Zephyr took no more than a few moments to clear the press and burst into the open ground on which the knights were reeling.

Bellamus had indeed deliberately created the gap in the Suthern line, seeking to draw the Anakim through where they would then be swept away by his heavy cavalry. But his ace had been destroyed, first by the unanticipated fervour of the legionaries, then by that extraordinary burst of lightning. It had only killed a score of the thousands who were charging against the Greyhazel, but the horses had been terrified and the knights shocked by their extraordinary ill-fortune. On any other day, on any other battlefield, Roper would have put that down to sheer chance. But on the Altar, this could only be divine intervention.

The Black Lord was the only Anakim horseman behind the Suthern line and he charged straight for the static knights. Faced with the swarming Greyhazel legionaries, many of these were pulling away and retreating. Roper spotted one who had not seen him, horse sideways-on to him and his charging mount. He raked back his spurs and held the mighty beast's head straight, forcing him to smash into the knight's horse. Zephyr's bulk was irresistible and the knight was knocked flat, horse and all. Zephyr staggered slightly but simply rode over the prone knight and horse, Roper casting around for his next target. Another knight came riding at him, lance held skilfully level to pierce Roper's heart. Killing this one was not difficult; Roper beat aside the lance and, once he was past its lethal tip, there was nothing the knight could do. Roper slashed Cold-Edge at the gap between the knight's chestplate and helmet hard enough to cut halfway through his neck. The knight toppled backwards off his horse and tumbled out of sight.

Almost every other Suthern warrior was in headlong retreat before Roper so he turned Zephyr round to look at the back of the Suthern line. A steady trickle of pikemen, assaulted from the flank and the rear, had dropped their weapons and fled while they could, and as Roper watched this became a flood. The Hermit Crabs had stayed in their ranks but were edging backwards under the pressure of the legionaries who assaulted them with renewed savagery. Like a collapsing dam, a massive block of the pikemen suddenly disintegrated, chased by a swift steel wave.

More horns were sounding: *Pursue Enemy.* Someone appeared to have taken command in Roper's absence and, under skilful manipulation, the Suthern line was being ripped apart. Those Sutherners who watched their fleeing comrades and the legionaries chasing them down knew the game was up and began to edge backwards. The hail still fell, the visibility was low and that meant the Suthern line collapsed more slowly than it might have done otherwise. But steadily, from the gap that had been of Bellamus's own engineering, the line was peeling backwards. Pikes were abandoned, plate armour and chain mail were torn off as Sutherners scattered across Harstathur, trying to outrun their dreadfully quick opponents.

The giants.

Monsters. Freaks, demons, destroyers. God could not be on the side of such unholy creatures: they had used some sort of evil magic to gain victory this day. The subjects of the Black Kingdom were as brutal and uncompromising as they had always been taught. They did not back down, they did not give up, and they had somehow snatched victory on this lightning-struck field. And rampant at the head of them all was this monstrous Black Lord on his armoured destrier.

23

Uvoren the Mighty

Helmec. Gray.

When the battle was won: when the Sutherners had swarmed back, some in good order, most panicked and weaponless, and the Black Legions had cut them down, Roper had returned to the site of the cavalry charge to search for his two friends. He found Pryce, who had outstripped the rest of the Sacred Guard, on the way back. 'Help me! Gray has fallen!' Pryce stumbled awkwardly over the bodies to join Roper, the two of them scanning the killing floor. Pryce, apparently still energetic after the day's exertions, began ripping bodies aside to reveal those lying beneath. Together, he and Roper located where they thought the knights had first struck the Greyhazel and searched the bodies there.

Dead faces stared up at them. Some with their helmets partially ripped off. Some carrying so many wounds that it was unbelievable that they had still been standing to sustain the last of them. Some with no obvious injuries at all. Many were alive, eyes shut and armoured chests still working. Roper passed all of these, his gaze so frantic that he was not sure his eyes would settle on one of his friends long enough to recognise them. Partly, he did not want to recognise them.

How could either have survived that terrible press of flesh? Pryce was still tearing around like a dog looking for a wounded deer, roughly upturning the dead and injured. And somehow the hands were the hardest things to look at. Clawed about weapons; loose and empty; frozen while reaching for something: all were more evocative of intention than even the slack faces.

Roper had an idea he might be sick. It might ease his nausea and make the search swifter. He looked up for a moment, panting and poking a filthy finger into his visor to clear the tears that had begun to gather there.

There was a figure moving beyond him. One of the bodies was stirring. It dragged itself clear of a corpse on top of it and then staggered to its feet, stumbling over again to collapse on top of a dead horse. Roper took a hesitant pace forward, straining his eyes. The figure was slumped, panting, against the body of the horse. Roper lurched forward, the movement triggering something familiar. 'Gray?'

The figure tilted its head drunkenly at Roper and then slipped feebly down on the horse, lying there. Roper was sprinting over but was overtaken by a dark blur as Pryce surged past him. Roper arrived just after the sprinter and the two knelt by Gray, Roper tugging off his own helmet. Gray had lost his some time during the charge and his eyes were only half-open. A huge bruise had already spread across his forehead but Roper could see no other sign of injury. Pryce laid a hand against Gray's chest, ignoring his attempts to stand up and pressing him back against the horse. 'Lie now, Gray. I'm with you.'

'Pryce?' Gray's voice was slurred.

'Yes,' said he. Gray's hand rose jerkily and clutched onto Pryce's wrist, groping to find his hand. Pryce clasped it with both his own. 'I'm here. Calm now.'

'Roper,' slurred Gray.

'He's here too,' said Pryce. Gently, Roper reached a hand forward and placed it on Gray's shoulder, gripping it a little.

Gray abandoned the attempt to open his eyes and rested his head back on the horse. 'Did we . . . did we win?'

Roper sat back on his haunches. His eyes travelled over the scene behind Gray, past the dead horse that he lay on, to the ocean of bodies beyond. There was random movement, with one of the bodies stirring every now and then, to little effect. 'Yes,' he said softly. 'We won.'

Gray exhaled slightly, apparently able to say no more.

'Will you take care of him, Pryce?' asked Roper. 'I must find Helmec.'

'I have him,' said Pryce.

Roper stood, turning away from Gray to continue searching for his friend. 'Helmec!' he called. Perhaps he would be conscious too. 'Helmec!' *He was further back than Gray*, thought Roper, scouting away from the Lieutenant of the Guard and his kneeling protégé. But in the end, he was not much further back. Helmec lay twisted beneath two dead legionaries, his neck unnaturally distorted.

He was dead.

With a clang, Roper brought his fist up to his helmeted forehead. He stared at the broken form of the guardsman for a moment. Then he dropped to his knees. 'Oh, my friend!' Helmec's stillness did not look restful, or at peace. It was disturbing. His armour now protected a cold relic. All expression had faded from his face, all recognition from his eyes and the familiarity that his form once evoked was now tainted by an alien lumpenness. Whatever it was that had animated his limbs and gazed out from behind his face had left, or died, or simply vanished.

Roper laid a hand on the chest. He stared at the face for a moment and felt his mouth begin to warp uncontrollably. His vision blurred. He hiccoughed, a spasm wracking through his shoulders. And then, he gave way and sobbed. Tears spilled down his cheeks and he covered his face with his hands and bowed his head. His shoulders heaved silently for a long moment, the only sound he uttered a brief strain as he drew another breath. He spoke into his cupped hands, mouth so twisted in grief he could barely talk. 'My love, rest easy . . . It's over.' He drew another laboured breath. 'My friend, goodbye.'

It was a long time before Roper had wept his fill. It was not just for Helmec. It was for Kynortas. For the warriors who, obedient to his wishes, lay silently around him. For his country, which had survived. For the relief of the heavy and lasting pressure of responsibility that had been lifted from him. For the closest thing to security that he had known for a year. For his two brothers, whose safety he had ignored for so long, wrapped up in his own affairs. He wept.

His tears were dry by the time Pryce came to fetch him. He was just sitting quietly by Helmec, holding the guardsman's hand. Pryce stood over the pair of them for a moment, looking down in silence. Roper had no desire to meet his eye, but Pryce held out a hand and, at last, Roper released Helmec and took it. Pryce hauled him to his feet and the two embraced over Helmec's body. Roper felt the tears almost restart, but controlled himself, breaking away from Pryce. 'Is Gray going to be all right?'

'He should be,' said Pryce. 'He's speaking more clearly now.'

Roper stared at Pryce for a moment, his lips twisting slightly. Then he placed his hand on Pryce's shoulder. 'You know why he's dead? Who ordered the Greyhazel through that gap?'

'Uvoren the Mighty,' said Pryce.

Roper shook his head, but not in disagreement. 'Get him for me, Pryce,' he said. He gestured at the banner of the Jormunrekur, the snarling wolf some way in the distance. 'I'll be there. Bring that snake to me. Tell him to come without helmet, without armour and without his war hammer. It's time he answered for his actions.'

'That would be my pleasure, lord,' said Pryce, savagely.

Roper nodded and turned away. He brought Zephyr over to where Gray sat propped on the dead horse and helped the guardsman up onto Zephyr's back. Roper sat behind so that he could hold him steady as he rode for his banner, where he knew the legates would have begun to cluster.

Pryce watched the two of them go, and then turned in the direction of the Almighty Eye, held aloft on a huge strip of silk. Beneath it, he knew he would find Uvoren. He had been walking no more than a few minutes when he found a caparisoned horse pulling at some tufts of grass between two bodies, flicking its ears calmly as he approached. He took its reins and mounted, turning the Suthern beast towards where the Sacred Guard had assembled, half a league across the plateau.

The Guard, already two-score understrength before the start of the battle, had lost another fifty warriors in their duel with the Hermit Crabs. Pryce arrived to find that the greatest fighting unit in the Known World was composed of barely two hundred souls. Though battered and bloody, they still stood in ranks. In front of them was Uvoren the Mighty, staring dead-eyed at the retreating Sutherners. Pryce thought he could hear the captain say something about 'giving them time to retreat' but Uvoren had fallen silent by the time he curbed the horse in front of him.

Pryce regarded Uvoren haughtily. 'Captain Uvoren. The Black Lord has summoned you to answer for your disobedience on the battlefield today. You are to come with me now without helmet, arms or armour and present yourself before him for discipline.'

Uvoren glanced at the Sacred Guard, back at Pryce and then let out a roar of laughter. He hefted Marrow-Hunter in his hands and chuckled at the expression on Pryce's face. 'I don't take orders from disgraced lictors whose allegiance flits from one man to another like a sparrow,' he said. 'Settling everywhere but at his captain. If the Black Lord wants to speak to me, he can come and find me here; with my Guard.'

Pryce rolled his eyes and swore tiredly. He dismounted and took a step towards Uvoren, ignoring the war hammer that was raised as he approached. 'I'm tired, sir,' he said softly, barely moving his lips. 'A friend of mine has died because of your stupidity. So I'm going to ask you one last time. Present yourself to the Black Lord. Face justice at his hand. Or at mine.' And he drew his shattered half-sword, holding it low before him.

Uvoren just laughed again. 'You propose to duel me?' He cast an eye over Pryce's truncated sword. 'With that? Is this a joke?'

Pryce was still a long moment. Still in the way that a snake's head is motionless as it gathers its coils behind it. He just stared at Uvoren, who had stopped smiling. Then he lunged at the captain with his astonishing speed: half-blade raking upwards towards Uvoren's face. It was not even a blow to kill: it was a blow to hurt and to maim.

But the captain had been expecting the attack and thrust his hammer forward, stepping close and body-checking Pryce forcefully. Pryce staggered, his blow deflected and his blade flying out of his hand with the force of Uvoren's parry. He tried to dance backwards but Uvoren had trodden on his foot which was now pinned to the ground and Pryce fell hard, twisting to the floor. He gave a little grunt as his ankle was forced into an unnatural extension by the pressure of Uvoren's foot, sprawling to the ground as Uvoren took a massive overhead swing at his head. Pryce twisted aside, ripping his foot free from beneath Uvoren's boot and rolling away from the war hammer, which hit the earth by his head with a flat smack.

Pryce scrambled away, staggering upright as his torn right ankle almost gave way beneath him. He hobbled back from Uvoren, unarmed and injured. Uvoren was smiling again. 'I didn't expect much, Pryce. But I expected more than this. You can't fight me.' Pryce was limping badly as he cast around on the floor for another weapon, but there were none in evidence. Uvoren stood between him and his shattered blade, war hammer raised.

Then the captain rushed at Pryce, checking just before he hit the guardsman, who attempted to retreat as Uvoren swung Marrow-Hunter at him. Pryce ducked, the war hammer moaning as it swept through the air just above his head, but Uvoren kept swinging and managed to manoeuvre Marrow-Hunter's weight so that the steel handle struck Pryce on the chin. Pryce staggered back, dazed, but his practised legs operated without input and, in an odd, hopping sprint, he managed to withdraw from Uvoren's range. His eyes swept the ground once more, seeking a weapon of some kind.

Then a voice shouted behind from behind him. 'Pryce!' Pryce turned and saw Leon, the guardsman who had killed Lord Northwic beside the sea, drawing his sword. He tossed it at Pryce's feet and Pryce stooped quickly to snatch it up, eyes always on Uvoren. The captain's eyes were wide at this display of support from Leon but he quickly recovered himself, giving a little snort.

'Come on, then, Pryce!' he roared. 'Come and face me!' Uvoren lunged forward. Pryce was struggling to manoeuvre himself on his injured foot and took a clumsy swing at Uvoren as he retreated. Uvoren blocked and countered in a diagonal blow that Pryce had to pivot to avoid, putting him off balance. Uvoren, poised and balanced still, mirrored Pryce's pivot with far more control and raised a leg, booting Pryce in the chest. The smaller man was sent sprawling backwards, where he almost lost his sword again. He re-gripped the handle and was on his feet once more before Uvoren had time to crowd him, sword raised and threatening.

There was something beneath Pryce's foot. Looking down, he saw that their latest exchange had placed him at the site he had lost his sword last time and that its blade's ragged edge was beneath his boot. Pryce stooped suddenly to snatch at it with his left hand, so that when he straightened, he was facing Uvoren with two blades.

Uvoren was standing off, looking hungrily at Pryce's injured ankle. Both of them knew that was an almost insurmountable weakness. A weapon of Marrow-Hunter's weight could not be blocked with a sword. At full swing, its momentum was too great. It had to be dodged: a task of exceeding difficulty with only one working foot. But Pryce did not look worried. He looked furious. One of Uvoren's blows had reopened the cut that Garrett had made on his jaw and it was bleeding freely again, with Pryce spraying a crimson fountain on each exhalation. 'With one foot or two,' he snarled at Uvoren. 'Half a sword or a whole one, I will break you apart, Captain.'

Then Pryce charged. He stuttered forward on his unstable ankle, twisting slightly as he surged towards Uvoren but maintaining his course. Uvoren used his greater mobility, stepping one way in a feint before bringing the hammer across in a sweeping final blow, designed to crush Pryce, who was too weak and moving too fast to change direction. Pryce twisted at the waist, trying to limit Marrow-Hunter's impact so that it clipped his shoulder instead of striking him full-on. There was a noise, somewhere between a crack and a pop, and Pryce's right shoulder buckled visibly beneath the blow, Leon's sword falling from his grasp and onto the ground.

But Pryce had not stopped, was still moving, and brought the savage shard of metal in his left hand up over the inside of Uvoren's wrist, sawing it into the flesh and screaming in fury. Uvoren bellowed, Marrow-Hunter falling from his weakened fingers as Pryce span away, his right arm swinging uselessly. Uvoren stooped and lunged for Marrow-Hunter with his left hand, but Pryce's broken sword came out of nowhere, spearing into the hand and driving through, deep into the ground. Uvoren leaned forward, his face screwed up against the pain, gasping. He took several deep breaths and spat on the ground, glancing at his useless right hand which was tilted back, fingers extended and unresponsive. He was pinned to the floor by Pryce's sword, driven through his left hand.

Pryce turned away from the stricken captain, breathing fast. His right shoulder still looked visibly depressed and he seized his own wrist, levering it upwards, face quivering with the effort until, with a pop, the shoulder resumed its socket.

'Help me!' gasped Uvoren, casting around at the guardsmen. 'Kill him! Kill him!' But nobody moved. The guardsmen looked on, expressionless, at the scene playing out before them. Leon was nodding slowly at what he saw. Not a man spoke out for Uvoren, as Pryce turned back towards the Captain of the Guard, his right hand held tight in at his chest for support. He picked up Leon's sword in his left hand, and walked to stand before Uvoren. The captain was on one knee, still pinned to the earth by that sword through his hand. Pryce stepped right into Uvoren, aggressively close so that the captain was forced to crane his neck upwards to look into Pryce's face.

'You bastard,' said Pryce. 'You total, total snake.' Blood was dripping from his chin and it splattered onto Uvoren's cheek.

Uvoren glanced at Pryce's right shoulder, relocated now but still grossly asymmetrical. 'You are a madman,' he said softly. Then he bowed his head. 'Make it quick.'

Pryce smiled. 'No. Look at me, Uvoren. Look up at me.' Pryce slid Leon's sword beneath the captain's chin and tilted his head upwards. 'My face is the last thing you will ever see.'

Uvoren stared upwards for a moment. Then he shut his eyes tight.

Many of the knights survived the lightning strike and subsequent slaughter on top of Harstathur. The momentum shift was so drastic and so evident that, to most, the prudent option had seemed retreat. They rallied by Bellamus and

Garrett, who had somehow found a horse on top of the plateau (though accounts differed as to whether the horse had already been riderless or whether Garrett had knocked a Suthern knight from his saddle to take it). With Garrett by his side, Bellamus had then shown extraordinary nerve by approaching Roper's banner with a white flag to bargain for the lives of his shattered army.

Roper received him on horseback, Gray and Tekoa on either side and a cluster of legates and aides waiting behind. Gray was slumped in his saddle, barely equal to holding his head up. Tekoa had a bandage round his head from where his eyebrow had been split by Uvoren's fist. 'Not a customary time for parley, Bellamus,' Roper observed as the two groups of horsemen met. He glanced at Garrett, mounted next to his master and covered in grime, with Heofonfyr still clutched in his hand. Bellamus looked calm and spread his hands in a gesture of regret to Roper.

'The victory is yours, my Lord Roper,' he said. 'I applaud you; it was quite a battle.' He paused and smiled ruefully. 'I thought I had you at the end.'

'But the Almighty intervened.'

Bellamus looked carefully at Roper. 'Fortune, more like. We could have played that game a thousand times. Only one of those times would the lightning have broken my knights. It might have struck the Sacred Guard.'

'But it didn't,' said Roper.

'No. It didn't.' The words were the same, but the two leaders meant entirely different things. 'But sometimes that'll happen if you dress men in steel and send them out with lances into a thunderstorm. So I think that makes the score between us one each, though both in curious circumstances. I'm looking forward to our next encounter.'

Roper smiled thinly. 'I think we both enjoy our encounters. But I doubt you enjoy them so much that you came here just to exchange these words.'

'I'm here for the lives of my soldiers. There is no need to

turn your fine victory into a farmyard slaughter. If you let the remainder of my army march home, I will send you two tons of steel from the south.'

Roper raised his eyebrows. 'I see you have learned to barter in steel rather than gold.'

'I speak your language,' said Bellamus with a smile.

'Steel would be welcome, but I want Bright-Shock back as well.' Roper glanced pointedly at the blade that Garrett clutched upright like a pennant.

Bellamus sighed. 'Heofonfyr is not mine to give. The king himself gave the sword to Garrett. I cannot deprive him of what is probably the best weapon in Albion.'

'It was not the king's to give in the first place,' said Roper harshly. He could see Garrett frowning as he struggled to translate the rapid dialogue.

'Oh yes it was,' said Bellamus. 'Even by your own laws, what is taken in battle is the property of the victor. Your father was killed by my forces and his army sent reeling from the field. His sword was mine, to use as I saw fit. I presented it to the king and he gave it to Garrett. The offer is two tons of steel for the lives of these men here.'

'We could kill you all and take Bright-Shock now,' suggested Roper, shrugging.

'You won't. As you have told me yourself, "not under a white flag".'

Roper stared at Bellamus for a long while, and Bellamus stared back. Garrett rolled his shoulders restlessly and then went still. A Hermit Crab with an amber beard on Bellamus's left moved his hand to the hilt of his sword.

'No,' said Roper at last. 'But a white flag can't be your defence for ever. Maybe when you've left here, you could escape. You and your Hermit Crabs could take your swiftest horses and go south as fast as the road permits. Perhaps you'd make it over the Abus and live to fight another day. But no other Sutherners will escape the Black Kingdom. On that, you have my word.'

Bellamus looked over the massed legions behind Roper, formed up and ready for pursuit. He let out a slow breath. 'I would deeply regret that,' he said. He looked back into Roper's eyes. 'And I certainly would not forget it.'

'After the destruction you have wreaked on my lands; after –' there was a brief pause in which Helmec's name hung in the air before Roper – 'after that; this was the very least you could expect,' Roper finished coldly. It would mean nothing to Bellamus. 'The whole of Albion will know what happens to armies who cross the Abus. They do not come back.' Bellamus was nodding grimly and Roper glanced at Garrett. He addressed the giant hybrid. 'One day, I will have my blade back. I hope you ride fast, Eoten-Draefend. Pryce Rubenson is very quick indeed and he wants your head.'

'We have other ideas for Pryce,' intervened Bellamus. 'We have not forgotten Earl William.'

'You had better start riding south, Bellamus. I will give you one Anakim hour before we pursue. After that, we will kill any Sutherner we see.'

'Then I must fly,' observed Bellamus. 'We shall meet again, Lord Roper.'

'Until then.'

After Bellamus and Garrett had departed, Tekoa spoke. 'You could have used that steel to help settle our debts, Lord Roper.'

'Two tons of steel is not worth this army making it back to Suthdal alive. We gain more through the fear of slaughter. I wanted them to refuse to give me Bright-Shock,' he said, watching Bellamus and Garrett retreat. Tekoa and Gray exchanged a glance.

They waited in silence for a time until Bellamus was nearly out of sight. He had done as Roper suggested and was at the far end of the field, he and his household guard mounted on well-fed coursers. They might escape. The Black Cavalry Corps rode destriers: too heavy to keep pace with the coursers that most Suthern warriors used. There were probably not enough mounted Skiritai to force Bellamus's party to stop either. But they would stay close and hound his party on the road. One wrong turning, or a mud-slide blocking the road, or poor travelling conditions and they would be caught. Bellamus must trust to the fortune which had abandoned him in this place.

There was no hope at all for the Suthern army. They had abandoned their armour and all but the lightest weapons on the battlefield. They streamed after Bellamus and his riders, hoping to stay ahead of the Anakim who still waited in calm ranks. Bellamus would soon be out of sight and then they would be left alone and leaderless in a foreign land. The Anakim would catch them; god alone knew what would happen then.

'My lord.' A voice spoke from behind Roper. He turned to see that Pryce was approaching on the back of a Suthern horse. Roper looked him up and down, blinking.

'Where is Uvoren, Pryce?'

'Uvoren fell on the battlefield, my lord. He will not be able to answer for his actions.'

Roper just stared. Pryce's face was expressionless, but he controlled the horse with his left hand; his right held tight into his chest and his right shoulder considerably lower than the left. His face was caked with blood and mud. 'A late casualty, eh?' said Roper at last.

'That's right, my lord.'

Roper nodded brusquely. 'Then Gray is Captain of the Guard. And you're a lictor again.'

'Thank you, lord.'

'I wish he had made it back here, Pryce,' said Roper, after a pause.

'He was never going to make it back here, lord,' said Pryce in barely more than a hiss.

The hail had stopped. Roper had promised an hour and by his reckoning that meant that the Sutherners still had two-twelfths to get off the Altar. Behind them was left a vast sprawl of corpses and a felled forest of pikes. Crows and gulls were beginning to arrive already and pick over the remains, eliciting cries of pain from those who were still alive. Heavy clouds still hung overhead, but the air felt fresher and clearer and the light was fading from the field. The Sutherners would be hunted through the night. By the time the sun next rose, most of them would be cold and still.

Bellamus made it across the Abus. It took him three days to ride clear of the Black Kingdom, and following him the whole way were the Skiritai. They did not harass or try to engage their more numerous opposition. They just watched and informed, and at night did their best to keep Bellamus's party awake with incessant horn-blowing and riding through the dark. His last view of the Black Kingdom came after he was across the broad river. Shivering and wet, he turned back to the barren hills beyond to see the Skiritai still watching him from the far bank. The Anakim side of the Abus was their beloved wilderness; more rugged by far than that tilled by the Sutherners. The gloomy forests that had once covered the whole of Albion spread over the hills like bristles atop a mighty slumbering boar.

They were not forests like those in Suthdal. Ivy, honeysuckle, roses and the plant known as 'moonlight' wound their way up the trunks of oak, ash, beech, hornbeam and elm; all enormous and ancient. It was more closed; the dense canopy creating shadows in which wolves, bears and lynx roamed. The timber grew straighter and truer towards the light above, a dense phalanx of pikes raised to the heavens. The Anakim hung giant eyes woven from willow-fronds from many of the highest trees (Bellamus had often wondered how they got them up there). The branches dripped with lichen. Handprints were evident in many of the trunks, as though the flesh of the tree was soft and yielding to the touch of the Anakim and only adopted its woody nature when faced by Suthern enquiry. The forests of the Black Kingdom did not rustle in the breeze; they shivered. They did not creak in storms; they groaned.

Bellamus had known as much as he possibly could about the Anakim before he had ever set foot in the Black Kingdom. He had known their laws, their customs, their economy, their technology, their leaders, their heroes, their language and their history. But now, looking back across the Abus at the dark wilderness, he realised what he ought to have known all along. The level of his ignorance. He had interviewed every Anakim that he could possibly find about their land, their laws and their mindset. He should have realised how much they had not told him; how much that it would not occur to an Anakim to tell him.

As he and Lord Northwic had pillaged the east of the country, he had expected the Anakim to swarm away from their force in the manner that his people would have done when facing invasion. It was true that some had fled to the Hindrunn, but most had simply stayed and died. They had no weapons, they had no defensive position and they knew they must face slaughter, but they had stayed nonetheless. Bellamus had been baffled. What was at the heart of this behaviour? Were they somehow incapable of seeing their doom in the armies that had crossed the Abus? Did they have a sense of imagination less acute than men of Bellamus's own race, or perhaps an inability to comprehend death? It had taken many more interviews before one of them, the border-dwelling woman named Adras, had thought to tell him what none of the others had. The Anakim were connected to their land in a way the Sutherners were not. They did not feel the need to travel or explore. Their one desire was to stay and grow familiar, and with each passing season they loved their home more. They had known they would die in the Suthern invasion, but had preferred death to the alternative. Like a pack of wolves, they knew their territory and would do anything to protect it.

Those who had fled were the younger families, whose love for their land was not yet so complete that it was unthinkable to uproot. Not one of the scores that Bellamus had spoken to had thought to tell him that; it had not occurred to them that a Sutherner would feel any different. They did not realise that the Suthern army was not crippled by wretched heart-sickness at the alien lands through which they marched. They did not realise that Sutherners, as a rule, do not love their homes as dearly as they love their families.

Through observation, trial, error and experimentation, Bellamus had come to know more. The Anakim did not seem to feel as acutely as the Sutherners. Cold was less bothersome, worry less sickening, pain less debilitating, fear less overwhelming and horror less shocking. Only love seemed to be felt quite as acutely, but still they rarely let it engulf them. Indeed, so different were they that cold was something they appeared to love. Bellamus had questioned this and found most unequal to an explanation. They just loved it. Could Bellamus explain why he was happier in the warmth? Why food was a pleasure when hungry? Why roses smelt sweet? A few had tried harder, stuttering something about cold making the feeling of *maskunn* (to be exposed) more intense. If you were cold, they explained, you felt more. There was less separation between them and their beloved land.

There must be so much more that he, Bellamus, did not know; that he might not find out for many years. It was what they lacked which was most obvious. They could conceive of no value to gold, so did not use money. They had to trade simply instead: one useful object for another. Perhaps this was because their understanding of art and symbolism was so crude. Everything that they painted or wove was in black and cream; they did not seem able to conceive the new dimensions that colour might add. Beyond a few specific symbols, they had no writing. Their language, Bellamus was finding, was frustratingly inexact where it ought to be precise, and pedantic where it ought to be obscure. It lacked equivalent words for the distinct colours of orange, red, blue and green, and concepts such as 'civilised', 'optimistic' or 'déjà vu'. To them, orange and red were simply considered two shades of the same colour, as were blue and green; civilisation was anathema; optimistic simply irrelevant, and déjà vu a phenomenon they appeared familiar with, but had no term to describe.

But they had words that the Sutherners had yet to imagine. They had a word for a stranger you feel you have met before; a word for a memory or thought that slips away as you grasp at it; a word for the feeling that something good is drawing to a close; a word for the sin of putting the short term above the long term; a word for wind strong enough to make branches in the forest rattle and smack together; a word for the sense of nostalgia initiated by a familiar smell; a word for feeling estranged from someone you were once close to. Their word for servant was unambiguously positive. Their word for 'lord' was related to that of 'father', 'lady' to that of 'mother', and both were more than anything else an expression of gratitude. It was not expressed with the deference that a Sutherner might associate with the words: rather, with appreciation. Bellamus had uncovered six different words for 'stream', four describing the silhouette of a tree, seven for how hard ground was to travel on. His favourite discovery was their term for a word that is pleasurable to say: *eulalaic*.

He had arrived in the north with libraries of questions, and the Black Kingdom had answered precious few. Instead, it asked its own of him, and then wrung the answers from him. What frightened him? Is anything inherent to the Sutherner? How do desperate men behave? How robust are your ideas of beauty? Decency? Honour? Truth? God?

Bellamus stayed in northern Suthdal. This was partly to keep eyes on the Abus and make certain that no vengeful legions came south, and partly because he did not want to face King Osbert's displeasure. It had taken an enormous effort of will to launch another invasion so soon after the last, and Bellamus had made promises that he should not have. He stayed away.

Legions did come south, but only to deliver the Suthern army back home. Fifty thousand heads, planted on the pikes that had been left on the battlefield, were erected on the Suthdal side of the Abus. There were enough to stretch, one every four yards, from one coast of Albion to the other. The crows found them and feasted, cutting the island in half with a turbulent wall of black. Bellamus saw it with his own eyes. He and Garrett, accompanied by Stepan and half a dozen Hermit Crabs, sat on horseback atop a hill that overlooked the Abus, in front of which the heads had been planted. There was no sign of Anakim north of the bank.

'This isn't the last of this,' said Bellamus. 'They're coming south, Garrett.'

'They are not as hard as the Unhieru,' was all Garrett said.

'The Anakim's bad cousins,' mused Bellamus. 'I find the Anakim infinitely more threatening. They have an eye to the long term that neither we nor the Unhieru possess and, given the right motivations and the right leader, they can bend everything towards a single cause. We have given them both.'

'The right leader and the right cause?'

'Exactly. And they and the Unhieru are natural allies. If the Anakim come south, we may have to face Gogmagoc as well.'

'I would like nothing more than to face Gogmagoc,' said Garrett.

'No doubt that would add to your considerable renown,' observed Bellamus.

'And that Pryce Rubenson . . .' Garrett let out a long, slow breath. 'He was the fastest thing I have ever seen.'

'I doubt you'll see Pryce again, but there are other Anakim champions you can test yourself against. Leon Kaldison is the next great hero, and Vigtyr the Quick is supposed to be the best of them. We must be prepared for a different class of warfare, big man. We have to find ways of matching the Anakim man-for-man. At the moment, the quality of their individual soldier is too good.'

'We have started a war that cannot be won,' said Garrett bleakly.

'No. We have ended a peace that masked a lie; we cannot live with the Anakim.' Bellamus glanced back at Stepan sitting behind, who, unseen by Garrett, dropped his hand to the hilt of his sword. 'Or, rather, I ended a peace that masked a lie.'

Garrett turned his head slowly to face Bellamus. 'What do you mean, you ended the peace?'

Bellamus smiled at him pleasantly. 'What you must understand about the Anakim, Garrett, is that they are too warlike for their own good. Battle is the only thing that keeps their numbers in check. They live such a long time that, though they breed more slowly than us, in the end they will outnumber us if they are not controlled by war.' Garrett was frowning and Bellamus turned back to face the bleak kingdom over the river. 'That was the realisation I came to a few years ago. All across Erebos, I've seen the frontier where Anakim meets Sutherner, and there is never peace. We are too different; there is too much mutual suspicion and misunderstanding. We have the advantage in numbers now, but it will not last. The sooner this war started, the more likely we were to win it. So I started it.'

'No you didn't,' said Garrett. 'They started raiding Suthdal. That brought God's wrath: the flooding, the plague, the snakes in the sky. That is why the war started.'

'And why did the Anakim raid south? Because I raided them first. We did,' said Bellamus, gesturing around at the Hermit Crabs. 'We provoked them, and they replied. There is always flooding. There is always plague. Every single year. The fiery snakes were a pleasant coincidence, but it was I who paid the priests to declare that they were signs of God's displeasure for allowing the Anakim to set foot in our lands. I know how the king works, Garrett. He's scared wicked of the Anakim. All he needed was the right push.' Garrett did not seem to have noticed that the Hermit Crabs were now very close behind him.

'I heard that you were counselling caution in King Osbert's court,' said Garrett, still suspicious. 'And that it was Queen Aramilla who championed the invasion.'

Bellamus waved the queen's intervention aside, not prepared to reveal everything. 'I did counsel caution,' he said. 'I did not want my hand detected and I did not want Earl William in charge, but fortunately that situation resolved itself early in the campaign.' Bellamus let silence fall for a time. 'So now that you know,' he said presently. 'I wondered whether you might join me in finishing this war. I can promise you more prestige than you will find anywhere else. Certainly more than you'll get sitting in King Osbert's court. You can have your chance against the greatest Anakim warriors ever to live. You can fight Gogmagoc. Or, you can do as His Majesty suggested and take my head back to him for my failure.'

Garrett was fixated on Bellamus, sitting very still in his saddle. 'What will His Majesty do when he discovers what's happened?' He spoke in a softer voice than Bellamus had heard him use before.

'Certainly I am out of favour now, and that makes me safer up here, even with your presence,' said Bellamus, casting an eye over the huge man. 'But in the inevitable slaughter when the Anakim come south, opportunity will arise and His Majesty will need me again. I just need to stay away until then. I'm looking forward to it. You say you want to fight Gogmagoc? I want Roper. This Black Lord is even better than his father.'

Silence fell for a time. Bellamus's horse tossed its head and twitched its ears and he soothed it.

Garrett imitated Bellamus and turned back to face the Black Kingdom. 'So you're testing me,' he said after a while. Bellamus thought that more perceptive than he would have given Garrett credit for. 'If you think your warriors could stop me before I killed you, you are mistaken.'

Bellamus wondered whether that was right. He sat

passively, waiting for the big man to finish. Tucked within his jerkin were two letters. One was in Aramilla's cypher, imploring him to stay away, describing King Osbert's terrified rage and suggesting that he stay very quiet in the north and hope to be forgotten until he was needed. *Wait for this storm to pass, my upstart. When it does, I will come north for you. I will not forget.*

The second had been addressed to Garrett, intercepted by one of Bellamus's men. It ordered the hybrid to decapitate Bellamus and take his head south to be displayed over Lundenceaster's gate. Now it was damp with Bellamus's sweat as he waited for the warrior's response. Garrett had Heofonfyr at his side, though the long-bladed tip was covered in a ghastly leather sheath of his own creation, made from Anakim skin. He was still staring straight ahead. The Hermit Crabs were pressing a little closer to him, readying themselves to stop his response. Stepan's sword was six inches clear of its scabbard. Bellamus was still. He must trust his men.

'I want what you want,' said Garrett at last. 'And the king is a grub. I do not follow men like him.'

Bellamus did not relax. 'But you will follow me? You cannot stay here if I can't trust you.'

'If I am first among your warriors then yes, I will follow you.'

'No one but you can make you first among my warriors,' said Bellamus.

'That I will do.'

Bellamus smiled gently. 'The legendary Eoten-Draefend,' he said. 'It's good to have you join us.' Silence fell again.

'There's nothing there,' said Garrett. He was staring over the Abus at the far rugged country. 'Barely even farmland. Just forests and mountains and rivers. Do they love it? The disorder? Or is it just sloth that stops them improving their land?'

'Oh, they love it.' *And so do I,* thought Bellamus. Gazing across the Abus, the upstart's eyes were fierce and tender in equal measure. Bellamus knew Stepan felt the same: both were bewitched by the Black Kingdom. Garrett, however, shared the view of most of his countrymen: the north was a barren wasteland. 'Wilderness is an essential part of their world,' said Bellamus. 'To them, tilled land is empty land. In the wild they feel more . . . well, they just feel more. To them, the world is outlines and shadows. They have absolutely no interest in colour. To them, memory is colour. In the wild, there is more on which to hang memories. If I could be granted any wish, it would be to see the world through Anakim eyes for just one day.'

Garrett glanced sidelong at his master and Bellamus regretted the words at once. The hybrid had turned against the Anakim with the certainty that only a man with a foot either side of the Abus could muster. He would never be welcome in the north. Here, in the south, his only chance of survival was to be more certain in his hatred of the Anakim than even the most resolute Sutherner. 'They are demons,' said the huge man slowly. 'It is a whole country of fallen angels.'

'Of course,' said Bellamus, quickly. 'It is a foolhardy desire, I suspect. But to fight your enemy, you must know your enemy. They will not be defeated unless we understand them.'

'As you said, we will never understand them,' said Garrett.

'So have you discovered any more about the Kryptea?'

Roper and Keturah sat opposite one another in his quarters; Roper at his desk, the battered equipment spread out before him bearing the signature of Harstathur; Keturah sitting on the bed and attempting to weave.

Keturah was silent for a moment as she fumbled with a line. Her movements became jerkier and clumsier and finally she dropped the malformed square of cloth in her lap with a tut. She stared at it for a while longer before answering Roper. 'Yes. I discovered that I will learn no more about them from the Academy.'

Roper looked up at her, frowning.

'I witnessed a chant on the third level while you were away,' she explained. 'The Kryptea and the Academy have an alliance, Husband. For the last four hundred years, the Academy has sent anything regarding the Kryptea to their Master for editing. That is why I was warned so heavily against enquiring about them. They protect each other.'

Roper stared at Keturah. 'What? The Academy is supposed to be fully independent.'

Keturah nodded. 'So are the Kryptea. It seems that the position of both as outsiders persuaded them they would be more secure together. So they struck a deal: the Kryptea gets to filter out any information that might turn people against its existence, and in return, it expanded its role to defend the Academy. So anyone now thought to be endangering the Academy is targeted.' Roper could do no more than stare and Keturah took up her weaving once more. 'It is as I heard in that first chant. The Kryptea are a toxic fungus, whose roots have spread too wide to ever be cut out. They are everywhere. They know I've been asking about them. They left me a cuckoo in my clothes.'

Roper's stillness was partly because Keturah had spoken so matter-of-factly. They had threatened her; they directly threatened him by their mere existence. And one day, they might do the same to the child she carried.

There came a knock at the door and Roper ignored it for a while, continuing to stare at Keturah. 'This is simply our first dead end, Wife. We will find a way to neuter that office. I broke Uvoren. Some day, I will break Jokul.' Keturah's head jerked up at him, eyes wide, but Roper had turned towards the door. 'Come!'

Roper expected to see Helmec's familiar face as the door opened but was instead presented with the less benign countenance of the guardsman Leon, who had been brought closer to Roper on Pryce's advice. Leon announced Gray's presence and stood back so the new captain could enter.

'Captain,' said Keturah, looking up with a smile. 'Thank you for the last time. You survived the battle unscathed?'

'I did, Miss Keturah. My head is still a little tender, but once again I am not seriously wounded.'

'Given the tales I hear of your bravery, that must make your skill quite remarkable. Pryce and my father returned fairly cut to pieces.'

'My fortune is quite remarkable. How is the pregnancy?'

Keturah grimaced. 'Morning sickness. Roper arrived in the middle of a bout earlier and it appears to hurt him almost as much as it does me.'

'It is disgusting,' confirmed Roper. He beckoned Gray forward. 'You're working on your list?'

'I am, lord,' said Gray, taking a seat opposite Roper. The Black Lord, his ear bent by the lictors, legates and captains throughout the army, had presented Gray with a sheet, covered in the arms of almost three hundred warriors. From those, Gray would pick the most worthy to join the Sacred Guard. He had been working on it for almost the whole journey back from Harstathur and would announce almost a hundred new guardsmen at the victory feast in just a few hours' time. As soon as Gray gave the word, messengers would scurry out across the fortress to invite the new guardsmen to the Honour Hall. Everyone knew there were many vacancies in the Sacred Guard, and every warrior with a reputation would be hoping desperately for a seat at the long benches that night.

'There is one crest here that does not fit with the others, lord,' said Gray. 'That of Vigtyr the Quick.'

'Ah . . .' Roper set down his quill and sat back in his chair, gazing at Gray. 'You're certain?'

'Quite certain. It would be an assault on the principles of the Guard. Vigtyr is an exceptional fighter, but his courage is insufficient. He is too self-serving, has too much of a love for gold and wealth. Questions would rightly be asked over his inclusion.'

'It is your decision,' said Roper, raising his palms. 'Vigtyr will not be invited to the Honour Hall if he is not to be made a guardsman. He would have to bear the disappointment in front of too many men. Better that he can do that in obscurity.'

'Agreed. How on earth do you intend to placate him?'

'I have given him an estate in the north and commissioned him an Unthank-silver blade.'

Gray looked at Roper for a while, face frozen in a grimace. 'You might find that new blade being shoved up your arse.'

Keturah, who had returned to fumbling at her weaving, laughed delightedly without looking up. Roper nodded seriously. 'It's a distinct possibility.'

'Remember the ease with which he dragged down the great men of the country? And that was without the benefit of a court full of Ephors who are looking for any excuse to punish you.'

'I couldn't have done this without Vigtyr. Uvoren's death at Harstathur would have triggered open civil war if his lieutenants hadn't already been disgraced. We had to leave his body there: it was in *bits*. I wish Pryce had held back a little. So it is what it is, and I will have to face Vigtyr's displeasure.'

Gray nodded slowly. 'I'm sorry to force this on you, lord.'

'That's all right, Gray. As long as you help me deal with him, now that he's incensed.'

Gray snorted. 'We can die together trying to untangle this fiasco. But what next? You are the Black Lord, without rival or challenge. What would you have this country do?'

Roper beamed. His whole body seemed to relax and he drummed his fingers excitedly. 'First, we are going to defend our home. Never again will a Suthern army be able to cross our borders and raid with such impunity. We're going to expand the canal, Gray. The Great Canal will stretch right across Albion and be controlled by a dam behind the Hindrunn. It will be impossible for an army to cross without building rafts or a bridge, and that will slow them enough to give us time to respond.'

Gray was listening with eyebrows raised. 'An ambitious legacy. The sums involved, my lord; where will the money come from?'

'I have already discussed it with Tekoa: the Vidarr will fund the construction.'

'And how shall you repay them?'

Roper pushed his chair back from the desk and stood, heading to a stand from which he took three goblets. 'Birch wine?' he asked Gray, beginning to fill the goblets.

'Before the feast?' Gray grinned. 'You like to live dangerously, lord.'

Roper did not need to ask Keturah, who had inherited her father's fondness for drink. He gave his two companions a goblet apiece and sat back down. He glanced at Keturah before he continued. The two had not spoken about this. 'The Vidarr are not the only debt waiting to be paid. My father promised that we would take Lundenceaster as revenge.' He paused to sip from his goblet. 'So we will go to Suthdal and the Sutherners will know we are there because they dared to start this war. But that is not all. The memory of Harstathur is still very raw, so it is difficult to say. But I think I have come to love war.' He stopped again to look at Gray, but the guardsman was impassive. 'I never thought I would. There is so much death; so many have their lives ruined and their loved ones taken away. My father died before my eyes. Helmec was crushed to death. It is blood and corpses and grief. But I find my mind travelling back to every battle, over and over again. It is so much starker than normal life. Everything is crystallised: you have one unalloyed purpose. Every action assumes a lifetime's significance. And in spite of it all, I love it. Nothing compares.'

'Battle is sacred for that reason,' said Gray. 'Death, euphoria and purpose combine altogether. There will never be an experience more moving. That reaction is far from unique to you, lord. Many of our peers love war. But do not lose sight of what it is. Do not allow it to consume the rest of your life.

If you allow yourself to forget to live when you are not at war and simply lust after your next fight, that is possession. You may think this once that life is dull by comparison; you cannot control your thoughts. But you can control your habits.'

'You're right.' Roper sipped his drink again. 'Of course you're right. And, as powerful as war is, our country becomes less and less under its influence. We are more outnumbered than ever by the Sutherners, and we must finish this war while we still have the strength. We're not just going to take Lundenceaster, Gray. We're going to take Albion. We're going to end this war, once and for all. No more tenuous peace treaties and double-crossed dealings. We will subdue Suthdal.'

'And what of the Sutherners who occupy it?'

'I have not thought that far,' confessed Roper. 'Perhaps we expel them. Maybe they would till the land and pay us a tithe, and be forbidden from creating weapons. I have not thought. But one way or another, the Black Kingdom will fall one day if we do not secure its future. And the only way to do that is to control the whole of Albion. Only when there is ocean between us and the Sutherners will peace prevail.'

'What of the Unhieru?' If the Anakim were to take Suthdal, it would open up a new border with Unhierea, in the west of Albion. At present, the Anakim had so little contact with them that they were almost mythical. Roper was not even sure that Gogmagoc, the man said to be their king, was a real figure.

'I would have them join us,' said Roper. 'We offer them the return of their ancestral lands if they march with our army. I do not think they are interested in expansion, as the Sutherners are. They are not so voracious, and may be satisfied with their small kingdom. With them, perhaps we could form a lasting peace. Do you have any experience of them?'

'None,' said Gray. 'But I have heard stories, and those suggest we will not find them easy to control. So loot from Suthdal will repay the Vidarr.'

'Yes. The south has become fat and wealthy. There is more than enough to settle our debts.'

'Well,' said Gray, at last taking a drink himself. 'At least the breadth of your military ambition matches your infrastructural ambition. It may save you from becoming known as Roper the Engineer.'

'A fine title,' said Roper.

'Wait, my lord, and you shall have finer.' Gray had spoken matter-of-factly. The Black Lord smiled and raised his goblet, Gray returning the salute.

'Will you help me?' Roper asked.

'Yes, lord,' said Gray.

Epilogue

There was a knock on the door. Vigtyr, sitting in a chair with his long legs outstretched towards the fire, a cup of wine in his hand, turned his head towards the sound. He was still for a moment, staring at the back of the door. The fire fluttered in the hearth next to him, animated by the wind that roared over the chimney above. He drained his cup, eyes always on the door. The knock came again. Vigtyr placed the cup carefully on the floor beside him and stood, stretching for a moment before answering. He opened the door to reveal a messenger behind; a short, stocky, black-haired legionary who carried something long, wrapped in lightest, softest leather. The messenger bowed.

'Lictor Vigtyr Forraederson of Ramnea's Own, I assume?'

Vigtyr nodded. The messenger beamed.

'Ah! An honour, Lictor. I come with Lord Roper Kynortasson's greatest compliments.'

Vigtyr stood aside with a knowing tilt of his head and gestured the messenger inside. The man hesitated, but Vigtyr's eyes were unwavering and the messenger gave way, muttering thanks as he entered.

The room was bizarre. Barely an inch of wall was visible;

hidden by dozens of tapestries. Not all of them were Anakim. Some were evidently Suthern work: less stylised, and coloured with all manner of reds, blues and golds; barely the same art form as the black and cream Anakim banners. Adornment was everywhere: on a dozen tables set around the room was a chalice of silver, richly engraved; pewter plates leaned against the wall; weapons so shiny and with edges so perfect that they could never have been used; unforgivably ornamented oil lamps, gleaming with care; a pair of mighty animal tusks; a tiny harp; carved wooden pieces a forearm in length that depicted bird-warriors, lion-headed men, and angels with giant, spidery hands. The floor was not covered with skins like most Anakim houses but with rugs, finely woven and intricate. Most extraordinary and unfamiliar of all was the heavy perfume that overlaid everything; a potent, fragrant miasma that was almost too thick to breathe.

The messenger faltered slightly. The room was uncomfortably crowded. There was too much to look at, too much to consider, and his eyes flickered from one object to another, then at Vigtyr, then back at an object and then, seeking familiarity, finally settled on the hearth. The messenger was blinking and spluttering slightly at the perfume but could see Vigtyr looking expectantly at him and so began, trying not to inhale the overwhelming fragrance. 'As I say, Lictor, I come bearing the Black Lord's compliments and reward for services to the Black Kingdom.' He held forth the long, leather-wrapped item. Vigtyr took it, unravelling the leather to reveal a sheathed sword of some splendour. The tang was the full width of the handle, each rivet set perfectly and the division between metal and elm blanks too small for human eyes to discern. Each binding and material of the scabbard was faultless and as tightly assembled as the handle; the only flourish the sheen of its constituent parts. Anakim craftsmanship, which was ill-fitted to this room.

'Unthank-silver,' said the messenger, seeing that Vigtyr had not unsheathed it, and struggling to keep his eyes open in the caustic atmosphere. 'The blade, however, is merely . . .' The messenger stopped and took a shallow breath. 'Merely a token of a fifty-hide estate granted you in the north. You have the Black Lord's very great gratitude.'

Vigtyr examined the sword for a while. 'Thank you for delivering this, Legionary,' he said, looking up after a moment. 'Anything else?'

'No more than that, Lictor, and to express the Black Lord's gratitude once more. He was quite specific on that.'

Vigtyr was looking back down at the sword and smiled at it. 'How pleasing,' he said. 'May I offer you wine, Legionary?'

The messenger's eyes flickered towards the hearth once more. 'I'm afraid I must decline, Lictor. I have other messages that I must see to.'

'What messages?'

The messenger tried a smile. 'Alas I cannot tell you, sir; business of the Black Lord.'

Vigtyr gazed at the messenger for a time. 'Come, now,' he said at last, turning away. 'You cannot refuse a single cup.' He poured birch wine from a silver pitcher that rested on a stand behind him before turning back to the messenger and holding the cup out before him. The messenger hesitated. Vigtyr was wearing that unshakeable look again and the messenger stretched out his hand, taking the cup.

'Thank you, Lictor.' He took a sip and Vigtyr smiled at him pleasantly.

'You were at Harstathur, I assume?'

The messenger nodded, lifting his eyebrows as he tried the wine. 'Yes, Lictor.'

'How was your battle?'

'It was hard on our portion of the line, if I may say, Lictor. The pikeline was exceedingly difficult to penetrate. We lost many men, and opportunities to strike back were few.'

'It is not a glorious place to fight,' said Vigtyr. 'I love to fight knights. They're so slow, they may as well not be armed at all. The only difficulty lies in penetrating their plate.'

'Slow to some of us, Lictor,' offered the messenger, taking another sip of wine.

'Well, indeed,' said Vigtyr. 'Pike. Knight. It's all the same to me, they're all too slow.'

The messenger made a polite sound.

'You wonder how many nobles you killed during a battle like that one,' continued Vigtyr. 'How many of them were thought of as among the best of the realm.'

'I imagine they'd be in the Hermit Crabs if they were the best,' suggested the messenger.

Vigtyr grunted and turned his attention to the sword. After inspecting the handle once more, he unsheathed it suddenly.

'Built with your hands in mind, I believe, Lictor,' said the messenger. It was hot in the room and perspiration had begun to stand out on his brow.

Vigtyr, holding the blade left-handed, gave it a graceful sweep. His eyes lingered on the messenger again and he switched the sword to hold it in his right. For a moment, he levelled the sword at the messenger. The eye contact was so forcible, the sword so threatening that the moment, no more than a heartbeat, was distorted beyond recognition. The messenger took a half-pace back. Then the sword was lowered and Vigtyr gave it another graceful swing. 'Well-balanced,' he commented. The instant had been so brief that the messenger might have imagined it.

Vigtyr turned to refill his own goblet, still holding the naked blade, and the messenger took the opportunity to drain the rest of his wine. 'So what are these messages you have to deliver?' pressed Vigtyr again, turning back to the messenger. The sword was still low but he was no longer holding his goblet. It sat on the table behind him.

'Outside of the fortress,' said the messenger, unwillingly.

'Ah. A little wilderness for you?'

'Yes, Lictor. I'm heading north.' Vigtyr looked at the

messenger expectantly through the long pause that followed. 'To the haskoli. I have a message for the Black Lord's brothers.'

Vigtyr raised his chin, his mouth slightly open. 'Ah . . . Roper's brothers.' He licked his lips. 'Yes. I'd forgotten they were still in the haskoli. Which one is it?'

'Lake Avon.'

'Beautiful. Telling them that they're safe, now that Uvoren's threat has been extinguished, I should imagine.'

'Something like that, Lictor.'

Silence prevailed. The perfume was stifling and the messenger had to look away from Vigtyr. Then the huge lictor smiled. 'Well, my friend: a long journey lies ahead of you. And I must take up no more of your time.' He laid the sword aside on another of those little tables. Relief broke over the messenger's face and he set down his goblet.

'Thank you very much for the wine, Lictor. I must indeed depart.' The messenger bowed and straightened rather suddenly, eyes on Vigtyr, who stood perfectly still. The messenger backed away slowly, smiling weakly, and then turned and trotted for the door. Vigtyr watched him go, not moving. He turned away then, moving for the fire which he fed with another log before straightening and staring into the flames, hands clasped behind his back. He frowned a little. Then he gave a low, tuneless whistle. After a pause, a short, squat legionary with the substantial hands of a workman entered from a door by the hearth. He glanced at Vigtyr, who was still staring into the flames.

'Sir?'

'I have work for you at Lake Avon, in the north. You leave before the feast.'

'Lake Avon?' said the legionary. 'At the haskoli?'

'Yes, at the haskoli.'

'What kind of work, sir?' asked the legionary, hooking his thumbs into his belt.

Vigtyr looked up at the soldier. 'A message,' he said.

Roll of Black Legions

Full Legions:
Ramnea's Own Legion
Blackstone Legion
Pendeen Legion
Greyhazel Legion
Skiritai Legion

Auxilliary Legions:
Gillamoor Legion
Saltcoat Legion
Dunoon Legion
Fair Island Legion
Ulpha Legion
Hetton Legion
Hasgeir Legion
Soay Legion
Ancrum Legion

Houses and Major Characters of the Black Kingdom

Major Houses and Their Banners:

Jormunrekur – *The Silver Wolf*
Kynortas Rokkvison *m.* Borghild Nikansdottir (House Tiazem)
Roper Kynortasson *m.* Keturah Tekoasdottir (House Vidarr)
Numa Kynortasson
Ormur Kynortasson

Lothbrok – *The Wildcat*
Uvoren Ymerson *m.* Hafdis Reykdalsdottir (House Algauti)
Unndor Uvorenson *m.* Hekla Gottwaldsson (House Oris)
Urthr Uvorenson *m.* Kaiho Larikkason (House Nadoddur)
Tore Sturnerson
Leon Kaldison
Baldwin Duffgurson

Vidarr – *Catastrophe and the Tree*
Tekoa Urielson *m.* Skathi Hafnisdottir (House Atropa)

Pryce Rubenson
Skallagrim Safirson

Baltasar – *The Split Battle-Helm*
Helmec Rannverson *m.* Gullbra Ternosdottir (House Denisarta)
Vigtyr Forraederson

Alba – *The Rampant Unicorn*
Gray Konrathson *m.* Sigrid Jureksdottir (House Jormunrekur)

Indisar – *The Dying Sun*
Sturla Karson

Oris – *The Rising Sun*
Jokul Krakison

Algauti – *The Angel of Madness*
Aslakur Bjargarson
Randolph Reykdalson
Gosta Serkison

Kinada – *The Frost Tree*
Vinjar Kristvinson *m.* Sigurasta Sakariasdottir

Neantur – *The Skinned Lion*
Asger Sykason
Hartvig Uxison

Rattatak – *The Ice Bear*
Frathi Akisdottir

Other Houses and Their Banners:

Eris – *The Mother Aurochs*
Atropa – *The Stone Knife*
Kangur – *The Angel of Divine Vengeance*

Alupali – *The Eagle's Talon*
Keitser – *The Almighty Spear*
Brigaltis – *The Angel of Fear*
Tiazem – *The Dark Mountain*
Horbolis – *The Headless Man*
Denisarta – *The Rain of Stars*
Hybaris – *The Mammoth*
Mothgis – *The Angel of Courage*
Nadoddur – *The Snatching Hawk*

Acknowledgements

It is fair to say that, since writing this, my image of the author as the lone creative dynamo behind each book is in smithereens. Particular thanks must go to my agent, Felicity Blunt, and my editor, Alex Clarke – both of whom not only had faith in this book, but also substantial creative input, helping to shape a much better novel than the one I originally submitted to them. Very many thanks must also go to the rest of the team at Wildfire, Headline and Curtis Brown, particularly Ella Gordon, Katie Brown and Jess Whitlum-Cooper.

Special thanks also to my mum, who has put a great many hours into the book and whose insight, opinion and support have been indispensable. There are very many more members of my family and my friends to whom I owe thanks for their inspiration and emotional support during the writing of this: too many to list, but they are no less appreciated for that.

Finally, very great thanks to Michael Dobbs, for some early and gratefully received support, and valuable words of wisdom.

Acknowledgements

It's a joy to see that, since writing [illegible] the [illegible] and time [illegible] each book is [illegible]. Particular thanks must go to my agent, Felicity Blunt, and my editor, Alex Clarke – both of whom not only had faith in this book, but also substantial creative input, helping it [illegible] much better [illegible] than the one I originally submitted to them. Very many thanks must also go to the rest of the team at Wildfire, [illegible] particularly [illegible].

Special thanks are due to my [illegible] hours into the book and whose [illegible] and support have been indispensable. There are very many more [illegible] of my family and my friends to whom I owe thanks for their inspiration and emotional support during the writing of this – too many to list, but they are no less appreciated for that.

Finally, very great thanks to Michael [illegible] for [illegible] and [illegible] support and valuable words of wisdom.

One Snowy Night

Rita Bradshaw was born in Northamptonshire, where she still lives today. At the age of sixteen she met her husband – whom she considers her soulmate – and they have two daughters, a son and six grandchildren. Much to her delight, Rita's first novel was accepted for publication and she has gone on to write many more successful novels since then, including the number one bestseller *Dancing in the Moonlight*.

As a committed Christian and passionate animal-lover her life is full, but she loves walking her dog, reading, eating out and visiting the cinema and theatre, as well as being involved in her church and animal welfare.

BY RITA BRADSHAW

Alone Beneath the Heaven
Reach for Tomorrow
Ragamuffin Angel
The Stony Path
The Urchin's Song
Candles in the Storm
The Most Precious Thing
Always I'll Remember
The Rainbow Years
Skylarks at Sunset
Above the Harvest Moon
Eve and Her Sisters
Gilding the Lily
Born to Trouble
Forever Yours
Break of Dawn
Dancing in the Moonlight
Beyond the Veil of Tears
The Colours of Love
Snowflakes in the Wind
A Winter Love Song
Beneath a Frosty Moon
One Snowy Night